UP FROM SLAVERY; AN UNFINISHED JOURNEY

The Legacy of Dunbar High School

ARCHIE MORRIS III, D.P.A.

authorHOUSE®

AuthorHouse™
1663 Liberty Drive
Bloomington, IN 47403
www.authorhouse.com
Phone: 1 (800) 839-8640

Published by AuthorHouse 03/20/2019

ISBN: 978-1-7283-0423-6 (sc)
ISBN: 978-1-7283-0422-9 (hc)
ISBN: 978-1-7283-0421-2 (e)

Library of Congress Control Number: 2019903061

CONTENTS

Part V
The End of an Era

PREFACE

Jean Jacques Rousseau said that "plants are shaped by cultivation and men by education. Man is born weak and needs strength. He is born totally unprovided and needs aid. He is born stupid and needs judgment. Everything he does not have at birth and which needs when he is grown is given him by education."[1] Rousseau's philosophy of education was one black people understood in the early days of the history of the United States; education meant freedom. One would travel far or lay down his life in the attempt to obtain learning. I suppose that is why I am writing this book, to tell the story of a journey to freedom.

Paul Laurence Dunbar High School stressed excellence in all things and never allowed the school to fall into the category of a black subculture or popular fads. Reminiscing, a while back, with a reporter from *The Washington Post*, Senator Edward Brooke (Class of 1937) said:[2]

> We sort of lived in a cocoon. Dunbar sort of had an intellectual élite.... We were not aware of what we were missing because of segregation. It was very competitive.... Dunbar took the cream of the crop. They did well at Howard where I went. Negro History Week was observed, and in American History they taught about the emancipation of the slaves and the struggle for equality and civil rights. But there was no demand by students for more, no real interest in Africa and its heritage. We knew about Africa as we knew about Finland.

The Dunbar culture is, to put it mildly, controversial even in current times. William Raspberry summarized in a column he wrote in the

Washington Post that if a room is filled with middle-aged blacks who grew up in Washington and someone mentions the word "Dunbar," that person will have to take cover. That one word will divide the room into two emotion-charged, outraged factions; those who did and those who did not attend Dunbar High School "when Dunbar was Dunbar."[3] The ensuing arguments are usually highly emotional and predicated on biased opinion and innuendo, with little knowledge or understanding of history. Slavery, Jim Crow segregation, family, the church, the community, and, now, U.S. welfare policy are all part of the "big picture" pertaining to the significance of Dunbar in urban education in the United States.

The achievements of M Street and Dunbar students might possibly have had some influence on questions about educating black children, had they not been ignored. No scholarly study of the school has yet appeared, and almost the entire literature on the subject consists of one slim volume, *The Dunbar Story*, printed privately in 1965 by Mary Gibson Hundley, a retired Dunbar teacher, at her own expense. Where the school has been noticed at all, it has been brushed aside as a "middle-class" black school, and local tradition in Washington suggests that its students were predominantly light-skinned blacks, many scarcely distinguishable from whites. The facts do not support either assertion, but the attempt to dismiss the accomplishments of the Dunbar experience is a significant phenomenon.[4] Why?

I was born and raised in the Washington, D.C. My father grew up on a farm in Virginia and had only a fourth-grade education. He obtained a GED when he came to Washington in his teens and worked a variety of vocations. Beginning as a laborer on construction sites, he learned bricklaying, carpentry, and truck-driving, and he worked as an automobile mechanic. Dad also was a religious man who heightened his reading skills by reading the Bible. He preached when he was called and sang and wrote gospel music. He was a self-taught musician who played guitar, several wind instruments, the piano, and drums.

My mother grew up in Washington, D.C. and graduated from Dunbar High School. She was a housewife during the early years of my childhood and, later, obtained a clerical job in the federal government. Dad's dream was to return to Virginia and have his own land when he and Mom retired. They were able to purchase some 22 acres in Orange County,

Virginia, a few years before they both had retired. Dad built the house from the ground up by himself, living on the site while he cleared the land and constructed the buildings. Several generations of our family enjoyed numerous visits to Orange County, Virginia, for decades.

The Morris nuclear family consisted of the father, the mother, two boys, and one girl. In the early days, we moved often and, as a result, we lived in most of D.C. at some time or other; Benning Ridge, Navy Yard, Anacostia, Truxton Circle, Shaw/Cardozo, and Brookland. As children, our "job" was to go to school, study hard, and stay out of trouble. The family had a lower income status when it started out, but we espoused the values characteristic of the middle class, even though we did not have the financial means to obtain this lifestyle. Plans for the future included retirement and a good education for the children.

Ours was an extended family in the literal sense. In addition to our nuclear family, we lived near relatives such as our grandparents, aunts, uncles, and cousins; most residing in the District of Columbia or nearby Virginia and Maryland. We respected family elders and looked to them for guidance as we looked to our parents. Cousins were as close to one another as siblings. My grandmother, my aunts and uncles, cousins and friends, all talked to me about Dunbar High School, and of Armstrong Technical, Cardozo, and Phelps Vocational. The latter were considered good schools with high standards for their missions. Furthermore, one could go to college upon graduation from any of these other schools, but their primary mission was not college preparatory.

Dunbar was a tradition in our family households. My grandmother had attended M Street High School in the early 1890s, transferring to Howard University before graduating. My mother and five of her siblings attended Dunbar High School, as did most of our cousins and friends. I was inspired by conversations about school and the importance of an education. We did not have televisions, but there were books, the public library and many books in the homes of family and friends that we could borrow. Someone was always reading or doing school homework.

I had done well in elementary and junior high school, skipping a couple of grades in the first six years. I was reading incessantly at a young age. My grandmother had started me reading *Readers Digest* cover-to-cover when I was 8-9 years old, thus expanding my comic book repertoire. My uncle, who was a student at Howard University, had given me Geoffrey Chaucer's *Canterbury Tales* to read, and I was checking out and reading 2-4 library books every week or two.

We also heard first-hand stories and history relating to the black community, the church, the family, the military, and politics. The family was the foundation of black people in D.C. It consisted of two parents and their children. The black father was the guardian of the household, stressing thrift, hard work, self-respect, and morality. We learned of slavery almost first-hand, but segregation was the active force in the black community. It was surpassed only by religion. The family elders told us of the 1919 race riots in D.C., when black veterans of *World War I* had to take up arms to secure their neighborhoods, and how the Ku Klux Klan marched down Pennsylvania Avenue in 1925. Ministers provided information and leadership on important issues, particularly race and politics. Most blacks were Christian and Republican, and, over the years, male family members served in both *World Wars*.

My father thought it would be a good idea for me to learn a trade, but it was pretty much a *fait accompli* that I would attend Paul Laurence Dunbar High School. We did not have money for college, but it was understood that we would find a way when it was time. The family moved from the projects in Southeast Washington to Northwest and, in 1952, I was enrolled for the 10th grade at Dunbar. I was 13 years old.

While attending Dunbar as a student, I did not appreciate the institution's high academic standing. I was, to some degree, quite immature and more "jock" than nerd. I got good grades, basically stayed out of trouble, and met a lot of new people because Dunbar students came from virtually every neighborhood in the city, some having moved to the city from several states. I was active in sports and a member of the Spanish Club and the Rex Club. My principal was Mr. Charles S. Lofton and the assistant principals were Mrs. Gladys W. Fairley and Mr. Howard F. Bolden. All the boys knew about the paddle kept in Mr. Bolden's office.

My homeroom teacher was Mr. Domingo A. Lanauze, who was also my Spanish teacher. I do not remember all my teachers, but some are: Mrs. Madeline S. Hurst, Mr. Madison W. Tignor, Miss Lillian S. Brown, and Mr. Warren B. Griffin in English; Mrs. Mary G. Hundley in Latin; Mr. Charles Pinderhughes, Mr. Jesse B. Chase, and Mr. L. J. Williams as coaches and Physical Education; Dr. James H. Cowan in Chemistry; Dr. A. F. Nixon in Biology; Mr. U. V. McRae in Mathematics; Mr. Don B. Goodloe and Mr. Frank H. Perkins in Social Studies; Mrs. Hortense P. Taylor in Music; and Mrs. Helen M. Cunningham in Art. I regret that there are others whom I cannot remember, but all my instructors were excellent teachers. To this day, I remember that I never met a Dunbar student or classmate who could not read or do basic mathematical computations. Also, I honed my writing skills at Howard University, but I learned them at Dunbar High School.

History was an important part of my studies at Dunbar. The coursework at school covered ancient and medieval history, European history, American history, Negro history, and Latin American history. Family and friends told many stories of the past and, for all practical purposes, we were living in a historical context daily; i.e., segregation was the law of the land and slavery was not far removed from our current existence. Moreover, in the churches and black households, discussions of the Bible were historic in their framework and this was reinforced during church attendance by ministers' sermons and Sunday School teachers. This combination of sources encouraged critical thinking and a motivation for knowledge and learning.

History helped put things in perspective. It provided a paradigm to compare and contrast current events in the present with an understanding of where black people had been and how far they had come. Black men and women, who became "the first" in many fields and endeavors, were role models because we understood how formidable the obstacles were that they overcame and the efforts each of them possessed in accomplishing their feat. This helped us to become strivers instead of victims.

I graduated in 1955 and, a couple of months after I turned 17, joined the U.S. Air Force. It did not take long for me to realize that Dunbar had prepared me well academically and for life. One of the most important things to happen to me in life occurred at my last USAF post. I had already been approached about re-enlisting and, while not greatly enthusiastic, was seriously considering it so I could continue playing sports, travelling the world, and maybe take some college courses. However, about a week later while working my shift in the Special Security Office (SSO), a white officer in my unit approached me. I had only a passing acquaintance with the man, but he told me that he had observed my work, my written reports and oral presentations, and noted that I had no college credits. He said I was very intelligent, and he urged me, instead of re-enlisting in the USAF, to enroll in a college.

Fortunately, or unfortunately, I took his advice and went on to earn the Bachelor of Arts (BA) and the Master of Arts (MA) from Howard University and the Master of Public Administration (MPA) and the Doctor of Public Administration (DPA) from Nova Southeastern University. I think that officer knew I needed a last push to keep going in the right direction.

I am uniquely qualified to write a book about the Dunbar experience and its beginnings. I am a native Washingtonian, an alumnus from the "old Dunbar" days and, currently, a volunteer with the Dunbar Alumni Federation (DAF). I have the life experience and cultural associations, a family history and background, and the education and the social science research skills to bring the elements together that will illustrate the larger picture. This tome brings together branches of social science using historical research techniques, comparative analysis, and qualitative observational methods as a base to help understand how black education, during slavery and Jim Crow segregation, affected urban education and, by extension, the ascension and decline of the M Street/Dunbar High School. I have taken an academic approach to this project, using an empirical research approach to observe and analyze real-life data and patterns of events. Thus, I have utilized several research techniques.

Historical research techniques are used to review data from the past and draw conclusions that impact the present or the future. This required a significant amount of reading, translating, researching, and discussion. Comparative analysis is used for comparison of changes in political and legislative activities over several governmental administrative periods together with detected emerging trends in an organization's operations and results. As the researcher, I am also a participant observer. Accordingly, qualitative observational methods are used so that the full range of individuals' responses to an environment can be documented and verified. First, the focus of the observations is deliberately left more open-ended and observations are much broader in contrast to quantitative observational strategies that focus on specific behaviors. Second, I do not necessarily strive to remain neutral about what I am observing and may include my own feelings and experiences in interpreting what happened.

The book is organized into five parts: I. The Roots, II. Dred Scott to Reconciliation, III. The Black Paradigm, IV. The Black Crown Jewel, and V. The End of an Era.

Part I of the book, "The Roots," provides a wide-ranging view of the system of slavery and bondage, and how it affected black people's roles in colonial times. There were free blacks, and some were as prosperous as their white neighbors (Chapter One). Early training and education made black men more useful and trustworthy servants, but it instilled in them a longing for freedom. They became better laborers and artisans, and many showed administrative ability adequate to manage business establishments and large plantations. Education and training provided blacks a general uplift in life (Chapter Two).

Part II, "Dred Scott to Reconciliation," deals with black people being declared by the U.S. Supreme Court to have no rights the white man was bound to respect and the circumstances of competition and conflict leading to the American Civil War (Chapter Three). The North won the Civil War militarily, but, when President Lincoln was assassinated, the Democrats were able to regain political control and implement Jim Crow segregation. Education was greatly affected by *de jure* segregation (Chapter Four). The churches played a large part in attempting to set up education opportunities for the newly freed slaves, providing a forum for the expression of black political views and a training ground for black political leadership (Chapter Five).

In Part III, "The Black Paradigm," the movement for the education of black youth begins and a quarrel starts as to whether their education should be "classical" or "industrial" (Chapter Six). The early 1900s were a time of a progressive breakdown of the black community in Washington, D.C., owing principally to the restriction of economic opportunity. Only the strongest individuals could avoid a general sense of despair (Chapter Seven). Education was a prized commodity even though one could not use it for economic advantage (Chapter Eight).

In Part IV, "The Black Crown Jewel," the city was a conglomeration of neighborhoods that were informally organized and had boundaries that, to some degree, separated them from each other (Chapter Nine). The black

Preparatory High School for Colored Youth opened its doors in 1870 as the first high school for black American students and, in 1892, it was renamed the M Street High School (Chapter Ten). The new building at 1st and O Streets, N.W., was dedicated January 15, 1917, and it was named Dunbar High School after the black poet Paul Lawrence Dunbar (Chapter Eleven). Dunbar was characterized by the *esprit* of its students, the dedication of its teachers, and the strong support of the community, both in everyday chores and in episodic crises. Indeed, the school's reputation and high standards were well known to parents and middle-school children throughout the black community (Chapter Twelve).

In Part V, "The End of an Era," The whole dual school system in Washington was reorganized around the concept of neighborhood schools, and the maintenance of educational quality at a black academic high school had no emotional appeal or political clout (Chapter Thirteen). The situation began changing in the 1970s when black professionals and the stable working class moved to higher-income neighborhoods in other parts of the city and the suburbs, leaving behind the most disadvantaged segments of the black community. This severely impacted the quality of education (Chapter Fourteen).

Washington, D.C.
January 2019

PART I

THE ROOTS

"In all of us there is a hunger, marrow-deep, to know our heritage- to know who we are and where we have come from. Without this enriching knowledge, there is a hollow yearning. No matter what our attainments in life, there is still a vacuum, an emptiness, and the most disquieting loneliness."

— Alex Haley, 1921-1992

CHAPTER ONE

SLAVERY AND BONDAGE

History provides the paradigm necessary for critical thinking. Without a reliable knowledge of times gone by, one's thinking may be biased, distorted, partial, uninformed, or down-right prejudiced. Yet, the quality of our life and that of what we produce, make, or build, depends precisely on the quality of our thought.

To understand the legacy of the black middle class and its link to Dunbar High School, one needs to understand the historical insinuations of what occurred before he can understand the implications for contemporary times. It is all about culture, that complex whole that anthropologist Sir Edward Burnett Tylor says includes knowledge, belief, art, morals, law, customs, and any other capabilities and habits acquired by man as a member of society."[1] Through the study of slavery, for example, we can investigate and interpret why the school developed as it did and determine what influences were determined by the past, and how history can be put to good use in the present. To quote philosopher George Santayana, "Those who cannot remember the past are condemned to repeat it."

From a historical perspective, slavery is a system in which one human being is legally the property of another. A slave can be bought or sold, is not allowed to escape, and must work for or serve the owner without any choice. The most crucial and frequently utilized aspect of the condition is that slave owner has a communally-recognized right to possess, buy, sell, discipline, transport, liberate, or otherwise dispose of the bodies and behavior of other individuals.[2] An integral element of the slave system is that children of a slave mother automatically become slaves.[3]

One is usually told that conflicts over slavery caused the Civil War. The problem is that there is disagreement regarding which kinds of conflict—ideological, economic, political, or social—were most important.[4] Conflict between groups requires some form of ethnocentric awareness of group differences. There is a sense of "we" versus "they" that becomes a struggle for control of the other group for resources, status, or scarce commodities. Conflicts between groups are disruptive and costly, and can take a variety of forms, including slavery and other forms of institutionalized discrimination. Thus, accommodations tend to move toward an institutionalized, stable relationship.

Bondage as an Economic Concept

Slavery is an established institution that can be traced back to such early records as the Code of Hammurabi (circa 1760 BC).[5] It does not include historical forced labor by prisoners, labor camps, or other forms of unfree labor in which laborers are not considered property. Moreover, it was rare among hunter-gatherer populations because slavery depended on a system of social stratification. Slavery archetypally requires a shortage of labor and a surplus of land to be viable. Furthermore, most of the history of slavery did not include the enslavement of people who were racially different from those who enslaved them. Frequently, indigenous people enslaved each other; i.e., Europeans enslaved other Europeans, Asians enslaved other Asians, Africans enslaved other Africans, and the indigenous peoples of the Western Hemisphere enslaved other peoples of the Western Hemisphere. People were enslaved not because of their racial differences, but because they were vulnerable.

Slavery between different peoples began only in recent centuries when both the technology and the necessary wealth existed that enabled one group of people to go from one continent to another to acquire slaves and transport them *en mass* across an ocean.[6] After it became both technologically and economically feasible to transport masses, whole populations of slaves of different races or ethnicities were transported from one continent to another. Europeans, as well as Africans, were enslaved and transported from their native lands to bondage on another continent. Pirates, alone, transported a million or more European slaves to the Barbary Coast of North Africa. This was twice as many European slaves as there were African slaves transported to the 13 colonies from which the United States was formed.[7] In fact, white slaves were still being bought and sold in the Islamic world as late as the 1900s, decades after blacks had been freed in the United States. It was the rise of the Christian society in medieval Europe that practically wiped out the slave-system of olden days preceding the Middle-Ages.[8]

Nevertheless, while exploring the coast of Africa in the 1440s, the Portuguese rediscovered slavery as a working commercial institution. The practice of slavery had always existed in Africa where it was operated by local rulers who were often assisted by Arab traders because slaves were exchangeable commodities. Slaves were captives, outsiders, or people who had simply lost tribal status.[9] Among West African peoples, sources of slaves included criminals and people pawned by their lineages as security for loans that had not been repaid and, most important, captives taken in war.[10]

The first Europeans to engage in the slave trade with sub-Saharan Africa were the Portuguese. When they took over the slave trade in the middle 15th century, the Portuguese transformed slavery into something more impersonal and horrible than it had ever been in antiquity or medieval Africa. This new-style slave business was characterized by the large scale and intensity with which it was conducted and by the cash nexus which linked together African and Arab suppliers, Portuguese and Lancado traders, and purchasers. The slaves were overwhelmingly male and were put to work in large-scale agriculture and mining activities.[11]

Even in these early times, perceptions of some black people were negative and little effort was made to acculturalize black slaves. The Arab geographer Muhammad al-Idrisi, for example, in concluding his account on the first climate zone with some general remarks about its inhabitants, repeated the old clichés about furrowed feet and stinking sweat and ascribed "lack of knowledge and defective minds" to black people.[12] The Arabo-Muslim historian, sociologist and philosopher, Ibn Khaldūn, distinguishing between white and black slaves, remarked: "the Black nations are, as a rule, submissive to slavery, because (Blacks) have little that is (essentially) human and possess attributes that are quite similar to those of dumb animals."[13]

The Portuguese had a virtual monopoly on the Atlantic slave trade. By 1600, 300,000 African slaves had been transported by sea to plantations; 25,000 went to Madeira, 50,000 went to Europe, 75,000 to Cape São Tomãé, and the rest to America. By then, four out of five slaves were heading for the New World.[14] The number of slaves who reached the New World in three and a half centuries is estimated to have been 10-15 million.[15] At this point, relatively late in world history, enslavement across racial lines occurred in America on such a scale as to promote an ideology of racism that has outlasted the institution of slavery itself.[16]

When the black man was first enslaved, his subjection was not justified in terms of his biological inferiority. Indeed, prior to the influences of the Enlightenment, human servitude was taken as an unquestioned element in the existing order of economic classes and social estates; a way of thinking that had been prevalent in feudal and post-feudal Europe. The historical literature on this early period records that the imported Negroes and captured Indians were originally kept in much the same status as white indentured servants.[17]

In America, the meeting and merging of two streams of Old-World immigrants, one voluntary and one forced, evolved from a society with slaves into, by the second third of the 18th century, a slave society. Ira Berlin, a leading historian of southern and black American life, argues the distinction between the two. In societies with slaves,

> slaves were marginal to the central productive processes; slavery was just one form of labor among many. Slave owners treated their slaves with extreme callousness and cruelty at times because this was the way they treated all subordinates, whether indentured servants, debtors, prisoners-of-war, pawns, peasants, or simply poor folks. In societies with slaves, no one presumed the master-slave relationship to be the social exemplar.[18]

When societies with slaves became slave societies, Berlin continues, "slavery stood at the center of economic production, and the master-slave relationship provided the model for all social relations,"[19] It was an all-encompassing system from which, in the words of Frank Tannenbaum, "Nothing escaped, nothing, and no one."[20]

The transformation from a society in which slavery was present, but not the dominant form of labor, into one in which it was central, began with the discovery of commodities like sugar, gold, rice, coffee, or tobacco. Such commodities commanded an international market, which also required a great deal of labor to produce. A second precondition was that slave holders in these societies could consolidate their political power, enacting comprehensive slave codes that gave them near-complete sovereignty over their slaves' lives. Slaveholding elites then erected impenetrable barriers between slavery and freedom and created elaborate racial ideologies to bolster their dominant position.[21]

The New World

The first slaves used by Europeans were among the participants of the Lucas Vásquez de Ayllón colonization attempt of North Carolina in 1526. The attempt lasted only one year and was a failure. The slaves revolted and fled into the wilderness to live among the Cofitachiqui people,[22] one of the most powerful and highly civilized tribes in the southeastern United States.[23] Accordingly, black people have been in the United States as long as the earliest white settlers, even before the *Mayflower* and the appearance of the first Africans in Virginia in 1619.[24] In fact, new information has surfaced in recent years regarding the first Africans to arrive in Virginia that indicates there were more Africans present in the Virginia colony by 1620 than the "20 and odd" negroes that John Smith and John Rolfe recorded as having been brought to Virginia in a Dutch ship in 1619. Thirty-two Negroes (15 men and 17 women) were listed in a census of 1619/20 recently discovered in the Ferrar Papers, Magdalene College, Cambridge.[25]

In 1619, three events occurred in the American colonies that made the year significant. First, to make the Jamestown colony more attractive to settlers, the London-based Virginia Company sent out a ship carrying 90 young, unmarried women. Any bachelor colonist could purchase one as a wife by paying 125 pounds of tobacco for the cost of her transportation. Second, the colonists were given their "rights of Englishmen;" a term referring to the rights granted English citizens in the *Magna Carta*. Third, a Dutch man-of-war, the *White Lion*, arrived and sold the colonists some 20 and odd black men who were not free, but strictly speaking, they were not slaves. These men were "indentured servants" whose indentures expired at the end of five years. Upon completion of their contractual agreements, they would become free men and could buy land and enjoy all the rights of free citizens of the colony. White laborers arrived from England under the same terms and signed indentures under identical conditions as payment for their passage to America.[26]

In practice, however, many indentured men acquired other financial obligations by borrowing money during their initial period of service. This usually extended their contract. It does not appear that any of these first 20 Africans ended up as free farmers in the colony. Most of the white servants, who struggled free of their indentures, did not fare much better and found themselves tenant farming on the Jamestown River. However, it was not impossible for a black person to become a free man in Virginia, and some are recorded as having done so.[27] One of them went on to become the first slave-owner of record in the New World.

When the first 20 blacks arrived in Jamestown in 1619, a statutory process to fix the legal standing of blacks did not yet exist.[28] Although the American colonists seemed to have practiced from the very beginning the "same discrimination which white men had practiced against the Negro all along and before any statutes decreed it,"[29] these first blacks were not exposed to the systematic degradation to which blacks later would be subjected. Yet, they were not free and their position in the larger society was not clear. After centuries of investigation and discussion, scholars are still unable to agree on that point.[30]

During 1624 and 1625, demographic records reveal that family life was a firmly rooted institution in Virginia.[31] Africans living in the area appear to have paired off and formed family units as well, for people of both sexes were present. Among whites, households often consisted of a married couple and one or more children, plus a small number of servants, including some who were of African origin.[32]

Throughout the 17th and 18th centuries, many families included the children from one or both parents' prior marriages. Step-siblings, half-siblings, and full-blooded relatives tended to progress with a parent or step-parent through a series of marriages almost always terminated by death. Servants (and later, slaves) would have accompanied household members whenever living arrangements changed. The accumulation of wealth through successive marriages and the hardships that were a part of frontier life probably made widows and widowers eager to remarry. As the colony became better established, more women came to Virginia and the number of marriages and births rose. Africans developed nuclear families and ties that extended well beyond the plantations on which they lived. These kinship networks were extremely important.[33]

There is ample evidence in historical records that people of mixed race could be accepted in communities if they were documented as exercising the rights of citizens to bear arms and vote. In early periods when few records were kept, social acceptance by the majority white community, rather than details about ancestry, was often the key as to whether a person was considered white.[34] For example, in 1652 "an unfortunate fire" caused "great losses" for the Anthony Johnson family and he applied to the courts for tax relief. The court reduced the family's taxes and on February 28, 1652, his wife Mary and their two daughters were exempted from paying taxes at all "during their natural lives." At that time, taxes were levied on people, not property. Under the 1645 Virginia taxation act, "all Negro men and women and all other men from the age of 16 to 60 shall be judged tithable."[35] It is unclear from the records why the Johnson women were exempted. The change gave them the same social standing as white women, who were not taxed.[36] During the case, the justices noted that Anthony and Mary "have lived Inhabitants in Virginia (above thirty years)" and had been respected for their "hard labor and known service".[37]

Most of the workers in colonial America in the 17th and early 18th centuries were indentured servants, white and black. Friendships between the races developed and, since there was not a clear distinction between slavery and servitude at the time, biracial camaraderie often resulted in children. The idea that blacks were property did not harden until around 1715 with the rise of the tobacco economy, by which time there was a small but growing population of free families of color. By 1860, it is estimated that there were 250,000 free black or mixed-race individuals.[38]

In 1618, the headright system was introduced to solve the labor shortage. It provided colonists already residing in Virginia could be granted two tracts of 50 acres each, or a total of 100 acres of land. The headright system fueled development of the plantation economy and, during the tobacco boom-times of the 1620s, successful planters amassed substantial quantities of land and reaped substantial profits. The labor of indentured servants was critical to their success. During the late 1610s and 1620s, the labor shortage was so critical that landowners often worked beside their servants in tobacco fields.[39]

As time went on, settlers continued to fan out in every direction and forest lands were converted to cleared fields that were used for agriculture. Small and middling farmsteads that were interspersed with the larger plantations of the well-to-do throughout the Tidewater area. Settlers moving into new territory vied for waterfront property that had good soil for agriculture and convenient access to shipping. Successful planters were those who managed to acquire several small tracts and consolidate them into relatively large holdings. Small freeholders sometimes hired freed servants to fulfill their need for labor. These workers, however, were not servants and not obliged to stay with a single employer. Moreover, they could bargain for higher wages.

Many freed servants could accumulate enough capital to rent or purchase land of their own during periods when tobacco prices were high. The prospect of social mobility was a great enticement to former servants. So was the prospect of marriage and family. Small planters' dominance in the Chesapeake had begun to decline by the 1680s. Fewer servants came to the colonies and the servant trade nearly died out after 1700. Between 1680 and 1720, when tobacco prices were unstable and the crop often was unprofitable, there were fewer opportunities to be upwardly mobile.[40]

A decline in English birthrates during the second third of the 17th century, and rising wages in the Mother Country, had also significantly reduced white laborers' interest in coming to the New World. By 1680, the relatively new colonies of Pennsylvania and South Carolina were competing with the Chesapeake colonies for prospective white servants interested in immigrating to Virginia.[41]

The gradual decline in the number of servants immigrating to Virginia transformed the labor system irrevocably. Planters, who almost continuously sought laborers to work in their tobacco fields, began substituting Africans for white servants. By 1700, African slaves were producing much of the

Chesapeake's tobacco. The long depression in tobacco prices gradually took its toll. Poorer farmers, who acquired land that was less well suited for tobacco production, and newly freed servants, who sought to develop their property, found themselves unable to compete. They lacked the capital needed to purchase the labor force they needed. Nevertheless, even though tobacco prices were low, relatively successful planters could afford to purchase servants and maximize production. This phenomenon widened the breach between the rich and the poor. Meanwhile, consistent with the laws of supply and demand, the price of a white male indentured servant rose in proportion to that of the more numerous black field hands and planters soon learned that African slaves could be at least as productive as white servants.[42]

As the 17th century wore on, the population of the colonies grew through natural increase and immigration. There was also a greater demand for laborers to work in the fields. Whether or not they preferred to employ white English servants, the planters were increasingly obliged to turn to non-English whites or Africans and, during the latter half of the 1690s, Chesapeake and Tidewater planters begin purchasing substantial numbers of Africans. Between 1695 and 1700, approximately 3,000 Africans were enslaved and put to work in the area. By 1700, most slave laborers were black and the number of native-born adults in the white population had increased significantly. Such people not only started life free, they frequently received inheritances from their families. They also tended to marry at earlier ages than did white servants and accumulated property more rapidly. Inheritance played a great role in amassing wealth and this allowed the successful to become even more successful because they could count on inheriting land and servants or slaves.[43]

The success with which landowners used blacks to work their tobacco plantations was a most ominous factor. It was not long before they were buying more men who were not indentured servants. Thus, they were buying chattel slaves; i.e., persons who were the personal property of an owner and could be bought and sold as commodities. With this situation, the first English colony in America embarked on two roads which proceeded in two totally different directions; one toward representative institutions leading to democratic freedoms, and the other toward the use of slave-labor leading to what came to be called the "peculiar institution" of the South. Large numbers of black chattel slaves did not arrive in North America until the 18th century, but the bifurcation was real and eventually produced a country that was divided into two castes of human beings, the free and the unfree. The two branches were relentlessly pursued for 250 years until their fundamental incompatibility lead to the great American Civil War that was fought from 1861 to 1866.[44]

The Colonial Perspective on Indentured Servitude

Early 17th century references to life in Virginia suggest that many colonists considered "slavery" synonymous with forced labor and the loss of freewill. Captain John Smith spoke of making men slaves to the colony for life, suggesting strongly that it was a severe punishment that was reserved for very serious crimes.[45] A May 1618 proclamation, issued by Deputy-Governor Samuel Argoll, made church attendance compulsory. Anyone who failed to do so would "be a slave the following week."[46]

In April 1620, a man in England said that in Virginia, the colonists were treated "like slaves."[47] Five years later, Captain John Martin claimed that were it not for him, "the colony and its future would have been sold for slaves."[48] In March 1622, when the Indians attacked the settlement of Martin's Hundred plantation and took captures, they reportedly detained 19 colonists "in great slavery." In the aftermath of the 1622 uprising, Virginia Company officials suggested that Native Indian warriors captured during retaliatory raids be sold as slaves. In 1623, Richard Frethorne of Martin's Hundred wrote his parents that fellow settlers had taken two Indians alive "and made slaves of them."[49]

On May 25, 1611, Sir Thomas Dale sent a letter to his superiors describing how he was strengthening the colony. He said that he had put the settlers to work, repairing and constructing new improvements, and that "All the Savages I set on work who duly ply their taske." His statement indicates that Indians were among those involved in the construction of Jamestown's improvements.[50] It is very unlikely that their labor was voluntary.

In 1624, a group of ancient planters, who had come to Virginia before May 1616, described the repression they endured while the colony was governed by Sir Thomas Dale. They said that they had been in "general slavery." In another portion of the same text, they said that they had endured living conditions that were "noe waye better than slavery."[51] Around the same time, Virginia's burgesses sent word to England that during Sir Thomas Smith's government, when the colony was under martial law, those who survived "who had both adventured their estates and persons were constrained to serve the colony (as if they had been slaves!) 7 or 8 years for their freedomes, who underwent as hard and servile labour as the basest fellow that was brought out of Newgate."[52] All of these statements indicate that the colonists considered slavery as punitive and degrading, a punishment that could be imposed upon those who disobeyed the law, required strict control, or extreme correction. However, it was a punishment that stopped just short of the death penalty.

Anthony Johnson was one of the first Africans to have finished his services as an indentured servant. He then became a landowner on the Eastern Shore and a slave-owner himself.[53] Johnson was captured in his native Angola by neighboring tribesmen and sold to Arab slave traders. He was eventually sold as an indentured servant to a merchant working for the Virginia Company.[54] He arrived in Virginia in 1621 aboard the *James*. The Virginia Muster (census) of 1624 lists his name as "Antonio not given," recorded as "a Negro" in the "notes" column.[55]

Sold to a white planter named Edward Bennet as an indentured servant, Johnson was put to work on Bennet's tobacco plantation near Warresquioake, Virginia. Servants typically worked under an indenture contract for four to seven years to pay off their passage, room, board, lodging and freedom dues. In the early colonial years, most Africans in the Thirteen Colonies were held under such contracts of indentured servitude. Apart from those indentured for life, they were released after a contracted period with many of them receiving land and equipment after their contracts expired or were bought out.[56] Most white laborers also came to the colony as indentured servants.

Antonio almost lost his life in the Indian massacre of 1622 when the Bennet plantation was attacked by the Powhatan, who were the dominant Native Americans in the Tidewater of Virginia. They attacked the settlement where Johnson was working when the settlement was attacked to repulse the colonists from their lands. Fifty-two of the 57 men were killed, with Johnson being one of the five survivors.[57]

In 1622 "Mary, a Negro Woman" arrived aboard the *Margrett and John* and, like Antonio, she was brought to work on Bennett's plantation. At some point, Anthony and Mary were married; a 1653 Northampton County court document lists Mary as Anthony's wife. It was a prosperous and enduring union that lasted over forty years and produced at least four children including two sons and two daughters. The couple was respected in their community for their "hard labor and known service," according to court documents.[58]

Sometime after 1635, Antonio and Mary gained their freedom from indenture. Antonio changed his name to Anthony Johnson.[59] Johnson first enters the legal record as a free man when he purchased a calf in 1647. He was granted a large plot of farmland after he paid off his indentured contract by his labor.[60] On 24 July 1651, he acquired 250 acres of land under the headright system by buying the contracts of five indentured servants (four white and one black). The land was located on the Great Naswattock Creek which flowed into the Pungoteague River in Northampton County, Virginia.[61] When he was released from servitude, Anthony Johnson was legally recognized as a "free Negro."

In 1653, John Casor, a black indentured servant whose contract Johnson appears to have bought in the early 1640s, approached Captain Samuel Goldsmith. He claimed his indenture had expired seven years earlier and that he was being held illegally by Johnson. A neighbor, Robert Parker, intervened and persuaded Johnson to free Casor. Parker offered Casor work, and he signed a term of indenture to the planter. Johnson then sued Parker in the Northampton Court in 1654 for the return of Casor. The court initially found in favor of Parker, but Johnson appealed. In 1655, the court reversed its ruling.[62]

Finding that Anthony Johnson still "owned" John Casor, the court ordered that he be returned with the court dues paid by Robert Parker.[63] This was the first instance of a judicial determination in the Thirteen Colonies holding that a person who had committed no crime could be held in servitude for life,[64] thus making Casor the first permanent slave and Johnson the first slave owner in the New World Colonies.[65]

Since the 1654 Johnson court case, free black people, at one time or another, have owned slaves "in each of the thirteen original states and later in every state that countenanced slavery."[66] Like their white neighbors, some were benevolent masters, granting their blacks special privileges, emancipating especially loyal servants, and respecting the sanctity of slave families. However, most considered their blacks as chattel property. They bought, sold, mortgaged, willed, traded, and transferred fellow blacks, demanded long hours in the fields, and severely disciplined recalcitrant blacks. A few seemed as callous as the most profit-minded whites, selling children away from parents, mothers away from husbands, and brutally whipping slaves who ignored plantation rules.[67]

For a time, free black people could even "own" the services of white indentured servants in Virginia as well. Free blacks owned slaves in Boston by 1724 and in Connecticut by 1783. By 1790, 48 black people in Maryland owned 143 slaves. One particularly notorious black Maryland farmer named Nat Butler "regularly purchased and sold Negroes for the Southern trade."[68] By 1860, black women in Charleston had inherited or been given many slaves and other property by white men. They used these slaves and the property to start successful businesses, consequently, they owned 70 percent of the black-owned slaves in the city.[69] Carter G. Woodson and a few assistants systematically examined records of the U.S. Census in 1830. The study recorded every single household where a black person was listed as "head of household" and the household owned slaves. According to Woodson's research, the 1830 Census listed 3,776 people as "free Negroes" who owned 12,907 slaves.[70]

Having economic interests in common with the white slaveholders, Negro owners of slaves often enjoyed the same social standing. It was not exceptional for them to attend the same church, to educate their children in the same private school, and to frequent the same places of amusement. Under these circumstances, miscegenation easily followed. While those taking the census of 1830 did not generally record such facts, the few who did, as in the case of Nansemond County, Virginia, reported a situation which today would be considered alarming. There appeared among the slaveholders in this County free Negroes designated as Jacob of Read and white wife and Syphe of Matthews and white wife. Others with white wives were not reported as slaveholders.[71]

Historians have been arguing for some time over whether free blacks purchased family members as slaves to protect them or whether, on the other hand, they purchased other black people primarily to exploit their free labor for profit, just as white slave owners did. The answers to these questions are complex, but the evidence shows that, unfortunately, both opinions are true. The great black historian, John Hope Franklin, states: "The majority of Negro owners of slaves had some personal interest in their property." Still, he admits, "There were instances, however, in which free Negroes had a real economic interest in the institution of slavery and held slaves in order to improve their economic status."[72]

Slavery in the Colonies

Slavery did not exist only in the South. John Winthrop's journal entry of 1638 is apparently "the earliest recorded account of black slavery in New England. Blacks may have been enslaved before that time, but earlier allusions to slavery are inferential. Even contemporaries apparently were no more certain of the facts."[73]

Slavery did not develop in New England haphazardly or in a piecemeal fashion. Virginia developed a legal framework for slavery in response to societal custom, but the Massachusetts and Plymouth colonies statutorily sanctioned slavery as part of the 1641 Body of Liberties a mere three years after the first blacks arrived. Accordingly, Massachusetts was the first colony to authorize slavery by legislative enactment.[74]

The 1641 Body of Laws outlawed "bond slaverie, villenage, or captivitie" among settlers, unless those held in bondage were:

> lawful captives taken in juste warres, and such strangers as willfully sell themselves or are sold to us. And these shall have all the liberties and Christian usages which the law of God established in Israel concerning such persons doth morally require. This exempts none from servitude who shall be judged thereto by Authoritie.[75]

Three types of servitude were expressly prohibited and three forms were, in turn, legislatively authorized. Massachusetts colonists could rightly enslave those captured in just wars, strangers who were voluntarily or involuntarily sold into slavery, and those individuals who were required by "authorie" to be sold into servitude. Thus, the statute provided a hint of the colonists' acceptance of and participation in the institution of chattel slavery.

Winning the war with England in 1781 forced the 13 States to pool their resources and minimize their differences. The *Declaration of Independence* in 1776 proclaimed that all men were created equal, and the only way to justify slavery was to depict those who were enslaved as being not fully men. An early battle that was lost in Thomas Jefferson's first draft of the document was the phrase that criticized King George III for having enslaved Africans and for over-riding colonial Virginia's attempt to ban slavery. The Continental Congress removed this phrase under pressure from representatives of the South:[76]

> He has waged cruel war against human nature itself, violating its most sacred rights of life and liberty in the persons of a distant people who never offended him, captivating & carrying them into slavery in another hemisphere or to incur miserable death in their transportation thither. This piratical warfare, the opprobrium of infidel powers, is the warfare of the Christian King of Great Britain. Determined to keep open a market where Men should be bought & sold, he has prostituted his negative for suppressing every legislative attempt to prohibit or restrain this execrable commerce. And that this assemblage of horrors might want no fact of distinguished die, he is now exciting those very people to rise in arms among us, and to purchase that liberty of which he has deprived them, by murdering the people on whom he has obtruded them: thus paying off former crimes committed again the Liberties of one people, with crimes which he urges them to commit against the lives of another.[77]

New Englanders had grown restive about the sin of slavery, but they were obliged to overlook it for the time being. John Adams, who was passionately opposed to slavery, agreed without argument to omit the slavery passage from the *Declaration of Independence*. This was done primarily to hold together the new American Republic, but it was clearly a defeat for the slaves. The worse, however, was to come in the process of writing the constitution.[78]

Despite the freedoms demanded in the *Declaration* and the freedoms reserved in the *Constitution* and the *Bill of Rights*, slavery was not only tolerated in the Constitution, it was codified. On the slavery question, this can be seen most clearly. The Convention had representatives from every corner of the United States, including, of course, the South, where slavery was most pronounced. Slavery, in fact, was the backbone of the primary industry of the South and it was accepted as a given that agriculture in the South without slave labor was not possible. The life of the average black slave in the South was worth a considerable amount. The average price for a black slave in 1860 was approximately $800, which, in 2001 dollars, would be approximately $20,000.[79] The economic power of a slave has been estimated by academics at $2.6 million, so a slave was a large investment for slaveholders. This helps explain why the life expectancy of slaves in the South was longer than that of "free" workers in the North.[80]

Although slaves were not cheap by any measure, they were cheaper than hiring someone else to do the same work. The cultivation of rice, cotton, and tobacco required slaves to work the fields from dawn to dusk. If the nation did not guarantee the continuation of slavery to the South, it was questionable whether they could form their own nation.[81]

Originally, the Framers were very careful about avoiding the words "slave" and "slavery" in the text of the *Constitution*. Instead, they used phrases like "importation of Persons" in Article 1, Section 9 for the slave trade, "other persons" in Article 1, Section 2, and "person held to service or labor" in Article 4, Section 2 for slaves. It was not until the Thirteenth Amendment slavery was specifically mentioned in the *Constitution*. There, the term was used to ensure that there would be no ambiguity as what exactly the words were eliminating. In the Fourteenth Amendment, the euphemism "other persons" (and the three-fifths value given a slave) was eliminated.

One sees "slavery" in the Constitution in only a few key places. The first is in the Enumeration Clause, where representatives are apportioned.[82] Each state is given representatives based on its population. In that population, slaves, called "other persons," are counted as three-fifths of a whole person.

This compromise was hard-fought, with Northerners wishing that slaves, legally property, be uncounted, much as mules and horses are uncounted. Southerners, however, were aware of the high proportion of slaves to the total population in their states and wanted them counted as whole persons despite their legal status. The three-fifths number was a ratio used by the Congress in contemporary legislation and was agreed upon with little debate.[83]

Alexander Hamilton said later that, without the federal ratio, "no union could possibly have been formed." It was true. The *Constitution* could not have gone through without the slavery compromise. The question before the Convention was not one of human rights, shall slavery be abolished? Rather, it was who shall have the power to control it, the states or the national government? The result, finally, was that Congress could control the traffic in slaves exactly as it controlled all other trade and commerce.[84]

Congress is limited, expressly, from prohibiting the "Importation" of slaves, before 1808.[85] The slave trade was a bone of contention for many, with some who supported slavery abhorring the slave trade. The 1808 date, a compromise of 20 years, allowed the slave trade to continue, but placed a date-certain on its survival. Congress eventually passed a law outlawing the slave trade that became effective on January 1, 1808.

The "Fugitive Slave Clause" is the last mention.[86] The problem that slave states had with extradition of escaped slaves was resolved. The laws of one state, the clause says, cannot excuse a person from "Service or Labour" in another state. The clause expressly requires that the state in which an escapee is found must deliver the slave to the state from which he escaped from "on Claim of the Party."

The Cancer in the Body Politic

The ideas of the American Revolution added their influence to disparaging the arguments of early Christian thinkers and preachers, particularly the Quakers. They gave an entirely new vision of society as it is and as it ought to be. This vision was dominated by a radically equalitarian political morality that could not possibly include slavery as a social institution. The philosophical ideas of man's natural rights merged with the Golden Rule of Christianity, "Do unto others as you would have them do unto you."[87]

How it looked in the minds of the enlightened slaveholders who played a prominent role in the revolution is well known. Since they were under the urge for intellectual clarity in their age, their pamphlets, speeches, and letters frequently discussed the troubles of their conscience. Most of them saw clearly the inconsistency between American democracy and black slavery. To these men, slavery was an "abominable crime," a "wicked cause," a "supreme misfortune," an "inherited evil," a "cancer in the body politic."[88] Jefferson, himself, made several attacks on the institution of slavery, and some of them were [politically] nearly successful. Later in his life (1821), he wrote in his autobiography:

> . . . it was found that the public mind would not hear the proposition [of gradual emancipation], nor will it bear it even at this day. Yet the day is not far distant when it must bear it, or worse will follow. Nothing is more certainly written in the book of fate than that these people are to be free. Nor is it less certain that the two races, equally free, cannot live in the same government . . .[89]

The *Constitution of the United States*, though it provided some basis for the federal government's support of slavery, contained no authority for federal discrimination against the black race. Yet, in 1792, Congress excluded blacks from the militia and, in 1810, denied them the right to work as mail carriers. By congressional action, free blacks in Washington, D.C., were disenfranchised, excluded from certain kinds of business activity, and made subject to many of the laws regulating slaves. From time to time, Congress also disenfranchised blacks in the territories. The executive branch, though it never developed a consistent and comprehensive racial policy, added discriminatory edicts of various kinds, such as those excluding blacks from the Navy and Marine Corps in 1798 and denying them pre-emption rights on public lands in 1856.[90]

CHAPTER TWO

PRE-CIVIL WAR EDUCATION OF BLACK PEOPLE

Frederick Douglass was a man who believed that all people are created equal. Nonetheless, he also believed we were not just born free: "We have to *make* ourselves into who we are." Thus, education and self-improvement were very important to him. In fact, Douglass argued that slavery and education are completely opposite things. He worked towards making himself free by expanding his horizons though reading, but he still had to physically escape from slavery. Of course, it was his education that gave him the strength of will to make the physical escape happen.[1]

The worst thing about slavery was that it prevented people from improving themselves through education. From Hugh Auld, his owner in Baltimore, Douglass got the notion that knowledge must be the way to freedom. Slave owners kept men and women as slaves by depriving them of knowledge and education. When Auld forbade his wife to teach Douglass how to read and write because education ruins slaves, he unwittingly revealed the strategy by which whites managed to keep people as slaves and the strategy by which blacks might free themselves. The ability to read was extremely important. Reading enabled Douglass to scrutinize newspapers, pamphlets, political materials, and books of every description. The knowledge he gained from reading created a new realm of thought that led him to question and condemn the whole institution of slavery.[2]

Douglass did not oversimplify the connection between his freedom and his education. He had no illusions that knowledge automatically rendered slaves free. Knowledge helped slaves to articulate the injustice of slavery and to recognize themselves as men rather than slaves. However, rather than providing immediate freedom from slavery, it awakened a consciousness that brought much anguish to those who pursued higher knowledge.[3]

Like many abolitionists, Douglass believed that education would be crucial for black people to improve their lives. This led him to become an early advocate for school desegregation. In the 1850s, Douglass observed that New York's facilities and instruction for black children were vastly inferior to those for whites. He called for court action to open all schools to all children, arguing that full inclusion within the educational system was a more pressing need for back people than political issues such as suffrage.[4]

Early Training and Education of American Slaves

Educating black people, both enslaved and free, was often discouraged during the era of slavery in the United States. Most southern states made it illegal because many whites believed that literacy was incompatible with the institution of slavery and would ultimately lead to rebellion. Furthermore, educated blacks would demand the same rights as whites.

In the early years of African enslavement in the American colonies, slave owners taught the slaves such things as English, music, and other humanities. They did this so the slaves could communicate with them and entertain in front of company. Often, however, slave owners feared that once slaves learned how to read and write, they could more easily organize escape plans. Consequently, laws of antiliteracy were passed to keep slaves from obtaining literacy skills. The laws were only casually enforced, but they played a big role in inhibiting the improvement of education among Blacks.[5]

According to Carter G. Woodson, the history of the education of ante-bellum blacks falls into two periods.[6] The first extends from the time of the introduction of slavery to the climax of the insurrectionary movement occurring about 1835. At this point, most the people in the country answered in the affirmative the question when asked if it would be prudent to educate their slaves. The second period occurred when the industrial revolution changed slavery from a patriarchal to an economic institution. Then, intelligent blacks, encouraged by abolitionists, made so many attempts to organize servile insurrections that the pendulum began to swing the other way. Most southern white people, by this time, had reached the conclusion that it was impossible to cultivate the minds of blacks without arousing too much self-assertion.

The heathen slaves brought from the African wilds to constitute the laboring class of a pioneering society in the New World had to be trained to meet the needs of their environment. Newly arriving Africans initially received industrial and social training in the homes of their masters. If they learned well and were compatible, they were seldom resold. The slaves were taught by example as they worked in the shops, houses, and fields beside their owners. When a master was rich enough to own a small business, black slaves sometimes fell under the tutorship of fellow white servants. New slaves also learned from white children in the household, a relationship which was institutionalized regarding catechism instruction.[7]

Little argument was required to convince intelligent masters that slaves, who had some concept of modern civilization and understood the language of their owners, would be more valuable than rude men with whom one could not communicate.[8] Therefore, a common language is indispensable for intimate association between members of a group and between groups.

The inability to speak a common language represents an insurmountable barrier to adjustment and adaptation within the major culture of a community. Adhering to the proposition "that every group has its own language," its peculiar "universe of discourse," and "its cultural symbols," will only limit communication, education, and integration. The unity achieved through a single language is not necessarily, or even normally, an indication of like-mindedness. Rather, it contributes to a unity of experience and of orientation, out of which may develop a community of purpose and action.[9] Any organized social activity, any participation in this activity, implies "communication." In human society, as distinguished from animal society, common life is based on a common speech. To share a common speech does not guarantee participation in the community life, but it is an instrument of that participation.[10]

The questions as to exactly what kind of training blacks should have and how far education should go, were a matter of much confusion to the white race. Not a few masters believed that slaves could not be enlightened without developing in them a longing for liberty. They maintained that the duller and more brutish the bondsmen, the more susceptible they would be for purposes of exploitation. It was this class of slaveholders that finally won most southerners to their way of thinking and, unfortunately, determined that blacks should not be educated.[11] Still, there was the need to adapt and function in the culture, so both freemen and slaves learned to read and write because of frequent secret efforts by blacks themselves.

Each plantation was a self-sufficient economy outside of its major crop export and food import. Therefore, it required craftsmen and people with the skills necessary to maintain what was essentially an agricultural community. A small portion of slaves received excellent training as artisans and handicraftsmen. Moreover, in the towns and cities, slaves worked in the commercial handicrafts and the artisan tradition was passed on from person to person. These skills usually did not require schools or the teaching of the more general arts, but there was the need for basic literateness.[12]

Despite the oppressive conditions of slavery in the United States, a relatively large population of slaves could read, write, and had specialized skills. Free black families living in northeastern areas had education equal to the average white family. Whites living in those areas were more liberal with their slaves. In New York, they were taught to read and write after their daily work was completed and, by 1708, as many as 200 slaves were being educated. Subsequently, blacks in the North were being educated much earlier than those in the South, even though Jim Crow laws were prevalent.[13]

Reading was encouraged in religious instruction, but writing was not. Writing was a mark of status and unnecessary for many members of society, including slaves. Memorization, catechisms, and scripture formed the basis of what education was available. Still, despite the lack of importance generally given to writing instruction, there were some notable exceptions. The most famous of these exceptions was probably Phillis Wheatley, whose poetry won admiration on both sides of the Atlantic Ocean. Two others of note were Jupiter Hammon and George Moses Horton.

Phillis Wheatley (1753-1784) was the first published African-American female poet. Born in Gambia, West Africa, she was sold into slavery at the age of seven or eight and transported to North America. She was purchased by the Wheatley family of Boston, who taught her to read and write and encouraged her poetry when they recognized her talent. The publication of Wheatley's *Poems on Various Subjects, Religious and Moral* (1773) brought her fame both in England and the American colonies. She was emancipated shortly after the publication of her book.[14]

Jupiter Hammon is widely considered one of the founders of the early American and black American writing traditions. The first black American poet to be published in the United States, he was born into slavery on October 17, 1711, in Lloyd Harbor, New York. The Lloyd family encouraged him to attend school, where he learned to read and write. He went on to work alongside his owner, Henry Lloyd, as a bookkeeper and negotiator for the family's business.[15]

In his early years, Hammon was heavily influenced by the Great Awakening, a major religious revival of the time, and became a devout Christian. Hammon published his first poem, "An Evening Thought. Salvation by Christ with Penitential Cries," as a broadside in 1761. Eighteen years passed before the publication of his second work, "An Address to Miss Phillis Wheatley." In this poem, Hammon addresses a series of quatrains with accompanying Bible verses to Wheatley, the most prominent black poet of the time. In 1782, he published "A Poem for Children with Thoughts on Death." His date of death is unknown, although he is believed to have died sometime around 1806, having been enslaved his entire life.[16]

George Moses Horton (1798–1884) was a black poet born in North Carolina, the first to be published in the Southern United States. He published a book in 1828, while he was still enslaved. He wrote both sonnets and ballads. His earlier works focused on his life in servitude. Such topics, however, were more generalized and not necessarily based on his personal experience. His poetic style was apparently influenced by contemporary European poetry and white contemporaries; possibly a reflection of his reading and work on a commission basis. However, he referred to his life on "vile accursed earth" and the "drudg'ry, pain, and toil" of life, as well as his oppression "because my skin is black." Horton gained his freedom in 1865.[17]

ARCHIE MORRIS III, D.P.A.

The Mission of Christianity

The history of black education before the Civil War can be divided into three distinct, though overlapping, stages. These are white philanthropy, black self-help, and public support.[18] Prominent whites such as Benjamin Franklin and John Jay supported educating blacks because the character of the country was established from the concept of individual freedom. Blacks should be able to take their "rightful place" among other citizens. Thomas Jefferson suggested a plan for instruction that provided training, under the supervision of whites, in agriculture and handicrafts. This would prepare slaves for liberation and colonization and give them the ability to care for themselves.[19]

Even though converting slaves had no impact on their status, missionary groups sought out blacks to educate them.[20] Formal education of the black population began with the Church of England and the "Propagation of the Gospel in Foreign Parts" whose primary function was to Christianize Native Americans in the colonies. However, blacks were educated as well. In 1695, Thomas Bray of the Church of England was sent to Maryland to promote the education of slaves. By 1696, Reverend Samuel Thomas was inviting slaves to his church to learn to read and write in South Carolina. South Carolina was a main point of entry for the slave trade and its population grew rapidly. In 1755, Hugh Bryan, a religious-minded slave-owner, opened a school for slaves in Virginia where slaves often gathered in large numbers to be taught from the Bible.[21]

During the U.S. colonial period, the English settlers' efforts to teach the Indians to read were almost invariably part of a missionary effort. Two religious groups were prominent during the time, Congregationalists and Anglicans. The Congregationalists were a type of Protestant church organization in which each congregation, or local church, had free control of its own affairs. The Anglicans were related to the Church of England. Both saw the conversion of slaves as a spiritual obligation and the ability to read scriptures was part of this process.[22] The "Great Awakening" was a period of great revivalism that spread throughout the colonies in the 1730s and 1740s. It de-emphasized the importance of church doctrine and put a greater importance on the individual and their spiritual experience. The

"Great Awakening" served as a catalyst for encouraging education for all members of society.

The Church of England established the Society for the Propagation of the Gospel in Foreign Parts (SPG) in 1701. The mission of the SPG was to convert unconverted blacks, Native Americans, and whites to Christianity. In pursuit of this mission, the church saw it as necessary that blacks be educated to make reading of the Bible possible. In 1704, the SPG founded in New York the first North American school for educating Blacks.[23] The school offered a strict religious education as a means of preparing its students for baptism. Instruction, however, was hampered by the fact that slaves worked long and hard hours.

It was difficult to teach tired students, who were often discouraged by masters, and only beginning to learn the language. Still, because of dedicated teachers like Ellis Neau, a young French-born evangelist, hundreds of New York blacks learned to read and write. Neau was especially effective as a teacher of slaves because it was known that, as a former Huguenot, he had been the victim of religious persecution. He had even been chained in the slave galley of a French ship. Neau was trusted by blacks who respected him not only for his past suffering, but, also, because he continued to suffer at the hands of those in the colony who believed it dangerous folly to attempt to educate blacks.[24]

Clerical educators hoped their efforts would encourage mandatory religious education for all slaves. However, many whites resisted any education which might lead to the Christianization of slaves, believing at that time, that baptism demanded emancipation. To allay these fears, colonial officials took steps to ensure that education and consequent baptism would not alter the status of a slave when they passed a law to that effect in 1706. Despite the difficulties they experienced, the number of black students continued to grow. By 1710, over 200 blacks were educated at Neau's school alone. The New York slave rebellion of 1712, a violent insurrection of slaves in New York City, confirmed the fears of many whites and black educational activities were temporarily halted. This revolt resulted in brutal executions and the enactment of harsher slave codes, but black education efforts ultimately continued throughout the colonial period.[25]

Thirty-nine years later, the SPG founded another school for blacks in Charleston, South Carolina. The Charleston Negro School employed two slaves who were purchased to serve as instructors in the hope that blacks would receive instruction from teachers of their own race with more facility and willingness than they would from white teachers. The school continued for 22 years and was closed only when the last black teacher died, and no one was found to fill the vacancy. The significance of the school was that it existed after South Carolina's Slave Code of 1740 which prohibited slaves from gathering without white supervision, learning to read and write, and growing their own food.[26] It also created harsher punishments for disobeying the law.

Toward the end of the 18th century, abolitionist organizations and wealthier members of the Quaker Church initiated the foundation of schools in New York, New Jersey, Pennsylvania, Rhode Island, Delaware, Maryland, Virginia, South Carolina, and Georgia. Meanwhile, schools were independently being opened by free blacks. The first official Catholic school open to blacks was founded in Washington D.C. by Sister Maria Becraft, a devout Catholic committed to the education of black girls. Two schools were opened in Charleston, South Carolina, by the Brown Fellowship Society, which was an organization for mulattos. One of the schools was for the children of the members of the society and the other was for darker, but free, blacks and orphans.[27]

Opposition and Support for Educating Slaves

Winning the war with England in 1781 forced the Thirteen States to pool their resources and minimize their differences. The *Declaration of Independence*, in 1776, proclaimed that all men were created equal and the only way to justify slavery was to depict those who were enslaved as being not fully men. An early battle that was lost in Thomas Jefferson's first draft was the phrase that criticized King George III for having enslaved Africans and for over-riding colonial Virginia's attempt to ban slavery. The Continental Congress removed that phrase under pressure from representatives from the Southern States.[28] New Englanders had grown restive about the sin of slavery, but they were obliged to overlook slavery for the time being. John Adams, for example, who was passionately opposed to slavery, agreed without argument to omit the slavery passage from the

Declaration of Independence, primarily to hold together the new American Republic. This was clearly a defeat for the slaves, but worse was yet to come in the process of writing the constitution.[29]

The list of restrictions on the everyday activities of slaves was extensive, but in comparison to teaching a slave to read and write, they were almost never enforced.[30] Essentially, slaves were given little or no formal education. It had been a crime to teach a slave to read because ignorance made for a more docile and tractable labor force. Particularly revealing, however, was the prohibition against teaching a slave to read or write—an act that elicited penalties of as much as 15 pounds sterling. It took the better part of a century to wipe out the mass illiteracy that was one of slavery's most crippling legacies.[31] In the opening year of the 20th century, almost half—45 percent—of the nation's black adults were unable to read and write and, in 1940, the proportion was still a sizable one out of nine.[32]

Public opposition to the education of black slaves was inferred from misgivings like those of the state. Reassurance for the rightness of such convictions was accompanied by self-serving assertions that Africans were not educable. Efforts to "civilize" and "Christianize," however well meaning, were ultimately doomed to failure because blacks were deemed to be incorrigible in their behavior, less than fully human, or by nature suited only to simple, mindless tasks. "Johny is the most constant churchgoer I have, "wealthy Virginia slave owner Landon Carter, a staunch churchman, noted, "but he is a drunkard, a thief and a rogue." When slaves experienced "new birth" through revival preaching, Carter bemoaned the consequences for all concerned: "I believe it is from some inculcated doctrine of those rascals that the slaves in this colony are grown so much worse."[33]

White opposition to education and conversion of slaves, Anglican complicity with slavery and neglect of the slaves, and the African's resistance to Anglican Christianity were clearly parts of the story, but not the whole story. The latter is more muddled, ambiguous, and complicated than most accounts would have it. Anglican parsons baptized slaves and thereby acknowledged not only their membership in the church, but their humanity as well. Black people attended Divine Service and parsons catechized them and sponsored efforts to extend their basic education.[34]

The early advocates of the education of slaves were of three classes. First, there were the masters who desired to increase the economic efficiency of their labor supply. Second, there were those sympathetic persons who wished to help the oppressed. And third, there were the zealous missionaries who, believing that the message of divine love came equally to all, taught slaves the English language that they might learn the principles of the Christian religion. Slaves had their best chance for mental improvement through the kindness of the first class. Each slaveholder dealt with the situation to suit himself, regardless of public opinion. Later, when measures were passed to prohibit the education of slaves, some masters, always a law unto themselves, continued to teach their slaves in defiance of the hostile legislation. Sympathetic persons were not able to accomplish much because they were usually reformers. They not only did not own slaves, but they resided in practically free settlements far from the plantations on which the bondsmen lived.[35]

The Spanish and French missionaries were the first to face this problem and they set an example which influenced the education of blacks throughout America. Some of these early heralds of Catholicism manifested more interest in the Indians than they did in blacks and advocated the enslavement of the Africans rather than of the Red Men. However, being anxious to see blacks enlightened and brought into the Church, they courageously directed their attention to the teaching of their slaves, provided for the instruction of the numerous mixed-breed offspring, and granted free blacks the educational privileges of the highest classes. Put to shame by this noble example of the Catholics, the English colonists had to find a way to overcome the objections of those who, granting that the enlightenment of the slaves might not lead to servile insurrection, nevertheless feared that their conversion might work toward emancipation. To meet this exigency, the colonists secured, through legislation in their assemblies and formal declarations of the Bishop of London, the repeal of the law that a Christian could not be held as a slave. This allowed access to the bondsmen and the missionaries of the Church of England, sent out by the Society for the Propagation of the Gospel among the Heathen in Foreign Parts, undertook to educate the slaves for the purpose of extensive proselyting.[36]

The liberal Puritans had directed their attention to the conversion of the slaves long before these early workers of the Established Church of England advocated abolition. Many of them justified slavery as established by the precedent of the Hebrews, but they felt that persons held to service should be instructed as were the servants of the household of Abraham. The progress of the cause was impeded, however, by the bigoted class of Puritans who did not think well of the policy of incorporating undesirable persons into a Church that was then closely connected with the state.[37]

The Quakers were the most significant group to uphold education of slaves. By 1735, they organized schools for black slaves in the South even though there was a tremendous opposition to teaching them to read and write. Slave owners asserted it would be useless to teach slaves because they were mentally inferior and were content with their present existence. Any attempt to educate them might make them aware of their real conditions and provoke them to unrest. However, the Quakers began a reactionary movement. They wanted slaves to be men and women who were capable of being active citizens. George Fox, a prominent Quaker and advocate for black education, spoke boldly about teaching blacks and Indians... how Christ died for all men. In addition, George Keith and William Penn supported religious training, opportunity for improvement, and preparation for emancipation.[38]

The Quakers were so adamant about the dissolution of the slave trade that they developed a plan for free slaves to return to Africa as missionaries. As a result, they were persecuted in slaveholding communities for their beliefs and actions. There was strict opposition to their ideas and laws were enacted to prevent them meeting with blacks and excluding them from the teaching profession by creating a proclamation they could not sign for religious reasons.[39]

Ironically, Quakers were vocal proponents of educating slaves even though they were slave owners themselves. In 1774, John Woolman published "Some Considerations on the Keeping of Negroes," where he admonished Quakers who founded and funded schools while retaining slaves of their own.[40] The Quakers continued to open schools for black children in areas such as Rhode Island before it became a free state.

The Quakers formed the Manumission Society to protect slaves from bounty hunters ("manu" was a term used interchangeably with abolish). In 1787, the manumissions group established the New York African Free School to empower blacks to protect themselves through education. The school began with 40 pupils whose parents were slaves. Four years later, a female teacher was hired, and girls were admitted. The first building was destroyed by fire and a second was erected in 1820 with land contributed by the City of New York to accommodate an additional five hundred students. Though this school was an important milestone in the lives of blacks, it was not widely supported by whites. In the Northeastern areas, blacks also were not thought to be equal to whites. To receive support, scholars from around the world were invited to observe their program. Students performed such skills as reading, essays, poetry, and prose for invited guests.[41]

During the 18th century, religious organizations such as the Episcopal Society for the Propagation of the Gospel, which worked in both the North and the South, and the Society of Friends, undertook rudimentary education of slaves and free blacks to enable them to read the bible. Some anti-slavery societies formed during the Revolutionary era also offered free blacks an opportunity for elementary education. In 1787, the New York Manumission Society opened the African Free School, which was so successful that six additional schools were added in the city by 1834. Ultimately, they became part of the public school system.[42]

Black Education Initiatives

Under the auspices of the black churches and mutual benefit societies emerging at the end of the 18th century, free blacks maintained their own schools. Even where white philanthropic support was solicited, the initiative came from blacks themselves. In Newport, Rhode Island, a white Episcopal rector established in 1763 a school for blacks. In 1807, eight years after the school had closed, the leaders of the black community reopened it through their newly organized African Benevolent Society. The institution was operated with varying degrees of success until the city took over. In 1787, in Boston, Prince Hall led a group of blacks in petitioning the Massachusetts General Court for a school because blacks "receive no benefit from the free schools." According to some authorities, a few black children did attend the public schools with whites at the end of the 18th century. However, most withdrew because of ridicule and mistreatment.[43]

In 1798, some black parents, supported by white friends, opened a private school in Prince Hall's home. Seven years later, the institution moved to the African Meeting House. Not until 1820, however, was a black public school opened, and within a short time blacks lost their right to use the white schools. Early in the nineteenth century, several black Philadelphia ministers organized schools in their churches and the Bethel AME Church founded the Society of Free People of Color for Promoting the Instruction and School Education of Children of African Descent. In 1812, the New York Society of Free People of Color established a school for orphans.[44]

In the South during the ante-bellum period, black education never went beyond the second stage. By the beginning of the 19th century, a substantial number of free blacks, having achieved a degree of economic security as mechanics and tradesmen, were financially underwriting their own schools. In the Deep South, the Brown Fellowship Society of Charleston, as early as 1790, provided educational facilities as part of its mutual-welfare program. Two decades later, the Minor Society was organized to educate indigent and orphaned children. In 1829, one of the youths trained by the Minor Society, Daniel Alexander Payne, opened a school of his own for black children. In New Orleans, the Roman Catholic Church educated some blacks, but that city's prosperous *gens de couleur* provided financial support for several schools of their own. Older children were sent to France for instruction and, in 1840, blacks established the École des Orphelins Indigents for the education of lower-class youth.[45]

As the Southern race system grew harsher during the 19th century, the education of free blacks was restricted, though never eliminated. In 1823, Mississippi forbade groups of blacks larger than five to study together. In Charleston, beginning in 1834, it became legally mandatory that a white person attend each class meeting. Payne closed his school and moved to the North, where he became a distinguished AME bishop. However, some of the free black schools continued to operate. In many other parts of the South, private classes were held, by both philanthropically minded whites and blacks, often in violation of state or city regulations.[46]

In the Border States, there was no such interference by public authorities, nor did white educators actively assist black schooling. The first two schools that blacks established in Baltimore were in existence by the beginning of the 19th century. One was under the auspices of the all-black Sharp Street Methodist Church and the other was conducted by Daniel Coker, the pioneer AME minister. Other black churches were soon operating education institutions and, during the 1820s, even adults received instruction at night in various subjects, including Latin and French. Some white philanthropists contributed time, money, and teachers to supplement these efforts. The first school for blacks in Washington was formed in 1807 by three illiterate black men, two of whom worked in the Navy Yard. They constructed a small frame schoolhouse and employed a white teacher. Beginning with the educational institution opened in 1818 by the Resolute Beneficial society, Washington's blacks were not without at least one well-administered school and, in their efforts, they obtained the cooperation of certain dedicated whites as well. It was not until 1862 that Washington municipal authorities undertook to create schools for blacks.[47]

Encouraging as were things after these early efforts, the complaints about the neglect to instruct the slaves showed that the cause lacked something to make the movement general. Then came the days when the struggle for the rights of man, based on principles of the *Age of Enlightenment*, aroused the civilized world. Most popular in France, where its leaders included philosophers like Voltaire and Denis Diderot, an important principle of the *Enlightenment* was that all people can reason and think for themselves and should not automatically believe what an authority says. Another important idea was that a society works best when everyone works together to create it. People with very little power or money, should have the same rights as the rich and powerful to help create the society within which they live.[48]

After 1760, the emerging social doctrine found response among the American colonists. They looked with opened eyes at the blacks and a new day dawned for the dark-skinned race. Patriots such as Patrick Henry and James Otis, who demanded liberty for themselves, could not but concede that slaves were entitled at least to freedom of body. The frequent acts of manumission and emancipation, which followed this change in attitude toward persons of color, turned loose upon the society many men whose chief needs were education and training in the duties of citizenship. To advance these schools, missions and churches were established by benevolent and religious workers. These colaborers included at this time the Baptists and Methodists who, thanks to the spirit of toleration incident to the *Revolution*, were allowed access to blacks, both slaves and freemen.[49]

For black Americans, as for Americans generally, education was both the foundation of freedom and one of its benefits. As blacks gained their freedom, they established schools, often building on the earlier efforts of white evangelical groups and Quakers. Quaker educational efforts in Philadelphia were especially extensive, beginning in the 1750s and continuing with the Friends African School, established in 1770 and the Association for the Free Instruction of Adult Colored People organized in 1789.[50] Under their auspices, black men and women in separate classrooms received a basic education on Sundays and weekday evenings at three different locations in the city until the War of 1812.

In 1790, members of the Pennsylvania Abolition Society formed a Committee on Education to support black education. They funded several schools started by blacks, including one begun by Eleanor Harris, a free black woman. They also assisted schools run by Absalom Jones, a black abolitionist and clergyman, Cyrus Bustill, a mulatto who was born into bondage and later purchased his freedom, Ann Williams, a school headmistress, and Amos White, a teacher. The committee led efforts to raise funds for the construction of a permanent black school. Clarkson Hall, named in honor of British abolitionist Thomas Clarkson, opened in 1813, educating black children during the day and adults in the evening. For 13 years, according to its abolitionist sponsors, this school provided "a decided refutation of the charge that the mental endowments of the descendants of Africa are inferior to those possessed by their white brethren."[51] Although the Clarkson school could not withstand competition from the public schools, many blacks believed their success in maintaining the private school helped encourage the establishment of public schools.[52]

Educational Rewards

With all these new opportunities, blacks displayed a rapid mental development. Intelligent colored men proved to be useful and trustworthy servants. They became much better laborers and artisans, and many of them showed administrative ability adequate to manage business establishments and large plantations. Moreover, better rudimentary education served many ambitious persons of color as a stepping-stone to higher attainments. Blacks learned to appreciate and write poetry and contributed to mathematics, science, and philosophy. Furthermore, having disproved the theories of their mental inferiority, some of the race, in conformity with the suggestion of the socially and politically influential Puritan minister, Cotton Mather, were employed to teach white children.[53]

William Syphax, son of Charles and Maria Syphax, was born in 1825 shortly after the troublesome days of the Missouri Compromise. He witnessed the growing hatred and sectional discords that resulted in the Compromise of 1850 and saw the devastating effects of the Kansas-Nebraska Bill, the Dred Scott Decision, and the John Brown Raid. He lived through the hectic days of disunion, civil war and subsequent reconstruction, and, through it all, he had an abiding faith in his people. At every possible opportunity, Mr. Syphax demonstrated a manliness and a fortitude in his efforts to champion their cause. He would go on to establish the first Preparatory High School for Colored Youth in the District of Columbia 45 years later.[54] Established in 1870, the Preparatory School became the M Street High School in 1891 and the Paul Laurence Dunbar High School in 1916,

Observing these evidences of a general uplift of blacks, certain educators advocated the establishment of special colored schools. The founding of these institutions, however, was not a movement to separate the children of the races because of caste prejudice. Rather, the dual system resulted from an effort to meet the needs peculiar to a people just emerging from bondage. It was easily seen that their education should no longer be dominated by religion but should unite the benefits of practical and cultural education. The teachers of black schools offered courses in the industries along with advanced work in literature, mathematics, science, and languages.[55]

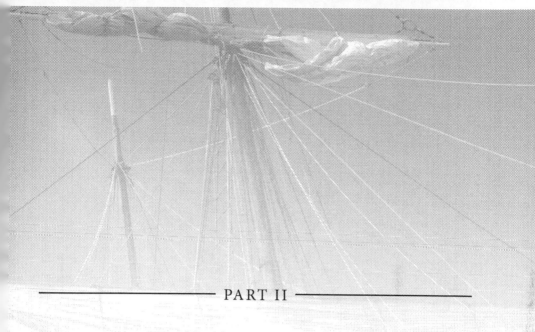

PART II

DRED SCOTT TO RECONCILIATION

"Racial hatred in America still exists but never was it anything like the time immediately after the Civil War. The western history of our nation would not be complete without the story of former slaves that helped develop the unique character of the West."

— William A. Silverman, 1930-2012

CHAPTER THREE

SPARKING THE INEVITABLE WAR

Competition is a common state of affairs in the world of living things. Under ordinary circumstances, it goes on unobserved even by the individuals who are most concerned. However, in periods of crisis, when men are making new and conscious efforts to control the conditions of their common life, when the forces with which they are competing get identified with persons, then competition is converted into conflict. It is in what has been described as the *political process* that society consciously deals with its crises.[1] War is the ultimate political process. It is in war that the big decisions are made. Political organizations exist to deal with conflict situations. Political parties, courts, public discussion, and voting are simply substituting for war.

The *U.S. Civil War* was fought in the United States from 1861 to 1865 and, as with most wars, there was no single cause. Historical revisionists have attempted to offer a variety of reasons for the conflict, but most academic scholars identify slavery as the central cause. .[2] It was the most terrible conflict that America has experienced during its comparatively short existence, resulting in 620,000 to 750,000 U.S. military deaths.[3]

For more than 80 years, people in the Northern and Southern states debated the issues that ultimately led to the war: economic policies and practices, cultural values, the extent and reach of the national government, and the role of slavery within the American society. Against the backdrop of these larger issues, individual soldiers had their own reasons for fighting. Their motivations often included a complex mix of personal, social, economic and political values which did not necessarily match the aims expressed by their respective governments or those of other members of their families. The latter, in some instances, resulted in siblings being pitted against one another in battles between the armies of the North and the South.[4]

The political conflict between the North and the South became clear in 1819, when Missouri applied for admission into the Union to become a state. Because the territorial laws of Missouri recognized and embraced slavery, Northern members of Congress refused to approve Missouri's application, while Southern congressmen fully backed Missouri for statehood. The confrontations in the halls of Congress over this issue were long and, often, heated. It was during this debate that tensions between the North and the South took center stage in United States politics and civil war became a distinct possibility.[5]

The Dred Scott Case

The *Missouri Compromise* held that Missouri would be admitted as a slaveholding state, but no slavery would be allowed anywhere else north of the Mason-Dixon Line. The Mason-Dixon Line runs west from Maryland to the Ohio River, then south along the river, finally turning west along latitude 36 degrees-30 minutes north, along the southern border of Missouri. It also included the "Bootheel," even though it extends below the line. The Missouri state legislature was infuriated at this because it imposed conditions upon Missouri that had not been imposed upon other states. Missouri became the only "Northern" state where slavery was legal and, as a result, the Missouri legislature resolved Missouri would side with the South, further fanning the fuels of North-South conflict.[6]

Another factor that contributed to the start of the war was the *Dred Scott* case of 1847 in St. Louis, Missouri. Fourteen years before Fort Sumter, Scott, a slave, sued for his freedom. He had attempted to buy his own freedom and that of his wife, Harriet, but was turned down. Scott then sought his freedom through the courts. The Supreme Court dealt abolition a stunning blow with its ruling in 1857.[7]

Scott, born a slave in Virginia, claimed his freedom after living for years outside the South with his master, who was a military man stationed in Illinois and in Wisconsin Territory where slavery was prohibited. The case passed through state and local courts and finally reached the Supreme Court where Chief Justice Roger B. Taney issued a ruling that greatly distressed black Americans and their allies. Taney concluded that Scott remained a slave and added that Congress had no right to legislate against slavery in the western territories. This effectively declared the *Missouri Compromise* of 1820 unconstitutional. Even more disturbing, Taney declared that blacks had no citizenship rights under the *United States Constitution*. Despite their service in the *Revolution* that won America's freedom and in the *War of 1812* that reinforced and defended it, no matter that they voted in New England and with qualifications elsewhere, and despite the fact that many blacks held American passports, Taney proclaimed that black people had never been, were not, and could never be citizens of the United States. They had "no rights which the white man was bound to respect."[8]

The decision and Taney's opinion infuriated black Americans. They had faced increasing attacks on their rights for the entire decade and were then told by the highest court in the land that they had no rights. Standing before a Philadelphia protest meeting in the spring of 1857, just one month after the decision, black abolitionist Charles Lenox Remond expressed the rage that so many felt. "We owe no allegiance to a country which grinds us under its iron heel and treats us like dogs. The time has gone by for colored people to talk of patriotism."[9]

At a New York meeting chaired by journalist and social reformer William Lloyd Garrison, Frederick Douglass continued to contend that the *Constitution* was a document that could be used to attack slavery. "As a man, an American, a citizen, a colored man of both Anglo-Saxon and African descent," Douglass argued, "I denounce the representation as a most scandalous and devilish perversion of the *Constitution*, and a brazen mis-statement of the facts of history."[10]

Political leader Robert Purvis disagreed, "I assert that the *Constitution* is fitting and befitting those who made it — slaveholders and their abettors." He further proclaimed that the federal government "in its formation and essential structure as well as its practice, is one of the basest, meanest, most atrocious despotisms that ever saw the face of the sun." Praising the antislavery society leading a new revolution against this despotism, Purvis continued, "I rejoice . . . that there is a prospect of this atrocious government being overthrown and a better one built up in its place."[11] In the aftermath of the *Dred Scott* decision, some blacks left the United States for Canada, but others redoubled their determination to stay and fight for the rights that the court had refused to recognize.

Lincoln, Douglas, and Slavery

A statistical report on the black ownership of slaves was done in 1921 when the Director of the Association for the Study of Negro Life and History (ASNLH) obtained from the Laura Spelman Rockefeller Memorial an appropriation to do research into certain neglected aspects of Negro History. This statistical report, however, was not the objective of the Research Department of the Association. Rather, it developed as a by-product. In compiling the statistics for the much larger report on free Negro heads of families in the United States in 1830, the investigators found so many cases of blacks owning slaves that it was decided to take special notice of this phase of the history of free blacks. The investigators were impressed with the frequent occurrence of wide separation of the master from the slave. In noting the cases of free blacks owning slaves, it was then a simple matter to record cases of absentee ownership, and it was done accordingly.[12]

The purpose of the report was to facilitate further study of this neglected group. Persons, supposedly well informed in history, are surprised to learn today that about a half million, almost one-seventh of the blacks in this country, were free prior to the emancipation in 1865. Furthermore, they find it incredulous that a considerable number of blacks were owners of slaves themselves and, in some cases, controlled large plantations.

According to Carter G. Woodson, the 1830 census records showed that most black slaveowners did so from the point of view of philanthropy. In many instances, the husband purchased the wife or vice versa. The slaves belonging to such families were few compared with the large numbers found among whites on the well-developed plantations. Slaves of blacks were in some cases the children of a free father who had purchased his wife. If he did not subsequently emancipate the mother, as so many such husbands failed to do, his own children were born his slaves and were thus reported by the enumerators.[13]

The Woodson thesis underestimated the materialistic side of black slaveholding when he stated that most free blacks owned slaves for benevolent reasons. Many black slaveowners were firmly committed to chattel slavery and saw no reasons for manumitting their slaves. To those colored masters, slaves were merely property to be purchased, sold, or exchanged. Their economic self-interest overrode whatever moral concern or guilt they may have harbored about slavery. Since the black slaveowners benefitted from slavery, they rationalized that, because the institution was profitable, they could not relinquish their valuable property without being reimbursed.[14] Free black slave owners resided in states as far north as New York and as far south as Florida, extending westward into Kentucky, Mississippi, Louisiana, and Missouri. The federal census of 1830 indicates free blacks owned more than 10,000 slaves in Louisiana, Maryland, South Carolina, and Virginia. Most black slaveowners lived in Louisiana and planted sugar cane.[15] Furthermore, black slaveowners continued to own slaves throughout the *Civil War*.

Having economic interests in common with the white slaveholders, the black owners of slaves often enjoyed social standing close to that of whites. It was not exceptional for them to attend the same church, to educate their children in the same private school, and to frequent the same places of amusement. Under such circumstances miscegenation easily followed. While those taking the census of 1830 did not generally record such facts, the few who did, as in the case of Nansemond County, Virginia, reported a situation which today would be considered alarming. In this county, there appeared among the slaveholders free Negroes designated as Jacob of Read and white wife and Syphe of Matthews and white wife. Others reported with white wives were not slaveholders.[16]

Still, slavery had become the nation's central political issue when Abraham Lincoln, a railroad lawyer and moderate Republican, challenged Stephen A. Douglas for his Senate seat in 1858. Their positions on slavery and the *Dred Scott* ruling were the critical factors. Douglas, a Democrat, accepted Taney's decision, while Lincoln argued that the ruling was a misreading of the intent of the framers of the *Declaration of Independence*. While acknowledging that the founders did not mean to "declare all men equal in all respects," Lincoln did believe that they recognized the right of all men to basic liberty. He argued that they placed it in the *Declaration of*

Independence, not because it was practical for their time, "but, for future use." Douglas and the Democrats referred derisively to the Republicans as "black Republicans," charging them with seeking to promote black equality.[17]

Republicans argued that keeping the West free of slavery would preserve it for free white labor and condemned the *Dred Scott* decision, calling it part of the "Slave Power Conspiracy" to subvert the federal government and extend slavery into all parts of the West.[18] Lincoln walked a fine line, condemning slavery and arguing for black rights without seeming to support race mixing. "Now I protest against the counterfeit logic," he declared, "which concludes that, because I do not want a black woman for a slave I must necessary want her for a wife."[19] Seven debates took the candidates thousands of miles crisscrossing the state of Illinois. Lincoln discussed the immorality of slavery, while Douglas focused only on the politics of the institution.[20]

Blacks could not vote in Illinois, and, hence, could do little to prevent Lincoln's defeat. In New York, however, propertied blacks could vote, and they faced a difficult choice. In the gubernatorial contest, they could either support the Republican, Edwin D. Morgan, or support Gerrit Smith who was running on the Radical Abolitionist ticket. At a meeting in Troy, black New Yorkers debated their options. Some voted their hearts by supporting Smith and his party, though he had no real chance of success. Others cast more practical and perhaps critical votes for the Republicans. A resolution advocating support for the Republicans was hotly debated and finally passed, although many like Reverend Dr. Henry Highland Garnet, president of the American and Foreign Anti-Slavery Society, asked that "their name [not be] identified with it." Despite their differences, New York blacks helped elect the Republican to the governor's chair.[21]

The seeds of the American civil war lay in the institution of slavery, which had already existed in America for over a century at the time the United States gained its independence. By the beginning of the 19th century, slavery was an exclusively Southern institution, with slaves providing the labor for the South's extensive staple-crop economy. During the first half of the century, increasing moral objections to the institution led to increasing defensiveness and hostility on the part of the South. A minority of Northerners espoused abolitionism, the position that slavery should be immediately abolished rather than be allowed to continue or even be phased out slowly. Abolitionists in the North condemned slavery. In response, Southerners, coming more and more to think that such views represented all Northerners, reciprocated with charges of bigotry and extremism.[22]

The coexistence of a slave-owning South with an increasingly antislavery North made conflict inevitable. Much of the political battle in the 1840s focused on the expansion of slavery into the newly created territories.[23] All of the organized territories were likely to become free-soil states, which increased the Southern movement toward secession. Both the North and the South assumed that if slavery could not expand, it would wither and die.[24] Sectional disagreements over the morality of slavery, the scope of democracy, and the economic merits of free labor versus slave plantations, caused the Whig and "Know-Nothing" parties to collapse, and new ones to arise in the form of the Free Soil Party in 1848, the Republicans in 1854, and the Constitutional Union in 1860. In 1860, the last remaining national political party, the Democratic Party at its convention in Charleston, South Carolina, split along sectional lines of North and South.[25]

Since the U.S. constitutional system clearly made the domestic institutions of the individual states their own concern, Northerners could do nothing about the existence of slavery in the already existing Southern states. However, many Northerners did hope to prevent slavery from spreading to new areas still under federal control. The political struggle thus came to focus on the status of slavery in the territories. When, in 1854, the Republican Party was born with the central theme of permitting no further spread of slavery into the territories, offended Southerners loudly declared that their states would secede from the Union should a Republican be elected president.[26]

In 1860, the electorate put Southern threats to the test by choosing Republican Abraham Lincoln in an unusual four-way election contest. Abraham Lincoln received not a single vote in the Southern states and received fewer than half of the popular vote. He nevertheless comfortably won the needed majority electoral vote by carrying every Northern state except New Jersey, where he split the electoral vote with Democratic candidate Stephen A. Douglas. Like many other Northerners, Lincoln believed that Southern talk of secession was empty bluster. Southerners, however, lost no time in making good their threat.[27]

Secession from the Union

On December 20, 1860, before Lincoln took office, South Carolina declared itself no longer part of the Union, and, during the next six weeks, six other Southern states, Mississippi, Florida, Alabama, Georgia, Louisiana, and Texas, followed suit. In February 1861, their representatives met at Montgomery, Alabama, and set up a government which they declared to be the Confederate States of America. They selected Jefferson Davis of Mississippi, a former army officer, secretary of war, and U.S. senator, as their president.[28]

Davis said that they had left the Union "to save ourselves from a revolution" that threatened to make "property in slaves so insecure as to be comparatively worthless." The Confederate secretary of state advised foreign governments that the southern states had formed a new nation "to preserve their old institutions" from "a revolution [that] threatened to destroy their social system."[29] Many Southerners still believed that the North would tamely accept their secession and that no war would follow, but Davis rightly suspected otherwise.

Lincoln had not proposed federal laws against slavery where it already existed. In his 1858 "House Divided Speech," he expressed a desire to "arrest the further spread of it and place it where the public mind shall rest in the belief that it is in the course of ultimate extinction."[30] In his inaugural address, he appealed for calm and reason. Asserting that states could not rightly withdraw from the Union, he nevertheless promised not to take aggressive action against them unless they fired the first shot. Significantly, he asserted that he would continue to hold the remaining federal outposts in the South.[31]

On April 14, 1861, the American flag came down and the Confederate stars and bars rose over Fort Sumter.[32] The North responded to the attack on Fort Sumter with expressions of outrage, patriotic rallies, and a rush to enlist in the military. The news galvanized the North. On April 15, Lincoln issued a proclamation calling 75,000 militiamen into national service for 90 days to put down an insurrection "too powerful to be suppressed by the ordinary course of judicial proceedings." The response from the free states was overwhelming.[33]

War meetings in every city and village cheered the flag and vowed vengeance on traitors. "The heather is on fire," wrote a Harvard professor who had been born during George Washington's presidency. "I never knew what a popular excitement can be. . . . The whole population, men, women, and children, seem to be in the streets with Union favors and flags." From Ohio and the West came "one great Eagle-scream" for the flag. "The people have gone stark mad!"[34]

In New York City, previously a nursery of pro-Southern sentiment, a quarter of a million people turned out for a Union rally. "The change in public sentiment here is wonderful—almost miraculous," wrote a New York merchant on April 18. "I look with awe on the national movement here in New York and all through the Free States," added a lawyer. "After our late discords, it seems supernatural." The "time before Sumter" was like another century, wrote a New York woman. "It seems as if we never were alive till now; never had a country till now."[35]

Declaring that a rebellion existed, Lincoln called for 75,000 three-month volunteers to put it down. The quota was met and exceeded within days. The South was excited, too, and pleased that their leaders had finally struck a blow against the hated Yankees. Davis called for 100,000 one-year volunteers, and Southern men responded with equal eagerness. The slave states of Virginia, North Carolina, Tennessee, and Arkansas, faced with the choice of fighting either for or against their fellow slave states of the Confederacy, chose to go with the South. Eager for the prestige that Virginia offered as the home of Washington, Madison, and Jefferson, the Confederacy transferred its capital to Richmond at the end of May.[36]

Four slave states remained in the Union. Delaware had few slaves and never seriously considered secession. Maryland possessed many slaves in the eastern part of the state, and that section was virulently pro-Confederate. When the Sixth Massachusetts Regiment passed through Baltimore on its way to Washington, a proslavery mob attacked it. Several fatalities occurred on both sides. Other Marylanders strove to take the state out of the Union and into the Confederacy, but Lincoln moved firmly to quash the secession movement in Maryland. When he did, he had to bend or temporarily set aside certain legal provisions. Among those was an order from U.S. Supreme Court Chief Justice Roger B. Taney, himself a Marylander, directing him not to jail a man who was endeavoring to recruit troops for the Confederacy within the state. Contrary to what Confederate propaganda maintained, however, Lincoln's infringements on civil liberties were few and slight, considering the exigency that faced the nation.[37]

Another slave state on the border between North and South was Kentucky, the home state of both Abraham Lincoln and Jefferson Davis. The Bluegrass State's populace was sharply divided between the Confederacy and the Union. On the other hand, a large segment was simply determined to go with Kentucky, whichever way it went. The result was that the state declared itself neutral and forbade either side to move troops into or through its territory. This bizarre arrangement was an enormous benefit to the Confederacy while it lasted, shielding the heartland of the South from Union invasion. Yet, both sides carefully observed the limitation, since, as Lincoln saw it, the loss of Kentucky would fatally tip the balance in the coming war against the North. Kentucky neutrality continued throughout the summer of 1861. Then, a Confederate general foolishly invaded the state in early September. Thereafter, Kentucky opted for the Union, although a few of its citizens wound up fighting for the South.[38]

The westernmost border slave state was Missouri. Swift and decisive action by federal authorities there staved off an early attempt by pro-Southern forces to snatch power in the state. Missouri remained bitterly divided and saw ferocious guerrilla warfare that sometimes degenerated into bloodthirsty banditry that continued beyond the end of the war. For the most part, however, the state remained Union territory, rarely visited by main-force Confederate armies.[39]

After the Union had assumed control of the border states, it established a naval blockade while both sides massed armies and resources. The navy was a little better prepared for war than the army. There were 42 ships in commission when Lincoln became president, and most were patrolling waters thousands of miles from the United States. Fewer than a dozen warships were available for immediate service along the American coast.[40]

Civil War

Union and Confederate troops fought the first major battle of the war at Bull Run (or Manassas Junction), Virginia, on July 21, 1861. It was the first test of strength and, by all odds, it was thought that the North should have won. Bull Run was both a repulse to Union armies and a rebuke to Northern expectations. It was nearly a home thrust, for it took place but a few miles from the Union capital whose inhabitants, from the time of the Baltimore riots in April 1861 through Jubal Early's raid of July 1864, lived in intermittent fear of being captured.[41]

No sooner had the armies, east and west, penetrated Virginia and Tennessee than fugitive slaves appeared within their lines. They came at night, when the flickering camp fires of the blue hosts shone like stars along the black horizon. They were old men, thin, with gray and tufted hair. They were women with frightened eyes, dragging whimpering, hungry children. They were men and girls, stalwart and gaunt, a horde of starving vagabonds, homeless, helpless, and pitiable in their dark distress.[42]

Two methods of treating these newcomers seemed equally logical to opposite sorts of minds. Said some, "We have nothing to do with slaves." "Hereafter," commanded Union Gen. Henry Halleck, "no slaves should be allowed to come into your lines at all; if any come without your knowledge, when owners call for them, deliver them." But others said, "We take grain and fowl; why not slaves?" Whereupon Maj. Gen. John Fremont, as early as August 1861, declared the slaves of Missouri rebels free. Such radical action was quickly countermanded, but at the same time the opposite policy could not be enforced. Some of the black refugees declared themselves freemen, others showed their masters had deserted them, and still others were captured with forts and plantations.[43]

Evidently, too, slaves were a source of strength to the Confederacy, and were being used as laborers and producers. "They constitute a military resource," wrote Secretary of War Simon Cameron, late in 1861, "and being such, that they should not be turned over to the enemy is too plain to discuss." So, the tone of the army chiefs changed. Congress forbade the rendition of fugitives, and the "contrabands" were welcomed as military laborers. This complicated rather than solved the problem. Now the scattering fugitives became a steady stream, which flowed faster as the armies marched.[44]

In 1862, the American Civil War battles, such as Shiloh and Antietam, caused massive casualties unprecedented in U.S. military history.[45] In the East, Confederate commander Robert E. Lee won a series of victories over Union armies[46], but Lee's defeat at Gettysburg in early July 1863, where he lost 30 percent of his army, proved the turning point in the war.[47] The capture of Vicksburg and Port Hudson by Ulysses S. Grant completed Union control of the Mississippi River and Confederate resistance collapsed after Lee surrendered to Grant at Appomattox Court House on April 9, 1865.[48]

The war was the deadliest in American history, causing 620,000 soldier deaths and an undetermined number of civilian casualties. It ended slavery in the United States, restored the Union by settling the issues of nullification and secession, and strengthened the role of the federal government. The social, political, economic, and racial issues of the war continue to shape contemporary American thought.

The Emancipation Proclamation

On July 22, Lincoln presented the *Emancipation Proclamation* to his cabinet. The president informed the cabinet of his intention to issue a proclamation of freedom and invited comment. Only Postmaster-General Montgomery Blair dissented, claiming such an edict would cost the Republicans control of Congress in the fall elections. Secretary of State William H. Seward approved the proclamation but counseled its postponement "until you can give it to the country supported by military success." Otherwise, the world might view it "as the last measure of an exhausted government, a cry for help . . . our last *shriek*, on the retreat." The wisdom of this suggestion "struck me with very great force," said Lincoln later. He put his proclamation in a drawer, having thus been persuaded to delay issuing it until after a Union victory.[49]

On September 22, five days after the battle of Antietam, Lincoln called his cabinet into session. He had made a covenant with God, said the president, that if the army drove the enemy from Maryland, he would issue his *Emancipation Proclamation*. "I think the time has come," he continued.

"I wish it were a better time. I wish that we were in a better condition. The action of the army against the rebels has not been quite what I should have best liked." Nevertheless, Antietam was a victory and Lincoln intended to warn the rebel states that, unless they returned to the Union by January 1, their slaves "shall be then, thenceforward, and forever free." The cabinet approved, though Montgomery Blair repeated his warning that this action might drive border-state elements to the South and give Democrats "a club . . . to beat the Administration" in the elections. Lincoln replied that he had exhausted every effort to bring the border states along. Now "we must make the forward movement" without them. "They [will] acquiesce, if not immediately, soon." As for the Democrats, "their clubs would be used against us take what course we might."[50]

Lincoln issued his *Proclamation of Amnesty and Reconstruction* on December 8, 1863. It contained his lenient "Ten-Percent Plan" for returning southern states to their proper relationship with the federal government.[51] In December 1863, Lincoln offered a model for reinstatement of Southern states called the *10 Percent Reconstruction Plan*. It decreed that a state could be reintegrated into the Union when 10 percent of the 1860 vote count from that state had taken an oath of allegiance to the United States and pledged to abide by emancipation. Voters could then elect delegates to draft revised state constitutions and establish new state governments. All Southerners except for high-ranking Confederate army officers and government officials would be granted a full pardon. Lincoln guaranteed Southerners that he would protect their private property, though not their slaves. By 1864, Louisiana, Tennessee, and Arkansas had established fully functioning Unionist governments.[52]

This policy was meant to shorten the war by offering a moderate peace plan. It was also intended to further his emancipation policy by insisting that the new governments abolish slavery. However, under Lincoln's plan, slavery could survive the war. His attitude toward the expedience and legality of emancipation, like that of many people in the Union, had shifted with the vicissitudes of war. By late 1863, however, his vision of the future of slavery held steady. He believed that when the war ended, those who had been slaves prior to the war would fall into two groups.[53]

The first would be slaves who had made their way to Union lines or who lived in areas occupied by Union armies and were included in the terms of the *Emancipation Proclamation*. These people would be free in the eyes of the Lincoln administration. The second group would be those slaves living in the Border States or areas exempted by the *Emancipation Proclamation*. These people would not yet be free, but they would likely be emancipated soon by postwar legislative and judicial action. This second group included slaves living in areas covered by the proclamation, but not yet occupied by Union armies. In Lincoln's view, the operation of the proclamation ceased with the war. Lincoln's expectations turned out to be well off the mark, because Union armies, in the aftermath of war, rarely awaited legal judgments and continued to emancipate slaves regardless of the location.[54]

Radical Republicans in Congress were pleased that the president had maintained his commitment against slavery, but they pushed harder than Lincoln to ensure that emancipation would be universal, immediate, and legally secure. To reach these goals, congressional Republicans worked on two distinct, related types of legislation. The first was a bill outlining the terms by which seceded states would rejoin the Union, and the second was a constitutional amendment abolishing slavery everywhere, including the Border States. Historians have usually detached these two efforts, seeing the first as the creative beginning of a reconstruction program and the second merely as the obvious final stage of wartime emancipation. However, the two initiatives were very much connected. Both involved creating a new Union cleansed of all traces of slavery. Despite historians' emphasis on the way in which Americans in the last years of the war considered how to restore the Union, most Americans during that period were just as interested, if not more interested, in the matter of how to make black freedom final.[55]

In April 1864, the Senate passed a resolution for the abolition amendment and sent it to the House of Representatives. Two months later, in June, the House voted on the measure, but failed to carry it by a two-thirds vote. Then, in July, Congress finally passed its reconstruction bill, the so-called Wade-Davis bill.[56]

The legislation is best known among historians for raising the bar for states seeking re-entry to the union above the mark set by Lincoln. Fifty percent of white voters rather than the 10 percent proposed by Lincoln would have to take a strict, "ironclad" oath before a new government could form and be readmitted. The bill also contained a crucial difference with Lincoln's plan in the matter of emancipation. Whereas the president's reconstruction proclamation left ambiguous the timing of emancipation for those slaves not freed by confiscation acts and the *Emancipation Proclamation*, the Wade-Davis bill granted immediate freedom to all slaves in the Confederacy.[57]

It was precisely this difference that Lincoln mentioned when he pocket-vetoed the Wade-Davis bill. Aside from objecting to the way that the bill would undermine unionist movements in Confederate states such as Louisiana and Arkansas, Lincoln protested that Congress did not have a "constitutional competency ... to abolish slavery in States." In other words, he applied the same standard by which he had judged the constitutionality of earlier wartime acts against slavery. The federal government could use its "war power" to free slaves owned by disloyal masters or residing in specific rebellious areas, but it could not abolish slavery everywhere in one or all the states; at least, not by statute. The proposed constitutional amendment, Lincoln declared, was the preferable—and legal—method of universal emancipation.[58]

Bringing the War to Conclusion

The Republican convention in Baltimore during the second week of June exhibited the usual hoopla and love-feast unity of a party renominating an incumbent. The assemblage called itself the National Union convention to attract War Democrats and Southern unionists who might flinch at the name Republican. Nevertheless, it adopted a down-the line Republican platform, including endorsement of unremitting war to force the "unconditional surrender" of Confederate armies and the passage of a constitutional amendment to abolish slavery. When this latter plank was presented, "the whole body of delegates sprang to their feet . . . in prolonged cheering," according to William Lloyd Garrison, who was present as a reporter for his newspaper *The Liberator*. "Was not a spectacle like that rich compensation for more than thirty years of personal opprobrium?"[59]

The platform dealt with the divisive reconstruction issue by ignoring it. Delegations from the Lincoln-reconstructed states of Louisiana, Arkansas, and Tennessee were admitted, while, with the president's covert sanction, the convention made a gesture of conciliation to radicals by seating an anti-Blair delegation from Missouri. The Missourians then cast a token ballot for Ulysses S. Grant before changing its vote to make Lincoln's nomination unanimous.[60]

The only real contest at the convention was generated by the vice-presidential nomination. The colorless incumbent, Hannibal Hamlin, would add no strength to the ticket. The attempt to project a Union party image seemed to require the nomination of a War Democrat from a southern state. Andrew Johnson of Tennessee best fitted this bill.[61] After backstairs maneuvers whose details remain obscure, Johnson was nominated on the first ballot.[62] This nomination had a mixed impact on radical-moderate tensions in the party. On the one hand, Johnson had dealt severely with "rebels" in Tennessee. On the other, he embodied Lincoln's executive approach to reconstruction.

The Democrat party met in convention in Chicago, Illinois, August 30, 1864, and nominated George B. McClellan for president. Their platform proclaimed that the war was a failure and called for immediate peace. McClellan muddied the issue by accepting the nomination but repudiating the platform.[63] McClellan possessed all the qualities which make for "availability." He had an extraordinary personal charm, enhanced by his comparative youth, his gracious manner, and his cultural background.[64]

Gen. William T. Sherman's successes in September and his continued progress through Georgia, swung opinion strongly back in Lincoln's favor. The increased desperation of the South, as expressed in terrorism, bank-raids, and murder in Northern cities, inflamed Northern masses and were strong vote-winners for the Republicans. The resentful George B. McClellan fared disastrously for the Democrats. Lincoln carried all but three of the participating states and was awarded 212 electoral votes out of 233. It was a resounding vote of confidence by the people.[65]

Convinced that he could reunite North and South by proposing a joint campaign to throw the French out of Mexico, Francis Preston Blair, the old Jacksonian, as quixotic in his own way as Horace Greeley, badgered Lincoln to give him a pass through the lines to present this proposal to Jefferson Davis. Lincoln wanted nothing to do with Blair's harebrained Mexican scheme, but he allowed him to go to Richmond to see what might develop. For his part, Jefferson Davis anticipated nothing better from negotiations than the previous demands for "unconditional submission." He did, however, see an opportunity to fire up the waning southern heart by eliciting such demands publicly. Davis thus authorized Blair to inform Lincoln that he was ready to "enter into conference with a view to secure peace to the two countries." Lincoln responded promptly that he too was ready to receive overtures "with the view of securing peace to the people of our one common country."[66]

A dramatic confrontation took place February 3, 1865, on the Union steamer *River Queen*. Lincoln's earlier instructions to Secretary of State William H. Seward had formed the inflexible Union position during four hours of talks:[67]

1. The restoration of the National authority throughout all the States.
2. No receding by the Executive of the United States on the Slavery question.
3. No cessation of hostilities short of an end of the war, and the disbanding of all forces hostile to the government.

In vain, Alexander H. Stephens, Davis's vice president of the Confederate States, tried to divert Lincoln by bringing up Blair's Mexican project. Equally unprofitable was General David Hunter's proposal for an armistice and a convention of states. Lincoln said there would be no armistice. Surrender was the only means of stopping the war. Hunter responded that even Charles I had entered into agreements with rebels in arms against his government during the English Civil War. "I do not profess to be posted in history," replied Lincoln. "All I distinctly recollect about the case of Charles I is that he lost his head."[68] On questions of punishing rebel leaders and confiscating their property, Lincoln promised generous treatment based on his power of pardon. On slavery, he even suggested the possibility of compensating owners to the amount of $400,000,000, about 15 percent of the slaves' 1860 value.[69]

Some uncertainty exists about exactly what Lincoln meant in these discussions by "no receding . . . on the Slavery question." At a minimum, he meant no going back on the *Emancipation Proclamation* or on other wartime executive and congressional actions against slavery. No slaves freed by these acts could ever be re-enslaved. The Southerners questioned how many slaves *had* been freed by those actions. Was it all the slaves in the Confederacy, or only those who had come under Union military control after the *Proclamation* was issued? As a war measure, would it cease to operate with peace? That would be up to the courts, said Lincoln. Seward informed the commissioners that the House of Representatives had just passed the Thirteenth Amendment. Its ratification would make all other legal questions moot. If Southern states returned to the Union and voted against ratification, thereby defeating it, would such action be valid? That remained to be seen, said Seward.[70]

In any case, remarked Lincoln, slavery as well as the rebellion was doomed. Southern leaders should cut their losses, return to the old allegiance, and save the blood of thousands of young men that would be shed if the war continued. Whatever their personal preferences, the commissioners had no power to negotiate such terms. They returned dejectedly to Richmond.[71]

Southern professions of shock and betrayal at the North's demand for "unconditional surrender" were disingenuous. Lincoln had given them no reason to expect otherwise. The three commissioners drafted a brief, matter-of-fact report on their mission. When Davis tried to get them to add phrases expressing resentment of "degrading submission" and "humiliating surrender" they refused, knowing that the president wished to use them to discredit the whole idea of negotiations. So, on February 6, Davis added the phrases himself in a message to Congress accompanying the commissioners' report. The South must fight on, said Davis that evening in a public speech that breathed "unconquerable defiance." We will never submit to the "disgrace of surrender," declared the Confederate leader. Denouncing the Northern president as *"His Majesty Abraham the First,"* Davis predicted that Lincoln and Seward would find that "they had been speaking to their masters." Southern armies would yet "compel the Yankees, in less than 12 months, to petition us for peace on our own terms."[72]

It is no depreciation of Lincoln's spiritual devotion to the Union cause to say that his policy was characterized by his usual grasp of the realities of the situation. His problem was to secure his reelection in November and that reelection involved the support of a diverse constituency. To retain that support, the policy he had devised earlier had to be maintained in a time of discouragement and despair. Even when a "peace simoon" was blowing dust in the eyes of Northern voters, he had to remain firm and unshaken.[73]

Lincoln remained true to his war and peace policy. His terms were stated in their briefest form in "To Whom It May Concern," the reply to the Confederate commissioners. He was willing to negotiate about details, as his outline for the mission of James Jaquess and James R. Gilmore showed. He talked of compensation for the slaves with a visitor to the White House in August, but, on the fundamental conditions of reunion and freedom, he never wavered.[74]

On the other hand, it may be said that in his letter to Charles D. Robinson and the instructions for a commission to Richmond, which he proposed as an answer to the Republican Executive Committee, there was an indication that he did modify his policy. In answering this assertion, the peace negotiations of July 1864 must be considered. If Lincoln had needed understanding of the issues of the war, the adventures of Greeley and Jaquess and Gilmore would have given it to him. The results of their missions had furnished renewed evidence of the fact that the Confederacy was fighting for independence and for independence alone. Strengthened by this reassurance, Lincoln could afford to be disingenuous in his letter to Robinson and omit from his unused instructions of August 24 all reference to slavery. Since the President saw the situation with unflinching clarity, he was justified in exploiting it for political purposes.[75]

The scene of Lincoln's second inauguration was a striking one. The morning had been inclement, storming so violently that, up to a few minutes before twelve o'clock, it was supposed that the Inaugural Address would have to be delivered in the Senate Chamber. The people gathered in immense numbers before the Capitol, despite the storm, and, just before noon, the rain ceased. The clouds broke away and the President took the oath of office administered by Chief Justice Salmon P. Chase. The blue sky appeared above and a small white cloud, like a hovering bird, seemed to hang above his head. The sunlight broke through the clouds and fell upon him with a glory, afterwards felt to have been an emblem of the martyr's crown, which was so soon to rest upon his head.[76]

CHAPTER FOUR

FROM ACCOMMODATION TO CONFLICT

The accommodations of slavery could have evolved into assimilation; e.g., "a process of interpenetration and fusion in which persons and groups acquire the memories, sentiments, and attitudes of other persons or groups, and, by sharing their experience and history, are incorporated with them into a common cultural life."[1] Instead, the accommodations of slavery persisted for a long period, were disrupted, and then dissolved into the conflict of civil war.

The worldwide industrial movement so revolutionized spinning and weaving that the resulting increased demand for cotton fiber gave rise to the plantation system of the South. This required a larger number of slaves. Becoming too numerous to be considered as included in the body politic conceived by John Locke, Baron de Montesquieu, and Sir William Blackstone, the slaves were generally doomed to live without any enlightenment whatsoever. Thereafter, rich planters thought it unwise to educate men who were destined to live on a plane with beasts. Besides, it was considered by some to be more profitable to work a slave to death for seven years and buy another in his stead rather than to teach and humanize him with a view to increasing his efficiency.[2]

The New Codes

The increase in the number of blacks raised fears among whites about lawlessness and insurrection. This led to the passage of stringent slave codes to regulate the activities of blacks.

Prohibitive legislation lasted over a period of more than a century, beginning with the South Carolina Assembly enacting the "Negro Act" in 1740 that established South Carolina's slave code. The code was passed in response to the Stono slave rebellion of 1739 led by a native African slave called Cato.[3] It was the most serious outbreak of the colonial period.[4]

The rebellion began Sunday, September 9, 1739, approximately 20 miles from Charlestown. A group of 20 black slaves met in secret near the Stono River in South Carolina to plan their escape to freedom. Shortly thereafter, they broke into a store, killed the two storekeepers, and stole the guns and powder inside. The group moved southward toward St. Augustine, burning and killing whites as other slaves joined the band. While riding on horseback to Charlestown, Lt. Gov. William Bull spotted the group and alerted the whites. The blacks had proceeded on, dancing, singing, and beating drums to attract other slaves. By afternoon, the group stopped after having traveled more than 10 miles and decided to wait until morning before crossing the Edisto River.[5]

Numbering some 60 to 100 participants, the group was met by a group of white planters numbering 20 to 100 men. A battle ensued and, according to some secondary accounts, the uprising was suppressed by nightfall. Other accounts show that a small assemblage of slaves had continued to the southern border and were met by whites the following Saturday. It is estimated that 21 whites and 44 blacks died in the Stono River Rebellion.[6]

The South Carolina act also served as a model for the Georgia slave code of 1755,[7] and remained largely unaltered until emancipation in 1865. The new code stripped enslaved blacks of any kind of protection under the law. Punishment for the murder of an enslaved person by a white, for example, was reduced to a mere misdemeanor punishable by a fine. Slaves could never physically attack a white person except in defense of the life of the slaveholder who owned them. They could be executed for plotting insurrection or conspiring to run away, burning a barrel of tar or a "stack of rice," or teaching another slave "the knowledge of any poisonous root, plant, [or] herb." Much of the Negro Act was devoted to controlling miniscule aspects of a slave's life. For instance, slaves were not allowed to dress in a way "above the condition of slaves." Their clothes could only be made from a list of approved coarse fabrics. They were prohibited from learning how to read and write and were not permitted to assemble with one another. Blacks in violation of these provisions were subject to flogging.[8]

While South Carolina and Georgia were prescriptive in their legislative measures, other states attacked the problem in various ways. Black people, beyond a certain number, were not allowed to assemble for social or religious purposes, except in the presence of certain "discreet" white men. Slaves were deprived of the helpful contact of free persons of color because the freemen were driven out of some Southern States. Masters, who had employed their favorite blacks in positions which required knowledge of bookkeeping, printing, and the like, were commanded by law to discontinue that custom. Private and public teachers were prohibited from assisting blacks to acquire knowledge in any manner whatsoever.[9]

By this time, many people of the South had concluded that intellectual elevation made men unfit for servitude and rendered it impossible to retain them in this condition. In other words, the more the minds of slaves are cultivated, the more unserviceable they become. They develop a higher relish for those privileges which they cannot attain and what is intended as a blessing becomes a curse. If they are to remain in slavery, they should be kept in the lowest state of ignorance and degradation. The nearer one brings them to the condition of brutes, the better chance they will retain their apathy. Finally, the measures enacted to prevent the education of blacks not only forbid association with their fellows for mutual help, but closed most colored schools in the South. In several states, these measures had made it a crime for a black person to even teach his own children.[10]

Mississippi laws passed in the South after the Civil War (1865-1867), were widely considered to be the first set of *Black Codes*; e.g., a body of laws, statutes, and rules enacted by Southern states immediately after the Civil War to regain control over the freed slaves, maintain white supremacy, and ensure the continued supply of cheap labor. These codes represented a concerted effort by white lawmakers to restore the master-slave relationship under a new name. Within a few months after Mississippi passed its first such law, Alabama, Georgia, Louisiana, Florida, Tennessee, Virginia, and North Carolina followed suit by enacting similar laws of their own.[11]

Under slavery, whites had disciplined blacks largely outside the law, through extralegal whippings administered by slave owners and their overseers. After the slaves were emancipated, panicky whites feared that blacks would seek revenge against them for their harsh and inhumane treatment on the southern plantations. Some states limited the type of property blacks could own. In others, blacks were excluded from certain businesses or from the skilled trades. Former slaves also were forbidden to carry firearms or to testify in court, except in cases concerning other blacks. Legal marriage between blacks was provided for, but interracial marriage was prohibited.[12]

Emancipation

From the first days of the Civil War, slaves had acted to secure their own liberty. The *Emancipation Proclamation*[13] confirmed their insistence that the war for the Union must be a war for freedom. It added moral force to the Union cause and strengthened the Union both militarily and politically. With this decree, Lincoln hoped to inspire all blacks and slaves in the Confederacy to support the Union cause. He also felt it was needed to keep England and France from giving political recognition and military aid to the Confederacy. Because it was a military measure, however, the *Proclamation* was limited in many ways. It applied only to states that had seceded from the Union, leaving slavery untouched in the loyal border states. It also expressly exempted parts of the Confederacy that had already come under Union control. Most important, the freedom it promised was dependent upon Union military victory.[14]

Although it did not end slavery in the nation, the *Emancipation Proclamation* did fundamentally transform the character of the war. After January 1, 1863, every advance of Federal troops expanded the domain of freedom. Moreover, it announced the acceptance of black men into the Union Army and Navy, enabling the liberated to become liberators. By the end of the war, almost 200,000 black soldiers and sailors had fought for the Union and freedom.[15]

By the time Confederate President Jefferson Davis was captured, Lincoln was already dead. On April 14, Good Friday, Lincoln attended the play "Our American Cousin" at Ford's Theater in Washington. He was assassinated by John Wilkes Booth, an actor, a pro-Confederate Marylander, and a member of a Confederate espionage ring. Simultaneously, Lewis

Powell, alias Lewis Paine, slashed and seriously wounded Secretary of State William H. Seward at Seward's home, where the secretary of state lay bedridden from injuries sustained in a carriage accident. Powell was a member of the same Confederate espionage cell as Booth. He was later hanged, along with three other accomplices. Booth, however, cheated the gallows by being shot or shooting himself to avoid capture, several days after his crime.[16]

The weeks after Booth fulfilled his vow passed in a dizzying sequence of events. Jarring images dissolved and reformed in kaleidoscopic patterns that left the senses traumatized or elated; particularly, Lincoln lying in state at the White House on April 19 as General Ulysses S. Grant wept unabashedly at his catafalque. Confederate armies surrendered one after another as Jefferson Davis fled southward hoping to reestablish his government in Texas and carry on the war to victory. Seven million somber men, women, and children lined the tracks to view Lincoln's funeral train on its way back home to Springfield.[17]

The steamboat *Sultana* returning northward on the Mississippi, with liberated Union prisoners of war, blew up on April 27 with a loss of life equal to that of the *Titanic* a half-century later. Jefferson Davis was captured in Georgia on May 10 and falsely accused of complicity in Lincoln's assassination. Imprisoned and temporarily shackled at Fortress Monroe, Virginia, he remained there for two years until he was released without trial. He lived to 81 years of age, becoming part of the ex-Confederate literary corps whose followers wrote weighty tomes to justify their Cause. The Army of the Potomac and Sherman's Army of Georgia marched 200,000 strong in a Grand Review down Pennsylvania Avenue on May 23-24 in a pageantry of power and catharsis before being demobilized from more than one million soldiers to fewer than 80,000 a year later. They reached an eventual peacetime total of 27,000. Weary, ragged Confederate soldiers straggled homeward, begging or stealing as they went.[18]

After Lincoln's assassination in April 1865, Southerners, stunned by their defeat and its possible consequences, were prepared for almost anything. As the editor of the Raleigh Press told the newspaperman Whitelaw Reid in the summer of 1865, they were "willing to acquiesce in whatever basis of reorganization the President would prescribe." Even black suffrage "would be preferable to remaining unorganized and would be accepted by the people."[19] President Andrew Johnson, however, missed this opportunity to inaugurate a policy that would at least have protected the minimum rights of the former slaves. He was forewarned. Blacks in Alexandria, Unionists in Maryland and Virginia, officials in Louisiana, among others, warned him through letters and petitions they sent to him. They cautioned him not to abandon the Unionists and blacks to the tender mercies of returning rebels.[20]

Reconstruction

It was the Northern reaction to the black codes, as well as to the bloody anti-black riots in Memphis and New Orleans in 1866, that helped produce Radical Reconstruction and the Fourteenth and Fifteenth amendments. Reconstruction did away with the black codes, but, after Reconstruction was over, many of their provisions were reenacted in the Jim Crow segregation laws.

Reconstruction was one of the most turbulent and controversial eras in American history. It witnessed America's first experiment in interracial democracy. President Andrew Johnson favored a lenient approach to Reconstruction, calling for an immediate return of the former Confederate states into the Union without any guarantee of black civil rights.[21] However, just as the fate of slavery was central to the meaning of the *Civil War*, so, too, did the divisive politics of Reconstruction turn on the status that former slaves would assume in the reunited nation.[22]

President Johnson announced his plans for Reconstruction at the end of May 1865. The plans reflected both his staunch Unionism and his firm belief in states' rights. In Johnson's view, the Southern States had never given up their right to govern themselves and the federal government had no right to determine voting requirements or other questions at the state level. Under his Presidential Reconstruction, all land that had been confiscated by the Union Army and distributed to the freed slaves by the army or the Freedmen's Bureau reverted to its prewar owners. Apart from being required to comply with the Thirteenth Amendment to the Constitution, swear loyalty to the Union and pay off war debt, Southern State governments were given free rein to rebuild themselves.[23]

The Republican-controlled Congress opposed the Johnson's plan and refused to admit Congressmen from the former Confederate states.[24] Over Johnson's vetoes, Congress renewed the Freedmen's Bureau and passed the *Civil Rights Act of 1866.* During the congressional election campaign later that year, Johnson took his case to the people in his "Swing Around the Circle" speaking tour.[25] He pressured Ulysses S. Grant, the most popular man in the country at the time, to go on the tour with him. Grant, wishing to appear loyal, agreed.[26]

Grant, however, believed that Johnson was purposefully agitating conservative opinion to defy Congressional Reconstruction. He found himself increasingly at odds with the president, and he believed Johnson's speeches were a "national disgrace." Publicly, Grant attempted to appear loyal to the President while not alienating Republican legislators essential to his future political career. Concerned that Johnson's differences with Congress would cause renewed insurrection, he ordered Southern arsenals to ship arms north to prevent their capture by Southern state governments.[27]

The election of 1866 decisively changed the balance of power, giving the Republicans control of Congress and enough votes to overcome Johnson's vetoes. Congress rejected Johnson's argument that he had war powers to decide what to do, because the war was over. Congress decided it had the primary authority to decide on how Reconstruction should proceed because the Constitution stated Congress had to guarantee each state a republican form of government.[28] The issue became how republicanism should operate in the South; i.e., how the newly freed blacks would achieve citizenship, what the status of the Confederate states should be, and what should be the status of men who had supported the Confederacy.[29]

By 1866, Johnson, a consistent Jeffersonian-Jacksonian Democrat, broke with the moderate Republicans and aligned himself more with the Democrats who opposed equality and the Fourteenth Amendment granting citizenship to former slaves.[30] Radicals attacked the policies of Johnson, especially his veto of the *Civil Rights Act of 1866,* which was intended to protect the civil rights of blacks. Congress ultimately prevailed. Overriding Johnson's vetoes became routine for Congress and, when he fired a cabinet member without the Senate's permission after Congress had passed a law denying him the power to do so, the House of Representatives impeached him. The Senate came within one vote of the two-thirds majority required to remove him from office.[31]

The Republicans established seven military districts in the South and used Army personnel to administer the region until new governments loyal to the Union could be established. They granted citizenship and suffrage to former slaves. Certain tracts of land were set aside exclusively to be worked and used by freedmen. These reservations were called Freedmen Labor Colonies. Schools were established, both in the Home colonies and in the Labor colonies.[32] They suspended the franchise for the estimated 10,000 to 15,000 white men who had been Confederate officials or senior officers.

With the power to vote, blacks started participating in politics. A Republican coalition of blacks and Southerners supportive of the Union, and Northerners who had migrated to the South, organized to create constitutional conventions and new state constitutions to implement changes affecting former slaves. Some were returning natives, but most were Union veterans. This group was snidely called "carpetbaggers." Many of them were agents for capital and went down from the North with the psychology of modern investment in conquered or colonial territory. They brought the capital, invested it, remained in charge to oversee the profits, and acquired power to protect these profits. Conversely, there were teachers who came down from the North, Army chaplains, social workers, and others, who whole-heartedly went into the social aspects of a new democracy.[33]

The constitutional amendments and legislative reforms that laid the foundation for the most radical phase of Reconstruction were enacted from 1865 until 1871. The Thirteenth Amendment abolished slavery. The Fourteenth Amendment addressed citizenship rights and equal protection of the laws for all persons. The Fifteenth Amendment prohibited discrimination in voting rights of citizens based on "race, color, or previous condition of servitude." The radical Republican governments in the South attempted to deal constructively with the problems left by the *Civil War* and the abolition of slavery. So-called carpetbaggers (Northerners who settled in the South), scalawags (Southern whites in the Republican party), and blacks began to rebuild the Southern economy and society. Agricultural production was restored, roads rebuilt, a more equitable tax system adopted, and schooling was extended to blacks and poor whites. The former slaves' civil and political rights were guaranteed. Blacks could participate in the political and economic life of the South as full citizens for the first time.[34]

The Ku Klux Klan

An increasing number of southern whites turned to violence in response to the revolutionary changes of Radical Reconstruction. The first branch of the Ku Klux Klan (KKK) was established in Pulaski, Tennessee, in May of 1866. A year later, a general organization of local Klans was established in Nashville. Most of the leaders were former members of the Confederate Army and the first Grand Wizard was Nathan Forrest, a Confederate general during the *Civil War*.[35] Through the years 1866-1871, the KKK acted as a secret society of vigilantes who wore white robes to conceal their identities and who rode by night to do "justice." They dressed to terrify the black community and, where terror failed, they used the whip and the noose.[36]

The KKK played a violent role against blacks in the South during the Reconstruction Era of the 1860s and, although there was little organizational structure above the local level, similar groups rose across the South and adopted the same name and methods.[37] Sporadic small-group nocturnal violence was a practical and effective tactic in the postwar rural South. It required little organization or planning, could respond quickly and easily to specific local conditions, and drew on community networks that the northerners interested in suppressing it found difficult to decipher.

Early in the postwar period, particularly in 1866 and 1867, former Confederate soldiers and others took advantage of the weakened state to spawn groups of "vigilantes" or "guerrillas" throughout the South. Most were nameless, but others took names, or had names given to them. The Black Horse Cavalry wore blackface while terrorizing laborers in Franklin Parish, Louisiana. The Pale Faces emerged in 1867 in Middle Tennessee. The Knights of the White Camellia began in Louisiana in the spring of 1867. Countless other groups of unnamed "slickers" roamed rural regions throughout the South in the early Reconstruction years.[38]

All these forms of violence, however, shared a significant shortcoming as a means of reasserting white racial dominance. Rather than representing the voice of a defeated-but-not-prostrate white South, they conveyed a message of inchoate southern white fury. Individual white-on-black attacks, riots, or slickers demonstrated and asserted local white control while intimidating black southerners. Yet, the same qualities that made these types of violence attractive in the early Reconstruction era, also neutered their coordinated political force. While their clashes skirted potential northern interference by being seemingly unplanned, sporadic, and deniable, the many thousands of individual white-on-black attacks, the several bloody riots, and the hundreds of slicker groups, failed to add up to a coherent whole.[39]

The KKK solved this problem. It revalued collective local nighttime attackers, allowing Ku-Klux to effectively remain small, local, and difficult to detect or suppress. In the meantime, this permitted them to imagine and present themselves as part of a single pan-Southern resistance movement. Combining small-scale organization with an insistent discursive claim to regional coherence, the many small groups that comprised the first KKK would become, together, the most widely proliferated and deadly domestic terrorist movement in the history of the United States.[40]

Essentially, the KKK was a vehicle for white southern resistance to the Republican Party's Reconstruction-era policies aimed at establishing political and economic equality for blacks. Its members waged an underground campaign of intimidation and violence directed at white and black Republican leaders. Though Congress passed legislation designed to curb Klan terrorism, the organization saw as its primary goal the reestablishment of white supremacy. This goal would be fulfilled through Democratic victories in state legislatures across the South in the 1870s.

In 1870 and 1871, the federal government passed the *Force Acts*, which were used to prosecute Klan crimes and suppress Klan activity.[41] In a few Southern states, Republicans organized militia units to break up the Klan. However, beginning in 1874, newly organized and openly active paramilitary organizations, such as the White League and the Red Shirts, initiated a fresh round of violence aimed at suppressing black voting rights and running Republicans out of office.[42] The activities of these various organizations contributed to segregationist white Democrats regaining political power in all the Southern states by 1877. They also disrupted Republican organizing and terrorized blacks to bar them from the polls.[43]

After a period of decline, white Protestant nativist groups revived the

Klan in the early 20th century, burning crosses and staging rallies, parades, and marches. They also denounced immigrants, Catholics, Jews, blacks, and organized labor. In 1924, the KKK found some moderate success getting Klansmen elected to political offices. Five were voted into the Senate, including Alabaman Hugo Black, a future Supreme Court judge who quickly became disenchanted with the Klan. However, the Klan did take hold in the political situation in Indiana, the only state in the country in which every county boasted a Klavern.[44]

The rapid growth of the KKK in the Hoosier State could be attributed greatly to Grand Wizard David Curtis Stephenson, who played on a virulent anti-Catholic sentiment. He founded a Klan magazine titled *The Fiery Cross*, which became immensely popular. Indiana political figures, who spoke out against the Klan, were certain to read about supposed gangsterism and prostitution in their cities or counties in the next issue of *The Fiery Cross*. Stephenson also organized a program in which the Klan researched the background of every candidate who ran for office, from school board to judge to mayor. Aggressive campaigns were conducted against all Catholics, blacks, Jews, and anyone else deemed undesirable by KKK. Moreover, before the 1924 election, the Indiana Klan sent out 250,000 sample ballots to its members, indicating the candidates for whom they should vote. The result was that Klansman Ed Jackson, an unknown before the primary, won the gubernatorial election in 1924 and other KKK members were also swept into office. Shortly afterward, the image of the Indiana Klan and the national organization was destroyed by accusations that Stephenson had murdered a young woman named Madge Oberholzer. The incident brought about the downfall of the Klan and spelled an end to the greatest era of KKK popularity in its history.[45]

During his trial, fellow Klansmen had encouraged Stephenson by claiming the jury had been fixed in his favor. Furthermore, even if it did judge him guilty, Governor Jackson would certainly pardon him. Stephenson was convicted of second-degree murder and Jackson did nothing. He feared that siding with his KKK buddy would be akin to committing political suicide. Angered by Jackson's refusal to help, the doomed Grand Wizard revealed to the media all the corruption that revolved around the 1924 election, including Indianapolis Mayor John Duvall's signing a document that he would not appoint anybody to the board of public works without Stephenson's consent and that Jackson took unreported campaign contributions from the KKK. The political careers of Jackson and Duvall were ruined, as were the careers of dozens of other Indiana politicians.[46]

By the time the investigations slowed to a crawl and the gavels stopped banging, membership in the Indiana Klan had plummeted from 350,000 to a meager 15,000. The national organization similarly took a huge hit as 600 Klansmen in New Haven, Connecticut, resigned in one fell swoop and sent a resolution to the Imperial Headquarters that they could no longer remain members and keep their self-respect. Correspondingly, the KKK lost nearly all its members in the Deep South.[47]

The Stock Market Crash of 1929 had ushered in the Great Depression. In 1930, the corporate owners of the landmark film, *Birth of a Nation*, placed it back in circulation with new soundtrack and sound effects. However, public reaction was hardly the same as 15 years earlier. Hardly anyone showed up aside from Klan recruiters hoping to find new members in a desperate, vain attempt to revitalize the organization. Not only had the illegal activities by the Indiana Klan and the attack and murder of a young woman by its leader in the 1920s proven abhorrent to the public, but Americans' preoccupation with the struggles of daily survival were now far more important than any thought to the Klan. What remained of the KKK leadership continued in its attempt to instill fear and anger amongst Americans by blaming Jews, Catholics, and blacks for the worst economic crisis in the nation's history. Few people gave any merit to KKK allegations.[48]

Eventually, the Klan found a cause in *New Deal* legislation created by President Franklin Roosevelt, who took office in 1933. They blamed Jews serving in the newly formed cabinet for policies the KKK deemed dangerous to American freedom and recruited from the labor unions that were gaining strength during the Roosevelt administration. Imperial Wizard Hiram Wesley Evans, who had remained at his post despite the almost total loss of public support, worked to tie unionism with Communism, but with little success. Just weeks after Roosevelt moved into the White House, Adolf Hitler and the National Socialist German Workers' Party (Nazis) assumed control of Germany and, unsurprisingly, comparisons were made between the philosophies and tactics of the KKK and the Nazis. Rev. Otto Strohschein, a former American Klansmen who moved to Germany in 1923, started a Klan Klavern there that eventually grew to 300 members. [49]

The feelings of those with Nazi sentiments were favorable toward the KKK. Klansmen in areas with large Jewish populations, particularly in New York, praised Hitler for his anti-Semitism and the anti-Jewish programs he was initiating in Germany. American Nazi Party leader, Fritz Kuhn, attempted to merge his organization with the Ku Klux Klan, but the talks ended in 1939 when he was convicted of embezzlement and sent to jail. His replacement, G. William Kunze, organized a joint rally of Nazis and Klansmen in the summer of 1940, which prompted a congressional committee to investigate what was considered a dangerous linking of right-wing extremists. In the end, it did not matter. The American Nazi Party was forced to disintegrate when the United States entered *World War II*.[50]

Individual Klansmen still operated throughout the South, but the organization was barely holding on by the early 1950s. However, a Supreme Court ruling in 1954 gave them a cause to rally around. The Court determined in *Brown v. Board of Education* that the separate-but-equal policies of the South were inherently unequal and voted to strike down school segregation. Southern states basically ignored the ruling, which prompted the Court to order in 1955 that districts practicing segregation must integrate "with all deliberate speed." That vague wording allowed those in charge of Southern schools to further delay implementation and gave the KKK an opportunity to gain membership and accelerate its violence against blacks.[51]

By 1957, the KKK numbered about 40,000 members, a clear majority of whom were racist, violent thugs who preyed on their perceived enemies. The civil rights movement had begun and, though most blacks followed the lead of Dr. Martin Luther King, Jr., a 27-year-old minister who eschewed violence, others had become angry enough to fight back. Robert Williams, a black war veteran and former marine, successfully integrated the library in Monroe, North Carolina, before setting his sights on swimming pools, restaurants, and other public places. The KKK responded by terrorizing the local black community, which motivated Williams to apply for and receive a charter from the National Rifle Association (NRA). He trained his friends how to use firearms and, in the summer of 1957, when hooded

Klansmen drove down his street honking their horns and bellowing out threats along the way, they were stunned to see Williams and other blacks firing at them with rifles. The Klansmen, who were not their equals in marksmanship, hightailed it out of the area quickly.[52]

The civil rights movement of the 1960s also saw a surge of KKK activity, including bombings of black schools and churches and violence against black and white activists in the South. Dr. Martin Luther King launched his campaign with a bus boycott in Montgomery, Alabama, where blacks had been forced to sit in the back of the buses. Official integration of Montgomery buses a year later proved to be the first in a long line of triumphs for Dr. King and other Southern blacks. Opposed to the civil rights movement and its attempt to end racial segregation and discrimination, the Klan capitalized on the fears of whites to grow to a membership of about 20,000. It portrayed the civil rights movement as a Communist, Jewish conspiracy and engaged in terrorist acts designed to frustrate and intimidate the movement's members.[53]

KKK adherents were responsible for acts such as the 1963 bombing of the Sixteenth Street Baptist Church in Birmingham, Alabama, in which four young black girls died and many others were injured, and the 1964 murder in Mississippi of civil rights workers Michael Schwerner, Andrew Goodman, and James Chaney. The Klan was also responsible for many other beatings, murders, and bombings, including attacks on the Freedom Riders who sought to integrate interstate buses. In many instances, the Federal Bureau of Investigation (FBI), then under the control of J. Edgar Hoover, is reputed to have had intelligence that would have led to the prevention of Klan violence and conviction of its perpetrators. However, the FBI did little to oppose the Klan during the height of the civil rights movement.

Democrats Solidify Political Control in the South

From 1865 through the 1870s, the general trend in the nation was toward wider acceptance of black patronage. The federal Civil Rights Act of 1866 guaranteed them "equal benefit of the laws."[54] This set off a flurry of test suits, but most state and federal court rulings between 1865 and

1880 held in favor of black rights. These rulings served as a steady pressure on business owners to relax racial bars.[55]

By 1870, all the former Confederate states had been readmitted to the Union and the state constitutions, written during the years of Radical Reconstruction, were the most progressive in the region's history. Black participation in Southern public life after 1867 would be by far the most radical development of Reconstruction, which was essentially a large-scale experiment in interracial democracy. It was unlike that of any other society that had abolished slavery. Blacks won election to Southern state governments and the U.S. Congress during this period. Among the other achievements of Reconstruction were the South's first state-funded public school systems, more equitable taxation legislation, laws against racial discrimination in public transport and accommodations, and ambitious economic development programs, including aid to railroads and other enterprises.[56] Reconstruction had made some progress in providing the former slaves with equal rights under the law, and blacks were voting and taking political office. Republican legislatures, coalitions of whites and blacks, established the first systems of public school systems in the South.

Abraham Lincoln strained the economic equilibrium and the political order of the United States. He first destroyed the traditional balance of economic power between the South and the North, and then broke up the political scheme of Southern control of slavery. Whatever may have been the immediate result of the *Civil War,* the more remote sources of the conflict must undoubtedly be sought in the great cosmic forces which have broken down the barriers that had formerly separated the races and the Democrat and Republican political parties. Booth's assassination of Lincoln, however, pushed the United States back into old political intimacies and the Democrats were able to regain political control and initiate new forms of competition, rivalry, and conflict; i.e., "Jim Crow" segregation.[57]

From 1873 to 1877, conservative white Democrats, calling themselves "Redeemers", regained power in state elections throughout the former Confederacy. Several states kept constitutions rewritten during Reconstruction years for many years. Others used separate legislation to overturn some of the Reconstruction progress. In 1877, Republican President Rutherford Hayes withdrew federal troops, causing the collapse of the remaining three Republican state governments. Through the enactment of disfranchising statutes and constitutions, and extralegal means, the white Democrats subsequently removed most blacks and hundreds of thousands of poor whites from voter rolls in every Southern state.[58] They established one-party rule and enforced a system of racial segregation that continued throughout the South until the 1960s. Bitterness from the heated partisanship of the era lasted into the 20th century. However, in other ways, whites in the North and South started reconciliation, which reached higher heights in the early 20th century.[59]

During the 1870s, no state in the Union, whatever its relation to the Mason-Dixon Line, had laws requiring separation of whites and blacks in places of public accommodations such as smoking cars on railroads or balconies in theaters. Instead, blacks sat beside white customers who could not afford first-class tickets. However, some Northern and Western establishments refused black patronage entirely.[60] The situation was much the same in the larger cities of the border states and in the Deep South. Most establishments admitted blacks to second-class facilities. Some gave first-class service to blacks with high social status, such as federal and state public officials, army officers, newspaper men, and traveling clergymen. On the other hand, many places, particularly in rural areas, were closed to black people whatever their wealth or status.[61]

Still, even with the federal Civil Rights Act and the three Constitutional amendments, U.S. Supreme Court Justice Joseph P. Bradley wrote in the opinion of the Court that Congress could not protect blacks against discrimination unless "state action" was involved.[62] As a result, reconciliation coincided with the nadir of American race relations during which time there was an increase of racial segregation throughout America. Along with segregation came disfranchisement of most blacks in the South and more incidents of racial violence. The Thirteenth, Fourteenth, and Fifteenth amendments were constitutional legacies of the Radical period. These established the rights on which black Americans, poor whites, and their allies based extensive litigation leading to U.S. Supreme Court rulings starting in the early 20th century. These court rulings struck down disfranchising provisions and civil rights legislation that was enacted in the mid-1860s.

The Struggle for Black Education

In the early days of the conflict, a move to ensure support for the Confederacy saw the dismissal of teachers who were not perceived to be fully behind Confederate goals. Other teachers left their posts to join the ranks and the Union blockade of Southern ports wrought havoc on schooling. Southern schools had relied on Northern textbook publishers for textbooks, but they found themselves with a severe shortage of them as the blockade progressed. Out of necessity, Mobile, Alabama, shortly became a center of textbook publishing in the South.[63]

From the first days of their freedom, however, freed slaves demanded formal education. Legislation passed in 1829 had made it a crime to teach slaves to read and white attitudes discouraged literacy within the free black community. Yet, when schools for freed people opened in early 1865, they were crowded to overflowing. Within a year of black freedom, at least 8,000 former slaves were attending schools in Georgia. Eight years later, black schools struggled to contain nearly 20,000 students.[64]

Service in the war and economic upheaval affected public education. For example, in Alabama, the state superintendent of education, Gabriel DuVal, could not devote full attention to that position because he was also captain of a company of Alabama volunteers. The $500,000 that had been spent on public education in 1858 decreased by almost half in 1861. By 1865, public education in Alabama received only $112,000.[65]

During Reconstruction, public schools in the South enjoyed greater funding than before and during the *Civil War*. Republican governments fostered educational growth, believing that education could be a key to social progress. Local governments greatly increased property tax rates, resulting in greater revenues despite lower post-war property values. In 1860, Alabama collected just $530,000 on property with an assessed value of $432 million, compared with more than $1.4 million on property assessed at $156 million by 1870. The average cost of state and local government from 1858 to 1860 was $800,000; by 1868, it exceeded $4 million.[66]

Racial hostility prevented the establishment of racially integrated schools. During the day, teachers, affiliated with the black schools, taught children. At night, they provided instruction to adults, many of whom were motivated to learn so they could read the Bible. White supremacists countered this development by burning black schools and terrorizing teachers and students. There was a tremendous thirst for education among blacks, however, and black churches often took over the task of providing it.[67]

By 1870, 41,300 blacks and 75,800 whites attended public schools. A year later, 54,300 blacks and 87,000 whites were attending public schools. Much of the increase in enrollment among former slaves came about because of the activities of the Freedman's Bureau, which assisted former slaves in their transition to free status.[68]

In March 1865, the U.S. Congress created the Bureau of Refugees, Freedmen, and Abandoned Lands to aid blacks undergoing the transition from slavery to freedom in the aftermath of the *Civil War*. The Freedmen's Bureau, as it was more commonly known, was the first organization of its kind, a federal agency established solely for social welfare. Under the direction of Major General Oliver O. Howard, the agency furnished rations to refugees and freed people displaced by the war. It established schools and hospitals, supervised the development of a contract labor system, and created military tribunals to adjudicate legal disputes. Though operations ceased in Georgia and other states as early as 1870, the bureau remained a functioning federal agency until 1872 when Congress allowed its authorization to expire.[69]

On May 20, 1865, Howard appointed Brigadier General Rufus Saxton to oversee the bureau's efforts in Georgia, South Carolina, and Florida. Saxton had spent the better part of the war on the Sea Islands of South Carolina as part of a Union occupation force that supervised abandoned plantations and their black residents. As the bureau's assistant commissioner, he largely continued his wartime efforts, encouraging freed slaves to resettle on abandoned or confiscated properties and touting land acquisition as an essential step on the path to self-sufficiency. His advocacy of free labor and written contracts helped shape the bureau's efforts for years to come.[70]

Saxton struggled to bring order to the state's inland territories and in September 1865 was relieved of his command in Georgia. The bureau's presence expanded under Saxton's successor, Brigadier General Davis Tillson, and, by September 1866, the agency had doled out more than

800,000 rations statewide. While much of the agency's rations went to blacks, a surprising number of poor whites benefited from bureau relief measures as well. In Georgia, whites received almost one-fifth of the agency's rations. Regionwide, whites received more than a fourth.[71]

Little success was achieved by the bureau in civil rights. The bureau's own courts were poorly organized and short-lived. Only the barest forms of due process of law for freedmen could be sustained in the civil courts. Its most notable failure concerned the land itself. Thwarted by President Johnson's restoration of abandoned lands to pardoned Southerners, the bureau was forced, by the adamant refusal of Congress to consider any form of land redistribution, to oversee sharecropping arrangements that inevitably became oppressive. Congress, preoccupied with other national interests and responding to the continued hostility of white Southerners, terminated the bureau in July 1872.[72]

CHAPTER FIVE

THE PHILOSOPHY OF EDUCATION

Education almost always has assimilation as its goal, the merging of two or more cultures into a single, shared set of traditions and memories. For emancipated American slaves, education was the path to freedom. However, public education in the South virtually ceased during the long *Civil War*. There were Southerners who did not seriously object to the enlightenment of black people, but timorous black Southerners soon had other reasons for an uncharitable attitude. During the first quarter of the nineteenth century, effective forces were rapidly increasing the number of local reactionaries who, through public opinion, gradually prohibited the education of colored people in all places except certain urban communities where progressive blacks had been sufficiently enlightened to provide their own school facilities.[1]

One rejoinder by intelligent blacks was the circulation of antislavery accounts pertaining to the wrongs done to black people and the well-portrayed exploits of François Dominique Toussaint Louverture, one of the leaders of the Haitian Revolution. Moreover, refugees from Haiti had settled in Baltimore, Norfolk, Charleston, and New Orleans, where they gave local blacks a first-hand story of how black men in the West Indies had righted their wrongs. At the same time, certain abolitionists were praising, in the presence of slaves, the bloody methods of the *French Revolution*. When this enlightenment became productive of such disorders that slaveholders lived in fear of servile insurrection, Southern States adopted the thoroughly reactionary policy of making the education for blacks virtually impossible.[2]

Influence from Abroad

The rapid strides made by black people in their mental development after the revolutionary era were so startling that some began to favor the backward-looking policy of educating them only on the condition that they would be colonized. The colonization movement was supported by some white men who, seeing the educational progress of the colored people during the period of better beginnings, felt that they should be given an opportunity to be transplanted to a free country where they might develop without restriction.[3]

In 1804, the Haitian government attempted to attract black Americans. By the late teens, it met with some success. In direct communication with New York City's black community, Haiti offered to pay passage and provide land to those who would settle there. When Prince Saunders introduced the idea at the 1818 meeting of the American Convention for Promoting the Abolition of Slavery in Philadelphia, it was enthusiastically received.[4]

Paul Cuffee was a black Quaker businessman, sea captain, patriot, and abolitionist. He was of Aquinnah Wampanoag and African Ashanti descent and helped colonize Sierra Leone. Cuffee built a lucrative shipping empire and, as well, established the first racially integrated school in Westport, Massachusetts.[5] A devout Christian, Cuffee often preached and spoke at the Sunday services of the multi-racial Society of Friends meeting house in Westport, Massachusetts.[6] In 1813, he donated most of the money needed to build a new meeting house. Many freed slaves had moved from the United States to Nova Scotia after the *American Revolution* and Cuffee became involved in the British effort to resettle them to the colony of Sierra Leone. He also helped establish The Friendly Society of Sierra Leone which provided financial support for the colony.

In 1816, Cuffee envisioned a mass emigration plan for black Americans, both to Sierra Leone and possibly to newly-freed Haiti.[7] Congress rejected his petition to fund a return to Sierra Leone. Many blacks began to demonstrate an interest in immigrating to Africa and some people believed this was the best solution to problems of racial tensions in American society. Cuffee was persuaded by Reverends Samuel J. Mills and Robert Finley to help them with the African colonization plans of the American

Colonization Society (ACS), but he was alarmed at the overt racism of many members of the ACS.

ACS co-founders, particularly Henry Clay, advocated exporting freed blacks as a way of ridding the South of potentially "troublesome" agitators who might threaten the plantation system of slavery.[8] Other Americans also became active with the ACS and found there was more reason to encourage emigration to Haiti where American immigrants would be welcomed by the government of President Jean-Pierre Boye.

James Forten and the Reverends Richard Allen and Peter Williams, along with many other supporters of Haitian emigration, had backed Cuffee's African emigration plans, but they were even more comfortable with the idea of nearby Haiti as an alternative. Forten's support was significant because he was a prominent black abolitionist, inventor, and entrepreneur, and one of the wealthiest Americans of his day.[9]

Prince Saunders, himself, had been one of Cuffee's original correspondents in the Boston African Institution. A native of Vermont, who had been educated at the Moor and Indian School attached to Dartmouth College, Saunders was ill and on leave from teaching at the African School in Boston. His doctor advised him to take a long trip to a warmer climate and, in 1815, acting partly on this suggestion, Saunders wrote to Cuffee informing him that he and several families from Boston were interested in immigrating to Sierra Leone. In preparation for emigration to Africa, Saunders went to London for training as a missionary. At that time, British abolitionists were exploring the possibility of Haiti as a destination for freed American slaves and, as well, Haitian ruler King Henri Christophe had expressed a need for teachers. Consequently, William Wilberforce persuaded Prince Saunders to go there to help establish schools.[10]

For the next few years, Saunders recruited teachers and promoted interest in Haiti, dividing his time between England, the United States, and Haiti, where Christophe appointed him minister of education. Saunders, British abolitionist Thomas Clarkson, and the king developed a plan for Haiti to provide asylum for emancipated American slaves as an alternative to the American Colonization Society plan. Saunders' efforts on behalf of Haiti were interrupted by personal conflicts with Christophe, a coup against the king, and Christophe's death in the fall of 1820.[11]

Early Black School Systemization

After the *Civil War*, there came a tremendous demand for education in the South. In the early 19th century, there was less opposition to education for blacks than in the years before the *Civil War*. However, early students tended to be privileged. Children of prosperous free blacks and servants of prominent families or government officials, attended private schools established by free blacks or benevolent whites.[12]

While Northern private benevolence and the federal government deserve credit for aid to black education in the South during Reconstruction, the primary impetus and sustaining force came from blacks themselves. The first postwar schools were former clandestine schools, operating openly by January 1865. Literate black men and women opened new self-sustaining schools. Northern freedmen's aid organizations began establishing schools in mid-1865. Nearly 50 aid societies were working in freedmen's education in the 1860s. These benevolent organizations raised funds, recruited teachers, and attempted to keep the future of freed slaves before the Northern public.[13]

The Freedmen's Bureau did not hire teachers or operate schools itself. Instead, it assisted the aid societies in meeting the escalating black demand for education. It rented buildings for schoolrooms, provided books and transportation for teachers, superintended the schools, and offered military protection for students and teachers against the opponents of black literacy. Native Southerners, black and white, along with Northern teachers, shouldered the task of teaching in the schools of free blacks.[14]

Of the nearly 600 teachers in Georgia schools during Reconstruction, more than one-fifth were native Georgians, including nearly 50 whites. Twenty-five percent of the teachers were blacks. More than half of the black teachers were Georgians, while other black teachers hailed from the Seaboard South, Pennsylvania, New Jersey, New York, Massachusetts, and Ohio. Although contemporary Southern teachers seldom had completed high school, many of the Northern freedmen's teachers had graduated from post-secondary institutions such as Dartmouth College in New Hampshire, Yale University in Connecticut, Oberlin College in Ohio, and Mount Holyoke in Massachusetts. The black teachers had attended such college as Oberlin, Wilberforce University in Ohio, and Lincoln University in Pennsylvania.[15]

Even where the bureau and Northern aid did not reach into the South, blacks provided a substantial amount of support for the schools. They paid monthly tuition fees, raised funds for teachers' room and board, purchased lots for schoolhouses, and donated material and labor to build them. They also created and supported schools that were independent of Northern efforts. Until 1870, blacks, who were nearly half of the state's population, sustained their own schools and, as well, paid school taxes to provide for white schools from which they were excluded.[16]

Adult blacks wanted the benefits of literacy for themselves as passionately as they wanted schools for their children. In Winter and in the slack times between planting and harvesting, fathers and mothers recited beside their children in the schools. To meet the demand of education for adults who could not attend regular classes, the teachers organized night schools and Sabbath-day schools. Throughout Reconstruction, teachers reported that adults often constituted one-third of their students. Adult students were also served by formal secondary and higher education institutions. These ranged from normal schools for teacher training in Macon, Columbus, Savannah, and elsewhere, to preparatory schools attached to colleges and the colleges themselves. Among the colleges were Atlanta University, Clark College (later Clark Atlanta University), and the Augusta Institute (later Morehouse College).[17]

In addition to providing for rudimentary instruction, the free blacks of the North helped their friends to make possible what we now call higher education. During the second quarter of the 19th century, the advanced training of blacks was almost prohibited by the refusals of academies and colleges to admit persons of color. Because of these conditions, the long-time efforts put forth to found black colleges began to be crowned with success even before the *Civil War.* Later, after the *War,* institutions in the North admitted blacks for various motives. Some colleges endeavored to prepare them for service in Liberia, while others, proclaiming their conversion to the doctrine of democratic education, opened their doors to all.[18]

The advocates of higher education for black people met with substantial opposition. The concentration in Northern communities of the crude fugitives driven from the South necessitated a readjustment of things. The training of blacks in any manner, whatsoever, was very unpopular even in many parts of the North. When prejudice lost some of its sting, friends of black people did more than ever to help in their education. In view of the changed conditions, however, most of these philanthropists concluded that blacks were very much in need of a practical education. Educators first attempted to provide such training by offering classical and vocational courses in what they called the "manual labor schools." When these failed to meet the emergency, they advocated actual vocational training. To make this new system extensive, blacks freely cooperated with their benefactors, sharing no small part of the real burden because they were, at the same time, paying taxes to support public schools that they could not attend.[19]

This very condition was what enabled the abolitionists to see that they had erred in advocating the establishment of separate schools for blacks. At first, the segregation of black pupils was intended as a special provision to bring the colored youth into contact with sympathetic teachers who knew the needs of their students. When the public schools, developed at the expense of the state transformed into a desirable system better equipped than private institutions, the antislavery organizations in many Northern states began to demand that the blacks be admitted to the public schools. After extensive discussion, certain states of New England finally decided to admit blacks into the public schools and experienced no great inconvenience from the change. In most other states of the North, however, separate schools for blacks did not cease to exist until the end of the *Civil War*.[20]

Black teachers at all levels were dependent on the white community leaders. This dependence was particularly strong in the case of elementary school teachers in rural districts. Their salaries were low, and they had no tenure. Moreover, they could be used as disseminators of the whites' expectations and demands on the black community.[21]

The extreme dependence and poverty of rural black school teachers, and the existence of blacks who were somewhat better off and more independent, practically excluded the teachers from having any status of leadership in the black community. So far as their teaching was concerned, however, they were more independent than it appeared. This was solely because the white superintendent and the white school board ordinarily cared so little about what went on in the black schools that there were counties where the superintendent had never visited most his black schools. If the black stool pigeons did not transfer reports that she puts wrong ideas into the children's heads, the rural black school teacher was usually ignored.[22]

The situation was different in cities. Black elementary and high schools were better; teachers were better trained and better paid. In the black community, teachers had a higher social status. As individuals, they also achieved a measure of independence because they were usually anonymous to the white superintendent and school board. The white community did not follow closely what happened among blacks. The black principal in a city school, however, was directly responsible to white officials and watched his teachers more closely than did superintendents of rural schools.[23]

One of the earliest black schools in the Washington, D.C. was the Union Seminary School, established by John F. Cook, Sr., on H Street near 14th Street, N.W. Born a slave, Cook gained his freedom when his remarkable aunt, Alethia Browning Tanner, purchased from the proceeds of her vegetable garden near Lafayette Square not only her own freedom, but that of her sister and Cook's four siblings. In 1834, Cook became master of Union Seminary. The school's curriculum included reading, composition, recitation, sculpture, physiology, and health. The building was partly destroyed by some of the District's white citizens in the 1835 Snow Riot.[24]

Cook sought protection in Pennsylvania, where he built another school. He returned to the District of Columbia in 1836 and, in 1841, Reverent Cook and Charles Stewart formally organized the Fifteenth Street Presbyterian Church, the first such denomination in the city. In 1843, Cook was elected to be the church's first pastor and created a school there. He served both until his death in 1855. A surviving son, George, ran the church school until its closing in 1867.[25]

After an act of Congress created the public school system in 1864, the black schools of Washington and Georgetown were organized under a black board of trustees. In 1874, this board was consolidated with three others to create a 19-member board of trustees for all the District schools.[26] After Washington lost home rule in 1879, the District commissioners appointed the board members and the black and white schools came under separate superintendents. George F. T. Cook, one of the sons of John F. Cook, Sr., was appointed superintendent of colored schools, a position he held until the schools were reorganized in 1900. Both the black schools and the white schools were directly responsible to the Board of Trustees, on which it was customary for three black men to serve. After 1895, women also served.[27]

Classical Versus Industrial Education

As soon as the movement for the education of black youth began, the quarrel started as to whether their education should be "classical" or "industrial."[28] If the white Southerners had to permit blacks to get any education at all, they wanted it to be the sort which would make them better servants and laborers, not one that would teach them to rise out of their "place." The New England school teachers, who did most of the teaching at first, wanted to train black people as they, themselves, had been trained in the North; the "three R's" at the elementary level, with such subjects as Latin, Greek, geometry, rhetoric coming in at the secondary and college levels.[29]

In 1868, General Samuel C. Armstrong, a Union officer during the *Civil War,* had established Hampton Normal and Agricultural Institute in the tidewater region of Virginia as an "agricultural institution." Armstrong wanted to continue the skilled artisan tradition that had existed among blacks before the *War* and, as the school's president wrote in the annual report for 1872: "Skillful agriculturalists and mechanics are needed rather than poets and orators." His most famous pupil, Booker T. Washington, founded the Tuskegee Institute in Alabama and became the apostle of industrial education for black people. In his famous 1895 Atlanta Compromise message to black Americans, he entreated blacks to "cast down your bucket where you are." Washington beseeched blacks to develop first and foremost their economic prospects, realizing that "there is as much dignity in tilling a field as in writing a poem." Armstrong and Washington maintained close personal ties throughout their lives, and, in fact, Armstrong helped to provide much-needed publicity and financial contacts for Tuskegee's success.[30]

There is no doubt that, quite apart from the pedagogical merits of this type of education, Washington's message was extremely timely in the actual power situation of the Restoration. It reconciled many Southern white men to the idea of black education and Washington probably had a large share in salvaging black education from the great danger of its being destroyed. Meanwhile, the New England advocates of a classical education and their followers carried on at Atlanta, Fisk, and a few other Southern centers of black college education. The elementary schools, there were practically no secondary schools for blacks in the South at this time, followed the patterns set by the dominant colleges.[31]

The struggle between the conservative and the radical group of black leaders became focused on the issue of "industrial" *versus* "classical" education for black people. In 1853, Frederick Douglass expressed himself as in favor of "an industrial school" when Harriet Beecher Stowe offered some money for this or for an "educational institution pure and simple." He wished established ". . . a series of workshops, where colored people could learn some of the handicrafts, learn to work in iron, wood, and leather, and where a plain English education could also be taught." His opinion was ". . . that *want* of money was the root of all evil to the colored people. They were shut out from all lucrative employments and compelled to be merely barbers, waiters, coachmen and the like at wages so low that they could buy little or neither."[32] However, Booker T. Washington became the champion for the former position, and he was backed by the white South and the bulk of Northern philanthropy.

William Edward Burghardt Du Bois, who received his Ph.D. in sociology from Harvard in 1895, headed a group of black intellectuals who feared that most often the intention, and in any case the result, of an emphasis on industrial education would be to keep black people out of the higher and more general culture of America. Du Bois was strongly influenced by the new historical work of German-trained Albert Bushnell Hart, a historian and a professor of government and history at Harvard University, and the philosophical lectures of William James, often called the father of American psychology. Other intellectual influences came from his studies and travels between 1892 and 1894 in Germany, where he was enrolled at the Friedrich-Wilhelm III Universität (then commonly referred to as the University of Berlin but renamed the Humboldt University after *World War II*). Because of the expiration of the Slater Fund fellowship that supported his stay in Germany, Du Bois could not meet the residency requirements that would have enabled him to formally earn the degree in economics, despite his completion of the required doctoral thesis (on the history of Southern U.S. agriculture) during his tenure.[33]

With the publication of *Souls of Black Folk*, Du Bois emerged as the most prominent spokesperson for the opposition to Washington's policy of political conservatism and racial accommodation. Ironically, Du Bois had kept a prudent distance from Washington's opponents and had made few overt statements in opposition to the so-called Wizard of Tuskegee. His career had involved several near-misses whereby he himself might have ended up teaching at Tuskegee. He applied to Washington for a job shortly after returning from Berlin, but had to decline Tuskegee's superior monetary offer because he had already accepted a position at Wilberforce. On several other occasions Washington, sometimes prodded by Hart sought to recruit Du Bois to join him at Tuskegee, a courtship he continued at least until the summer of 1903 when Du Bois taught summer school at Tuskegee.[34]

Early in his career, moreover, Du Bois's views bore a superficial similarity to Washington's. In fact, he had praised Washington's 1895 "Atlanta Compromise" speech, which proposed to Southern white elites a compromise wherein blacks would forswear political and civil rights in exchange for economic opportunities. Like many elite blacks at the time, Du Bois was not averse to some form of franchise restriction, so long as it was based on educational qualifications and applied equally to white and black.[35]

This dispute was important in the development of black ideologies, but it scarcely meant much for the actual development of black education in the South that was dominated by the whites. If black education in the South did not turn entirely into industrial education on the elementary level, the main explanation was, as we shall see, the growing expense of such training after the Industrial Revolution and the competitive interest of white workers to keep blacks out of the crafts and industry. On the higher level, a nonvocational black education had, as Du Bois always emphasized, its chief strength in the fact that the Tuskegee institute and other similar schools had raised the demand for teachers with a broader educational background.[36]

Du Bois and Washington had overlapping goals in education and in society, but different emphases. Both recognized the very low standards of education skills, behavior, and hygiene among most blacks at the end of the nineteenth century. After all, they were just one generation removed from the world of the slave plantation.[37] During this era, Du Bois criticized the extravagant spending habits he found among blacks. In his study, *The Philadelphia Negro*, he also spoke more generally of "the Great Lack which faces our race in the modern world, Lack of Energy," which he attributed to "indolence" that had now become a kind of "social heredity."[38] Even if whites were to lose their racial prejudices overnight, it would make little difference in the economic position of most blacks, according to Du Bois. Although "some few would be promoted and some few would get new places" as a result of an end of discrimination, nevertheless, "the mass would remain as they are" until the younger generation began to "try harder" as the race "lost the omnipresent excuse for failure: prejudice."[39]

Du Bois saw many of the blacks as being drawn into "listless indifference or shiftlessness, or reckless bravado."[40] Like Washington, Du Bois saw an enormous need for self-improvement among blacks at this juncture in history. The big difference was that Washington made self-improvement the principal and over-riding goal of the kind of education he established at the Tuskegee Institute.[41]

Students at Tuskegee were taught job skills, including the skills that enabled them to build many of the buildings at the institute itself. They were taught deportment, hygiene, and other mundane, but important, things that were needed to take control of their own lives and advance in the world. Contrary to legend, Washington never renounced equal rights. "It is important and right that all privileges of the law be ours, but it is vastly more important that we be prepared for the exercises of these privileges," he said in his historic Atlanta Exposition speech.[42] By linking rights and responsibilities, Washington was able to address both the blacks and the whites in the audience on common ground. By linking the fates of the two races, he was able to enlist the support of some whites by arguing that blacks would either help lift up the South or help drag it down.[43] Du Bois, likewise, said to the Southern whites: "If you do not lift them up, they will pull you down."[44]

Although the two men said many things that were very similar at the time, their differing emphases were clear as well. Beginning with education, Du Bois emphasized academic education for those he called "the talented tenth"[45] of the race. These were largely people like Du Bois himself, educated and cultured descendants of the antebellum "free persons of color." For the "talented tenth," vocational education would have been a step backward. The very phrase "talented tenth" implicitly acknowledged that this was not what was most needed by most blacks at the time. Although Du Bois acknowledged the necessity and the achievements of vocation education, "accomplishments of which it has a right to be proud,"[46] he was promoting a very different kind of education for a very different class of people. This education and this class of people were intended to spearhead political agitation for civil rights, as exemplified by the National Association for the Advancement of Colored People (NAACP), which Du Bois helped found.[47]

Just as Du Bois acknowledged the need for vocational education for many blacks, so Washington acknowledged the need for academic education for other blacks. He served on the board of trustees for Howard University and Fisk University, whose educational missions were very different from that of Tuskegee Institute. He used his influence to get financial support for Howard and other black academic institutions such as Talladega College and Atlanta University.[48] Though he saw most blacks of his time as needing to acquire practical work skills first, Washington declared: "I would say to the black boy what I would say to the white boy. Get all the mental development that your time and pocket-book will allow of." Still, he said, "I would not have the standard of mental development lowered one whit for, with the Negro, as with all races, mental strength is the basis of all progress."[49] Kelly Miller, the first Black mathematics graduate student, saw the controversy over differences in educational philosophy to be the work of "one-eyed enthusiasts,"[50] rather than of men like Du Bois and Washington, who saw the need for both.

Booker T. Washington saw his own primary task as "the promotion of progress among the many, and not the special culture of the few."[51] He saw his work as an educator in his times as preparatory, as "laying a foundation for the masses,"[52] but not to confine the whole race to the work for which Tuskegee Institute would immediately prepare its students. After speaking proudly of a Tuskegee graduate whose knowledge of chemistry had increased the average yield of sweet potatoes several-fold, he said, "My theory of education for the Negro would not, for example, confine him for all time to farm work, to the production of the best and most sweet potatoes. However, if he succeeded in this line of industry, he could lay the foundations upon which his children and grand-children could grow to higher and more important things in life."[53] Even in the present, he said, "we need professional men and women"[54] and he looked forward to a time when there would be more successful black lawyers, Congressmen, and music teachers."[55]

As regards civil rights, Booker T. Washington wrote in 1899, "I do not favour the Negro's giving up anything which is fundamental and which has been guaranteed to him through the Constitution of the United States."[56] His general public posture was that he was too busy with the self-improvement of blacks to become involved in political controversies. Yet, when his papers were examined after his death, it became clear that he had privately goaded other blacks to crusade for civil rights, and had even secretly financed legal challenges to the Jim Crow laws in the South."[57]

Washington was fully aware that to have done these things publicly would have jeopardized the white financial support upon which Tuskegee Institute depended. This was not simply a matter of protecting his own interests. He understood the repercussions for others if he made explosive statements in the volatile racial atmosphere of the times. "I could stir up a race war in Alabama in six weeks if I chose," he said, but to do so "would wipe out the achievements of decades of labor."[58] Yet, he also understood that open challenges to racial discrimination had to be made. As he wrote to Oswald Garrison Villard, one of the founders of the N.A.A.C.P., "there is work to be done which no one placed in my position can do."[59]

Although Du Bois could not have known of all the things that Washington was doing secretly, he did have an insight into the man, himself, and he knew where Washington's loyalties lay. Du Bois said of Washington: "He had no faith in white people, not the slightest."[60] Booker T. Washington practiced what a later generation of black militants would only preach, to advance the cause of blacks "by all means necessary."[61] Howard University dean, Kelly Miller, said of Washington that the advancement of the black race "is the chief burden of his soul."[62]

Despite differences between Du Bois and Washington, and rivalries between their respective followers, this did not prevent civility between the two men themselves. In Booker T. Washington's autobiography, *Up from Slavery*, he wrote of a meeting arranged by some "good ladies in Boston" in 1899 where, in addition to "an address by myself, Mr. Paul Lawrence Dunbar read from his poems and Dr. W.E.B. Du Bois read an original sketch."[63]

An Educational Proclamation

The District of Columbia school system became an early magnet for black teachers, as salaries were relatively high. Moreover, the segregated school system diminished the effects of discrimination and the amenities of Washington black society provided an attractive way of life for teachers. By 1869, half of the teachers in the black schools were black and, by 1901, the last white teacher would withdraw.[64]

The head of the group that founded the first high school for black people was a remarkable man named William Syphax. Syphax grew up as a free man, having been freed in infancy in 1826, and became a civil rights activist in the Washington black community in the mid-19th century. He was described as a man of "dauntless courage and unwavering integrity" who "dared to demand what was due his race, fearing no man regardless of position or color." The substance and tone of his messages to municipal and federal officials clearly support this description. He was hardheaded on education. While the group he led preferred black teachers for black children, they were not prepared to compromise quality for the sake of racial representation. They deemed it a "violation of our official oath to employ inferior teachers when superior teachers can be had for the same money." Syphax was equally frank in telling the black community that its parents would have to send their children to school with respect for teachers and a willingness to submit to discipline and hard work if their education was to amount to anything.[65]

Only detached, incoherent, and inconclusive reports have been preserved and passing years have dimmed the memories of many of Syphax's descendants. Those who lived and associated with him have passed away. He was born shortly after the troublous days of the *Missouri Compromise* and witnessed the growing hatred and sectional discords that resulted from the *Compromise of 1850*. He likewise saw the devastating effects of the *Kansas-Nebraska Bill*, the *Dred Scott Decision*, and the John Brown raid. He lived through the hectic days of slavery, disunion, civil war, and subsequent reconstruction. Through it all, however, Syphax had an abiding faith in his people and, at every possible opportunity, he clearly projected a manliness and fortitude in his efforts to champion their cause. He was honest, courageous, and thrifty in all his dealings, and he never descended from his lofty pedestal.[66]

Syphax was not blind to the shortcomings of his own people. In a circular to the black people of Washington and Georgetown on September 10, 1868, he urged them to cooperate with the trustees in their efforts to render the schools as efficient as possible to "the great end for which they were established."[67] This circular was sent to the ministers and prominent blacks of Washington and Georgetown. In his zeal for parental cooperation, Syphax expressed a vision and an interpretation of school values that placed him well ahead of his time. He easily could have been living in the 20th century when he established a system of belief, principles, or opinions for black schools that became a philosophy of early black educators, parents, and students. His circular proposed to the ministers and citizens that:

1. Ministers should hold before their congregations the necessity of education to fit their children for the new duties of freedom and civil equality in order to fill worthily positions of honor and responsibility. This cannot be done in ignorance

2. Parents should send their children to school promptly on the first day of the year, in order that the school is organized quickly and to prevent certain students from getting an early start on the latecomers.

3. Parents were urged to send their children regularly and punctually to school. Many parents, not fully appreciating the importance of regular school attendance, had frequently kept their children at home for trivial reasons to the great injury of their children and the whole school. Tardiness, too, was a great vice. The habit of rising early and getting to school on time would cultivate the habit of early rising and punctuality that would be of value to children and parents through life.

4. Parents should be advised always to sustain the regulations and the good discipline of the schools. They should never be disrespectful to a teacher in the presence of their children; nor take sides with students against a teacher until after a visit and a calm inquiry into the matter of complaint has been made and the teacher found to be clearly in the wrong. Even in such instances the parent should speak to the teacher privately or to the superintendent or to the trustees, rather than blame the teacher in front of the students.

5. Parents should visit the schools, make the acquaintance of the teachers and see how the schools were conducted. This would indicate an interest in their children's progress and would stimulate the teachers to a greater interest in their work.

6. The ministers would set a good example by visiting the schools also; the children would then feel that harmony existed between the church and the school.

7. All should sustain the trustees in their determination to elevate the character of the schools by insisting on a high standard of qualifications for teachers regardless of color. Preference would be given colored teachers, their qualifications being equal, for we "deem it a violation of our official oath to employ inferior teachers when superior teachers can be had for the same money." Black teachers would be employed as rapidly as they became competent after they had enjoyed "equal advantages for a sufficient length of time."

These were the exhortations and admonitions of William Syphax to his people,[68] as he attempted to move blacks toward assimilation. The early period of competition and conflict in colonial days had been followed by the institutionalization of slavery, an accommodation that began to emerge in the 1660s and finished at the end of the *Civil War* in 1865. After a brief period of renewed conflict occurring during Reconstruction, a second accommodation, *de jure* segregation, stabilized black-white relations with whites still in a position of power. Every advance in education and intelligence would put blacks in possession of the white man's technique of communication and organization and, thus, contribute to the extension and consolidation of the black world within the white world.[69]

Many other blacks who were educators in the District of Columbia Public Schools made important contributions to black education. In 1864, Congress passed an act that provided for part of all funds raised in Washington and Georgetown to be set aside for colored schools in proportion to the number of children of this race between the ages of six and 17 who constituted a part of the entire school population. Five schools (1866-1868) opened with seven teachers and 400 students.[70]

PART III

THE PARADIGM

"The foundation of all free government and all social order must be laid in families and in the discipline of youth. Young persons must not only be furnished with knowledge, but they must be accustomed to subordination and subjected to the authority and influence of good principles. It will avail little that youths are made to understand truth and correct principles, unless they are accustomed to submit to be governed by them."

— Noah Webster, 1758-1843

CHAPTER SIX

THE CULTURE OF THE BLACK COMMUNITY PRIOR TO 1960

The cultural environment in which people live is a basic factor that both aids and restricts human progress. For blacks in the United States, slavery and, later, segregation were a dynamic force in the black community's development. So, blacks watched with despair while the foundations for the Jim Crow system were laid and the walls of segregation mounted around them. Their disenchantment with the hopes based on the *Civil War* amendments and the reconstruction laws was nearly complete by 1890.

The American commitment to equality, solemnly attested to by three amendments to the *Constitution* and several elaborate civil rights acts, was virtually repudiated. What had started as a retreat in 1877, turned into a rout. Northern radicals and liberals had abandoned the cause; the courts had rendered the *Constitution* helpless, and the Republican Party had forsaken the cause it had sponsored. A tide of racism was mounting in the country unopposed. Blacks held no less than five national conventions in 1890 to consider their plight, but all they could do was to pass resolutions of protest and confess their helplessness.[1]

In 1896, *Plessy v. Ferguson*, the Supreme Court ruled that it was not wrong for a state to use discriminatory seating practices on public transportation and that each state may require segregation on public transportation. This sustained the transportation law that ordered separate but equal transportation facilities for blacks and whites.[2] Essentially, the Court endorsed segregation with inconsistent rationales because it accorded with the "established usages, customs and traditions of the people." It went on to make several other significant decisions sanctioning racial segregation in other circumstances and in other places. One of these decisions subsequently ruled to authorize racially segregated schools. Segregation, the Court said, was not discrimination.[3] *Plessy v. Ferguson* remained the law of the land for exactly 58 years, from May 18, 1896, to May 17, 1954, when it was finally recognized that separate was not equal.

There are certain types of behavior which are considered essential to the welfare of a community; i.e., folkways, mores, and values. They involve moral judgments by the society as to what is right and what is wrong. They also relate to important aspects of life such as honesty and fairness in dealing with others, relationships between the sexes, safety of life and property, and loyalty to the nation. To further the important interests of the black community as a group, a social paradigm grounded on a complex pattern of behaviors was established based on the church, loyalty to country, and family. These three factors were the central interests and needs of the community and contributed greatly to what was considered the "good life" and the general welfare of black people.[4]

Religion

With few exceptions, the black slaves brought to America had not been converted to Christianity.[5] For nearly a century, many slaveholders were reluctant to let black slaves receive religious instruction because they believed that a baptized Christian could not be held as a slave. However, when theologians, legislatures, and courts declared, around the year 1700, that conversion to Christianity was not incompatible with the worldly status of a slave, many slaveholders went out of their way to provide religious teaching and places of worship for their slaves. Others simply did nothing to hinder missionary work among them.[6]

Undoubtedly, the slaveholder's primary motive was that the Christian religion, as it was expounded, suited their interests in keeping the slaves humble, meek, and obedient. The Christian duty to spread the gospel was taken quite seriously; particularly to compensate for many other deprivations to which blacks were subjected. The idea of free worship was too strong. Slaves were allowed into most white churches and could even meet by themselves if a white minister led them or if any white observed them. Essentially, the only religious meetings completely free of whites were secret ones.[7]

The church service was one of the few occasions when slaves could congregate. Here, they could feel a spiritual union with other blacks. They could feel that they were equal to the white man in the eyes of God and they could see one of their own number, the preacher, rise above the dead level of slavehood and even, occasionally, be admired by white people. The slaves on a plantation could regard the black preacher as their leader, one who could go to the white master and beg for trivial favors.[8]

In the North, the few black churches existing before the *Civil War* continued the same functions they had previously performed. Many of them, like some white churches, were "stations" in the "underground railroad," at which an escaping slave could get means either to become established in the North or to go on to Canada. The Northern black church was also a center of black abolitionist activities. The slavery issue in the national politics of these times gave the black church in the North as great an interest and stake in worldly affairs as it has today.

Probably only a minority of the black slaves were nominal Christians at the time of the Emancipation.[9] At the end of the *Civil War,* there was, on the one hand, an almost complete and permanent expulsion of blacks from the white churches of the South. On the other hand, there was a general movement among blacks themselves to build up their own denominations. This period witnessed another wave of conversion of black people to Christianity and the firm establishment of the independent black church. Southern black religious leaders were helped by white and black missionaries from the North. Observing the church situation in the 1870s, Sir George Campbell gives the following picture of this religious activity:

> Every man and woman likes to be himself or herself an active member of the Church. And though their preachers are in a great degree their leaders, these preachers are chosen by the people from the people, under a system for the most part congregational, and are rather preachers because they are leaders than leaders because they are preachers. In this matter of religion, the Negroes have utterly emancipated themselves from all

white guidance—they have their own churches and their own preachers, all coloured men—-and the share they take in the self-government of their churches really is a very important education. The preachers to our eyes may seem peculiar. American orators somewhat exaggerate and emphasize our style, and the black preachers somewhat exaggerate the American style; but on the whole I felt considerably edified by them. They come to the point in a way that is refreshing after some sermons that one has heard.[10]

Many black political leaders during the Reconstruction were recruited from the preachers. After Reconstruction, many of them returned to the pulpit. Under the pressure of political reaction, the black church in the South came to have much the same role as it did before the *Civil War*. Black frustration was sublimated into emotionalism, and black hopes were fixed on the after-world. Black preachers even cautioned their flocks to obey all the caste rules. However, there was a new factor, which increased the possibility of the black church to serve as a power agency for black people. The white preachers and the white observer in the black church disappeared. There remained, nevertheless, the black stool pigeon who reported to the whites on the activities of blacks in the church and elsewhere in the black community.[11]

In the 1890s, the move to reform the larger society led naturally to reforms aimed at combating racial discrimination. Under the Reverend Walter H. Brooks, Nineteenth Street Baptist entered a new phase of conflict for the black church and, by the same token, for privileged blacks. As racism and segregation increased in American society in the 1890s, the white church began to absorb some of these ideas. Black ministers found themselves forced to defend organized Christianity against charges of hypocrisy to a leadership that was beginning to realize that assimilation would not come any time soon.[12]

Blacks began to advocate racial solidarity, realizing that this was the only way to escape dependence on whites. The black church led the way in creating parallel black institutions that would relieve this dependence.

Brooks was particularly vocal in the disputes between the black Baptist church and its white counterparts in the late 1880s and 1890s,[13]

The main organizations for Baptists in the country were the Northern and Southern Baptist Conventions, which were controlled by white Baptists. Most black Baptist churches were affiliated with the Northern Baptist Convention. The Convention ran the foreign missionary efforts, the American Baptist Home Mission society (ABHMS), and distributed denominational literature through the American Baptist Publication Society. During the 1880s, blacks began to agitate for the appointment of black faculty at schools for blacks run by the ABHMS. In addition, black ministers and churchwomen, who were active in the movement for education, complained that the American Baptist Publication Society would not accept works by black theologians, and that the only Sunday school literature available for black churches was written by whites. Walter H. Brooks was among those black ministers who protested the Convention policies.[14]

Brooks had already made a name for himself as an advocate for education before his arrival in Washington. In 1881, he had written a widely read article advocating the expansion of the curriculum in the black Baptist colleges beyond the current theological courses; he wanted to see them include the sort of courses being offered by Howard and Fisk universities. He particularly emphasized the importance of education for black women. In response to his and others' pleas, Northern whites established Hartshorn Memorial College in Richmond, Virginia, for the education of black women.[15]

In Washington, Brooks led a group of black ministers in protesting the administration of the white president of the Baptist-affiliated Wayland Seminary, George Merrill Prentie King. They accused King of arbitrary corporal punishment and abuse of black female students of Wayland. Despite their protest, the ABHMS did not remove King.[16] The lack of resolution led to black demands for separation from white Baptists in much the way the African Methodist Episcopal (AME) church had separated from the Methodists in the early 19th century.[17]

By the turn of the century, black churches had established distinct identities with a strong reputation for race leadership. What middle-class blacks had sought for themselves in the 1880s, they now sought for the rest of the race. The black church led the movement for education for blacks and for the building up of independent institutions.[18]

The ideal of a progressive church dedicated to racial uplift was the Fifteenth Street Presbyterian Church under Francis J. Grimké. The church had been organized in 1841 by none other than John F. Cook. Early ministers included such notables as Benjamin Tanner, William B. Evans, and Henry Highland Barnet. In 1878, Francis J. Grimké took over ministerial duties, and apart from a 3-year hiatus in Jacksonville, Florida, in the 1880s, he served as minister for nearly 50 years. Although black Presbyterians never established a hierarchy separate from their white counterparts, ministers such as Grimké kept the issue of racism constantly before the church synods. According to one contemporary historian, Grimké's arrival at the Fifteenth Street Presbyterian heralded "a great spiritual awakening as the result of his forceful preaching."[19]

Grimké was a brilliant, fiery orator who became the first black leader to challenge Booker T. Washington's policy of accommodation. He argued that black people needed to fight for the justice they deserved. He denounced the racist policies of the "federation of white churches" and singled out the Young Men's Christian Association (YMCA) for its segregationist policies. Grimké also challenged the racial hierarchy and discriminatory practices of the Presbyterian Church. An early supporter of the Niagara Movement, Grimké helped found the American Negro Academy and served as a trustee to Howard University.[20]

During Grimké's first year, many new people joined the congregation, most of whom had recognizable middle-class status. Nor were these newcomers inactive in the church. Four years after joining, James H. Meriwether was elected elder; two years later, Furman J. Shadd became a trustee. The church weeded out members who had not participated actively and were still on the rolls. By 1890, it was clear that the Fifteenth Street Presbyterian Church had become an influential, activist church.[21] Grimké regularly preached special sermons on racial topics during inauguration week because, at that time, many representatives of the race came to his church from all over the country and he could reach a larger audience.[22]

Grimké typified the new generation of ministers. He was educated and he quoted poetry and scientific theory in his sermons. In addition, having grown up during Reconstruction, he felt confident of the abilities of his race and of the capacity of the white race to recognize those abilities. Thus, he did not hesitate to remind white churches of their duty to the black race and, while his tone remained essentially polite, he did not hesitate to speak out against injustice.[23]

Grimké believed that the church should be the center of moral and spiritual life and, as well, the source of information on what was good. Members should inspire goodness and fulfill this ideal in their personal characters and lives. The minister, himself, should be above reproach. His chief purpose was to teach and preach and, therefore, he should be thoroughly prepared both intellectually and spiritually.[24]

While Grimké was willing to speak out on the issues, he could propose few spiritual solutions to his congregation. In his sermons, "Signs of a Brighter Future" and "God and Prayer as Factors in the Struggle," he noted with pride that the race had moved beyond simply collecting material goods and had begun to stand up for its rights. However, the biggest reasons he could give for hope were, first, that God existed and so injustice could not prevail, and, second, that prayer was a powerful force that could help right wrongs.[25] For a sophisticated audience such as that at the Fifteenth Street Presbyterian Church, the thought was consoling but offered little practical advice.

Although the black church was orientating the affluent blacks to their responsibilities, other changes were taking place. American society was embracing the scientific method and religion was losing its authority. Racial prejudice within American churches caused disillusionment among black leaders. Finally, as the black middle-class took advantage of educational opportunities, a new leadership class developed. It was centered on black professionals, other than ministers, and on businessmen who had the economic means and practical knowledge necessary to sponsor movements for racial uplift outside the church.[26]

Religion remained important spiritually to the black community in the 20th century, but it played an increasingly smaller role in day-to-day life. Black churches adapted their programs to address the social welfare interests of their congregations, but they were not always able to compete with secular organizations. As the black middle-class became increasingly educated and professional, they expected more from the churches than the churches were able to give. The professionals became the community leaders that the ministers had once been, even though the church still played an important role in shaping the values of these leaders. Gradually, racial uplift took on a more secular aspect, and, in some ways, it displaced religion. Booker T. Washington sought "to imbue these young men who are going forth as leaders of their people with the feeling that the great task of uplifting the race, though it may be for others merely a work of humanity, for them, and every other member of the Negro race, it is a work of religion."[27] Nonetheless, individual members of the black community, particularly women involved in reform activities, found active participation in the church to bring forth both spiritual and secular benefits.

It should be no surprise that M Street and Dunbar High School classes began in the morning with a recitation of the Lord's Prayer. The school, like the black church, both reflected and reinforced middle-class ideals. In the 1880s, the church searched for an identity to differentiate itself from the masses, as did its more affluent members. In the 1890s, it took the lead in protesting discrimination, establishing independent institutions, and shaking off white control. In the 20th century, it became involved in social welfare reform to retain the interest of members who had become active in racial uplift. Although the church lost much of its influence on the secularization of society, it was the church that ultimately shaped the values of middle-class blacks and led them to embrace secular reform. By providing social status while promoting racial pride and uplift, the black church created leaders with a greater commitment to their community and to their race.[28]

Patriotism and Fighting for the Republic

The black community was a patriotic community. The military heritage of black Americans is as long as the history of a black presence in North America. There is little wonder that the Pledge of Allegiance was recited in black schools every morning. Moreover, the first black high school Cadet Corps was organized in 1888 at M Street High (which would later become Dunbar High School) by Christian Fleetwood and it was a great source of school and community pride. The purpose of the corps was to teach disciple and leadership.

From the first recorded visit in 1528 of a black person to what is now the United States, blacks, slave and non-slave, participated in military or quasi-military actions. Such participation has not received extensive coverage in general history books, nor was such participation undertaken without difficulty. White Americans have been ambivalent over the years about black participation in military organizations and, in most instances, have encouraged or allowed blacks in military activities only when forced by circumstances to do so. Still, black people have fought for the United States of America in every war in the history of this republic.[29]

Some black people fought in the *American Revolution* (1775-1783) because they saw it as a fight their own liberty and freedom from slavery. Others responded to the Earl of Dunmore's Proclamation[30] and fought for their freedom as black loyalists. Benjamin Quarles believed that the role of blacks in the *American Revolution* can be understood by "realizing that loyalty was not to a place or a person, but to a principle."[31] Regardless of where the loyalties of black people lay, it is often overlooked that they contributed much to the birth of the United States. During the *American Revolutionary War*, blacks served in both the Continental Army and the British Army. It is estimated that 5,000 black Americans served as soldiers for the Continental army,[32] while more than 20,000 fought for the British cause.[33]

The *Civil War* was no exception; official sanction was the difficulty. In the fall of 1862, there were at least three Union regiments of black troops raised in New Orleans, Louisiana: the First, Second, and Third Louisiana Native Guard. These units later became the First, Second, and Third Infantry, Corps d'Afrique, and then the 73rd, 74th, and 75th United States Colored Infantry (USCI). The First South Carolina Infantry (African Descent) was not officially organized until January 1863. However, three companies of the regiment were on coastal expeditions as early as November 1862. They would become the 33rd USCI. Similarly, the First Kansas Colored Infantry (later the 79th [new] USCI) was not mustered into service until January 1863, even though the regiment had already participated in the action at Island Mound, Missouri, on October 27, 1862. These early unofficial regiments received little federal support, but they showed the strength of black people's desire to fight for freedom.[34]

The first official authorization to employ blacks in the federal service was the Second Confiscation and Militia Act of July 17, 1862. This act allowed President Abraham Lincoln to receive black persons into military service and gave permission to use them for any purpose "he may judge best for the public welfare." However, the President did not authorize the use of black soldiers in combat until issuance of the *Emancipation Proclamation* on January 1, 1863: "And I further declare and make known, that such persons of suitable condition, will be received into the armed service of the United States to garrison forts, positions, stations, and other places, and to man vessels of all sorts in said service." With these words, the Union army changed.[35]

In late January 1863, Governor John Andrew of Massachusetts received permission to raise a regiment of black American soldiers. This was the first black regiment to be organized in the North. The pace of organizing additional regiments, however, was very slow. To change this, Secretary of War Edwin M. Stanton sent Gen. Lorenzo Thomas to the lower Mississippi valley in March to recruit blacks. Thomas was given broad authority. He was to explain the administration's policy regarding these new recruits, and he was to find volunteers to raise and command them. Stanton wanted all officers of such units to be white, but that policy softened to allow black surgeons and chaplains. By the end of the war, there were at least 78 black officers in the Union army. Thomas's endeavor was very successful and, on May 22, 1863, the Bureau of Colored Troops was established to coordinate and organize regiments from all parts of the country. Created under War Department General Order No. 143, the bureau was responsible for handling "all matters relating to the organization of Colored Troops."[36]

By 1865, more than 37,000 black soldiers had died in the Civil War, almost 35 percent of all blacks who had served in combat. This heavy toll reflected the fact that black units had served in every theatre of operations and in most major engagements, often as assault troops. Some of these casualties were due to poor equipment, bad medical care, and the "no quarter" policy followed by Confederate forces facing them. To the black troops themselves, these casualties reflected their great desire to prove to an uncaring nation their right to full citizenship and participation after the war. They were fighting to be free, not to return as slaves.[37]

The black community was galvanized by *World War I* in their effort to make America truly democratic by ensuring full citizenship for all its people. Black soldiers, who continued to serve in segregated units, were involved in protests against racial injustice on the home front and abroad. While many black troops were eager to fight, most provided support services. Only a small percentage was involved in combat. Yet, the black American presence in France, helping in any capacity, often elicited overwhelming gratitude from the French. Both the French and the American troops enjoyed listening to black bands that introduced blues and jazz rhythms previously unknown to their listeners.[38]

World War I also caused many social and economic changes within the United States. Black men emerged from the war as a cohort with rising expectations. They were no longer willing to accept passively the indignities and abuses of Jim Crow laws and other forms of racial discrimination. They now had a new determination to gain practical realization of constitutional and civil rights granted a generation earlier in the years following the *Civil War.*

In 1919, Dr. George E. Haynes, an educator employed as director of Negro Economics for the U.S. Department of Labor, wrote: "The return of the Negro soldier to civil life is one of the most delicate and difficult questions confronting the Nation, north and south."[39] One black veteran wrote a letter to the editor of the *Chicago Daily News* saying the returning black veterans:

> . . . are now new men and world men, if you please; and their possibilities for direction, guidance, honest use and power are limitless, only they must be instructed and led. They have awakened, but they have not yet the complete conception of what they have awakened to.[40]

Consequently, the stage was set in 1919, when the District of Columbia erupted into what newspapers called a "race riot." After winning the Great War, Washingtonian veterans returned home to a city where steady jobs were hard to find for workers of any race. White sailors panhandled downtown in their uniforms. Black soldiers who had fought in France listened incredulously as wives explained that there were no jobs available to them.[41] Nobody knows exactly how or where it started, but on a muggy Saturday night, July 19, 1919, the word began to spread among the saloons and pool halls of downtown Washington, where crowds of soldiers, sailors, and Marines just home from the Great War were taking weekend liberty.[42]

A black suspect, questioned in an attempted sexual assault on a white woman, had been released by the D.C. Metropolitan Police. The woman was the wife of a Navy man. So, the booze-fueled mutterings about revenge flowed quickly among hundreds of white men in uniform. The mob drew strength from a seedy neighborhood off Pennsylvania Avenue NW called "Murder Bay," known for its brawlers and brothels. The crowd crossed the tree-covered Mall heading toward a predominantly poor black section of Southwest. They picked up clubs, lead pipes and pieces of lumber as they went. Near Ninth and D streets SW, they fell upon an unsuspecting black man named Charles Linton Ralls, who was out with his wife, Mary. Ralls was chased down and beaten severely. The mob then attacked a second black man, George Montgomery, 55, who was returning home with groceries. They fractured his skull with a brick.[43]

The violence drew only scattered resistance in the black community and the police were nowhere to be seen. When the Metropolitan Police Department finally arrived in force, its white officers arrested more blacks than whites, sending a clear signal about their sympathies. Thousands of white veterans in uniform snatched black people from streetcars and sidewalks and beat them mercilessly. Black women cried in the streets for God to save them. "Before I became unconscious," recalled 17-year-old Francis Thomas, "I could hear [two black women] pleading with the Lord to keep them from being killed." A 22-year-old black man, Randall Neale, was walking near 4th and N Streets NW when a white Marine shot and killed him from a passing trolley car.[44]

By Sunday night, black Washington had had enough. Veteran sharpshooters cleaned their rifles before scaling walls to the roof of Howard Theatre. U Street, N.W. was their Rubicon and they defended it against white invasion. *The Washington Post* reported: "In the Negro district along U Street from Seventh to Fourteenth Streets, the Negroes began early in the evening to take vengeance for the assaults on their race in the downtown district the night before." After securing their neighborhoods, some black men went on the offensive, pulling unsuspecting white riders from streetcars and viciously beating them. Black and white men fired at each other from moving cars.[45] When the violence ended, a total of 15 people had died: 10 whites, including two police officers; and five blacks. Fifty people were seriously wounded and another 100 less severely injured. It was one of the few times when white fatalities outnumbered those of blacks.[46]

Over 400,000 blacks served in uniform during *World War I* (1914-1918). Of these, approximately 10 percent were assigned to combat units, the remainder to stevedore, depot, and other laborer units. Despite segregation and discriminatory assignments, over 1,300 blacks were commissioned as officers (less than one percent of all officers), most as 2nd or 1st Lieutenants, but some as Captains. The highest-ranking black officer, Colonel Charles Young had been forcibly retired at the beginning of the war for medical reasons. Some people suggested that given his seniority and the expanding size of the Army, he was cashiered in order to prevent him from being promoted to brigadier general. Three other black officers achieved field grade rank during the war; two in the 370th Infantry and one in the 9th Cavalry which did not see overseas action.[47]

During *World War II* (1941-1945), black soldiers and civilians fought a two-front battle. There was the enemy overseas and, additionally, the battle against prejudice at home. "Soldiers were fighting the world's worst racist, Adolph Hitler, in the world's most segregated army," says historian and *National Geographic* explorer in residence Stephen Ambrose. "The irony did not go unnoticed." As they had been in *World War I*, black soldiers were relegated to service units supervised by white officers, often working as cargo handlers or cooks.[48]

Black soldiers were generally restricted from combat, but the realities of war would soon blur the lines of race. One breakthrough came during the Battle of the Bulge in late 1944. General Dwight D. Eisenhower, faced with Hitler's advancing army on the Western Front, temporarily desegregated the army and called for urgent assistance on the front lines. More than 2,000 black soldiers volunteered to fight. Similarly, demands in Italy called the Tuskegee Airmen to action. In 1944, they began flying with white pilots in the European theatre, successfully running bombing missions and becoming the only U.S. unit to sink a German destroyer. Black women also fought to serve in the war effort as nurses. Despite early protests that black nurses treating white soldiers would not be appropriate, the War Department relented and the first group of black nurses in the Army Nurse Corps arrived in England in 1944.[49]

In 1941, A. Philip Randolph threatened President Franklin D. Roosevelt with a 100,000-person march on Washington, D.C. to protest job discrimination. In response, Roosevelt issued *Executive Order 8802*, prohibiting discrimination in defense jobs or the government. As the war dragged on, it affected American society at nearly every level. It shook up the society and disrupted old patterns of social and economic segregation that had relegated black Americans to an inferior role. In 1948, President Harry S. Truman signed *Executive Order 9981*. The order desegregated the army and the civilian government.[50]

The Black Family: Controversy and Stability

In 1891, Frederick Douglass noted that "where there is no family there is no morality, no truth, and no happiness."[51] That the institution of family was important to black people, there is little doubt. It was the first and primary influence that a child felt. It provided protection against the pressures of society. For those with an old family background, it created identity. When more affluent families combined, they reconfirmed their social status. Plus, for the Washington, D.C. black middle-class at the turn of the century, the family was an incubator for the leaders of the next generation.[52] Today, however, that concept of the black family has changed, and it warrants some discussion because of the M Street/Dunbar High School student family psyche.

Black families in the early 20th century exhibited the typical values characteristic of the middle class even when they did not have the financial means to obtain this lifestyle. Typical values associated with a black middle-class lifestyle included a plan that foresaw retirement, a desire to be in control of their future, respect for and obedience to the law, and a desire for a good education for themselves and their children. The way to move forward in socio-economic status was through a good education and hard work. The values consistent with this life style included a desire to protect their families from various hardships such as health issues, financial difficulties, and crime.[53]

In the times before the 1950s, the black family taught values that had changed little between 1880 and 1920. Reinforced by those taught in the church, these values were the cornerstone of "respectability," thrift, hard work, self-respect, and righteousness. Fathers had a valuable role to play in the family. They brought home the paychecks that housed and fed their families and provided a little extra for dance lessons, sports uniforms, and bicycles for the kids. Bringing home a paycheck was vitally important because nothing is more devastating to the lives of children than poverty. Keeping children fed, housed, and out of poverty was significant.[54]

The black father was the family's moral guardian, the symbol of masculinity for his sons and a harsh disciplinarian. Furthermore, in the two-parent black family, the father played many roles including that of companion, care provider, spouse, protector, model, moral guide, and teacher.[55] Yet, the family also taught responsibility to the race. Parents were the example for children to follow and, if the parents became involved in racial uplift efforts, the children would probably do likewise. Even if the parents were simply paying lip service to the ideal of racial solidarity, the children took them at their word.[56]

The natural affection of the black people for their children gave them what they saw as a personal opportunity to elevate the race by raising intelligent, educated sons and daughters who would, in turn, continue the work their parents had begun. The closeness of these families may have been a defense mechanism in reaction to discrimination from the outside world, but it was undoubtedly legitimate. The warmth they created in the home environment provided a shelter, but, correspondingly, it nourished the growth of happy children and provided continuity and hope for the future. Most marriages were partnerships forged to further family goals as well as to perpetuate status. Divorce was not unheard of, but it was rare. Separations were not uncommon. The black family in Washington was a line of defense against society and its values and strategies ensured that family status would continue through succeeding generations.[57]

The current controversy over the disintegration of the black family and the reasons for high rates of female-headed families among blacks can be traced back to the publication of the *Moynihan Report*[58] on the black family in 1965. In the *Report*, it was argued that family patterns among black Americans were fundamentally different from those found among whites and that family instability among blacks was the root cause of the social and economic problems suffered by blacks. Family patterns of blacks were attributed to slavery and racial oppression, which focused on humbling the black male. The *Report* generated bitter debate because, based on a comparison of 1950 and 1960 Census data, it characterized the black family as "crumbling" and as "a tangle of pathology." In so doing, the *Report* echoed the message of the classic work of sociologist E. Franklin Frazier, *The Negro Family in the United States.*[59]

Frazier argued that family instability among blacks resulted from the effects of slavery on black family life. Accordingly, because of the lack of marriage among slaves and the constant separation of families as males and older children were sold, slavery established a pattern of insecure and unstable black families. Slavery, therefore, destroyed all family bonds except for those between mother and child, leading to a pattern of black families centered on the mother.[60] Frazier argued, further, that newly freed blacks were rural folks with the typical family patterns of traditional agricultural society, out-of-wedlock childbearing, and marital instability. When these simple folks migrated to the North in large numbers, they encountered unfamiliar ways of life in the industrial cities. They were unable to cope with the new conditions and their family lives became disorganized, resulting in spiraling rates of crime, juvenile delinquency, and so on.[61]

On the other hand, in response to the *Moynihan Report*, historian Herbert Gutman undertook an extensive study of black families. His book, *The Black Family in Slavery and Freedom, 1750-1925*, was published in 1976. Gutman reasoned that if Moynihan was right, then there should have been a prevalence of female-headed households during slavery and in the years immediately following emancipation. Instead, he found that at the end of the *Civil War*, in Virginia, most families of former slaves had two parents, and most older couples had lived together for a long time (See Tables 6-1 and 6-2). He attributed these findings to resiliency among black Americans who created new families after owners sold their original families apart. Gutman concluded that Moynihan and Frazier had "underestimated the adaptive capacities of th enslaved and those born to them and their children."

Composition of Black Households with Two or More Residents, Montgomery, York, and Princess Anne Counties, Virginia, 1865-1866

Montgomery	*York*	*Princess Anne*

Type of household	County	County	County
Husband-wife	18%	26%	17%
Husband-wife-children	54	53	62
Father-children	5	5	4
Mother-children	23	16	17
Number	498	997	375

Source: Herbert G. Gutman, *The Black Family in Slavery and Freedom, 1750-1925*. p. 11.

Table 6-1

Length of Slave Marriages Registered
In Nelson and Rockbridge Counties, Virginia, 1866

Years married	Nelson County	Rockbridge County
Under 10	45%	49%
10-19	24	18
20-29	16	22
30-39	8	7
40 +	7	4
Number	616	230
Unknown	4	6

Length of Slave Marriages and Ages of Male and Female
Registrants, Rockbridge County, Virginia, 1866

Years Married In 1866	Age of Registrant in 1866					Number
	15-19	20-29	30-39	40-49	50+	
Under 2	50%	9%	9%	5%	1	30
2-9	50	82	46	24	16	194
10-19	0	9	38	17	9	84
20-29	0	0	7	50	34	102
30+	0	0	0	4	40	50
Number	6	114	113	111	116	460

| Age unknown | | | | | | | | 12 |

Source: Herbert G. Gutman, *The Black Family in Slavery and Freedom, 1750-1925.* p. 12.

Table 6-2

Conversely, Erol Ricketts, a demographer and sociologist with the Rockefeller Foundation, found that National Census data covering the decennial years from 1890 to 1920 show that blacks out-married whites despite a consistent shortage of black males due to their higher rates of mortality.[62] In three of the four decennial years, there was a higher proportion of currently married black men than white men (Table 6-3). Even in those years, the rate of female-headed families was higher among blacks than among whites, but the cause was high rates of widowhood, not lower rates of marriage.

Marital Status of the Population Aged 15 Years and Over, 1890-1920

	Blacks				Whites-Native Parentage			
	1890	1900	1910	1920	1890	1900	1910	1920
Single								
Male	19.0	19.2	15.4	32.6	41.7	40.2	39.0	35.3
Female	20.0	29.9	26.6	24.1	32.0	31.4	30.1	27.7
Married								
Male	55.5	54.0	57.2	60.4	53.9	54.6	55.7	59.1
Female	54.6	53.7	57.2	59.6	57.0	57.3	59.0	60.7
Widowed								
Male	4.3	5.7	6.2	5.9	3.9	4.5	4.4	4.6
Female	14.4	15.4	14.8	14.8	10.5	10.7	10.1	10.7
Sex ratio	99.5	98.6	98.9	99.2	105.4	104.9	106.6	104.4
% urban	---	21.0	27.0	34.0	---	42.0	48.0	53.0

Source: Decennial Census, U.S. Census Bureau

Table 6-3

Considering the continued debate about the origins of family formation problems among blacks, including female-headed families, it is useful to examine the available historical data covering the decennial years from 1890 to 1980, presented in Table 6-4. The data show, contrary to widely held beliefs, that through 1960, rates of marriage for both black and white women were lowest at the end of the 1800s and peaked in 1950 for blacks and 1960 for whites. What is more, it is dramatically clear that black females married at higher rates than white females of native parentage until 1950.[63]

Comparison of Marriage Patterns of Blacks and Whites, 1890-1980

(Percentage of ever-married women aged 15 years and over)

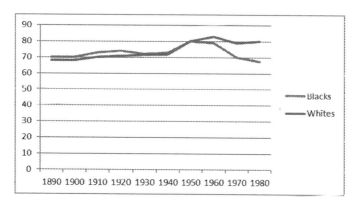

Source: Decennial Census, U.S. Census Bureau

Table 6-4

Furthermore, the decennial series on female-headed families covering the years 1930 to 1980 (presented in Table 6-5) show that the rate of female-headed families among blacks in 1980 was the highest in the series. Interestingly, the data show that rates of black female-headed families declined to their lowest level in 1950, only to rise sharply thereafter.[64]

Female-Headed Families, 1930-1980

	White Female Heads As % of White Families					Black Female Heads As % of Black Families				
	All	Urban	Rural-Nonfarm	Rural-Farm	% White-Population Farm That is Urban[a]	All	Urban	Rural-Nonfarm	Rural-Farm	% White-Population Farm That is Urban[a]
1930	12.0	14.4	12.0	5.0	59.4	19.3	25.2	20.6	10.5	47.4
1940[b]	14.5	17.3	13.1	7.2	65.2	22.6	29.5	21.7	11.5	52.3
1950[b]	8.5	9.7	7.2	4.3	65.9	17.6	19.8	18.1	9.2	66.2
1960	8.1	9.0	6.5	4.2	70.2	21.7	23.1	19.5	11.1	76.5
1970	9.0	10.0	6.3	n.a.	72.1	27.8	29.3	20.1	n.a.	83.3
1980	11.2	12.8	7.6	n.a.	70.2	37.8	39.6	26.8	n.a.	86.1

Source: Decennial Census, U.S. Census Bureau

[a] Percentage of total population, not merely female-headed families.

[b] Figures for blacks are for nonwhites.

n.a. = not available.

Table 6-5

So, what happened to destabilize the black family? Black Americans were moving forward on a path to family stability, even in a segregated society, when it was decided to begin subsidizing illegitimacy. Many people knew that granting widows' benefits to unmarried women with illegitimate children would have disastrous consequences.[65] An early twentieth century social welfare advocate, Homer Folks, warned back in 1914 that to grant pensions for "desertion or illegitimacy would have the effect of a premium upon these crimes against society."[66] Yet, this is exactly the system that was implemented under Lyndon B. Johnson's "Great Society."[67]

The tragic legacy of the Great Society is the violence inflicted upon the family as an institution. Through a series of actions, calculated or not, the family has been devalued as the bedrock of civil society and replaced with the government acting *in loco parentis* not only for the children it encounters, but for the parents as well. The "suitable home" requirements for welfare, such as having a husband, were jettisoned as irrational and racist by liberal progressives in the federal Bureau of Public Assistance.[68] By 1960, only eight percent of welfare benefits intended for widows or wives with disabled husbands were being collected by such. More than 60 percent of Aid to Families with Dependent Children (AFDC) payments went to "absent father" homes. That was the year that black marriage rates began its precipitous decline, gradually at first, with the marriage rate for black women falling below 70 percent for the first time in 1970.[69] Even as late as that, however, a majority of black children were still living with both parents.[70] As Ricketts says, "The argument that current levels of female-headed families among blacks are due directly to the cultural legacy of slavery and that black family formation patterns are fundamentally different from those of whites is not supported by the data."[71]

Social Change and Unrest

In the late 1960s and early 1970s, there was a violent cultural upheaval in the United States. Many young white people began to call for revolutionary change and they were joined by many young black people who apparently saw this as an extension of the civil rights movement. Old-fashioned values, norms, and folkways were swept aside. The social loyalties of religion, patriotism, and family commitment were "out." Dysfunctional behavior was "in."

Many Americans adopted anti-capitalistic, anti-imperialist political perspectives and, as American boys died in Vietnam, they carried Cuban and Vietcong flags while chanting derisively, "Ho Ho Chi Minh, the NLF [National Liberation Front] is gonna win."[72] An antiwar movement flourished on elite college campuses such as Columbia, Harvard, and Berkeley, which themselves were in an uproar over issues of curriculum, governance, and the universities' relationships to the federal government. By 1967, President Lyndon B. Johnson could not travel in the country without facing picketers, foul-mouthed chanters, and threats of violence.

Confounding the political problems on college and high school campuses was the so-called countercultural or hippie movement, in which young people abandoned middle-class values all together as they "turned on, tuned in, and dropped out." America witnessed the proletarianization of a dominant minority that set the value standard for the larger society through imitation of those at the bottom of society.[73] Thus, the cultural divide between the classes proved smaller than one may have expected as imitation of and respectfulness toward lower class behavior manifested itself in several ways.

In a few short years, many young Americans, and young people in Europe as well, let their hair grow long and traded in their high heels and skirts, their ties and button-down shirts, for torn jeans, tie-dyed T-shirts, and dirty sneakers. They talked openly about, and practiced, "free love." They listened to music that was incomprehensible to their parents, smoked marijuana, and rejected authority. However, while most young Americans were not foul-mouthed hippies, dope users, free-lovers, members of antiwar coalitions, or Marxists, there were enough telegenic countercultural, anti-establishment types at Columbia, Harvard, and Berkeley to suggest that the next generation of the establishment might not be like the last.[74] The pre-1960 values of God, country, and family were abandoned; God is dead,[75] "The working men have no country,"[76] and dysfunctional families have become the norm.[77]

CHAPTER SEVEN

THE WASHINGTON-GEORGETOWN LOCALITIES

A community consists of a group of people who live in a local area and have certain interests and problems in common and, because they have certain interests and problems in common, the members of a community must cooperate and organize. After the *Civil War*, the Washington-Georgetown black community made a conscious effort to control the conditions of their common life by identifying the forces with which they were competing and in conflict. The cultural environment of the black community shaped the structure of the education ideologies that were publicly shared in the iterations of what eventually became the Paul Lawrence Dunbar High School in the District of Columbia. In this respect, the school became part of a political process to deal with the limits of competition blacks had in dealing with whites.

The Washington-Georgetown black community had witnessed the *Missouri Compromise of 1820*, the *Compromise of 1850*, the *Kansas-Nebraska Act of 1854*, the *Dred Scott Decision*, and the John Brown raid. The *Civil War*, Lincoln's assassination, and the subsequent elections had decisively changed the situation into one of Jim Crow segregation. Whites and blacks were making the necessary internal adjustments to social situations which had been created by competition and conflict. These socially inherited accommodations grew up in the pains and struggles of previous generations and were transmitted to, and accepted by, succeeding generations as part of the natural, inevitable social order. These forms of control limited competition regarding the status of blacks in a racially segregated society; socially, politically, and economically.[1]

Georgetown

Georgetown is bounded by the Potomac River on the south, Rock Creek to the east, Burleith and Glover Park to the north, with Georgetown University on the west end of the neighborhood. Much of Georgetown is surrounded by parkland and green spaces that provide recreation and serve as buffers from development in adjacent neighborhoods. Rock Creek Park, the Oak Hill Cemetery, Montrose Park, and Dumbarton Oaks, are located along the north and east edge of Georgetown, east of Wisconsin Avenue.[2] The neighborhood is situated on bluffs overlooking the Potomac River. Thus, there are some rather steep grades on streets running north-south. The famous *"Exorcist* steps" connecting M Street to Prospect Street were necessitated by the hilly terrain of the area. The primary commercial corridors of Georgetown are M Street and Wisconsin Avenue, whose high fashion stores draw large numbers of tourists as well as local shoppers year-round. Between M and K Streets, runs the historic Chesapeake and Ohio Canal.

In 1632, English fur trader Henry Fleet first documented a Native American (Nacotchtank) village called Tohoga on the site of present-day Georgetown and established trade there.[3] At the time of its incorporation in 1751, Georgetown was part of the British colony of the Province of Maryland. The Maryland legislature authorized purchase of 60 acres (240,000 m[2]) of land from George Gordon and George Beall for the price of £280,[4] and a survey of the town was completed in February 1752.[5]

Situated on the fall line, Georgetown was the farthest point upstream to which oceangoing boats could navigate the Potomac River. Sometime around 1745, Gordon constructed a tobacco inspection house along the Potomac. Tobacco was already being transferred from land to waterways at this location when the inspection house was built. Warehouses, wharves, and other buildings were then constructed around the inspection house and it quickly became a small community. It did not take long before Georgetown grew into a thriving port, facilitating trade and shipments of tobacco and other goods from colonial Maryland.[6] One of the most prominent tobacco export businesses was Forrest, Stoddert and Murdock, formed in 1783 in Georgetown, by Uriah Forrest, Benjamin Stoddert, and John Murdock.[7]

Since Georgetown was founded during the reign of George II of Great Britain, some speculate that the town was named after him. Another theory is that the town was named after its founders, George Gordon and George Beall. The Maryland Legislature formally issued the town charter and incorporated the town in 1789.[8] Robert Peter, who was among the first to establish a business (tobacco export) in the town, became Georgetown's first mayor in 1790.[9]

Benjamin Stoddert was a major figure in early Georgetown history, having previously served as Secretary to the Board of War under the Articles of Confederation. Arriving there in 1783, he partnered with General Uriah Forrest to become an original proprietor of the Potomac Company. He ultimately owned Halcyon House at the corner of 34th and Prospect Streets. Stoddert purchased stock in the federal government under Alexander Hamilton's assumption-of-debt plan. Hamilton's assumption proposal was a plan that asked for federal "assumption" of the state debts within the United States so that the economy could be stimulated and so that the nation could be strengthened as a unified front. Hamilton would later submit a request for a national bank to help circulate currency and make financial transactions simpler for the government.[10]

The terms of the land transfer to the federal government to create the national capital were worked out by Stoddert and other Potomac landowners during a dinner at Forrest's home in Georgetown on March 28, 1791. Stoddert bought land within the boundaries of the federal district, some of it at the request of George Washington, for the government and some on speculation. Washington frequented Georgetown, including Suter's Tavern, where he worked out many land deals to acquire land for the Federal City.[11]

In the 1790s, City Tavern, the Union Tavern, and the Columbian Inn opened and were popular throughout the 19th century.[12] Of these taverns, only the City Tavern remains today. The speculative purchases were not, however, profitable and caused Stoddert much difficulty before his appointment to the post of Secretary of the Navy by John Adams. Stoddert was rescued from his debts with the help of William Marbury, later of *Marbury v. Madison* fame, and a Georgetown resident. The Forrest-Marbury House on M Street is currently the Embassy of Ukraine.

Col. John Beatty established a Lutheran church on High Street that was the first church in Georgetown. Stephen Bloomer Balch established a Presbyterian Church in 1784 and, in 1795, the Trinity Catholic Church was built, along with a parish school-house. St. John's Episcopal Church was built in 1803.

Several banks were established in Georgetown. The Farmers and Mechanics Bank was established in 1814. Other banks included the Bank of Washington, Patriotic Bank, Bank of the Metropolis, and the Union and Central Banks of Georgetown. Newspapers in Georgetown included the first paper, the *Republican Weekly Ledger*, started in 1790. *The Sentinel* was first published in 1796 by Green, English & Co. Charles C. Fulton began publishing the *Potomac Advocate*, which was started by Thomas Turner in 1838. Other newspapers in Georgetown included the *Georgetown Courier* and the *Federal Republican*.[13]

William B. Magruder was appointed the first postmaster on February 16, 1790, and a custom house was established on Water Street in 1795. General James M. Lingan served as the first collector of the port.[14] Thomas Jefferson lived for some time in Georgetown while serving as vice president under President John Adams.[15]

Georgetown also was home to Francis Scott Key, who arrived there as a young lawyer in 1808 and resided on M Street. Dr. William Beanes, a relative of Key, captured the rear guard of the British Army while it was burning Washington during the War of 1812. When the mass of the army retreated, they retrieved their imprisoned guard and took Dr. Beanes as a captive to their fleet near Baltimore. Key went to the fleet to request the release of Beanes. He was held until the bombardment of Fort McHenry was completed. It was during this bombardment that Key gained his inspiration for "The Star-Spangled Banner".[16]

By the 1820s, the Potomac River had become silted up and was not navigable up to Georgetown. Construction of the Chesapeake & Ohio Canal began in July 1828, to link Georgetown to Harper's Ferry, Virginia (now part of West Virginia). The canal was completed on October 10, 1850, at a cost $77,041,586. With the construction of the Baltimore & Ohio Railroad, the canal turned out to be unprofitable and never lived up to expectations.[17] Nevertheless, it did provide an economic boost for Georgetown.

In the 1820s and 1830s, Georgetown was an important shipping center. Tobacco and other goods were transferred between the canal and shipping on the Potomac River. Salt was imported from Europe, and sugar and molasses were imported from the West Indies.[18] These shipping industries were later superseded by coal and flour industries, which flourished with the C & O Canal providing cheap power for mills and other industry.[19]

Georgetown historically had a large black population, including both slaves and free blacks. Slave labor was widely used in construction of new buildings in Washington and to provide labor on tobacco plantations in Maryland and Virginia. Slave trading in Georgetown dates to 1760, when John Beattie established his business on O Street and conducted business at other locations around Wisconsin Avenue. Slave trading continued until the mid-19th century, when it was banned.[20] Other slave markets ("pens") located in Georgetown included one at McCandless's Tavern near M Street and Wisconsin Avenue.[21] Congress abolished slavery in Washington and Georgetown on April 16, 1862, when President Abraham Lincoln signed the *District of Columbia Emancipation Act* ending slavery in the District of Columbia. Passage of this law came eight and a half months before President Lincoln issued his *Emancipation Proclamation*.[22] Many blacks relocated to Georgetown following the Civil War and they established a thriving community.

In the late 18th century and 19th century, blacks comprised a substantial portion of Georgetown's population. The 1800 census reported the population in Georgetown at 5,120, which included 1,449 slaves and 227 free blacks.[23] A testament to the black history that remains today is the Mount Zion United Methodist Church, which is the oldest black congregation in Washington. Prior to establishing the church, free blacks and slaves went to the Dumbarton Methodist Church where they were restricted to a hot, overcrowded balcony. The church was originally located in a small brick meetinghouse on 27th Street, but it was destroyed by fire in the 1880s. It was rebuilt on the present site.[24] Mount Zion Cemetery offered free burials for Washington's earlier black population.[25]

After the *American Revolution*, Georgetown became an independent municipal government of the federal District of Columbia, along with the City of Washington, the City of Alexandria, and the newly created County of Washington and County of Alexandria (now Arlington County, Virginia). It was officially known as "Georgetown, D.C." In 1862, the Washington and Georgetown Railroad Company began a horsecar line running along M Street in Georgetown and Pennsylvania Avenue in Washington, easing travel between the two cities. Georgetown's corporate charter, along with Washington corporate charter, was formally revoked by Congress effective June 1, 1871. At this point, its governmental powers were vested within the District of Columbia.[26] The streets in Georgetown were renamed in 1895 to conform to the street names in use in Washington.[27]

By the late 19th century, flour milling and other industries in Georgetown were declining due, in part, to the fact that the canals and other waterways continually silted up.[28] Nathaniel Michler and Silvanus T. Abert led efforts to dredge the channels and remove rocks around the Georgetown harbor. However, these were temporary solutions and Congress showed little interest in the issue.[29] In 1890, a flood and the expansion of the railroads brought destitution to the C&O Canal and Georgetown. The municipality became a depressed slum, with alleys choked by tiny houses lacking plumbing or electricity. Shipping trade vanished between the *Civil War* and *World War I*[30] and, as a result, many older homes were preserved relatively unchanged. Alexander Graham Bell's earliest switching office for the Bell System was located on a site just below the C&O Canal and it remains in use as a phone facility to this day.

In 1915, the Buffalo Bridge (on Q Street) opened and connected this part of Georgetown with the rest of the city east of Rock Creek Park. Soon thereafter, new construction of large apartment buildings began on the edge of Georgetown. In the early 1920s, John Ihlder led efforts to take advantage of new zoning laws to get restrictions enacted on construction in Georgetown.[31] A 1933 study by Horace Peaslee and Allied Architects laid out ideas for how Georgetown could be preserved.[32]

The C & O Canal, then owned by the Baltimore & Ohio Railroad, formally ceased operations in March 1924. After severe flooding in 1936, the B & O Railroad sold the canal to the National Park Service in October 1938.[33] The waterfront area retained its industrial character in the first half of the 20th century and Georgetown was home to a lumber yard, a cement works, the Washington Flour mill, and a meat rendering plant. Its skyline was dominated by the smokestacks of a garbage incinerator and the twin stacks of the power generating plant for the old Capital Traction streetcar system, located at the foot of Wisconsin Avenue. The plant closed in 1935, but it was not razed until October 1968. In 1949, the city constructed the Whitehurst Freeway, an elevated highway above K Street, to allow motorists entering the District over the Key Bridge to bypass Georgetown entirely on their way downtown.

Legislators largely ignored concerns about historic preservation of Georgetown until 1950, when Public Law 808 was passed and the historic district of "Old Georgetown" was established.[34] The law required that the United States Commission of Fine Arts be consulted on any alteration, demolition, or building construction, within the historic district.[35]

As the only existing town at the time, Georgetown was the fashion and cultural center of the newly-formed District of Columbia. As Washington grew, however, the center of societal Washington moved east across Rock Creek to the new Victorian homes that sprang up around the city's traffic circles and to the Gilded Age mansions along Massachusetts Avenue. While many "old families" stayed on in Georgetown, the neighborhood's population became poorer and more racially diverse by the early 20th century. Its demographics started to shift again when gentrification began during the 1930s. Many of the members of the administration of President Franklin D. Roosevelt moved into the area and, by the 1950s, a wave of new post-war residents arrived. Many of these new residents were well-educated and from middle-class backgrounds. They took a keen interest in the neighborhood's historic nature.

Washington

The District of Columbia was a conglomeration of neighborhoods that were informally organized and had boundaries that, to some degree, separated them from each other. The people who lived in the different neighborhoods tended to share a similar culture and were acquainted with one another. The federal district was the major unit of social organization and it provided most of the services that the inhabitants required in the day-to-day routine of their lives. Washington and Georgetown were viewed as communities, but, within the overall scheme of things, Georgetown was more of a neighborhood than a community.

The variety and complexity found in the neighborhoods makes it difficult to neatly classify them based on common characteristics. The Washington communities and neighborhoods did not have a high degree of cultural or economic homogeneity with an extreme contrast existing between slum areas on the one hand and exclusive residential districts on the other. Furthermore, their economic life rested on a having good number and variety of industries and occupations.

In 1870, the Washington black community was unique. The slaves of the District of Columbia had been emancipated by the Congress in April 1862, but the Washington black community was much older than that. As far back as 1830, half the blacks in Washington were free. Before the *Civil War* started, 78 per cent of the blacks in Washington were free. However, as the slave states of the South progressively tightened up their restrictions on the "free persons of color" in the decades preceding the *Civil War*, Washington became something of a Mecca for free blacks seeking a better life. The federal government's presence made Washington less oppressive than the Southern slave states. It also offered employment opportunities through government jobs that were better than those open to black people elsewhere.[36]

It was a common occurrence in the 1880s for foreign travelers and Northern visitors to comment, sometimes with distaste and always with surprise, on the freedom of association between white and black people in the South. Yankees were unprepared for what they found and sometimes had underestimated. Many forget that while slavery was not prevalent in the North, northern commercial and industrial centers, particularly textiles industries, had a vested interest in the survival of slavery in the South.

Consequently, tens of thousands of black people poured into the city. No longer enslaved, they were looking for a new life. Some found a place to live in the hastily built and crowded alley dwellings; small houses situated in alleys behind large homes that faced the main streets. In early times, these dwellings housed the slaves and servants of the more prominent citizens. Residents often shared the alleys with workshops, stables, and other accessory buildings. During the *Civil War's* severe housing shortages, alley housing was one of the few options available to the poor and working-class residents in Washington. They were interracial in that conditions below the Potomac were better than those above. Segregation was, after all, a Yankee invention.[37]

U Street

The U Street area is largely a Victorian-era neighborhood, developed between 1862 and 1900. The majority of it has been designated a historic district. The area is made up of row houses rapidly constructed by speculative builders and real estate developers in response to the city's high demand for housing following the *Civil War* and the growth of the federal government in the late 19th century. The corridor became commercially significant when a streetcar line operated there in the early 20th century, making it convenient for government employees to commute downtown to work and shop.[38]

While always racially diverse, the area was predominately white and middle class until 1900. As Washington became progressively more segregated, the U Street Corridor and neighboring Strivers' Section emerged as fashionable neighborhoods for Washington's black residents. It became the city's most important concentration of businesses and entertainment facilities owned and operated by blacks. The surrounding neighborhood became home to many of the city's most prominent black Americans.[39]

U Street predates New York's Harlem as a Mecca for blacks. The *Civil War* encampments in the area had sheltered freedom seekers in the 1860s and the mission churches they founded live on today. Howard University, just north of this neighborhood, began to attract the nation's black intellectual and artistic leadership in the 1870s. By the early 20th century, this was the center of the city's black community, home to businesses, places of entertainment, and the major social institutions of black Washington. Until the 1920s, when Harlem surpassed it, the U Street neighborhood was the largest urban black community in the nation. All the great entertainers played at its lively theaters and clubs.[40]

In its cultural heyday in the 1920s and 1930s, U Street was known as "Black Broadway." It held its own against Harlem in terms of its influence on black culture and a major setting for luminaries such as Langston

Hughes, Zora Neale Hurston, Jean Toomer and Sterling Brown, to hold forth. D.C. native Duke Ellington and other jazz greats like Cab Calloway, Ella Fitzgerald, and Dizzy Gillespie, Louis Armstrong, Billie Holiday, Miles Davis, John Coltrane, Count Basie, and Thelonious Monk, turned the neighbourhood into a major entertainment destination. Duke Ellington's childhood home was located on 13th street between T and S Streets. The Lincoln Theatre opened in 1921 and the Howard Theater in 1926.[41]

LeDroit Park

LeDroit Park is a neighborhood in Washington, D.C., located immediately southeast of Howard University. Its borders include W Street to the north, Rhode Island Avenue and Florida Avenue to the south, Second Street NW to the east, and Georgia Avenue to the west. The neighborhood was developed by Amzi Barber (Board of Trustees, Howard University). In the 1870s, LeDroit Park was one of the first suburbs of Washington.

Many of the area's Victorian mansions, houses, and row-houses were designed by architect James McGill. Originally, the neighborhood did not follow the scheme for street names used in the rest of Washington D.C. LeDroit Park was developed and marketed as a "romantic" neighborhood with narrow tree-lined streets that bore the same names as the trees that shaded them. Extensive focus was placed on the landscaping, as developers spent a large sum of money to plant flower beds and trees to attract high profile professionals from the city. The neighborhood was even gated, with guards to promote security for its hopeful residents.

At the beginning, LeDroit Park was primarily a whites-only neighborhood. Efforts by many residents and multiple actions by students from Howard University lead to the area becoming integrated. In July 1888, the students tore down the fences that separated the neighborhood in protest of its discriminating policies. Consequently, by the 1940s, LeDroit Park became a major focal point for black professionals and many prominent black figures resided there. Griffith Stadium was located here until 1965, when the Howard University Hospital was built where it used to stand. LeDroit Park includes Anna J. Cooper Circle, named for the education pioneer who taught at Dunbar.

Notable LeDroit Park residents are listed below:

- General William Birney – *Civil War* veteran owned the stately mansion on Anna J. Cooper Circle. (T and 2nd Streets)
- Senator Edward Brooke – First black American to win a U.S. Senate seat by popular vote since Reconstruction, was born in a LeDroit Park house in 1919. (1938 3rd Street)
- Dr. Ralph J. Bunche – The first black American to receive the Nobel Peace prize for his mediation in Palestine; resided in LeDroit Park during his professorship at Howard University. (No address found)
- General Benjamin O. Davis, Sr. – The first black general in the U.S. Army; father of Benjamin O. Davis, Jr., who was commander of the *World War II* Tuskegee airman. (No address found)
- Hon. Oscar De Priest – First black U.S. Congressmen since reconstruction; lived here for his three terms in office. (419 U Street)
- Paul Laurence Dunbar – Black Poet Laureate and Howard University Alumnus for whom Dunbar High School was named. (321 U Street)
- Duke Ellington – Jazz legend, lived in the neighborhood with his family during his early childhood. (420 Elm Street)
- Major Christian Fleetwood – One of the first blacks to be awarded the Congressional Medal of Honor. (319 U Street)
- Julia West Hamilton – Civic leader and member of the National Association of Colored Women (N.A.C.W.). (320 U Street)
- Ernest Everett Just – Professor in biology, researcher in biogenetics with significant contributions to zoology and biogenetics. (412 T Street)
- Dr. Jesse Lawson and Dr. Anna J. Cooper – Both prominent educators who founded Frelinghuysen University to educate black working-class adults. Lawson also was a lawyer (Howard University Law, 1881) who advocated for the rights of poor D.C. residents. (201 T Street)
- Willis Richards – Prominent playwright credited with having the first serious play to be performed on Broadway. (512 U Street)
- Mary Church Terrell – Heiress and activist for civil rights and women's suffrage. (326 T Street - National Historic Landmark)

- Walter Washington – The first mayor of the District of Columbia elected under home rule. (408 T Street)
- Clarence Cameron White – A prominent violinist, educator in fine arts, and Howard University Alumni. (No address found)
- Dr. Garnet C. Wilkinson – Superintendent of Colored Schools during the period of Jim Crow segregation. (406 U Street)
- Octavius Augustus Williams – U.S. Capitol barber and first black to move into LeDroit Park in 1893. (338 U Street)

Anacostia

High atop a hill in Anacostia overlooking Washington is a beautiful old mansion. At the foot of the hill is the 19th-century village of Anacostia, still with many of its gingerbread houses and a tiny town square. From late 1877 until his death in early 1895, Frederick Douglass was the most prominent resident of Anacostia. An internationally known writer, lecturer, newspaper editor, and social reformer, Douglass was a man of his neighborhood. He spoke regularly at nearby churches, invested in the area's first street car line, and opened his Victorian mansion (1411 W Street, SE) in Cedar Hill to students from Howard University, where he served on the Board of Trustees. Douglass lived at Cedar Hill for more than 20 years in the 19th century. The home still contains many of Douglass's personal effects, including original furnishings and artwork.[42]

In the 1920s, Anacostia was far more rural than it is today and boasted a higher percentage of home ownership than other sections of the District of Columbia. In a study of residential building in the District during the 1920s, the National Capital Parks and Planning Commission found that for the city, 23 percent of its dwellings were multifamily apartment buildings. Broken down by planning districts, in the central part of the city, 32 percent of all dwellings were apartment buildings; in northwest D.C., 25 percent; in the northern area, 61 percent; in northeast, 4.5 percent; and, in the eastern section, 7.0 percent. In Anacostia, apartments accounted for only one half of one percent of all residential structures.[43]

At the time, Anacostia accounted for only five percent of the city's total population, but it possessed 40 percent of the District's vacant land. Considering these figures, Anacostia's low number of apartment houses is understandable. However, Anacostia's population was increasing. From 1920 to 1926, there was a 56 percent growth rate (the lowest was 10 percent and the highest was 187 percent), fourth highest among the planning districts. Yet, during that time, only four apartment houses were constructed there, compared to 1,820 detached and row houses.[44]

Evidently, Anacostia was a place intended for homeowners, but it was also a place proposed for private businesses. In 1928, 673 acres of Anacostia land was in commercial and industrial use, compared with 454 acres for residential dwellings. Few other areas of the District were as well-balanced. In a regional study of produce farms encompassing roughly 1,600 square miles, Anacostia possessed more than double the acreage under cultivation than any other location in the region.[45]

Less than 50 years later, Anacostia's schools were 83 percent over capacity (D.C. schools elsewhere were 16 percent over capacity); the federal and D.C. governments owned more buildings through foreclosure than in any other part of the district; and over 75 percent of Anacostia's land was zoned for apartments. D.C. zoning law prescribed an 80 percent rate of single-family occupancy in the other parts of the city.[46]

The radical transformation of Anacostia could be a simple story of rapid population growth and extremely poor zoning laws with unintentional consequences. However, it is likewise the story of urban renewal, the expansion of bureaucracy on one side of the river, and the creation of racialized public housing ghettos on the other. The role of the federal government in the creation of ghettos elsewhere in the country through Federal Housing Administration (FHA)/Home Owners' Loan Corporation (HOLC)/Veterans Administration (VA) loans, the Housing Acts of 1949 and 1954, and subsidies for infrastructure improvements connecting city to suburb, has been well documented by historian Arnold R. Hirsch and sociologists George Lipsitz, Douglas S. Massey, and Nancy A. Denton, among others. Their work shows that the federal government provided the funds and enabling legislation for local authorities to create racialized urban black ghettos (RUG). Anacostia provides an illustration of the role the federal government played directly, and self-interestedly, in creating an isolated or segregated area of the city to be inhabited by a socio-economically deprived minority.[47]

Neighborhood Mix among Students

Communities and neighborhoods in the District of Columbia varied greatly in character, size, culture, and had different socio-economic values. The factors that brought about the greatest degree of unity and the most homogeneous cultural patterns for black people in the city were segregation and racism.

Because it was not a neighborhood school during the 1870-1955 period, no one was automatically assigned to M Street/Dunbar. Students lived in different neighborhoods throughout the Washington-Georgetown area and the surrounding counties. No one was automatically assigned to M Street or Dunbar during the 1870-1955 period and no one just happened to enroll there. Admissions was open to all black D.C. residents and there were no tests or special entrance requirements. Moreover, the academic performance standards and graduation requirements were universal in that they were the same standards used in white America; no affirmative action.

In an alumni survey of M Street and Dunbar alumni who attended and graduated prior to 1960,[48] respondents lived throughout the city in all the major neighborhoods except the Penn Quarter/Chinatown locality. As indicated in Table 7-1 below, most of the respondents had a long daily commute to and from school. Fifty-eight percent travelled more than three miles one-way to school each day.

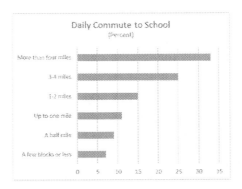

Source: Morris, Archie III., "Advancing Urban Educational Policy: Insights from Research on Dunbar High School," *Journal of the Case Studies in Education*, May 2017.

Table 7-1

Most of the survey respondents, 32 percent, lived in the LeDroit Park area. Seventeen percent in each of three other neighborhoods: Capitol Hill, U Street, and Anacostia/Southwest. See Table 7-2 below.

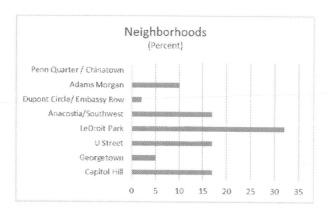

Source: Morris, Archie III., "Advancing Urban Educational Policy: Insights from Research on Dunbar High School," *Journal of the Case Studies in Education*, May 2017.

Table 7-2

Since M Street High and Dunbar High drew upon the entire black community of Washington-Georgetown for its students, the school was a focal point for black people in the area. It's reputation and standards were well known to parents and middle-school children throughout the black community, including nearby Maryland and Virginia and other more distant states in the South.[49] Each community and neighborhood sent children who had different values and cultural backgrounds, but all of them saw academic excellence as the key to a better life. Consequently, they established as their crown jewel, a high school that would prepare black children for higher education and employment. Blacks established their own schools because they were not entirely welcome at white schools, even up North. Subsequently, an education at M Street or Dunbar High School was the way to a better future and racial uplift.

The Values of the Washington-Georgetown Black Community

Washington had a community of black people that demanded academic excellence, even in 1870. This community continued to fight tenaciously for that academic excellence over the years. As early as 1807, the approximately 500 "free persons of color" in the District of Columbia built a small schoolhouse for their children. Over the next several decades, they sent their children to private schools because blacks were not allowed in the public schools. When the "colored trustees" of the D.C. public school system established the first school in 1870, they planted it in fertile ground.[50]

The black middle-class set the tone for the black community after the *Civil War* with values and goals typically characteristic of the white-middle class lifestyle; basically, moving from accommodation to assimilation.[51] This lifestyle was much more than just a matter of household income. Rather, it was a way of life complete with values, goals, and desires to attain a better quality of life. Even blacks with lower incomes sought a middle-class lifestyle. Families exhibited the typical values characteristic of the middle-class, even if they did not have the financial means to obtain this lifestyle. Typical values associated with the black middle-class lifestyle included a tendency to plan for retirement, a desire to be in control of their future, respect for and observance of the law, and a desire for a good education for themselves and their children. The way to move forward in socio-economic status was through a good education and hard work. These values also included a desire to protect their families from various hardships such as health issues, financial difficulties and crime.

Reflecting on his days as a student at Dunbar High School, Senator Edward Brooke (Class of 1937) told a reporter from *The Washington Post*:[52]

> We sort of lived in a cocoon. Dunbar sort of had an intellectual elite.... We were not aware of what we were missing because of segregation. It was very competitive.... Dunbar took the cream of the crop. They did well at Howard where I went. Negro History Week was observed, and in American History they taught about the emancipation of the slaves and the struggle for equality

and civil rights. But there was no demand by students for more, no real interest in Africa and its heritage. We knew about Africa as we knew about Finland.

The values of the Washington-Georgetown Black community middle-class served as broad guidelines in all situations for M Street/Dunbar students, faculty, staff, and principals and were the major influence on the behavior and attitudes of the institution. M Street High/Dunbar High School faculty and principals insisted on high academic standards, neat dress, and proper behavior. They instilled a confidence in students that they could succeed, even in a racially segregated society.[53]

CHAPTER EIGHT

LIVING A SEGREGATED LIFE IN THE NATION'S CAPITAL

Life for the over-all black community became increasingly more difficult between 1880 and 1900. Most of the gains of the Reconstruction period were lost as whites began to draw *de facto* racial barriers and soon followed these with legal ones. Owners began to segregate areas of public accommodations, the federal government hired fewer blacks, and job opportunities became more limited.[1]

Segregation

The "separate but equal" ruling of *Plessy* legitimized the move towards the segregation practices that had begun earlier in the South.[2] Along with Booker T. Washington's Atlanta Compromise address, delivered the same year, which accepted black social isolation from white society, *Plessy* provided an impetus for further segregation laws. In the ensuing decades, segregation statutes proliferated, reaching even to the federal government in Washington, D.C., which re-segregated during Democrat President Woodrow Wilson's first term in office. Several of Wilson's cabinet members were Southerners and they demanded that segregation be introduced into the federal government. Wilson permitted such efforts to go forward. Protests by the recently formed National Association for the Advancement of Colored People (NAACP) compelled the administration to drop some of the more blatant discriminatory measures, such as "white" and "colored" restrooms.[3]

Wilson's new postmaster general, Albert Burleson, ordered that his Washington offices be segregated, with the Treasury and Navy Departments soon doing the same. The numbers and percentages of blacks in the federal workforce were sharply reduced, a practice that continued under Northern-dominated Republican administrations in the 1920s. Wilson further soured his relations with blacks by permitting a well-publicized White House screening of David Wark Griffith's artistically ambitious but overtly racist film *The Birth of a Nation* (1915). The only move Wilson made toward improving race relations came in July 1918, during his second term, when he eloquently but belatedly condemned lynching.

The new Democrat House of Representatives passed a law making racial intermarriage a felony in the District of Columbia. Photographs were now required of all applicants for federal jobs. When pressed by black leaders, Wilson replied, "The purpose of these measures was to reduce the friction. It is as far as possible from being a movement against the Negroes. I sincerely believe it to be in their interest."[4]

The early 1900s were a time of "progressive disintegration of Washington's Negro world," owing principally to the restriction of economic opportunity. Only the "strongest individual able to draw upon deep inner resources" can avoid a prevailing sense of despair within the black Washington community.[5] "Nameless mulatto nobodies," as black journalist Roi Ottley called them, tried in vain to gain entrance. Moreover, while a superior education was available to the brightest youths of black Washington, possession of a light complexion was no guarantee of advancement to the upper reaches of black society.

Possession of an education, however, especially if it was coupled with refined manners, could get even one of humble origins admitted to the social elite. Because of restricted occupational opportunity, education was both a mark of status in the society and a way to "mark off social divisions *within* the same general occupational level." In 1909, when a student applied for and was admitted to the M Street High School, it was the most prestigious public school for black Americans and one of the best high schools in the country, period. An education here put a person on a level playing field with the aristocrats of color and opened opportunities to him that were available to few young people of any race.[6]

Caste and color torments were muted in part by the peculiar nature of segregation in Washington. Segregation in public accommodations was rigidly enforced, but one could buy licorice or peppermint sticks in the candy store at 20th and M streets because blacks did not sit in the store and eat sweets. At the drugstore soda fountain at 19th Street and Pennsylvania Avenue, a black person could not get counter service, but he could get an ice cream cone to go. At one neighborhood establishment, after the rare black person was served, the owner smashed the dishes from which the black person had eaten. For most black families, however, it was the laws of economics, more than the laws of segregation that kept them out of the places they were not allowed to enter. The only restaurant in town that served both whites and blacks was at Union Station, but prices there were prohibitive.[7]

Jim Crow laws and customs did not regulate several areas of public life. The streetcars were not segregated. Neither was the zoo nor the ballpark, so blacks could buy some inexpensive amusement *and* go there without experiencing the petty indignities of segregation that saturated the black experience in other Southern towns. More important was the fact that neither the public library nor the Library of Congress was segregated. This arrangement helped nudge many a black student toward a career in academia.[8]

Business and Occupational Security

From Colonial times to the pre-*Civil War* era, blacks were quite conspicuous in the skilled crafts and trades. In his 18th century travels around the United States, Isaac Weld observed that "Amongst their slaves are found tailors, shoemakers, carpenters, smiths, wheelrights, weavers, tanners, etc."[9] James Weldon, the novelist, wrote, "The Negroes drove the horse and mule teams, they laid the bricks, they painted the buildings and fences, they loaded and unloaded ships. When I was child, I did not know that there existed such a thing as a white carpenter or bricklayer or plasterer or tinner."[10]

In 1800, the civilian work force in Washington, D.C., was primarily engaged in the traditional trades and crafts involved with shipbuilding and refurbishing – carpenters, shipwrights, joiners, mast makers, blacksmiths, sail makers, rope makers, and caulkers.[11] Unions were nonexistent and there was no legislation that guaranteed any worker's wage or conditions of employment.[12]

There were many more skilled black people in 1865 than there were skilled white people. When skilled work became wage work, white workers moved into that niche with the help of unions. John Stephen Durham wrote about union exclusion of blacks from skilled crafts in the late 1800s:

> In the city of Washington, for example, at one period, some of the finest buildings were constructed by colored workmen. Their employment in large numbers continued sometime after the war. The British Legation, the Centre Market, the Freeman's Bank, and at least four well-built schoolhouses are monuments to the acceptability of their work under foremen of their own color.
>
> Today, apart from hod carriers, not a colored workman is to be seen on new buildings, and a handful of jobbers and patchers, with possibly two carpenters who can undertake a large job, are all who remain of the body of colored carpenters and builders and stone-cutters who were generally employed a quarter of a century ago.[13]

Early black professionals were heavily concentrated in the fields of teaching and the ministry, two professions that were open to educated blacks. By the turn of the century, however, greater educational freedom provided blacks with opportunities to study in a wider variety of fields. The black physicians and lawyers gradually assumed the positions as community leaders that the ministers and teachers had once held. In addition, as the professions opened to black people, more members of the younger generation trained as professionals rather than entrepreneurs, realizing that fewer risks were involved in professional employment.[14]

Thousands of manumitted and freeborn blacks had moved to the city decades before the *Civil War*, allowing a sizable black professional and working class to evolve well before emancipation. As early as 1827, black carpenters, plasterers, tanners, and pump makers had opened shops in the city. Surveys from the 1840s reveal many free black tradesmen in the city, mostly barbers, blacksmiths, and shoemakers. The steadiest employer of black people in this period, however, was the federal government, where blacks commonly worked as messengers and cooks.[15]

Many former slaves who moved to Washington during the Reconstruction years, more than 50,000 between 1870 and 1900, competed with demobilized Union soldiers for federal employment. Inevitably, blacks began to be excluded from government jobs. As a result, black Washingtonians were forced, in the words of one historian, "to work out schemes for solving their problems another way." That other way was independent business.[16]

Whether free or enslaved, blacks in American history have always showed an entrepreneurial spirit. Washington's black business boom began in the late 1880s. By the end of the decade, black Washingtonians owned two steamboat companies, several grocery stores, and several heating-fuel businesses. The black-owned Adams Oil and Gas Development Company invested in Oklahoma's oil fields. Within ten years, the city contained a black-owned bank, Capital Savings; two black-owned insurance companies, Douglas Life and the National Benefit Company; and, at least 11 black employment agencies.[17]

By 1892, the number of black businesses was large enough to support the Union League, the first black radical Republican organization in the southern United States. This was an association for "colored mechanics, business and professional men and women," whose self-described aim was "to better our moral and material status and make the conditions of success in the industrial and professional pursuits more easy." As a pamphlet from the organization, aimed at the city's growing black middle class, promised: "If you are employed in a store and aspire to be a clerk or salesman where you may learn the art of business from actual experience, we can help you. If you want to find such employment, we can help you."[18]

Each year, the Union League printed a directory of black-owned businesses that those looking for work or a place to shop could consult. "There is no better index to the character and development of a people than the number and nature of organizations they sustain," declared the directory's editor. The booklet soon ran to more than 100 pages and other leaders encouraged blacks to patronize black businesses as well. "If the colored people are to have their quota in the skilled trades, in business and in professions," editorialized one black newspaper in 1894, "colored people must have more confidence in the ability of men and women of their own race to fill these positions than they have yet shown."[19]

Many of these businesses were run by self-made entrepreneurs like Daniel Freeman, who had come to the city in 1881 from Virginia, penniless and looking for work. By 1901, at the age of 33, Freeman, a successful portrait artist, dominated the photography business in Washington during the first half of the twentieth century along with Addison Scurlock, his friend and stiffest competitor. Freeman owned a bicycle shop, a framing business, and a photography studio on 14th Street downtown. He also was a Mason, president of the Social Temperance League, and, according to contemporary accounts, the ninth-best rifle shot in the country. At the turn of the century and for decades after, Washington was home to hundreds of Daniel Freemans who became established in the Washington community. His life and work as a photographer chronicled the struggle and accomplishments of the local black community only 30 years after emancipation.[20]

Black businessmen realized that they could not compete with white businesses financially and invoked racial solidarity to ensure the patronage of the black community. Black professionals were slower to realize the importance of good relations with the black community, since they offered services few could duplicate. Nonetheless, after being denied entrance to white professional organizations and facing lowered estimations of their abilities because of their race, they soon found themselves in the vanguard of racial uplift. Black government workers and appointees depended on good race relations and the patronage of Booker T. Washington to keep their positions, but as segregation increased within the federal government and the influence of Tuskegee declined, they were only too happy to protest racial discrimination. Their livelihoods depended on fair treatment in the workplace.[21]

While one most often associates higher status with wealth, economic security was more important to the black upper classes of Washington. Economic security meant employment. In the black community plagued by insecurity, a steady job could qualify one for higher status. Although many among the older influential blacks had earned their status through business enterprises, the Washington middle-class counseled their children to enter the professions as well as to patronize black businesses. They also sought government positions that brought long-term security.[22]

The occupational structure of the black middle-class changed over time to reflect larger trends in society. Before the rise of segregation in the late 19th century, black businessmen found it difficult to compete with more established white businesses. After the rise of Jim Crow, when many white shopkeepers refused to serve black patrons, black entrepreneurs could find a steady market for their goods and services by appealing to racial solidarity.[23]

In the late 19th and early 20th centuries, salaries for blacks remained far lower than those for whites doing comparable work. Many blacks found it necessary to hold more than one job at a time and it was not uncommon for numerous members of the black middle-class to don two caps simultaneously. This was the dilemma of the teacher forced to teach night school to maintain a decent standard of living. Many lawyers, for example, also worked as clerks in the government departments. Moreover, the evolution of black businesses in the District reflected changing objective conditions. By the 1890s, most towns had a black business district like the Shaw neighborhood in Washington that was centered on Seventh Street and Georgia Avenue, N.W., and stretched roughly between Florida Avenue and Howard University. The proximity of Howard University was not coincidental. It attracted a large community of educated blacks who came to teach or study there and resided close by. They provided a ready market for black-owned businesses and created a demand for new services.[24]

Segregation did create opportunities for some black businesses. It provided them with a captive clientele. However, segregation also endangered the very existence of these enterprises. Black entrepreneurs were often unable to get goods of the quality available to whites and could not offer services comparable to those of white businesses that still served blacks. Other problems that black entrepreneurs faced were the low purchasing power of their clients, the difficulty of obtaining investment capital, and the lack of opportunities to gain modern business experience outside fraternal organizations.[25]

Blacks in Politics

The Democratic Party had become the dominant political party in America in the 1820s.[26] In May 1854, in response to the strong pro-slavery positions of the Democrats, several anti-slavery members of Congress formed the Republican Party. The party began as a coalition of anti-slavery "Conscience Whigs" and Free Soil Democrats opposed to the *Kansas–Nebraska Act*, submitted to Congress by Stephen Douglas in January 1854. The *Act* opened Kansas Territory and Nebraska Territory to slavery and future admission as slave states, thus implicitly repealing the prohibition on slavery in territory north of 36° 30' latitude, which had been part of the *Missouri Compromise*.[27]

The Democratic Party split over the slavery issue in 1860 at its Presidential convention in Charleston, South Carolina. Incumbent President James Buchanan was a northerner with sympathies for the South. He recommended that Supreme Court Justice Robert Grier vote proslavery in the *Dred Scott v. Sandford* case of 1857, a move so unpopular that it backfired on Buchanan's presidency. It allowed the Republicans to win a majority in the House in 1858 and full control of Congress in 1860. Buchanan declined to seek re-election in 1860 and these issues broke the Democratic Party into Northern and Southern factions. In the face of this divided opposition, the newly created Republican Party secured an electoral vote majority, putting Abraham Lincoln in the White House with virtually no support from the South.[28]

The South remained a one-party region until the civil rights movement began in the 1960s. Northern Democrats, most of whom had prejudicial attitudes towards blacks, offered no challenge to the discriminatory policies of the Southern Democrats. Republicans "waved the bloody shirt" in the late 19th century to associate the Democrat Party with the *Civil War* rebellion of the Confederacy. Democrats, on the other hand, warned white voters that Republicans were trying to install a regime of "Negro Supremacy" in the South. At that time, most blacks lived in Southern states and most black men voted for the Republican Party. Thus, the race issue was closely tied to partisanship.[29]

One of the consequences of the Democrat victories in the South was that many Southern Congressmen and Senators were almost automatically re-elected every election. Due to the importance of seniority in the U.S. Congress, Southerners could control most of the committees in both houses of Congress and kill any civil rights legislation. Even though Franklin Delano Roosevelt was a Democrat and considered a relatively liberal president during the 1930s and 1940s, he rarely challenged the powerfully entrenched Southern bloc. Thus, when the House passed federal anti-lynching bills in the 1930s, Southern senators filibustered them to death.[30]

Basically, President Roosevelt was not helpful to blacks. Some of his *New Deal* programs did involve blacks, even against the prevailing traditions of segregation, but he did little to advance civil rights. For example, why did he refuse to endorse the antilynching bills that were filibustered by southern Democrats in the Senate in 1937 and 1939? His endorsement would have been politically possible and politically desirable for a popular president determined to promote liberal ideas.[31]

Roosevelt issued *Executive Order 8802*,[32] which banned discrimination (selection based on race) in defense plants and established the nation's first Fair Employment Practice Committee, only after A. Phillip threatened to have 50,000 blacks march on Washington, D.C., to protest the exclusion of black American workers from jobs in the industries that were producing war supplies.[33] Some activists, including Bayard Rustin, felt betrayed because Roosevelt's order applied only to banning discrimination within war industries and not the armed forces. After the war, a similar technique led to President Harry S. Truman's order desegregating the army.[34]

A handful of blacks were able to achieve political office. This happened initially in the South during the Reconstruction that lasted from 1865 to 1877. In Southern states where large black populations had suddenly gained the status of free men and women, black men began to run for seats in the House of Representatives and the Senate. The *Reconstruction Act of 1867* emboldened them to attend political conventions and join political clubs.[35]

Hiram Rhoades Revels and Joseph Hayne Rainey were the first black Americans to sit in the U.S. Congress. In 1870, Revels, a Republican from Mississippi, was sworn in as the first black senator. He was born in Fayetteville, North Carolina, in approximately 1827 (the 1850 Census lists "about 1825") to free parents of mixed African and Croatan Indian heritage. An exact birthplace has not been identified. An educator and member of the clergy, Revels organized black troops in the *Civil War* and was a Mississippi state senator before being elected to the U.S. Senate. Revels took his seat in the Senate, after contentious debate, on February 25, 1870, and served through March 4, 1871. Returning to Mississippi in 1871, Revels was named president of Alcorn College, the state's first college for black students. He died on January 16, 1901, while attending a church conference in Aberdeen, Mississippi.[36]

Joseph H. Rainey, a Republican from South Carolina, was the first black American to sit in the Congress. He was born in Georgetown, Georgetown County, South Carolina, June 21, 1832, and received a limited schooling. He followed the trade of barber until 1862, when, upon being forced to work on the Confederate fortifications in Charleston, South Carolina, he escaped to the West Indies and remained there until the close of the war. Rainey was a delegate to the State constitutional convention in 1868 and a member of the State Senate in 1870. He was elected as a Republican to the 41st Congress to fill the vacancy caused by the action of the House of Representatives in declaring the seat of B. Franklin Whittemore vacant. He was reelected to the 42nd Congress and to the three succeeding Congresses. He served from December 12, 1870, to March 3, 1879. Appointed to be an internal revenue agent in South Carolina on May 22, 1879, he served until July 15, 1881, when he resigned. He then engaged in banking and the brokerage business in Washington, D.C. Rainey retired from all business activities in 1886 and returned to Georgetown, South Carolina.[37]

Robert Smalls, a Republican representative from South Carolina was born in Beaufort, S.C., April 5, 1839. As a youth, he moved to Charleston, S.C., in 1851 and worked there in a variety of jobs. The *Civil War* brought him his chance. On the morning of May 13, 1862, long before the sun was up and while the ship's white officers still slept in Charleston, Smalls smuggled his wife and three children aboard the *Planter* and took command. With his crew of 12 slaves, Smalls hoisted the Confederate flag and with great daring sailed the *Planter* past the other Confederate ships and out to sea. Once beyond the range of the Confederate guns, he hoisted a flag of truce and delivered the *Planter* to the commanding officer of the Union fleet. Smalls explained that he intended the *Planter* as a contribution by black Americans to the cause of freedom. The ship was received as contraband, and Smalls and his black crew were welcomed as heroes.[38]

Later, President Lincoln received Smalls in Washington and rewarded him and his crew for their valor. He was given official command of the *Planter* and made a captain in the U.S. Navy. In this position, he served throughout the war. Smalls was a member of the State constitutional convention in 1868 and served in the State house of representatives from 1868 to 1870, as a member of the State senate from 1870 to 1874, and as a delegate to the Republican National Convention in 1872 and 1876. He was elected as a Republican to the 44th and 45th Congresses (March 4, 1875-March 3, 1879) and then had a series of successful and unsuccessful election efforts. Smalls was an unsuccessful candidate for reelection in 1878 to the 46th Congress, but successfully contested the election of George D. Tillman to the 47th Congress where he served from July 19, 1882, to March 3, 1883. An unsuccessful candidate for reelection in 1882, he was elected to the 48th Congress to fill the vacancy caused by the death of Edmund W. M. Mackey. Reelected to the 49th Congress, Smalls served from March 18, 1884, to March 3, 1887. He was unsuccessful for reelection in 1886 to the 50th Congress. He was collector of the Port of Beaufort, S.C. from 1897 to 1913, and retained his interest in the military. Smalls was a major general in the South Carolina militia and died in Beaufort, South Carolina, February 22, 1915.[39]

Senator Blanche Kelso Bruce, another Republican black U.S. Senator from Mississippi, was elected in 1874. He had been born a slave in Farmville, Virginia, in 1841 and was the first black to serve a full term in the U.S. Senate. While rebuffed by some in Washington's white society, he and his wife, Josephine Willson Bruce, a prominent dentist's daughter, were early leaders in Washington's black society during the late 19th century. President James Garfield appointed Senator Bruce to the position of register of the treasury, a position he held until he died in Washington in 1898. The Blanche Kelso Bruce house is located at 909 M Street, N.W.[40]

Between 1870 and the late 1890s, nearly two dozen blacks served in the U.S. Congress. Others among them were John Langston of Virginia, Jefferson Franklin Long of Georgia, Robert Carlos DeLarge of South Carolina, Benjamin S. Turner of Alabama, Josiah Walls of Florida, Jeremiah

Haralson of Alabama, John Lynch of Mississippi, and George H. White of North Carolina. All of them were Republicans. While elected office did not promise wealth or acceptance within the white social structure, it did bring lasting prestige to certain family names. In Washington, these included names like Terrell, Pinchback, and Grimké. Prominent families socialized with one another, built businesses with one another, and intermarried to establish well-to-do and well-respected family dynasties.[41]

When Reconstruction was halted due to the compromise of 1877, a purported informal, unwritten deal that settled the strongly disputed 1876 U.S. presidential election and effectively allowed the stoppage of minority voting rights in the South, the growing stream of blacks elected to office virtually ground to a halt. By the late 1890s, most Black Americans had either been barred from or abandoned electoral politics in frustration. After Representative White's departure from the House of Representatives in March 1901, no black American served in the U.S. Congress for nearly three decades.[42]

By the late 1890s, most Black Americans had either been barred from or abandoned electoral politics in frustration. After Representative White's departure from the House of Representatives in March 1901, no black American served in the U.S. Congress until Oscar De Priest of Illinois in 1928. Then, Adam Clayton Powell Jr. of New York was elected in 1945 and served 12 terms.[43] However, during the entirety of the 20th century, there were just two black senators: Republican Edward W. Brooke of Massachusetts (1967-1979) and Democrat Carol Mosely Braun of Illinois (1993-1999). Senator Brooke was a graduate of Dunbar High School, Class of 1936.[44]

Housing Ownership

As early as 1881, there were complaints about a shortage of housing for black people. The crisis was especially acute for those blacks who were fairly well off because respectable homes were simply out of reach for anyone classified as black. Cottages and median-sized dwellings in desirable locations were scarce and white residential areas were closed to people of color. Still, despite the difficulties of purchasing property in a desirable section, many of a select few blacks managed to secure commodious residences in "fashionable quarters." The Douglass home at "Cedar Hill" in Anacostia, the Langstons' "hillside Cottage," and the Pinchbacks' 13-room house on Bacon Street, were among the largest and most elegantly furnished homes of the black community. Others were only a little less so. Henry P. Cheatham, the congressman from North Carolina who later became recorder of deeds, purchased a home on T Street Northwest, in 1897, that was described as "one of the best pieces of property owned by a colored man in the District."[45]

On the same street lived the Terrells and Alice Strange Davis, whose "at homes" were among the most exclusive social gatherings in Washington. The Daniel Murrays, who resided nearby, were for many years the only black residents in the 900 block of S Street, but, by 1912, the block had become all black, including two physicians and several Howard University professors. Perhaps "the most commodious house owned by a black person in Washington was the one built in 1899 by Mr. and Mrs. John F. Cook on 16th Street between L and M Streets. A 3-story structure of buff brick and stone, it was decorated inside with "finely finished oak" and contained "all modern conveniences." Some of the old families such as the Cooks, Wormleys, and Francises had acquired extensive real estate in the city before the *Civil War* and kept it in the family. By the turn of the century, such property had appreciated enormously in value. Dr. John Francis, who had inherited property from his father, invested extensively in real estate that included an elegant home on Pennsylvania Avenue adjoining his private hospital. For most blacks, however, regardless of their education, wealth, refinement, or fairness of complexion, the securing of housing, other than that already "discarded by discriminating people," involved considerable trouble.[46]

Housing for the Underprivileged

Housing in the District was dear and in short supply, even for those of modest means. Among the city's nonprofessional adult blacks, over 40 percent lived with boarders or lodgers. Over a third of the nonprofessional black family households consisted of extended families, two or more related nuclear families, or a family or families with boarders or lodgers. The city's black professionals were not immune to such pressures. More than a quarter either were boarders or lodgers or maintained boarders or lodgers in their homes. Over a third of the professional households were consanguineous in nature, either with one parent and children, or with unmarried siblings.[47] A fifth of the black population lived in the District's alley dwellings. Three quarters of the alley-dwelling families earned less than $800.00 a year. The average worker experienced 6.6 weeks a year of unemployment, while for 45 percent of the alley residents, that figure jumped to 13.4 weeks lost for reasons other than illness.[48]

Washington's poorest citizens lived in tenement housing in the alleys of the Nation's Capital. At the turn of the 20th century, blacks comprised two-thirds of the alley population. Various acts of Congress dating back to 1872, including the 1914 *Alley Dwelling Act*, which was declared unconstitutional, attempted to eradicate the alley population that persisted into the 1940s. In 1930, the alley population stood at 11,000-13,000 people, down from its high of 25,000. [49]

In 1880, the typical alley home had four rooms with a small back yard, a water pump, a privy, and a shed. These areas were generally without water, heat, electricity and sewerage service.[50] Black Washington's housing situation was another area where intra-race class divisions were obvious. Often, immigrants and impoverished Washingtonians were forced to live in the city's alleys. Already isolated from the outside world by a narrow passage to the main streets, living in these alleys meant being psychologically removed as well; thus, these residents were rendered invisible. Alley residents had to go outside to use the community water hydrant or backyard "privy"; they had to reside in a community which bred conditions of "vice, crime and immorality"; and they were exposed to a galaxy of other health risks.[51] Most alley dwellers were blacks that worked at low-paying jobs in construction or as domestics.

The National Capital Parks and Planning Commission (NCPPC) addressed the alley problem in its 1930 comprehensive plan for the District. The NCPPC called for a Congressional act which would give the president and local agencies of the federal government the power to purchase or condemn alley buildings and to relocate alley residents primarily to vacant street dwellings elsewhere in the District. The Commission strove "to assure street property owners and tenants that the character of their neighborhoods would not be injured. The search for vacant houses was confined to Negro blocks so as not to raise any question as to the population of a given square."[52]

The NCPPC justified the demolition of alley dwellings on the grounds of code violations and building obsolescence and through a moral appeal that alley tenants were particularly disposed to crime, delinquency, and communicable disease. The Commission's intent to relocate these tenants exclusively in black neighborhoods ignored the minority of white alley dwellers as well as the class-based heterogeneity of black neighborhoods. The Commission added, "Also, it is recognized that there are differences among the Negroes and it is not proposed to give respectable colored neighborhoods a new character by flooding them with undesirable new tenants. This is a difficult problem. All alley dwellers are not undesirable neighbors. The transition must be handled with consideration and tact."[53]

There was not enough vacant housing to accommodate the displaced families; thus, public housing in the District was born. Congress created the Alley Dwelling Authority (ADA) in 1934, which became the National Capital Housing Authority (NCHA) during the 1940s. Its responsibilities included construction of housing for war workers during *World War II*, eradication of alley dwellings, and construction of public housing in the District. The NCHA oversaw the construction of 943 public housing units throughout the city during the years of *World War II*. Congress's 1945 *D.C. Redevelopment* Act gave slum reclamation in Washington additional impetus and placed both the NCHA and the D.C. commissioners squarely under the authority of the NCPPC.

The NCPPC membership body included the chairmen of the District committees in the House and the Senate; presidential appointees like the director of the National Park Service, the chief of the Forest Service, and the Chief Engineer of the U.S. Army; and four presidentially-appointed city planners, one of whom had to be a resident of the District of Columbia. The *Redevelopment Act* provided for the clearance of substandard housing, but it also allowed the federal government to acquire land for federal development through the NCPPC.

In its 1950 *Comprehensive Plan*, the NCPPC mentioned that the *Redevelopment Act* would facilitate the clearance of a large area "to accommodate public buildings and an extension of the Mall east of the Capitol."[54] The process of redevelopment began with the NCPPC, which targeted certain areas of the city for clearance and redevelopment in accordance with its comprehensive plan for Washington. The D.C. Commissioners were given 30 days to approve or amend the proposal. Following approval, the Redevelopment Land Agency acquired the property through purchase, condemnation, or eminent domain. The NCPA constructed and administered public and subsidized housing when the area was to be redeveloped for low-income residential use. Marshall Heights, an Anacostia neighborhood, was the first community targeted for redevelopment, but the testimony of residents before a Congressional committee resulted in Congress refusing to fund the project.

With the beginning of *World War II*, the Authority suspended its work and concentrated attention on providing additional dwellings for defense workers and, later, for war workers. Expansion of military facilities, such as the Navy Yard and a military highway, displaced resident low-income families and necessitated that provisions be made for them. *Executive Order 9344*, of May 21, 1934, established the authority as an independent agency and changed the name to National Capital Housing Authority (NCHA).

After the war, NCHA continued as the public housing agency for the District of Columbia, attempting to provide an adequate supply of proper housing for low-income families and individuals. In addition to building and acquiring housing, the Authority managed and maintained the properties and provided social services, such as day care, tutoring and recreational activities, for residents. On March 13, 1968, by *Executive Order No. 11401*, the President designated the Commissioner of the District of Columbia as the Authority to carry out the provisions of the *District of Columbia Alley Dwelling Act*. The *Executive Order* stated that in carrying out his functions as such Authority, the Commissioner would be known as the "National Capital Housing Authority." The *District of Columbia Home Rule Act* (87 Stat. 779) of December 24, 1973, abolished the agency, effective July 1, 1974.

Some black families attempted to distance themselves from the black lower classes by seeking housing in integrated neighborhoods. Turn-of-the-century Washington had no ghettoes and, instead, was more a checkerboard of racial neighborhoods. Although blacks and whites might live on neighboring streets, they rarely crossed over, except for the black domestic servants and a minuscule number of black professionals who worked on white blocks. The block of 20th Street, between K and H streets, in 1900, was integrated, as was the surrounding neighborhood in the northwest section of Washington. About a third of the families were black, and their homes were interspersed with those of the white families. Residents for the most part coexisted peacefully, and some black and white children played together. The children got along despite their parents, who often did not want their children to be around the "niggers."[55]

An example of the resultant race situation in some neighborhoods occurred when the Logan family arrived, simultaneously with six other black families, on 20th Street and caused some ripples in the normally calm racial waters. The new mix of residents created an occasion for racial confusion. Some of the block's white residents considered the seven black families to be an invasion of sorts. The Logans hoped to avoid any sticky situations in their new neighborhood and, Martha Logan, a church-going woman and stern disciplinarian, made sure that her children stayed in line and out of trouble. The Logans also hoped their light complexion would help them avoid the hostility that would be visited upon a darker family.

Fair-skinned as they were, the Logans and the Simmses were, except for Rayford's brother, Arthur Jr., of a slightly browner shade than the Prices and the Grays, two of the block's established black families. Apparently, the Prices and the Grays were the darkest shade tolerable to the white residents. Soon after they moved in, a gang of white children began throwing rocks at the Logan residence. Another time, Rayford, Arthur, Jr., Robert Simms, Jr., and some friends fought a group of white boys their own age after "they called us 'niggers' and we retaliated by calling them 'poor white trash.'"[56] It was equally as confusing for fair-skinned blacks that lived in black lower income neighborhoods or the projects. They often had to fight with dark-skinned blacks because they were too light-skinned and, when they ventured a couple of blocks out of their own neighborhood, they had to fight with whites because they were "niggers."

Given the general predominance of mulattoes among the "free persons of color" and their descendants, it seems probable that the light-skinned mulatto stereotype was applicable to the early M Street and Dunbar students and teachers. This group continued for many years to be over-represented among the schools' students and teachers, but they did not necessarily constitute a majority. A study of old yearbook photographs at

Dunbar High School shows the great bulk of the students to have been very much the color of most American blacks. Any bias in the photography of that period, before black was beautiful, would be toward printing the pictures lighter than real life.[57]

Social and Leisure Activities in the District of Columbia

The social activities of selected groups tended to be exclusive, creating distance between the members of the group and the rest of society. Membership in certain social clubs was often one of the ascribed, or subjective, characteristics of a select few. One would expect such clubs to be the least likely areas in which to discover connections with the larger community, but Washington's black social clubs indeed developed such ties at the turn of the century.

While exclusivity remained an enduring legacy in the social and cultural organizations of the black privileged, the nature of these organizations underwent a transformation. Concerned only with creating social status in the 1800s, these organizations began to embrace concepts of racial pride and racial solidarity in the early 1900s. Excluded from white social institutions, advantaged blacks increased their pride in their racial heritage when they created their own social institutions. Even in activities designed to provide escape from daily struggles of an oppressive life, blacks became more aware of the need to uplift the race.[58]

All forms of culture and recreation were readily available to black citizens of the District at the turn of the century, particularly to those with the means to enjoy them. Black residents attended their own plays, musicales, poetry readings, lectures, and special exhibitions. They prided themselves on their literary organizations and annual galas. While some private facilities, such as theaters and restaurants, were segregated, the public museums and libraries in Washington, unlike those in some other Southern cities, were open to blacks.[59]

The U Street neighborhood was the center of Washington's black community with many black owned businesses, entertainment venues, and social institutions. Homes that had been built on U Street were converted to commercial uses about 10 years after their erection. An example is the townhouse at 1355 U Street that became Republic Gardens in the 1910s, a club by the same name that remains there today. Major entertainment venues catering to a black crowd began as early as 1909, when the Minnehaha Theater was built at 1213 U Street; Ben's Chili Bowl is there today. In 1910, the Howard Theater was constructed with a capacity of 1,200, predating the famed Apollo in Harlem by nearly a decade. The impressive True Reformer Building at 1200 U Street was begun in 1902 and hosted a myriad of social functions, parties, and even the first paid performance of the neighborhood's own Duke Ellington.[60]

Until the 1920s, when it was overtaken by Harlem, the U Street Corridor was home to the nation's largest urban black community. In its cultural glory days, U Street was known as "Black Broadway", a phrase coined by singer Pearl Bailey. With ample space for performances in the area's many theaters, the corridor continued to expand in the 1920s with additional smaller clubs, after-hours venues, and private gatherings for musicians, jazz performers, and the black cultural elite. Other theaters were constructed, including the Booker T Theater in the 1400 block of U Street and the famed and elegant Republic Theater in the 1300 block. Both have since been demolished.[61]

The Lincoln Theater was built between 1921 and 1923 as a first-run movie house and performance stage at 1215 U Street. Club Crystal Caverns opened in 1926 in the basement of 2001 11th Street in a cave-like setting that hosted performers from Pearl Bailey to Aretha Franklin during its prime. It operated under several different names until the mid-1970s and still exists today. Speakeasies in private basements and the Lincoln Colonnade often kept patrons entertained long after the official last call in the clubs.[62]

Sports Activities

Sports were popular among the black elite, who enjoyed them both as spectators and participants. Since there was no professional black baseball team in Washington, fans had to attend games at the American League baseball park, Griffith Stadium, one of the few public places never racially segregated. Here, blacks waited in the same food and ticket lines as everyone else, a circumstance that perhaps accounted for the popularity of the sport among black Americans. Beginning in 1925, however, the ballpark began to refuse to sell tickets to black fans whose names they recognized. The practice continued despite protest in the press.[63]

Golf and tennis were popular participation sports among the black elite. Originally, the white golf courses set aside certain days of the week for blacks to play, but white golfers complained that they did not like being restricted to certain days only. The black players petitioned for a separate black golf course, but, again, encountered opposition from the white community. Ultimately, the city agreed to build a 9-hole course for blacks in Potomac Park near the Lincoln Memorial. The course was so beautifully kept that problems arose when white players tried to use it.[64]

It was difficult for blacks outside the elite circle to play tennis, since the courts designated for use by blacks were located far from most black neighborhoods. By the 1920s, however, the city boasted five black tennis clubs, most of them affiliated with the schools or Howard University. The most prestigious was the James E. Walker Club, which held regular smokers to promote tennis and organized annual tournaments. The club was also instrumental in building new courts, first in Le Droit Park and, later, at 13th and T Streets, N.W., near the Terrell home. The Howard University Club also held annual tournaments, at which silver loving cups donated by local businessmen were awarded to the winners.[65]

Exclusive social clubs were an important part of black elite life because they restored a sense of prestige to their members. In the 1880s, black social clubs such as the Lotus Club focused on excluding those with darker skin or dividing social groups between longtime residents of the area and newcomers. While light skin did remain an important indicator of privileged status well into the 20th century, so many darker-skinned blacks were rising to the ranks of the elite that social clubs no longer made this distinction.[66]

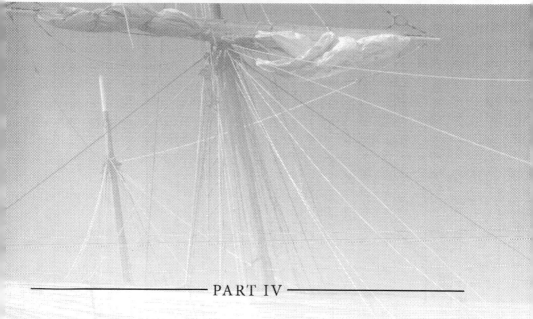

PART IV

THE CROWN JEWEL

He who opens a school door, closes a prison.

Victor Hugo, 1802-1885

CHAPTER NINE

THE COMMENCEMENT OF LIBERATION

There was a sense of uplift as a liberation theology flourished after emancipation and during the Reconstruction period. Policies of group advancement would be kept alive by generations of blacks singing "Lift Every Voice and Sing," its lyrics written in 1900 by James Weldon Johnson. The song was immensely popular in the black community and sung by school assemblies and church congregations from the days when black people celebrated the anniversary of the emancipation each year.[1]

For the black middle class, uplift meant an emphasis on self-help, racial solidarity, temperance, thrift, chastity, social purity, patriarchal authority, and the accumulation of wealth. This emphasis on class differentiation as race progress, however, often involved struggling with the culturally dominant construction of "the Negro problem." Amidst legal and extralegal repression, many blacks sought status, moral authority, and recognition of their humanity by distinguishing themselves from the presumably under-developed black majority; hence, the phrase, often of ambiguous significance, "uplifting the race."[2]

The Colored Public Schools

In 1866, there were five colored public schools. They opened with seven teachers and 400 pupils.[3] George F. T. Cook was appointed Superintendent of Colored Schools in 1868 and given charge of black schools in the District of Columbia. He was the first and last Superintendent of Colored Schools, as those who succeeded him were designated Assistant Superintendent in

Charge of Colored Schools. When Superintendent Cook commenced his term, the colored branch of the school system consisted of 41 schools, 41 teachers, and 2,300 pupils. At the close of his administration in 1900, there were 273 public schools for black children with 352 teachers and 12,748 pupils.[4]

Cook's administration was characterized by a philosophy that emphasized, as a fundamental objective, a respect for personality and character education by example as well as by precept.

Educators, under his leadership, recognized the philosophy espoused by William H. Kirkpatrick, an eminent educator at Columbia University, that:

> Men are, first of all, men, not animals, servants or tools. The first aim of education therefore must be to make not efficient workers but better men, better citizens, and better Christians. A nation which aims primarily to develop to the fullest possible extent the character and intellect of its citizens may find that material prosperity and commercial success are added to it.[5]

With this objective for education, Cook's administration was a noble and efficient endeavor for more than 30 years.

Cook was more than the scholarly product of Oberlin College. Rev. Francis J. Grimké, himself one of the foremost scholars of his day and one who knew Cook intimately, said of him in a discourse delivered at the Fifteenth Street Presbyterian Church on August 10, 1918, that he was the soul of courtesy, a gentleman, thoroughly honest, and straightforward in all his dealings with others. He was modest and shrank from all publicity. He preferred to do his work quietly and to let the work speak for itself. He was a clean, pure man, one of high ideals and noble aspirations, who commanded the respect of the community.[6]

Many able men and women of superior character and training worked side by side with Superintendent Cook. Among these was Martha B. Briggs, who, beginning in 1879, was the first woman of color to be appointed principal of the Miner Normal School. It was said of her by an educator:

Miss Briggs was a born teacher, and her work showed those qualities of head and heart that have made her name famous in the annals of education in the character of the graduates. The student teachers caught her missionary spirit and went forth from her presence stronger souls full of sympathy to magnify the teacher's vocation and inspire the learner.[7]

Miss Briggs was succeeded by Dr. Lucy E. Moten, who taught youth to be teachers rather than to merely act the part of a teacher when in the presence of students. Dr. Moten emphasized cleanliness, punctuality, accuracy, and thoroughness. Under her, the Miner Normal School developed into one of the best two-year teacher-training institutions in the United States. State superintendents throughout the country sought her graduates because of the efficient services they rendered wherever they were employed. Among the teachers who helped Dr. Moten lay the foundation for the fine work she did were Miss Ada C. Hand, Miss Jesse A. Wormley, Miss Mary Dickerson, Miss A. J. Turner, Charles M. Thomas, Miss Marie Bowie, George Jenifer, Miss Clara H. Shippen, and Eugene A. Clark.[8]

The great majority of the teachers and officers of the school system in 1932 were products of the Cook administration's outstanding 25 years leading the black school system in the District of Columbia. Three of the four men who rose to the highest office of First Assistant Superintendent were George F. T. Cook, Roscoe C. Bruce, and Garnet C. Wilkinson. Three of the four persons who served as assistant superintendents were Miss M. P. Shadd, Eugene A. Clark, and Alfred K. Savoy. There also were three supervising principals, John C. Bruce, Miss Minecola Kirkland, and Leon L. Perry, one of the three senior high principals. Robert N. Mattingly and four of the five junior high principals, Mrs. M. H. Plummer, Walter L. Savoy, Harold A. Haynes, and the Principal of the Randall Junior High School, were products of the public schools of the District of Columbia and they subsequently graduated from some of the leading colleges of the United States.[9]

Archie Morris III, D.P.A.

The Preparatory High School for Colored Youth

Education was regarded as the key to liberation. A new black school providing an education beyond the eighth grade was necessary to emphasize the black middle class ideals of racial uplift, espouse a vision of racial solidarity, and unite black elites with the masses.[10] The centerpiece of this mandate was the black Preparatory High School, established two years before the establishment of any white public high school in the District of Columbia.[11]

The first high school for black American students opened its doors in 1870, when Congress defeated a bill sponsored by Senator Charles Sumner (a Massachusetts antislavery Republican) for an integrated school system for the nation's capital city. While reaffirming the principle of a dual system of education in the nation's capital, Congress promised equal standards and a proportional representation on the governing body that oversaw the school system.[12] Initially, Alonzo E. Newton was superintendent of schools and William Syphax and William H. A. Wormley were trustees of the colored schools of Washington and Georgetown. Shortly thereafter, Syphax, the first chair of the Board of Trustees of the Colored Public Schools in the District of Columbia, instigated the Preparatory High School for Colored.[13]

In November 1870, the Preparatory High School for Colored Youth was established in the basement of the Fifteenth Street Presbyterian Church at 15th Street between I and K Streets, N.W., in Washington, D.C. First supported by means of private philanthropic funds, it became a tax-supported institution within a few years, actually preceding the establishment of the public high schools for whites. The Preparatory High School was the first black high school in the United States, and it was an academic school from the beginning. It fiercely resisted recurrent pressures upon it to become vocational, commercial, or "general." It taught Latin throughout this period and, in some early years, Greek as well. The school was never "relevant" to the passing fads, but it instilled individual and racial pride in its students and in the District of Columbia's black community. From the beginning it functioned, as its name implies, as a college preparatory school for the "Talented Tenth."[14]

The "Talented Tenth" is a concept espoused by W.E.B. Du Bois in *The*

Negro Problem. Du Bois, a black educator and author, felt it was necessary to have higher education to develop the leadership capacity among the most able 10 percent of black Americans. He was one of several black intellectuals who feared that an overemphasis on industrial training (as evidenced, for example, by the plan proposed by Booker T. Washington in his 1895 Atlanta Compromise speech) would confine blacks permanently to the ranks of second-class citizenship. In order to achieve political and civil equality, Du Bois stressed the importance of educating black teachers, professional men, ministers, and spokesmen, who would earn their special privileges by dedicating themselves to "leavening the lump" and "inspiring the masses."[15]

This beginning high school for black youth was, in fact, not a high school at all. It was mainly composed of students completing the last two years of the grammar grades, with a small number of students pursuing high school courses. The new institution labored under several decidedly obvious disadvantages. First, the teaching force was inadequate, as there was only one instructor for 45 students. Enough time for advanced studies was not provided and the school suffered from a loss of students who were recruited and employed to meet the growing demand for black teachers in the lower grades. The first class would have graduated in 1875, but the demand for teachers was greater than the supply. Thus, the first classes were drawn into the teaching corps before they had completed the prescribed coursework. It was not until 1877 that the first high school commencement was held, with 11 students being awarded diplomas.[16] This first graduating class was immediately hired to teach the other classes,[17] because of the demand for teachers and the lack of a normal school. The achievements of these first pupils, who became efficient teachers, attest to the high standard of instruction in the school from its inception.[18]

Given the extreme scarcity of educated blacks in 1870, the school's performance could not readily be duplicated elsewhere within any reasonable span of years. The first black woman to receive a college degree in the United States, Mary Jane Patterson, graduated from Oberlin in 1862 and taught at the Preparatory High School. The first black man to graduate from Harvard, Richard T. Greener, received his degree in 1870 and became principal of the Preparatory High School in 1872. The first principal of the Preparatory High School, however, was Emma J. Hutchins, a white woman who was a native of New Hampshire. Like many white men and women who came from the North at that time, Miss Hutchins was fired with zeal to do everything in her power to educate and uplift the youth of the newly emancipated race. She served as Principal of the O Street School, now the John F. Cook School, and was placed in charge of the Preparatory High School in 1870.

After one year, Miss Hutchins resigned to accept a position in Oswego County, New York. There was no dissatisfaction with her on the part of the people whom she served. She resigned because, as she said, there were, among the black people themselves, teachers thoroughly equipped to take up the work and carry it on while she could find employment elsewhere. Her term of service in the Washington public schools was brief, but the impression she made upon those with whom she came into contact remained indelibly fixed through the years that followed. She emphasized high ideals, conscientious performance of duty under adverse conditions, and loyalty to the interest of her students. It was said, "Hers was indeed the spirit of the true teacher."[19]

Miss Hutchins was the first teacher and the first four students in her class were Rosetta Coakley, John Nalle, Mary Nalle, and Caroline Parke. The Preparatory High School curriculum was, at first, mainly classical and English. The course of study included arithmetic, geometry, trigonometry, astronomy, English grammar, composition, literature and elocution, United States, English and general history, science, foreign languages, mental and moral philosophy, drawing, penmanship, and bookkeeping.[20] Technical and business courses were added later. The high school set of courses took three years up until 1894, when it was increased by electives to four years.[21]

In 1871, Mary Jane Patterson succeeded Miss Hutchins as principal of the high school, which was then located in the Thaddeus Stevens School building on 21st Street, N.W. Miss Patterson not only was the first black woman in the United States to earn a college degree, but she did it by spurning the usual courses for women at Oberlin and taking, instead, a program of Greek, Latin, and higher mathematics designed for "gentlemen." As principal, she was "a strong, forceful personality," noted for "thoroughness," and for being "an indefatigable worker."[22]

After Miss Patterson had served one year as principal, Richard T. Greener was appointed in 1872 to take her place. Just as Miss Patterson was the first woman of color to be graduated from Oberlin College, so Greener had the distinction of being the first black man to be so honored by Harvard College. He received his preparatory education in Boston, Oberlin, and Cambridge, and was graduated from Harvard in 1870. A scholar and lawyer by profession, Greener attracted attention through his essays and orations. He held several important positions, having served as a professor in the University of South Carolina during the Reconstruction Period, Dean of the Law School of Howard University, Chief Civil Service Examiner for New York City, and the United States Consul at Vladivostok, Russia. After serving as principal of the high school for nearly a year, Greener left for fields of broader opportunity. Miss Patterson was then reappointed principal of the Preparatory High School and served for a dozen more years in the formative period of the school. She was succeeded in 1884 by Francis L. Cardozo, Sr.[23]

When Cardozo was appointed to the principalship of the high school, the standard of scholarship required of the principals was certainly maintained. Born free in antebellum South Carolina, he had the rare distinction of being educated at Glasgow University in Glasgow, Scotland. There, he won two scholarships of $1,000 each in Greek and Latin. He also took a course in the London School of Theology in London, England, where he completed the three-year program in two years. He was, on one occasion, pastor of the Tremont Street Congregational Church in New Haven, Connecticut. Later, he went to Charleston, South Carolina, where he engaged in missionary work while employed by the American Board of Missions. Cardozo founded the Avery Institute in Charleston and served as its principal until he became Treasurer of the State of South Carolina in 1870. Under Governor Daniel Henry Chamberlain, he was Secretary of State for two terms.[24]

From the basement of the Fifteenth Street Presbyterian Church, the school was moved to the Thaddeus Stevens School for one year, 1871 to 1872. The Charles Sumner School at 17th and M Streets, N.W., was its home from 1872 to 1877. It then was moved to the Myrtilla Minor School on the corner of 17th and Church Streets, N.W. It remained there until 1891, when it became the M Street High School on M Street between First Street and New Jersey Avenue, N.W.[25]

From 45 students in the first year, the enrollment increased to 83 learners two years later. In the first graduating class of 1877, there were 11 pupils:[26]

Dora F. Barker

Mary L. Beacon

Fannie M. Costin

Julia C. Grant

Fannie E. McCoy

Cornelia A. Pinckney

Carrie E. Taylor

Mary E. M. Thomas

James C. Craig

John A. Parker

James B. Wright

By 1884, there were 172 students in the school and, two years later, enrollment had increased to 247. From 1887 to 1888, when the enrollment was 361, there were nine teachers, exclusive of the instructors in music and drawing. There was an increase of two teachers in 1888 to 1889. From 1877 to 1894, the high school curriculum consisted of three years of work. In 1894, the curriculum was enriched and enlarged by the addition of several electives and then lengthened to four years. The commercial department was established in 1884-1885 and, in 1887, a business course requiring two years of study was added. Girls were given an opportunity to take up domestic science and boys, military drill.[27]

In 1886, the business program was introduced in the old Miner School Building at 17th and Church Streets, N.W. Because of the growth of the academic department at M Street, the business department was transferred to the Garnet School Building at 10th and U Streets, N.W., where it remained for two years. It was then moved to the Douglass School Building at 1st and Pierce Streets, N.W. and, in turn, to Old Mott, Phelps, Dunbar, and finally Cardozo.[28]

M Street High School

As far back as 1874, Superintendent of Colored Schools George F. T. Cook had urged the construction of a suitable building for the high school.[29] Finally, an appropriation was made for the construction of a building known as the M Street High School. It was erected on M Street, N.W., near the intersection of New York and New Jersey Avenues. The 1904-1905 Report of the Board of Education of D.C. indicates the site of the building cost $24,592.50. The building itself cost $74,454.88 and the fixtures cost $9,862.44. The total expenditure for the new school was $109,909.82.[30]

Until 1892, the Preparatory School for Colored Youth had been housed at various sites around the city. The school was then moved into the new building at 128 M Street, N.W., and renamed the M Street High School. The old M Street High School became the Perry Elementary

School. Perry closed its doors with the instillation of desegregation laws in 1954.[31] The new M Street building was a large brick structure built in the Romanesque Revival style. It was designed by the Office of the Building Inspector of the Central Municipal Design and Construction Agency and housed 450 students.

The Engineer Commissioner supervised Office of the Building Inspector, among others, during a time when the city was governed by three appointed commissioners. The three-story brick building provided special rooms appropriate to the offerings of the high school. They included a "drill room" in the basement, scientific laboratories, and of study halls at the rear of the building. A large assembly hall was situated in the front portion of the third floor, which provided a stage and rows of opera chairs. At the time of its completion, the M Street High School building was "the first colored high school ever constructed from public funds. Other schools had been put up from private subscription, but this building was built from a public appropriation expressly made for that purpose...."[32]

The credentials of the M Street High School and its successor Dunbar High School faculty were formidable. The school system provided equal and relatively high salaries for all teachers regardless of gender or race, and the nation's best black educators were attracted to the District of Columbia because they faced limited professional opportunities elsewhere.

The M Street High School and Dunbar faculty were arguably superior to the white public schools, whose teachers typically were graduates of normal schools and teachers' colleges. With the school's emphasis on the classics, the M Street High School and its successor Dunbar High School were viewed by many as the equivalent of the public Boston Latin School[33] or other exclusive prep schools.[34] In fact, Rayford W. Logan, M Street graduate and historian, declared the M Street High School to be "one of the best high schools in the nation, colored or white, public or private."[35]

The achievements of Dunbar reflect the personal qualities of individual leaders during the institution's formative years. A special kind of confidence and courage must have been required for a black man or a black woman to pioneer at Oberlin or Harvard in the middle of the 19th century when even liberals, who were opposed to slavery, openly questioned the very capacity of the race for tutelage and education. The M Street and Dunbar principals had to be individuals not easily discouraged, frightened, or inclined to compromise about quality. This is how historical accounts describe them and, certainly, this became the dominant tradition of the school.[36]

Principals at M Street High School

Francis L. Cardozo, Sr. holds the distinction of being the last principal of the Preparatory High School for Colored Youth and the first principal of the new M Street High School.

In 1896, Dr. Winfield Scott Montgomery was appointed principal of the M Street High School and held that position for three years. Born in 1853 as a slave on a plantation in the vicinity of New Orleans, he had the great fortune to be liberated by the Union Army. He made his way as a camp follower to Virginia and Vermont, where he entered Leland and Gray Seminary in Townshend, Vermont. In the Fall Semester of 1873, he matriculated at Dartmouth College, but, lacking adequate funds, dropped out for a year and taught at Washington's Hillsdale School.

Dr. Montgomery graduated from Dartmouth College in 1879, earning the degree of A.A. with *Phi Beta Kappa* honors. He had the distinction of being the only black American to be elected to membership in the *Kappa Kappa Kappa* (Tri-Kap) social fraternity until after *World War II*. In June 1906, the honorary degree of Master of Arts was conferred on him by

Dartmouth College. Dr. Montgomery successfully studied medicine at Howard University and was awarded the degree of Doctor of Medicine in 1890. He was licensed to practice in both the District of Columbia and Michigan. In 1899, he was made assistant superintendent for the colored schools and held that position for seven years. A colleague referred to Dr. Montgomery's tenure at M Street High School as ". . . marked by a period of constructive work. He stood for high scholarship with a leaning toward the classical high school."[37]

Judge Robert H. Terrell succeeded Dr. Montgomery in 1899. He was the second principal of the high school to hold a degree from Harvard College. When he was a boy, he was a student in the public schools of the District of Columbia and was a member of one of the early classes in the old Preparatory High School. Terrell finished his preparation for college at Lawrence Academy in Groton, Massachusetts. In order to pursue his college education, Terrell worked in a dining hall at Harvard. He was one of seven *magna cum laude* scholars to graduate from Harvard in June 1884. In the fall of that year, he was appointed a teacher in the high school and held that position for five years. In the fall of 1889, he was appointed chief of a division in the United States Treasury Department where he served four years.

In the meantime, Terrell studied law. He practiced that profession until 1889. In 1902, President Theodore Roosevelt nominated him for a judgeship for one of the City Courts of Washington and Terrell resigned the principalship to accept this position. As principal, he "devoted most his time out of school to preparing boys for college," with the result that "a goodly number" later "completed their education at Harvard."[38] He started a tradition that continued as the school changed principals and buildings. In the period 1918 to 1923, Dunbar graduates earned 15 degrees from Ivy League colleges and universities, and 10 degrees from Amherst, Williams, and Wesleyan.[39]

Judge Terrell's successor was Anna J. Cooper, a native of Raleigh, North Carolina, who was a graduate of Oberlin College, class of '84 and held an M.A. from Oberlin. In 1925, she was awarded the degree of Doctor of Philosophy by the Sorbonne. She taught Latin, mathematics, and science, and wrote a popular book, *A Voice from the South*, which was widely acclaimed in the national press. She instilled in her pupils high ideals of scholarship, racial pride, and self-improvement.[40]

Dr. Cooper strove unceasingly to prepare her pupils for acceptance at nonsegregated Northern and Midwestern universities. The typical route to a prestigious northern college for gifted black American graduates of segregated schools included a stop, after high school graduation, at a New England prep school. Earnest Everett Just, the gifted marine biologist, for example, graduated from the Classical Preparatory Department of South Carolina State College in 1899, and then attended Kimball Union Academy in New Hampshire before entering Dartmouth College in 1903.[41]

Under Dr. Cooper's principalship, graduates who passed rigid entrance examinations were admitted directly. Edwin French Tyson, class of 1903, passed Harvard's exam and was the first pupil to thereby enter Harvard College from the M Street High School. In 1899, the pupils of the M Street High School scored higher than the students of the white Eastern and Western high schools on standardized tests in English and general subjects. Of the 30 faculty at this time, 20 "had degrees from top-flight Northern colleges and universities and five others had graduated from Howard."[42] Nor was any of this an isolated fluke, M Street and Dunbar had an impressive academic record throughout an 85-year period.[43]

The new school continued its rigorous academic curriculum. First-year students were required to take English, history, algebra, Latin, and physics or chemistry. English and Latin were the only required subjects for third- and fourth-year students. Most students took a typical academic load, including two years of Greek, three of French, four of Latin, two of English and geometry, trigonometry and higher algebra. There were other options, as well, including courses in German, Spanish, and political economy.[44]

Students who graduated from the M Street High School were spared the extra time and expense of attending another prep school. The M Street faculty so thoroughly prepared the special tutorials to assist students in their studies for college entrance examinations that Brown, Harvard, Yale, and Oberlin agreed to admit students based on the test results, without requiring further preparation.[45] Dr. Cooper also succeeded in obtaining scholarships for many of her students.[46]

Though a capable teacher, scholar, and administrator, Dr. Cooper had her detractors. In a series of factual and penetrating articles in 1905, the

Washington Post scrutinized her role as principal. For more than a year, formal charges regarding the methods of discipline and the efficiency of the high school's faculty had been on file at the board of education. An investigation followed in which Dr. Cooper was accused of being a poor disciplinarian. Charges of intoxication and smoking by male pupils on the school's premises, as well as the admittance of some pupils who were not prepared for high school studies, were aired.[47]

Dr. Cooper absolved herself of the charges regarding student drinking by demonstrating that there was no evidence to sustain them. She was upheld by the influential M Street High School Alumni Association, the Reverend Francis O. Grimké, minister of the prestigious Fifteenth Street Presbyterian Church, former Congressman George H. White of North Carolina, and Mrs. A. M. Curtis, who represented the mothers of the pupils of the high school.[48]

Dr. Cooper was the victim of a cabal. Certain persons in the local community strenuously opposed her on the grounds that she stood for strict equality of curriculum in the dual school system and that she had allowed W. E. B. Du Bois, in the Winter of 1903, to speak to the high school's pupils. In his speech, Dr. Du Bois, an ardent opponent of the industrial and social views of Booker T. Washington, remarked that he discerned a tendency in the United States to restrict the curriculum of black schools.[49] With the construction in 1902 of the Armstrong Manual Training School, located in the cluster of black schools a few blocks to the north of M Street High School, the college preparatory goals of the latter school were more easily reaffirmed.[50] The practical concerns of those advocating vocational classes were mollified with the opening of Armstrong.

Dr. Cooper adamantly opposed any lowering of academic standards in the high school. Her position placed her on a collision with Percy M. Hughes, the white director of high schools. Hughes had asserted that the pupils of the M Street High School were "incapable of taking the same studies in the same time as the other schools of like grade in the city."[51] He claimed that M Street students were ineligible for college scholarships and when Dr. Cooper continued to recommend students for scholarships, Mr. Hughes charged her with insubordination.[52]

Mr. Hughes claimed that M Street students did not seem prepared for

English and algebra upon entering the school, and recommended changes in the curriculum to remedy this situation. In 1904, he acknowledged attacks from the black community, but, nonetheless, recommended an increase in manual training, particularly for M Street students, who needed to learn the "dignity of labor." They would be "better educated men and women and therefore better fitted to win out in life's battle if properly trained in the use of tools as well as books."[53] Considering the magnificent academic achievements of the graduates of the high school during a period of Jim Crow segregation, it would appear that Hughes's ideas were racially motivated. Moreover, because of Dr. Cooper's in activist role in the black community, sexism may also have been a factor.[54]

For Dr. Cooper, charitable and reform activities took the place of occupation as the key to transformation of values and it is certain that Hughes knew of her activism in the black community. Many black women held jobs, but they did so more for freedom as women than for racial uplift. Some women combined work with racial uplift through their lectures on race issues, but they were not moved to feel sympathy for the race by their employment. It was charitable activities that brought the more privileged black women closest to the rest of the black community and provided the strongest link to racial uplift.[55] The outcome of the investigation was the retention of Dr. Cooper as principal. Her administrative methods were, however, rebuked and her loyalty to the director of high schools questioned.[56]

William Tecumseh Sherman Jackson succeeded Dr. Cooper in 1906. Jackson was a native of Glencairn, Virginia, and was educated at Amherst College, which conferred upon him the degrees of A.B. in 1892, and A.M. in 1897. Jackson owed his college education to U.S. Senator George Frisbie Hoar of Massachusetts, who paid Jackson's tuition and expenses. Jackson never forgot that kindness. He devoted his life to helping others obtain the same opportunities. He shepherded many of his students to Amherst, which graduated more Dunbar students than any other college outside of the nation's capital.[57]

Thereafter, Jackson pursued postgraduate studies at the Catholic University of America. His 25 years of service were all in the high school. He was a teacher of mathematics from 1892 to 1904, principal of M Street High School from 1906 to 1909, and head teacher in the Department of

Business Practice from 1912 to 1917. In commenting upon Jackson's work, one of his superior officers declared that he "introduced the individual promotion system, stimulated interest in athletics and fostered the school spirit." In 1902, Jackson married May Howard, the talented sculptor, who taught Latin.[58]

The last principal of the M Street High School was Edward Christopher Williams, who succeeded Jackson as principal of the M Street High School in 1909. Mr. Williams was born in Cleveland, Ohio, and graduated from the Central High School there. He held the degree of B.L. from the Western Reserve University, where, in his junior year, he was awarded the *Phi Beta Kappa* key.[59]

Upon his graduation with distinction from Adelbert College of Western Reserve University in 1892, Williams was appointed Assistant Librarian of Hatch Library at Western Reserve University and an instructor in bibliographical subjects in the Library School. In 1898, Williams took a sabbatical leave to pursue a master's degree in librarianship at New York State Library. He completed the 2-year program in one year, and went back to resume his responsibilities at Western Reserve University as Librarian and Instructor.[60] Williams was promoted to librarian of the Hatch Library where he worked until 1909. He resigned to assume the responsibility of Principal of M Street High School in Washington, D.C. [61] After serving seven years as principal of M Street High School, he resigned in June 1916 to accept a position at Howard University as Librarian and Director of the Library School. Williams achieved success as an administrative officer while principal of the M Street High School.[62]

Teachers at M Street High School

No educational institution can exist solely with administrators at the helm. Teachers and students represent two-thirds of the total entity.[63] In 1891 to 1892, the faculty at M Street High School numbered 17, and in 1914 to 1915, it was 35.[64] Among the high school's "talented Tenth" were Henry L. Bailey, Parker N. Bailey, Ulysses S. G. Bassett, Percival D. Brooks, Hugh M. Browne, Mary P Burrill, Harriet Shadd Butcher, John W. Cromwell, Jr., Jessie Fauset, Ida A. Gibbs, Amplias Glenn, Angelina Grimké, Edwin B, Henderson, William T. S. Jackson, Lola Johnson,

Mineola Kirkland, Julia Mason Layton, Caroline E. Parke, Harriet E. Riggs, Nevalle Thomas, Garnet C. Wilkinson, and Carter G. Woodson.[65] Let us examine briefly the careers of some of these outstanding teachers.

One of the most distinguished teachers was Hugh Mason Browne, who was born into a prominent free black family in Washington, D.C., in June 1851. His parents, John and Elizabeth Wormley Browne, and other relatives were established members of the local black middle-class as a result of their entrepreneurial, educational, and political activities in the nation's capital. After receiving his early education in the local colored public school system, Browne attended Howard University, graduating with a B.A. in 1875 and an M.A. in 1878. He also received a B.D. degree from Princeton Theological Seminary in 1878 and was ordained for the ministry in the Presbyterian Church. During the next two years, Browne traveled to Germany and Scotland and pursued additional studies. He then returned to the United States to pastor Shiloh Presbyterian Church in New York City for a brief period. In August 1883, he went to Liberia where he was appointed to a professorship in intellectual and moral philosophy at Liberia College. While in the country, Browne learned about the challenges involved in the assimilation of former slaves into an African setting and about the problems and cultural differences affecting Liberian social, economic, and educational development.[66]

Browne returned to Washington after nearly two years in West Africa and taught physics for the next two years at the M Street High School. There, he introduced an innovative system of instruction that emphasized student experimentation. Next, he taught at Hampton Institute in Virginia from 1898 to 1901. Then, he served as principal of the Colored High School in Baltimore, Maryland. In each of these settings, Browne sought to improve educational systems and services to black Americans through a balanced approach of theory and practice. He advocated academics with industrial training and equal development of the mind and body through intellectual stimulation and physical education.[67]

Theoretical and intellectual, Browne was nonetheless committed to the practical application of ideas to specific needs. While he commanded the respect of more well-known thinkers and leaders such as Washington and Du Bois, he also spent time turning abstract ideas into tangible inventions in the manner of George Washington Carver and Elijah McCoy. He was credited with patenting a device for preventing the back flow of water in cellars on April 29, 1890, and cited in the July 8, 1893, issue of *The Colored American*, which included "a partial list of patents granted by the United States for inventions by colored persons."[68]

Angelina Weld Grimké was born into one of the most prominent American families of the 19th century. She was named for her white great aunt, a leading abolitionist and women's rights advocate, Angelina Grimké Weld, who died four months before Grimké was born on February 27, 1880. Her father, Archibald, a child of Weld's brother and one of his slaves, was a lawyer, an important Republican Party activist (first in Boston and, afterwards, in Washington, D. C.) and a leader of the National Association for the Advancement of Colored People (NAACP). In 1879, Archibald married Sarah Stanley, a socially prominent white Bostonian, with whom he had one child, Angelina. The couple separated several years after Angelina's birth, with Stanley gaining custody of their daughter over Archibald's opposition. However, Stanley proved unable to take care of her. By the time she was seven years old, Angelina was her father's sole responsibility.[69]

In 1902, with her father's help, Miss Grimké was hired as a physical education teacher at the Armstrong Manual Training School in Washington, D. C. When she had a falling out with the school's principal five years later, she was transferred to the city's more prestigious Dunbar High School where some of the other writers of the Harlem Renaissance also worked. During this time, she spent summers as a student at Harvard. Miss Grimké strove to measure up in her father's eyes by excelling as an English teacher at Dunbar for almost 20 years and through the fame she gained as a writer.[70]

Miss Grimké was a noted writer from the 1900s through the 1920s and the first black American to have a play, *Rachel* (1916; published in 1920), staged. It was produced as a vehicle for the NAACP to rally allies against the effects of the motion picture *Birth of a Nation*. Her poetry regularly appeared in journals, newspapers, and anthologies during the era now known as the Harlem Renaissance. She apparently stopped writing by the end of the 1920s and faded into near obscurity soon thereafter. Her work was rediscovered in the 1980s and 1990s by lesbian, gay, and bisexual scholars, who recognized that Miss Grimké was attracted to women and men and that her inability to act on these desires both inspired her writing and contributed to her ultimately abandoning it.[71]

Garnet C. Wilkinson was a committed educational and civic leader for more than 60 years. Born in South Carolina, he moved to Washington as a child. He attended M Street High School, class of 1898, and received his Bachelor of Arts from Oberlin College in 1902. He earned his Bachelor of Law from Howard University in 1909 and, later, went on to earn his master's degree from the University of Pennsylvania. In 1902, Wilkinson was appointed to the faculty of his high school *alma mater* as a teacher of Latin and mathematics. He devoted much of his time after school hours to the training and instructing of the football and baseball teams, and in assisting the school's cadet corps. He later served as principal of the Armstrong Manual Training School and the Dunbar High School and was one of the first high school coaches in the city as well.[72]

In collaboration with Edwin Henderson, Wilkinson helped form and promote the Inter-Scholastic Athletic Association of Middle Atlantic States (I.S.A.A.) which resulted in various black basketball teams and players from schools, athletic clubs, churches, colleges, and Colored Y.M.C.A. branches emerging in and around Washington, D.C., and the East Coast. I.S.A.A. basketball games launched the spread of the young sport among black Americans and, because of the pioneering work of Henderson and Wilkinson, "black basketball" was born.[73]

Born in 1875 near the end of Reconstruction, in Buckingham County, Virginia, Carter Godwin Woodson was the fifth child of James Henry and Anna Eliza Woodson's seven surviving children. His parents had been born into slavery in Virginia, but his father had escaped during the *Civil War* and served in the Union Army. A skilled carpenter like his father, James Henry was unable to support himself with his craft and was forced into sharecropping. Later, he managed to buy 20 acres near his father's farm and, although the family was extremely poor, their status as landowners afforded them a measure of freedom that contributed to the young Woodson's strong self-reliance.[74]

The Woodson children worked hard on the family farm. Four months out of the year, between harvesting and planting, they attended the nearby school run by their uncles, John Morton Riddle and James Buchanan Riddle. While his uncles served as important role models, Woodson, on the other hand, credited his father, who was illiterate, with teaching him his most valuable lessons; i.e., be polite to everyone, but demand respect as a human being and never betray "the race." Woodson's mother, who had learned to read and write, expected Carter, her favorite child, to work hard and do well in his studies.[75]

In 1892, when he was 17, Woodson followed his older brothers to West Virginia, where they had moved several years earlier to work in the coal mines. There, Woodson fell in love with "the history of the race" through his association with Oliver Jones, a former cook and *Civil War* veteran from Richmond, Virginia. When Jones learned that the younger man could read, he engaged him to read the daily newspapers to him and his customers in exchange for free treats. By subscribing to "black" and "white" newspapers, Jones sought to keep abreast of the news in the black community, as well as in the nation and the world. In acknowledging the educational value of this experience, Carter wrote:

> I learned so much myself because of the much more extensive reading required by him than I probably would have undertaken for my own benefit. ... In seeking through the press information ... for Oliver Jones and his friends, I was learning in an effective way ... history and economics.[76]

To further pursue this interest, Woodson resolved to return to school, and, at the age of 20, moved into his parent's home in Huntington to attend the Frederick Douglass High School. Completing his high school studies in just two years, Mr. Woodson enrolled in Berea College in Kentucky in 1897 with only enough funds to attend full-time for two quarters. Yet, over the next 15 years, Mr. Woodson earned a bachelor of letters degree from Berea. However, because the University did not accept the credits he had earned from Berea College, he earned a second B.A. and the M.A. degree from the University of Chicago. In 1912, He earned the Ph.D. in history from Harvard University. He was the second black in the U.S. to receive a Doctor of Philosophy degree from Harvard.[77] The honor of "first" belongs to W.E.B. Du Bois.

Dr. Woodson did all this while teaching full-time in Malden, West Virginia from 1898 to 1900, serving as principal of Huntington's Frederick

Douglass High School from 1900 to 1903, and teaching in the Philippines from 1903 to 1907. In 1907, while traveling on a six-month world tour, he conducted research at various libraries and studied for a semester at the Sorbonne in Paris. While completing his doctoral dissertation, Dr. Woodson taught in the District public schools, including M Street High School where he taught French, Spanish, English, and history. He travelled widely in Europe and Asia.[78]

Dr. Woodson had a quiet dignity and paid strict attention to discipline. In 1915, he established the Association for the Study of Negro Life and History (ASNLH) and began publishing the *Journal of Negro History* in 1916. From 1919 to 1920, he served as dean of liberal arts at Howard University and was a graduate faculty head and a professor of history. Determined to foster public appreciation of the history of black life and culture, Dr. Woodson and the ASNLH created Negro History Week in 1926. It became Black History Month 50 years later.[79]

In 1933, Dr. Woodson published *The Mis-Education of the Negro*, which argued for making education relevant to blacks in order to counter feelings of inferiority. He created the *Negro History Bulletin*, an informational magazine for school teachers, in 1937.[80]

The M Street High School teachers were as exceptional as the students. Initially, the Board of Trustees sought qualified black college graduates from all over the country, attracting, among others, the young Mary Church and Anna J. Cooper, fresh from Oberlin, as well as Charlotte Atwood, Mary P. Burrill, and Ida Gibbs. Miss Atwood was a graduate of Wellesley College. Miss Burrill was a graduate of Emerson College and the sister-in-law of assistant school superintendent Roscoe C. Bruce. Miss Gibbs was a graduate of Oberlin College in 1884.[81]

By 1905, however, an abundance of young women and men trained at Myrtilla Minor Normal School were available to teach. Eventually, there were many more applicants than openings, so the quality of teachers was assured. Indeed, the number of college and normal school graduates teaching at M Street exceeded those teaching in the white high schools.[82] M Street High School sent black boys and girls to the best colleges in the north for decades; among them, Amherst, Dartmouth, Wellesley, Smith, and Harvard. Black middle-class families felt that there was no black high school in the nation that compared to it.[83]

CHAPTER TEN

THE PAUL LAURENCE DUNBAR HIGH SCHOOL

The new Dunbar High School building at 1st and O Streets, N.W., was dedicated January 15, 1917. It was a magnificent brick, sandstone-trimmed building of Elizabethan architecture with a frontage of 401 feet. The architectural style of the building contained elements of Roman and Greek architecture styles with symmetrical lines and the motif was mixed with Flemish decorative work, such as strapwork, and late-Gothic mullioned and transomed windows. It was christened in honor of the black poet, Paul Lawrence Dunbar, and represented an outlay of more than a half a million dollars. The grounds cost the government $60,000 and the building and equipment, $550,000. There was a faculty of 48 teachers, many of them graduates from the leading colleges and universities in the country. There were 1,252 students, 545 boys and 707 girls.[1]

The Physical Facility

The auditorium had a large stage and a seating capacity for 1,500. It was dominated by a verse written by the school's namesake:

> *Keep a-pluggin' away,*
> *Perseverance still is king;*
> *Time its sure reward will bring;*
> *Work and wait unwearying—*
> *Keep a-pluggin' away.*
> *Keep a-pluggin' away.*

From the greatest to the least
None are from the rule released
Be thou toiler, poet, priest,
Keep a-pluggin' away.

Provisions were made for presenting motion pictures and a pipe organ in the auditorium offered musical advantages that the students had never enjoyed previously. The lunchroom had an up-to-date kitchen for the preparation of hot foods, a factor that contributed greatly to the health and comfort of both teachers and students. The effectiveness of the music department was greatly enhanced by five pianos. Standing on the balconies provided for visitors, one could see the large gymnasiums for both boys and girls. Dressing rooms in each gymnasium were provided with shower baths and the latest equipment available. The printing plant was valued at $4,000. The classes in bookkeeping and accounting had the great advantage of receiving instruction in a real bank, for a banking department had been provided with a safe, windows, and all the other modern facilities found in such an institution.[2]

There was a dining room and a living room, each having contemporary furniture. The girls in the domestic science course could learn by actual experience; how to set a table, arrange furniture, and keep house. Botany, zoology, chemistry, and physics were taught in the laboratories and lecture rooms that occupied practically the whole basement floor. In the department of physics, there was some particularly fine science equipment that represented the careful collection and selection of many years. A wireless outfit was installed to greatly increase the advantage enjoyed by the students.

The library on the second floor was complete in its appointments, with a capacity for 4,337 volumes and facilities for the accommodation of 185 students. On the first floor, were the administration offices and a study hall which had a seating capacity of 106 students. In the armory under the auditorium, the cadets had space enough for several companies and there was a rifle range for target practice. The new building had 35 classrooms, five retiring rooms, an emergency room, seven locker rooms and locker accommodations for 1,500 students. A greenhouse and a roof garden were being constructed and it was hoped that Congress would soon make an appropriation for building a stadium in the areas behind the school.[3]

As the years passed, however, time and the lack of financial and logistical support for the facility took its toll. Blackboards began to crack with confusing lines resembling a map. The cafeteria was dark and crowded. On Mondays, the school was cold. Other inadequacies existed that represented the insensitivity and neglect often found in racially segregated schools. For example, while the colored teachers and their pupils accepted the inconveniences as a matter of course, schools for white citizens were comfortable because an additional staffing of custodians came on duty at 2:00 a.m. to provide heat for the schools opening on Monday after fires had been banked for the weekend.[4]

With the growth of the community and the decay of 40 years, the Dunbar plant was seldom adequate to meet current needs. Even as a new school, it had no stadium. On the other hand, Central High School, which was built the same year for white students as Dunbar had been built for black students, had a beautiful stadium at 13th and Clifton Streets, N.W. Dunbar waited through 10 years of protests and lobbying, while the school's athletic events were held in the city's baseball park, Griffith Stadium. Eventually, a stadium was built that provided for both athletic events and military drill activities for the Cadet Corps.[5]

Each evaluation revealed a shortage of books. A lending service was available from the D.C. Public Library where the Dewey Decimal System[6] was used. There were 4,500 bound volumes, together with magazines, pamphlets, clippings, and pictures in 1944. In 1945, a contribution of $900 was made after a successful project was sponsored by the Student Government Association. As an assignment aimed at vocational guidance, a staff of 10 students assisted the librarian. Books available for home study and fiction could be borrowed for one week.[7]

Another example of the neglect of community needs was the swimming pool. Requests for repairs had been repeatedly denied and it was closed in 1954. The pool was needed for both school and community use, as the immediate neighborhood was underprivileged and far removed from the river. The pool remained closed until 1963, when efforts by several religious groups and the personal interest of Robert F. Kennedy, United States Attorney General, were finally successful.[8]

In the 1940s, several classrooms on the first floor were replaced by new guidance offices and a new emergency room. A registered nurse supervised the clinics held by school physicians, examined pupils following absences for illness, and assisted in many other ways. Near the biology classrooms, a greenhouse provided materials during all seasons, especially in the spring when vegetable plants were sold at reasonable prices to pupils to take home for their "victory gardens." The 1940s also brought a track to the stadium and a modernized cafeteria to the building[9]

In a survey of alumni from classes during the 1930s through 1955, the adequacy of the Dunbar High School building was rated good to excellent by 85.4 percent of the survey respondents and the classrooms were rated good to excellent by 85.5 percent. Among the physical and support facilities in general, only two had higher ratings of excellent than of good. The auditorium was rated excellent by 41.5 percent and the armory rated excellent by 47.5 percent. Most of the other physical and support facilities for the school rated highest in the category of good (see Table 10-1 below).

Rating of Dunbar Physical and Support Facilities (Percent)							
	Excellent	Good	Average	Below Average	Inadequate	Do Not Know	Total
School building	29.3	56.1	12.2	2.4	0	0	100
Classrooms	24.4	61	14.6	0	0	0	100
Laboratories	27.5	42.5	17.5	5	0	7.5	100
Lunchroom/ cafeteria	12.8	48.7	28.2	7.7	0	2.6	100
Auditorium	41.5	39	14.6	4.9	0	0	100
Nurse's Office	19.5	41.5	19.5	0	0	19.5	100
Armory	47.5	30	12.5	7.5	0	2.5	100
Library facilities	32.5	45	10	7.5	0	5	100
Gymnasiums	17.1	43.9	26.8	9.8	2.4	0	100
Printing plant	5.9	26.5	8.8	0	0	58.8	100
Rifle range	17.1	25.8	17.1	0	0	40	100
School stadium	29	42.1	15.8	10.5	0	2.6	100
Swimming pool	30	25	20	15	2.5	7.5	100

Source: Morris, Archie III., "Advancing Urban Educational Policy: Insights from Research on Dunbar High School," *Journal of the Case Studies in Education*, May 2017.

Table 10-1

Despite limitations and deprivations, the school developed its facilities and made the most of its situation. The congestion characteristic of colored schools had been cited as early as 1868, when the Board of Trustees urged parents to send their children to school on the first day of the term, because "we fear that we shall be unable to provide teachers or schoolrooms for more than a third part of the children in these cities" (Washington and Georgetown); and, of course, those who first present themselves will be first entitled to seats." Large classes and crowded buildings were usually expected in colored schools.[10]

The course of study at Dunbar High School included all the academic and business subjects taught in similar schools of accredited standing, as well as domestic science, printing, physical training, and military science.[11] Despite a standard of 25 students per class, Dunbar had student loads of 35 to 40 students per class; occasionally, some classes had enrollments as high as 90.[12] As far back as 1877, there were 40 students per teacher, and a survey in 1953 showed Dunbar's student-teacher ratio to be higher than that of any white senior high school in Washington. This was not a matter of principle, but one of necessity because of the inadequate financial support the black schools received from the white-controlled Board of Education. Obviously, class size was less of a handicap with self-selected and highly motivated students than it would have been with average students or with students lacking self-discipline.[13] In the Dunbar alumni survey, class sizes during the 1930s through 1955 were as shown in Table 10-2 below.

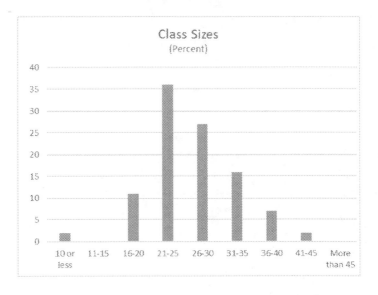

Source: Morris, Archie III., "Advancing Urban Educational Policy: Insights from Research on Dunbar High School," *Journal of the Case Studies in Education*, May 2017.

Table 10-2

Interestingly, Dunbar students' textbooks frequently were hand-me-down books. When the white schools received new editions of their textbooks, their old editions were passed off to the colored schools. Textbooks were issued at the beginning of the semester and collected from the students at the end of the semester. If a textbook was lost or not returned, the student had to pay for its replacement.

Dunbar had its methods and educational philosophy. A large segment of the enrollment consisted of highly motivated, middle-class students whose emphasis on intellectual accomplishment and competitiveness helped maintain the high academic standards the teachers set.[14] Tardiness and absenteeism were not tolerated. Students and teachers respected each other and demonstrated this in their day-to-day demeanor by good manners and courtesy toward one another. At Dunbar, the teachers called everyone by a prefix and their last name, Mr. Jones or Miss Jones. Students referred to teachers by their last name and the appropriate prefix, Dr., Mr./Mrs./Miss. [15]

Dunbar Principals

Dunbar High School was not a neighborhood school. It drew upon the entire black community of Washington for its students. It was in a similarly favorable position to recruit its teachers and principals. Dunbar had its choice of teachers with outstanding academic credentials for decades. Four of its first eight principals graduated from Oberlin and two from Harvard. Some had graduate degrees as well. In fact, Dunbar had three Ph.Ds. on its teaching staff in the 1920s, due to the almost total exclusion of blacks from most college and university faculties. It was 1942 before there was a black senior faculty member at any major white university and that faculty member, Dr. William Allison Davis, was a Dunbar graduate.[16] Dr. Davis was granted tenure at the University of Chicago in 1947 and became a full professor in 1948.

Garnet C. Wilkinson became principal of Dunbar High School in 1916. He was educated in the public schools of the District of Columbia, finishing coursework at the M Street High School in June 1898. Mr. Wilkinson graduated from Oberlin with the degree of A.B. in 1902, and from the Law Department of Howard University in 1909. In 1902, he was appointed as a Latin teacher in the M Street High School and discharged his duties in this new endeavor with enthusiasm and zeal. In November of 1912, he was promoted to the principalship of the Armstrong Manual Training School and transferred to the principalship of the Dunbar High School on July 15, 1916.[17]

Walter Lucius Smith, a graduate of Howard University, succeeded Mr. Wilkinson in 1921. He earned his A.B. in the College of Arts and Sciences in 1902. Mr. Smith had taught mathematics at M Street and Dunbar High Schools since 1905. He was married to Mary Annette Anderson, a professor of English grammar and history at Howard University, who was the first black woman elected *Phi Beta Kappa* at Middlebury College in 1899.[18] During Smith's administration, the school had on its faculty three of the first black women to earn Ph.D. degrees: Georgiana Simpson, Eva B. Dykes, and Anna Julia Cooper. Dunbar also reached its peak enrollment of 1,724 students in 1927 and, for the next decade, the school continued to score above the national average on standardized tests.[19]

Mr. Smith served for 22 years and died in office. He was influential in the development of the football team and the High School Cadet Corps. His high ideals of scholarship inspired many students to enter various colleges throughout the land. No matter what fields of endeavor students entered upon leaving Dunbar, Smith encouraged them to do their best.[20]

In 1943, Dr. Harold A. Haynes, a graduate of the University of Pittsburgh and the University of Chicago, began his term as principal and served for five years.[21] Dr. Haynes graduated from M Street High School in 1906. He and his wife, Euphemia Lofton Haynes, the first black woman to receive a doctorate in mathematics, devoted their lives to education in the District of Columbia. Dr. Haynes received an undergraduate degree in electrical engineering from the University of Pittsburgh in 1910, a master's degree in Education from the University of Chicago in 1930, and a Doctor of Education from New York University in 1946. He taught at Howard University from 1912 to 1918, and then moved to the District public schools where he taught Applied Electricity at Armstrong High School from 1919 to 1932. Dr. Haynes served as principal at Browne Junior High School from 1932 to 1940, Armstrong High School from 1940 to 1943, and Dunbar High School from 1943 to 1947.[22]

In 1948, Dr. Haynes was named associate superintendent of schools and, in 1951, he became the first Assistant Superintendent of Schools in Charge of District 2, also known as the Superintendent of Colored Schools in the District of Columbia's segregated school system. He continued in that position until the Supreme Court's *Brown vs. Board of Education* decision forced the reorganization and integration of the District's school system. After the reorganization of the District of Columbia's public school system in 1955, Dr. Haynes was named deputy superintendent, a post he held until he retired in 1958.[23]

Charles Sumner Lofton, who was a graduate of Dunbar, became principal of the high school from 1948 to 1964. Mr. Lofton graduated from Howard University and received a master's degree in history there in 1934. He taught the next year at what was then known as Virginia State College in Petersburg, and then became a history teacher at Armstrong High School in Washington. During *World War II*, he was an assistant professor of history in the Army's specialized training program at Howard while still working at Armstrong. In 1946, he became the first principal of the Veterans High School Center, a facility set up to educate veterans in academics and trades. Two years later, he was appointed principal of Dunbar.[24]

During his appointment as principal of Dunbar High School in 1948, Mr. Lofton insisted on high academic standards, neat dress, and proper behavior. He instilled confidence in his students that they could succeed, even in a racially segregated society. During the 1950s, when all black schools in the district were racially segregated, Dunbar sent 80 percent of its graduates on to higher education. In 1964, Mr. Lofton was named executive assistant to the superintendent of schools, the position from which he retired in 1970. He then became executive assistant to the president of the District of Columbia Teachers College for the next 10 years, during the period in which D.C. Teachers College, Federal City College, and the Washington Technical Institute were merged into the University of the District of Columbia. He retired in 1980.[25]

While he was a principal, Mr. Lofton continued to study, taking classes at Catholic, Georgetown, and New York universities. He also received a diploma from the Alliance Francaise in Paris. He traveled to Stockholm and Russia, as part of a Eugene and Agnes Meyer Foundation fellowship, and visited Israel and Jordan on an Israeli Foundation Travel Award. Mayors Walter Washington and Marion Barry both gave him the Mayor's Distinguished Service Award. He also served on several city committees and boards and consulted for the education and defense departments. Mr. Lofton was on the boards of the Woodward Foundation, the D.C. Chapter of the United Nations, the Metropolitan Police Boys Club, the Southeast Neighborhood House, the D.C. Youth Orchestra Program, and the Society for the Prevention of Cruelty to Animals. He was a past chairman of the Eugene and Agnes Meyer Foundation Fellowship committee and the Cafritz Foundation Fellowship committee, past president of the Columbian Educational Association, and the first black president of the D.C. chapter of the National Association of Secondary School Principals.[26]

Dunbar Faculty

Among the better-known faculty members were Mary Church Terrell; Jessie Fauset, later the literary editor of the *Crisis*; Ida A. Gibbs, who later became a leader in the Pan African movement after *World War I* and married William Henry Hunt, the U.S. consul to Tamafare and France; Angelina Grimké, political activist, abolitionist, women's rights advocate, and supporter of the women's suffrage movement; and Carter G. Woodson, historian, author, journalist, and the founder of the Association for the Study of Negro Life and History (ASANH). These teachers were also members of quite prominent families in the community.

Twenty of the 30 faculty members at the school between 1916 and 1921 had degrees from prestigious northern colleges, including Harvard, Yale, Oberlin, Amherst, Dartmouth, and Bowdoin. Five others had degrees from Howard University, the premier black school of higher education in the United States. The faculty was as committed to excellence among the students as it was distinguished. Students were admitted based on their academic promise and they were not promoted unless they continued to display that promise. One student reportedly took seven years to graduate. The faculty and administration were not about to promote him just to push him through the system. However, if he adhered to the school's values of discipline and good behavior, he could stay until he could *legitimately* pass.[27]

Graduate study was not required to teach before 1920, but, even then, Dunbar had several teachers with advanced degrees in liberal arts, medicine and law. Among these were Henri L. Bailey, John W. Cromwell, Mary E. Cromwell, Juanita P. Howard, William T. S. Jackson, Harriet E. Riggs, Louis H. Russell, Nelson E. Weatherless, and Carter G. Woodson. In the 1920s, Dunbar had three teachers with Ph.D. degrees: Anna J. Cooper, University of Paris; Eva B. Dykes, Radcliffe; and Georgiana R. Simpson, University of Chicago. Many other teachers took courses in methods and kept their professional zeal alive, while some enhanced their personal experience with continuing study and travel abroad.[28]

The Commitment of the Dunbar Teaching Staff

Dunbar High School faculty members were committed to their students and worked hard to inspire and train black youth for successful careers and responsible citizenship. They were dedicated in their efforts to develop students' talents in academics, dramatics, music, and art, and instilled in them a sound sense of values and morals.[29]

In the 1930s, there was a marked decline in the number of Dunbar graduates entering Northern and Ivy League colleges. There was a revival of the tradition in the 1940s when Principal Harold Haynes and a committee of teachers, known as the College Bureau, developed a coaching program that was conducted after school hours. During the normal school hours, crowded classes and heterogeneous groups often prevented intensive classroom work for honor students. This after-hours project prepared promising students for college entrance examinations.[30]

Mrs. Mary G. Hundley, chairperson of the College Bureau, and her committee of teachers overcame many obstacles in the 1940s. From 1947 to 1955, Mrs. Hundley gave an annual Christmas party at her home (125 Thomas Street, N.W.) for promising seniors and students returning from colleges for the holiday break. The potential college students were inspired and encouraged by informal contact with recent Dunbar graduates who were currently matriculating at such prestigious schools as Yale, Vassar, Sarah Lawrence, and Skidmore. These schools gave their first scholarships to Dunbar during this period when *World War II* had brought about more interracial contacts throughout the country. Americans were becoming aware of the limitations of Jim Crow segregation.[31] Separate but equal facilities for each race did not provide equal public services; i.e., schools, hospitals, prisons, etc.[32]

As a member of the College Bureau, Miss Mary E. Cromwell, a mathematics instructor and home room teacher of ambitious girls, guided each group through three years of college preparation. She encouraged them to apply early, visited their homes, and advised parents on financial problems.[33] Colonel Harry O. Attwood, military instructor, encouraged boys to apply to West Point and Annapolis. He helped ease racial prejudice in these federal institutions where black males had not been welcome.[34]

In music, many talented black youths were discovered and developed by dedicated teachers. The Boys' Glee Club was organized in 1904 by Mr. Gerald Tyler and regrouped by Mr. Ernest R. Amos a decade later. Operettas were presented and special choruses for boys and girls in the 1920s were followed by an orchestra conducted by Mr. Henry L. Grant. Miss Mary L Europe arranged annual assembly programs where the Howard University School of Music performed on various occasions. These assemblies inspired Dunbar students to prepare for musical careers. In gratitude for her inspiration and encouragement in his youth, Lawrence

Whisonant (Larry Winters), an internationally known baritone, sang at Miss Europe's funeral. Calm, smiling, and faithful, Miss Europe was affectionately called "Little Mary" by the students whom she trained in music theory and choral expression.[35]

Always interested in developing musical talent, Miss Europe organized a special chorus of boys and girls as early as 1919. Later, she formed a kantoren group of students who continued to sing even after graduation from Dunbar. Miss Europe's work with students extended into the localities and churches, hospitals, community centers, service clubs, and camps that enjoyed programs that she sponsored. Her work in the school was not confined to her department alone, for she assisted in numerous projects. In 1918, to spread Christmas cheer and to afford students the opportunity to manage a school institution modeled after a government department, she established the Dunbar Post Office.[36] Furthermore, The *Alma Mater* for Dunbar was composed by two teachers at Dunbar; Dr. Anna J. Cooper wrote the words and Miss Europe wrote the music.[37]

Mary P. Burrill, a 1901 M Street High School alumnus who taught English and drama, gave many years of outstanding service in teaching dramatics and stagecraft. As an early 20th-century black female playwright, two of her best-known plays were published in 1919. "They That Sit in Darkness" was published in the *Birth Control Review*, a monthly publication advocating reproductive rights for women, and the other, "Aftermath," was published in the *Liberator*, edited by socialist Max Eastman. In training students in speech and acting, she included play performances and interpretative readings. Miss Burrill emphasized speech and diction and held her charges to very high standards.[38] Correspondingly, Helen C. Nash, an English teacher at Dunbar from 1931 to 1944, sponsored The House Beautiful Club that gave both boys and girls the opportunity to learn what constituted good taste in furnishing and decorating the home. She quietly brightened the lives of many students.[39]

Boys and girls, who had never entered or appeared on a platform, surprised their classmates and themselves by playing roles on stage under Miss Burrill's direction in the school auditorium. Students from disadvantaged homes, whose race barred them from the customary cultural influences, found themselves developing in speech, posture, and poise. At one period, Miss Burrill persuaded Principal Walter Smith to introduce a daily program of posture drill at the beginning of each class period throughout the school.[40] One of her prized students was Willis Richardson, who would later become the first black dramatist to have a play produced on Broadway. Another was May Miller, who published her first play, *Pandora's Box*, while still a student at Dunbar.[41]

With the growth of oratorical contests in the 1920s and 1930s, Lillian S. Brown, who taught English, became well known for training contest winners. Plus, before racial barriers were lifted in the 1940s, Maude B. Allen, a teacher of speech, brought to the school contacts with Northwestern University, with actors Maurice Evans (an English actor noted for his interpretations of Shakespearean characters), and local theater managers. Refusal to admit blacks to theaters was accompanied by problems of renting costumes. James V. Mulligan, a local jeweler who sold class rings to Dunbar senior students for many years, was a tactful intermediary. Acting as a "straw man," he obtained costumes for Dunbar plays by alleging that he was acting on behalf of white students in Virginia.[42]

In art, the tradition of excellence and dedication was faithfully upheld by Thomas W. Hunster, William D. Nixon, and Samuel D. Milton. They developed and encouraged talented black youth to enter local contests and to prepare for careers in teaching and commercial art. Stage settings for all school plays were produced by these art teachers and their students. In the 1940s, Helen Cunningham produced an annual tableaux and elaborate murals for the Christmas season. These teachers brought light and inspiration to many underprivileged youths whose traditional contacts were limited by their racial environs.[43] Mr. Nixon also designed the school seal, a handsome bronze plaque. It was classic in its conception and carefully hand-chased to bring out the natural beauty of the metal. Its cardinal features were the class motto, *Carpe Diem*, and a *fleur-de-lis* enshrined between two cornucopias overflowing with fruit.[44]

Many Dunbar teachers contributed aid to needy students or bought equipment for their work with money from their own limited income. Funds for various student loans were sponsored by the Dunbar faculty who, from their own resources, gave an annual scholarship of $250 to a promising student for many years. Dunbar graduates also offered annual scholarships to worthy students. The College Alumnae Club, *Phi Delta Kappa* Sorority, the Elks, and several college fraternities offered aid and educational programs to students at various times. Anna L. Costin, a school teacher, willed $10,000 for scholarships for black female high school graduates of merit and promise. Caroline E. Parke, an algebra teacher for nearly fifty years, bequeathed a scholarship fund to the school; she had entered the Preparatory School for Colored Youth in 1870.[45]

The contributions of Julia E. Brooks, who taught English and Spanish from 1916 to 1922 and was assistant principal from 1922 to 1948, were outstanding and especially noteworthy. As dean of girls at Dunbar, Miss Brooks handled the problems of more than 1,000 girls, female faculty, and the entire school. She had an attractive office with flowers, plants, current literature, a stamp collection, and books and literature reflecting her travels. She managed the lunchroom, posted slogans on table manners, and sold candy to equip the faculty dining room. Miss Brooks sponsored the *Handbook* that provided information for new students and rules of conduct and etiquette. She subsidized the school Christmas tree and stayed late to supervise the distribution of baskets of food to needy families.[46]

Miss Brooks found part-time jobs for students, patronized community projects, and promoted worthy causes. She also sponsored the Dunbar Alumni Scholarship, sold candy to buy a set of encyclopedias for Dunbar, and gave freely of her means on all occasions. She chaperoned dances, trips, and senior picnics, always staying until the last pupil had left. Her account with the florist covered emergencies of illness or death among the faculty and staff. She supported homeroom programs of discussion and cultural projects, directed the clubs, and provided guidance and leadership for sundry extra-curricular activities.[47]

Dunbar principals and faculty lived in the District of Columbia, primarily in such neighborhoods as Georgetown, Le Droit Park, and the U Street Corridor. The teachers knew the people in their communities and, often, their family circumstances. They were respected professionals in their communities. Thus, Dunbar teachers had civic interests and a public spirit that led them to promote noble causes for the benefit of their students. Neval H. Thomas, a history teacher, spent ten years protesting and lobbying to secure an appropriation by Congress for a stadium behind the school. A colorful figure, he gave illustrated lectures on his travels in the Middle East and served as president of the local chapter of the National Association for the Advancement of Colored People (NAACP) in the 1920s.[48] William Nixon served the community for 20 years after his retirement. He was president of the Oldest Inhabitants, Inc., a leader in many civic organizations, and was active in the struggle to end racial discrimination in local restaurants.[49]

James C. Wright, who taught typewriting, also was a lobbyist on behalf of students. In the 1930s, he spent a decade securing the 3-cent carfare law for local school children. A pen used to sign the bill was given to him by President Franklin D. Roosevelt. The pen is a cherished possession of Dunbar. It is framed with a diamond medal awarded to Mr. Wright by the Underwood Typing Company for his skill in teaching Cortez Peters, Jr., a contest winner who later founded a local business school.[50] Mr. Peters won twelve international typing contests throughout the course of his life. He set a typing world record of 225 words per minute without a single mistake (an average of 18.75 keystrokes per second). His top recorded finger speed was 297 wpm.

Haley G. Douglass was a grandson of the abolitionist, Frederick Douglass, and taught science and history for 46 years. He had played football at Harvard and coached football teams in the 1910s and 1920s. His teams had an enviable record and photographs of the teams hung on the walls of a school corridor near the entrance to the Dunbar building.[51] He also was the mayor of Highland Beach, Maryland, from 1928 to 1953.

Alumni Assessment of Faculty and Staff

The alumni survey respondents believe the strengths of the Dunbar High School academic program were its faculty and principals (44 percent), its students (32 percent), and its curriculum (24 percent). They thought the teachers and principals were very well qualified and were dedicated to their students.

Thirty percent of the survey respondents felt that faculty had an impact on the success of the school's efforts to prepare students to function in the mainstream American society and the black community. For 12.5 percent, it was important that black teachers stressed the importance of education and excellence as a means of improving the status of the Negro. Another 20 percent felt the students were generally well prepared, despite a lack of resources, because teachers stressed the development of self-confidence, self-discipline, and perseverance as valued traits. Graduates were fortunate to have teachers at the Dunbar High School who were the cream of the crop because the opportunities for jobs in the larger society were limited or nonexistent. A special benefit was that the faculty that taught in the segregated schools and lived in the segregated black communities.

The survey respondents have very positive impressions of the Dunbar faculty as a group. Ratings in knowledge of their respective subjects, preparation for class, and communications in class were 95+ percent in the range of above average to outstanding. The lowest ranked categories were effective use of outside speakers in the classroom, which was rated 84.2 percent for average or above, and the opportunity to interact socially with the faculty, which was rated 77.5 percent for average or above. See Table 10-3 below.

Rating of Dunbar Faculty (Percent)						
	Out-standing	Above Average	Average	Below Average	Inadequate	Total
Exposure to a variety of points of view	65	27.5	7.5	0	0	100
Preparation of your teachers for class	73.8	19	4.8	2.4	0	100
The faculty's knowledge of their respective subjects	80.9	14.3	4.8	0	0	100
Ability to communicate clearly in class	64.3	30.9	4.8	0	0	100
Accessibility of the faculty outside the classroom	30	40	27.5	2.5	0	100
Opportunity to interact socially with the faculty	17.5	27.5	32.5	20	2.5	100
Assistance by the faculty in gaining college/university entrance and/or employment assistance	55	22.5	15	5	2.5	100
Effective use of outside speakers in the classroom	18.4	39.5	26.3	10.5	5.3	100
The quality of academic advising	57.5	27.5	10	2.5	2.5	100

The quality of career advising	35	30	27.5	5	2.5	100
The fairness of grading systems used	48.9	31.7	14.6	2.4	2.4	100

Source: Morris, Archie III., "Advancing Urban Educational Policy: Insights from Research on Dunbar High School," *Journal of the Case Studies in Education*, May 2017.

Table 10-3

The principal for 90 percent of the survey respondents when they attended the Dunbar High School was Charles S. Lofton. Five percent had Dr. Harold A. Haynes as their principal and another five percent had Walter L. Smith. The school principal supervised, in addition to faculty, the assistant principal(s), a secretary/clerical staff, the Reserve Officers' Training Corps (ROTC) instructor, and the janitorial staff. The survey respondents, as students, apparently had positive experiences across the board with the Dunbar High School principals and their administrative staff (see Table 10-4 below).

Rating of Dunbar Principals and Administrative Staff (Percent)						
	Out-standing	Above Average	Average	Below Average	Inadequate	Total
Principal	90.2	4.9	4.9	0	0	100
Assistant principal(s)	76.3	18.4	5.3	0	0	100
Secretary/clerical staff	57.1	25.8	17.1	0	0	100
ROTC instructor	50	33.4	13.3	3.33	0	100
Janitorial staff	37.1	51.5	11.4	0	0	100

Source: Morris, Archie III., "Advancing Urban Educational Policy: Insights from Research on Dunbar High School," *Journal of the Case Studies in Education*, May 2017.

Table 10-4

The Dunbar High School faculty, overall, was highly praised by all survey respondents. While 50 percent of survey respondents did not name a specific teacher as most outstanding, several teachers were named because they were admired for individual reasons:

Lillian S. Brown	15.8%
Frank Perkins	13.2%
Madison W. Tignor	5.3%
Mary G. Hundley	5.3%
Bertha McNeil	5.3%
Dorothy D. Lucas	5.3%

The survey respondents had a high regard for the Dunbar High School faculty as a group, but there were 83.8 percent who had specific reasons to remember individual teachers. Some 37.8 percent remembered faculty members for their general knowledge, teaching ability and subject matter expertise. Teachers made certain that students understood the subject matter and related the subject concepts to the real world. Many took every opportunity to make classes a teachable moment and build student self-confidence. Faculty was believed by 5.4 percent of the respondents to have put a great deal of preparation and effort into their work.

Members of the faculty were perceived by 5.4 percent of the respondents to be strong people who served as mentors and role models. In fact, 5.4 percent said they were inspired by their teachers and 8.1 percent indicated faculty helped prepare them for life experiences after they completed high school. Students were respected by the faculty, but teachers also insisted that all their pupils behave as ladies and gentlemen. The teachers called everybody by a prefix and their last name, Mr. Jones or Miss Jones, and students referred to teachers by their last name and the appropriate prefix, Dr., Mr./Mrs./Miss.

Neither faculty or staff were tolerant of tardiness, absenteeism, misbehavior, or disruptions in Dunbar High School classes, but 10.8 percent of survey respondents felt their teachers were kind and interested in the students.

CHAPTER ELEVEN

THE DUNBAR PARADIGM

The Dunbar student body was young and above average in their mental development. Thus, students tended to be at grade level for their age group, or higher if they had skipped grade levels in elementary or middle schools. In earlier times, District of Columbia school policy allowed students to be placed in classes according to their progress and accomplishments rather than simply by age. In this respect, one cannot ignore the basic elementary school training that students got before they entered Dunbar. Old-time elementary school teachers did not have a broad education, but they knew what they knew. They knew arithmetic and they knew English grammar. Most of all, they were totally dedicated to teaching. Without that, black students would not have excelled at Dunbar.[1]

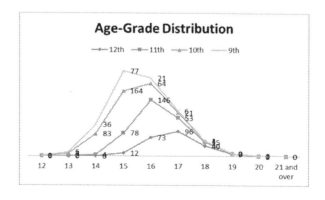

Source: Mary Gibson Hundley, *The Dunbar Story,* p. 25.

Table 11-1

On their way to Dunbar High School, alumni survey respondents indicate that they basically came through the segregated District of Columbia Public School system. Ninety-two percent attended elementary school in Washington, DC, six percent in Baltimore, Maryland, and two percent in Mechanicsburg, Pennsylvania. Ninety-eight percent attended middle school/junior high school in Washington and two percent in Mechanicsburg.

Statement of Philosophy and Objectives

In November 1944, the Dunbar faculty prepared a statement of its philosophy and objectives for an evaluation by the Commission on Secondary Schools of the Middle States Association of Colleges and Secondary Schools.[2]

The Philosophy of Dunbar High School

1. We believe that, in a democracy, free secondary education should be provided for all, regardless of race, except those whose physical or mental abnormalities make such training impossible.

2. Adapted to their capabilities, the curriculum should be broad and modern enough to meet the requirements of all pupils according to their present and future interests and needs. It should be differentiated, yet socially integrated, providing opportunities for pupils in acquiring, organizing, and evaluating knowledge and skills. Through co-curricular activities he should acquire training in leadership and social adjustment.

3. We believe that each pupil should be treated as a distinct personality, who should be assisted in achieving the maximum development of which he is capable. Methods should be used which would assist his systematic learning through actual participation, with the teacher cooperating with an attitude of cooperation characterized by constructive and sympathetic helpfulness.

4. The staff should be adequate to meet the needs of the pupil population. It should be secure in tenure and salary. Preparation

should include a liberal education, comprising subject matter specialization as well as professional resourcefulness. The teachers should represent a cross-section of colleges and ages. The staff should be highly intelligent and professionally minded with undiminishing interest in educational problems. The ethics of the profession should always be meticulously observed. Social consciousness should be included, for upon the teachers of youth in our peculiar social pattern rests the responsibility of protesting against injustices in the social order.

5. The pupil should be developed into a social-minded citizen with emphasis on appropriate conduct in the home, community, nation and the world. The secondary school should emphasize the relationship of the pupil to his immediate and future environment. The pupil should be willing to cooperate with others in obtaining and maintaining a democratic society, regardless of differences in race, nationality, or religion. For its outcomes, the school is directly responsible to society.

6. As objectives, the pupil should be physically fit, emotionally poised, morally conscious, and mentally alert. He should have an adequate preparation in ideals, skills, knowledge, and habits for more advanced training that will make him economically successful. He should be trained in habits of accurate thinking, which will permit him to make wise decisions. He should have a wide range of interests, a worthwhile philosophy of life, esthetic appreciations, the ability to become well integrated socially, a sensitiveness to his peculiar social problems and the ability to use his leisure in a worthy manner.

The faculty also established objectives for the school.[3]

Objectives of the Dunbar High School

1. To provide opportunity for progressive intellectual development, taking into consideration individual differences.
2. To develop interests, appreciations, knowledge and skills that enrich and beautify life.

3. To develop attitudes that will result in good health habits.
4. To provide situations that will encourage the development of desirable character and personality traits.
5. To provide opportunities for the development of attitudes and habits of good citizenship, in terms of honest respect for all human personality.

Curriculum

The curriculum through the years consisted mainly of the usual academic courses; English, Latin, French, Spanish, German, history, mathematics, and science. Greek was taught before 1920. Physical education, music and art were minor subjects, while, in the 1920s, major music and art were introduced. German was eliminated in the 1920s and 1930s. Later additions were home economics, aviation, and driver education as electives.[4] At M Street and Dunbar, there was no thought of an Africa-based learning situation. Questions of immigration and back to Africa movements had been debated at length since the days of slavery and questions of black relocation had been settled. Citizenship was unequivocally granted to black Americans in 1868 with ratification of the Fourteenth Amendment to the *U.S. Constitution*. Thus, black education was equated with freedom and assimilation, and Dunbar students were being prepared to live in the United States of America.

Ostensibly, Dunbar education was influenced by the early New England school teachers who, after the *Civil War*, taught the first of the newly freed slaves. They wanted to train black people as they, themselves, had been trained in the North; the "three R's" at the elementary level, with such subjects as Latin, Greek, geometry, and rhetoric coming in at the secondary and college levels.[5] As 80 percent of the graduates entered higher institutions, college entrance requirements had a direct influence upon the choice of electives. Advanced classes in foreign languages were often lost because Congress required at least 15 pupils in a class. Latin was the exception, with four years always offered. In the 1920s and 1930s, third-year French and Spanish were taught regularly, fourth-year French only once.[6]

Pupil enrollment grew from 45 in 1870 to 1,387 in 1945. The school outgrew the physical plant several times. In June 1877, there were 11 graduates; in June 1945, there were 213. The peak enrollment after 1945 was approximately 1,700 before the opening of Spingarn High School in 1952 to alleviate the overcrowding. While, at first, the school was traditionally classical in its curriculum, new courses were developed to meet vocational needs and to provide for individual differences. The required English courses were supplemented by courses in speech, dramatics, journalism, and formal grammar. Major art and music courses, including orchestra, developed artistic and musical talent. Physical education included a constructive health program with a school nurse and visiting physicians and dentists. The school kept pace with community growth and needs.[7]

From its inception in 1870 as the Preparatory High School for Colored Youth, Dunbar was the only opportunity among black people of the nation's capital to prepare for leadership. These were a people who had been recently freed from slavery and they were being guided by friends of the abolitionist tradition to develop to their utmost potential. The curriculum was designed in the tradition of a reputable, quality American school. The students' achievements represented the struggle and progress of an underprivileged people who lived in a paradoxical situation of federal support without franchise or municipal autonomy.[8]

The curriculum at M Street/Dunbar represented learning as derived from the concept of a classical education, a three-part process of training the mind. This classical pattern is called the *trivium*, which consists of grammar, dialectic, and rhetoric. The students learn the grammar of each subject and that subject's "particulars." They next learn dialectic, or the relationships of these to one another, and then go on to learn rhetoric; i.e., how to express what they have learned in an effective and coherent fashion. The purpose of following this pattern is not to teach the student everything there is to know, but rather to establish in the student a habit of mind which instinctively knows how to learn new material when the formal schooling process is only a faint memory. The student is not so much taught what to think, he is shown how to think.[9]

In classical learning, the 12 years of education consist of three repetitions of the same four-year pattern: the ancients (5000 B.C.-A.D. 400), the medieval period through the early Renaissance (400-1600), the late Renaissance through early modern times (1600-1850), and modern times (1850-present). Youth learn these four time periods at varying levels; simple for grades through 4, more difficult in grades 5 through 8 (when the student begins to read original sources). Learning takes an even more complex approach in grades 9 through 12, when the student works through these time periods using original sources (from Homer to Hitler) and, also, can pursue an interest (music, dance, technology, medicine, biology, creative writing) in depth.[10]

The other subject areas of the curriculum are linked to history studies. The student who is working on ancient history will read Greek and Roman mythology, the tales of the *Iliad* and *Odyssey*, early medieval writings, Chinese and Japanese fairy tales, and (for the older student) the classical texts of Plato, Herodotus, Virgil, Aristotle. He will read *Beowulf*, Dante, Chaucer, and Shakespeare the following year, when he is studying medieval and early Renaissance history. When the 18th and 19th centuries are studied, he starts with Swift (*Gulliver's Travels*) and ends with Dickens. Finally, he reads modern literature as he is studying contemporary history.[11]

The sciences are studied in a four-year pattern that roughly corresponds to the period of scientific discovery: biology, classification, and the human body (subjects known to the ancients); earth science and basic astronomy (which flowered during the early Renaissance); chemistry (which came into its own during the early modern period; and basic physics (very modern subject).[12]

The M Street/Dunbar curriculum followed the classical pattern of the *trivium*. This is readily discerned when one examines the coursework offered from the school's foundation as a college preparatory institution. For example, in the first semesters of 1943-44 and 1944-45, students were enrolled in the following curriculum subjects shown below in Table 11-2:[13]

Dunbar High School Subject Matter (First Semester 1943-44 and 1944-45	
English 1-8	Ancient History 1
Formal Grammar	Medieval History 2
Dramatics 1-2	Modern European History 3-4
Journalism	American History 7-8
Creative Writing	International Relations
	Civics
	Economics
	Sociology
	Latin American History

Elementary Algebra 1-2 Plane Geometry 3-4 Solid Geometry 5 Intermediate Algebra 6A-6B Trigonometry 7	Music Appreciation Choral Music Piano Music Theory Orchestra Minor Music
French 1-2 Pre-Induction French German 1-3 Pre-Induction German Spanish 1-4 Pre-induction Spanish Latin 1-7	Biology 1-2 Chemistry 1-3 Physics 1-2 Aviation 1-3 Electricity Mechanics
Typewriting 1-3 Shorthand 1-2 General Business	Major Drawing Minor Drawing Mechanical drawing

Source: Mary Gibson Hundley, *The Dunbar Story,* pp. 26-29.

Table 11-2

The requirements for graduation were 32 points.[14] Required courses were:

English 1-8	American History 7-8
Algebra 1-2	Biology 1-2 or
Health Education 1-8	Physics 1-2 or
(minor)	Chemistry 1-2

Additional electives had to be taken so that the entire number of points, both required and elective, would be 32 at the time of graduation. A point equaled ½ units or one semester major. A major equals five hours a week. A minor equaled two hours a week. Ninth grade art and music were required minor subjects. Electives were offered at various school levels.[15]

Alumni remember Dunbar as a college preparatory school. However, as its students developed interests pertaining to manual arts and business, programs were spun off which resulted in the establishment of two other high schools, Armstrong Technical High School and Cardozo High School. Courses available to the Dunbar students and the percentage of participation by the survey respondents are listed in Table 11-3 below.

Courses Studied by Students at Dunbar High School					
Course	Percent	Course	Percent	Course	Percent
English	93	Typewriting	50	Orchestra	0
Formal Grammar	59	Shorthand	4	Minor Music	9
Dramatics	2	General Business	9	Biology	72
Journalism	9	Ancient History	28	Chemistry	59
Creative Writing	9	Medieval History	9	Physics	24
Elementary Algebra	52	Modern European History	11	Aviation	2
Plane Geometry	72	American History	78	Health Education	43
Solid Geometry	20	Negro History	20	Electricity	2
Intermediate Algebra	50	International Relations	7	Mechanics	2
Trigonometry	20	Civics	37	Major Drawing	2
French	33	Economics	9	Minor Drawing	4
Pre-Induction French	0	Sociology	20	Mechanical drawing	9
German	17	Latin American History	0	Military Science	30
Pre-Induction German	2	Music Appreciation	33	Other (please specify)	
Spanish	22	Choral Music	17	Driver Education	4
Pre-induction Spanish	0	Piano	0	Gym for health	2
Latin	65	Music Theory	7		

Source: Morris, Archie III., "Advancing Urban Educational Policy: Insights from Research on Dunbar High School," *Journal of the Case Studies in Education*, May 2017.

Table 11-3

Cadet Corps Drill Teams

If any single activity epitomized the discipline and high standards of the schools and the black community in Washington, it was the high school Cadet Corps Drill Teams. The Cadets Corps, a precursor of the Junior ROTC, was comprised of male high school students. The purpose of the corps was to teach disciple and leadership.

Like most of America at that time, the Cadet Corps was segregated. In 1882, two companies of High School Cadets were organized for white high schools and the first competitive drill for white students was held in 1888. The first colored high school cadets were organized in 1888 at M Street High by Christian Fleetwood. It was largely through the efforts of Mr. Fleetwood that the Colored High School Cadet Corps was established in the Preparatory High School for Colored Youth six years after its founding in the white schools. [16]

Mr. Fleetwood had joined the Union army in 1863 and served as a sergeant major with the Fourth U.S. Colored Infantry until May 1866. For saving his regimental colors at the battle of Chaffin's Farm, Virginia, on September 29, 1864, he received the Medal of Honor. After the war, he organized and commanded units in the District of Columbia Militia and the D.C. National Guard. He lived in a house on U Street in Northwest with his wife Sara and became a leading citizen in the Washington black community, particularly in its churches. Mr. Fleetwood helped establish the cadet training for blacks primarily to benefit black aspirants to West Point, who, by and large, were not admitted to military prep schools. [17]

The Cadet Corps was a great source of school and community pride. Cadets marched in parades, including presidential inaugural parades, escorted dignitaries, and participated in drills. Being in the high school Cadet Corps was a family tradition for many households. One of the highest honors was to be commissioned as an officer in one's senior year. In addition to being in command, an officer wore a saber while lesser ranks carried a heavy rifle. On the day of the drill competition, thousands of black pedestrians passed through the streets of the city carrying the colors of the school of their choice. Hundreds of automobiles, elaborately decorated with school colors and loaded with merrymakers, raced noisily through the streets resounding the joy of their occupants. The competitive drill not only accentuated the popularity of the winning school for the successive year by increasing attendance and strengthening the morale of the student body, but it enhanced the status of the successful officers. This status, which the individual won in the competitive drill, remained with him for many years in all his future activities. [18]

By the 1930s, the Cadet Corps had become interwoven into the fabric of the school system, with 30 companies and seven bands distributed among the District's seven high schools. A faculty member, who was either an Army reserve officer or had military training, ran the cadet organization in each school. A retired Army officer served as professor of military science and tactics and supervised the entire corps. District regulations made "drill" compulsory for boys over 14 years of age, and cadets received credit for physical education. Only participation in varsity athletics, physical unfitness, or parental objection excused a boy from serving. Administrators and faculty found that the best cadets were also the best students, so they supported the corps and emphasized its physical and social benefits.[19]

Each of Washington's black high schools, Dunbar, Armstrong, and Cardozo, had several cadet companies that, together, formed the Twenty-Fourth Regiment. The black units had black instructors and a separate professor of military science and tactics. Black cadets did not participate in the annual competitive drills with whites, but, beginning in 1902, held their own annual competitive drill at the District's Griffith Stadium. The annual drill was a major event in the black community, drawing thousands of spectators, including black leaders like Mary McLeod Bethune. Dunbar units usually dominated the competition and distinguished members of Washington's black community presented the awards.[20]

The U.S. Infantry Drill Regulations were used for instruction of the cadets. The program taught discipline, stressed comportment, and rewarded scholastic achievement. A request from the faculty adviser was a command to be obeyed and a cadet treated it as he would a request from a parent. Cadets began their careers as privates and promotions were based strictly upon performance. The cadets were highly competitive and determined to safeguard their school's honor. Participation in the Cadet Corps was more than a casual activity and students learned to compete and work as a team. Cadets wore their dress uniforms to school.[21] They drilled twice a week from 7:30 to 9:00 in the morning. As the annual competition approached, they drilled three times a week.[22]

Military drill also became an important part of the curriculum at Dunbar High School for girls as well as for boys. There was a cadet corps for girls in the 1920s and 1940s that was closely aligned with the Physical Education Department. The suffragist movement of the 1920s may have inspired this. Several companies engaged in intramural competition, essentially imitating the boys' drill. Good posture and respect for authority were tangible effects of cadet training for girls.[23]

Forty percent of the alumni survey respondents participated in the Washington High School Cadet Corps Drill Teams program while at the Dunbar High School. Sixty percent did not. Twenty percent of the participants considered the Dunbar ROTC program to be outstanding. It was indicated by 48 percent of the respondents that the ROTC program developed leadership skills, discipline, and citizenship. Another 18 percent said it instilled self-discipline and responsibility. Thirteen percent regretted not being able to participate due to the distance travelled to and from school and the requirement to arrive before the start of classes.

Discipline

Dunbar used corporal punishment to discipline students and parents supported this practice. Many of the male students specifically remember the large paddle in the administrative offices at Dunbar. When a principal in a black school is given the authority to administer corporal punishment at the insistence of the parents, there is clearly more here than meets the eye. The important question was not whether corporal punishment was good or bad, any more than the important question about Dunbar students really needing Latin. The point is that certain human relations are essential to the educational process. When these conditions are met, then education can go forward regardless of methods, educational philosophy, or physical plant.[24]

A large majority of Dunbar students lived in a setting of a traditional, two-parent family. The mother was the more emotionally available, loving, physically affectionate, and more patient than the father. However, the father had a unique disciplinary role to play; especially for boys. The father established the moral standard for the children and contributed the most to their language and cognitive behavior. Thus, discipline at Dunbar was effective largely because of family pride. No one wanted to embarrass their family by being a discipline problem or, for that matter, being a poor student. Sitting on the principal's bench brought shame on a student, as did any other chastisement, assignment to study hall, or penalties.

Worse of all was having one's parents called by a teacher or principal when there was any violation of school rules or standards. It was important to a student that he or she have a good reputation in front of his or her peers, both personally and in school. Frequent discipline problems in front of one's family or within the black community was literally a statement of that pupil's cultural values. To be chastised or disciplined in the presence of one's family and peers was a very damning indictment. The student lost his sense of pride, his reputation was compromised, and his self-respect was lost.

During class periods, no student was out of the classroom and in the halls without a hall pass. Students served as hallway and building exits monitors during an open period in their class schedule and were stationed throughout the building in pairs. They reported any student using building exits or wandering the halls without a hall pass from a faculty member, an assistant principal, or the principal.

Although Dunbar, as a college preparatory high school, had few discipline problems, its history is not wholly irrelevant here. The importance of parental attitudes and parental involvement was recognized literally from the inception of the school. Although Washington in 1870 had many black families who were ready and eager for a first-rate school, it also had many who were not. The recent abolition of slavery had swelled the black population of Washington with many new arrivals from the South and the Border States. As of 1868, only about one third of the black children of the District of Columbia were attending any school at all. In this setting, William Syphax's admonitions to black parents to send their children to school, with a respect for learning and a readiness to work, were very much to the point.[25]

The types of punishment employed were the principal's bench, study hall after school, corporal punishment, chastisement, penalties, and parental involvement. In rating the effectiveness of the several forms of punishment in maintaining discipline, the alumni survey respondents found the principal's bench and involving the student's parents to be the most effective. They rated each of these forms of punishment to be 94.1 percent very effective or effective; being kept in study hall after school was next at 85.7 percent. See Table 11-4 below.

Types of Discipline Employed at Dunbar High School (Percent)						
	Very Effective	Effective	Somewhat Effective	Not Very Effective	Ineffective	Total

Principal's bench	52.9	41.2	5.9	0.0	0.0	100.0
Study hall after school	40.0	45.7	14.3	0.0	0.0	100.0
Corporal punishment	13.0	34.8	21.7	21.7	8.7	100.0
Chastisement	25.0	35.7	25.0	10.7	3.6	100.0
Penalties	10.7	60.7	17.9	10.7	0.0	100.0
Parental involvement	58.8	35.3	5.9	0.0	0.0	100.0

Source: Morris, Archie III., "Advancing Urban Educational Policy: Insights from Research on Dunbar High School," *Journal of the Case Studies in Education*, May 2017.

Table 11-4

While there was no dress code for Dunbar High School students, dressing for school attendance was not taken lightly. Among the alumni survey respondents, 51 percent classified their dress for school as casual and 44 percent as respectable; there is little different between the two. Most of the girls wore skirts and blouses or dresses with socks and shoes, such as loafers and oxfords. They were neat and appropriate. The boys wore pants, shirts and sweaters, sometimes coats and ties or ROTC uniforms. Their shoes were loafers or oxfords. There were no jeans, t-shirts, tank tops, tennis shoes or sneakers worn to school.

Extra-Curricular Activities

The pupil-activity program at Dunbar was comprehensive and carefully planned to inspire and develop the talents and interests of the students. Cultural aims in the early days were supplemented through a variety of activities. The Emerson Club, organized in 1904, became the Fleur-de-Lis Club of senior girls, grouped according to their interest in dramatics, music, and social service. Members of this club served as advisors to entering students in the 1940s and 1950s. The Rex Club, organized in 1916 for senior boys, was mainly social and cultural, but eventually undertook the direction of traffic problems in the building. A Boys Glee Club was organized in 1904 and a Girls Glee Club in 1910. In the 1920s, there was the Special Chorus of mixed voices.[26]

The Dunbar High School Savings Bank, organized in 1917, had three main objectives: (1) to encourage thrift and systemic saving; (2) to provide business training and (3) to keep financial records of school activities. Students saved for textbook purchases, Christmas or Easter outlays and donations, and graduation expenses. The bank was active in War Bond Drives and it received four awards from the U.S. Treasury Department for outstanding salesmanship in 1943 and 1944.[27]

In the 1940s, a large variety of clubs reflected the broad scope of the school programs: Banking, Biology, Chemistry, Commercial, Contemporary Literature, Current Topics, Debating, Dramatics, News Reel, Girl Reserves, Golf, Home Nursing, Foreign Languages, Library, Music, Negro History, Red Cross, Race Relations, Social Service, Stamp Collection, Short Story, and Travel Clubs. A faculty committee annually audited the finances of all activities and committees. Many clubs had accounts in the school bank, with a bonded teacher as treasurer, and students of bookkeeping as bank clerks.

Only nine percent of the alumni survey respondents did not participate in some form or other of these activities. Most popular among them was the Mixed Glee Club, the Foreign Languages Club, and the Music Club at nine percent each and the Red Cross Club at eight percent. See Table 11-5.

Clubs or Extracurricular Activities for Students at Dunbar High School					
Activity	Percent	Activity	Percent	Activity	Percent
Emerson Club/ Fleur-de-Lis Club	5	News Reel Club	4	Other (specify)	
The Rex Club	8	Girl Reserves	0	Cheerleading Squad	1
Boys Glee Club	0	Golf Club	5	Honor Society	3
Girls Glee Club	1	Home Nursing Club	1	Year Book	3
Mixed Glee Club	9	Debating Club	3	German Club	0
Biology Club	1	Library Club	1	French Club	1
Chemistry Club	1	Music Club	9	Latin Club	1
Commercial Club	0	Negro History Club	3	Dance Club	1
Contemporary Literature Club	0	Red Cross Club	8	Girl Scouts	1
Current Topics Club	3	Race Relations Club	0	Hockey Club	1
Foreign Languages Club	9	Intramural Sports	5	Boosters Club	1

Savings Bank/ War Bond Drive	3	None	9	Liber Anni	1
Dramatics Club	5			Quill and Scroll	1

Source: Morris, Archie III., "Advancing Urban Educational Policy: Insights from Research on Dunbar High School," *Journal of the Case Studies in Education*, May 2017.

Table 11-5

Athletics included baseball, football, basketball, track, tennis, and swimming for boys; basketball and swimming for girls. Varsity and intramural events were held in several fields. Dunbar graduates became outstanding athletes in many American colleges and participated in national and international competitions.[28] There was also a rifle team in which both boys and girls participated. A rifle range was in the basement and team members were able to practice there.

The alumni survey indicates that the Dunbar High School male and female students were well-rounded. A full range of sports activities was available to students and 65 percent of the alumni survey respondents participated at the varsity level. Baseball and football were most popular among boys with participation rates of 12 percent each, followed by basketball and track and field at eight percent each, and golf at seven percent. Basketball, field hockey, and swimming were the major sports for Percent girls. See Table 11-6 below.

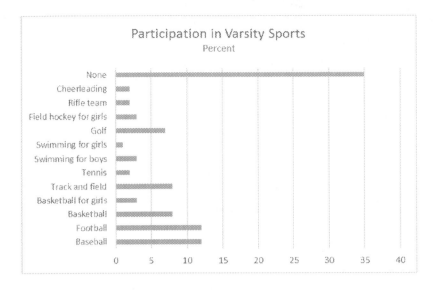

Source: Morris, Archie III., "Advancing Urban Educational Policy: Insights from Research on Dunbar High School," *Journal of the Case Studies in Education*, May 2017.

Table 11-6

Eligibility for varsity sports at Dunbar required that a student maintain a cumulative grade point average of 2.5. A failing grade (F) in any given class would result in one being suspended from an athletic team.

Parental Involvement

The Parent-Teachers Association (PTA) was not the major means of parental involvement in the Dunbar High School setting. Parental involvement was particularly important in black schools, for the black culture was not a permissive culture. If black kids misbehave, it is because their parents do not know or do not care. Dunbar students' parents did not tolerate any philosophy allowing black youths to "do their own thing." Where black parents have become involved in a school, they have sometimes urged a stricter discipline than the school was prepared to impose. Moreover, parental involvement did not mean taking "community control" through either an ideological dogma or a public relations ploy.

Where a community has a high rate of residential turnover, "community control" can mean the unchallenged dominance of a handful of activists who are not accountable to any lasting constituency. At Dunbar, it was important to have the widespread involvement of individual parents and the support of the church.[29]

Some 74 percent of the alumni survey respondents found the Parent-Teachers Association (PTA) to be average to above average. Twenty-one percent found it to be outstanding. See Table 11-6 below.

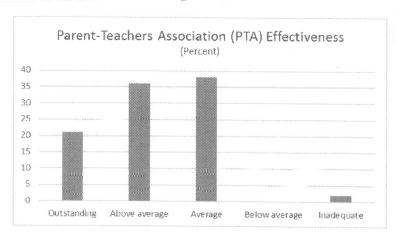

Source: Morris, Archie III., "Advancing Urban Educational Policy: Insights from Research on Dunbar High School," *Journal of the Case Studies in Education*, May 2017.

Table 11-6

Strengths and Weaknesses of the High School Academic Program

Segregation was considered a problem by 18 percent of the respondents and 21 percent felt there was a lack of resources and support for students. However, 61 percent felt there were no weaknesses except for the impatience of teachers for some students who did not prepare for class or do their homework; some may see this as a strength. Still, the city had a segregated school system and the funds to maintain supplies, books, and materials in black schools were limited. Specific weaknesses cited were overcrowded classes, run-down physical facilities, lack of money, and the distance to school that students needed to travel for attendance. Moreover, some places open to whites did not welcome black students and this affected students' opportunities to expand knowledge outside the black community.

The survey respondents believe the strengths of the Dunbar High School academic program were its faculty and principals (44 percent), its students (32 percent), and its curriculum (24 percent). They thought the teachers and principals were very well qualified and were dedicated to their students. Some of the faculty held doctoral degrees and they cared about student achievement. They also felt that students were focused on academics and held to high standards.

CHAPTER TWELVE

THE DUNBAR MILIEU

Throughout the period of its academic ascendancy, Dunbar was characterized by the *esprit de corps* of its students, the dedication of its teachers, and the strong support of the black community, both in everyday chores and in episodic crises. Special efforts were made to get college scholarships for bright, but poor, youngsters and special efforts were also needed to help the parents of such youngsters to keep them in high school. There was often a need to send teenagers to work so they could bring home some much-needed help for family finances. One concrete indicator of student attitude is the record of attendance and tardiness. A spot check of old Board of Education records in both categories shows Dunbar's record to have been superior to the average of its white counterparts, both around the turn of the century (1901-1902) and around mid-century (1952-1953).[1]

The Dunbar student's primary "job" was to go to school, study hard, and stay out of trouble. Many students had part-time jobs to help their families make ends meet. Fifty-one percent of the Dunbar alumni survey respondents had a job while they were attending high school. Forty-five percent of them worked 16-20 hours a week and three percent worked 21 or more hours per week. See Table 12-1 below.

Source: Morris, Archie III., "Advancing Urban Educational Policy: Insights from Research on Dunbar High School," *Journal of the Case Studies in Education*, May 2017.

Table 12-1

The School Environment

Because it was not a neighborhood school during the 1870-1955 period, no one was automatically assigned to Dunbar. One did not simply happen to enroll there. The school's reputation and standards were well known to parents and middle-school children throughout the black community. Indeed, some black youngsters from nearby Maryland and Virginia were known to give false D.C. addresses in order to attend.[2] Others, from more distant states in the South, were sent by their parents to live with relatives or friends so they could attend Dunbar High School. Additionally, students lived in different neighborhoods throughout the Washington-Georgetown area and the surrounding counties and traveled anywhere from a few blocks to several miles to attend class daily.

Homeroom classes began in the morning at 9:00 a.m. with a recitation of the Lord's Prayer and the pledge of allegiance to the flag of the United States of America. From 9:00 a.m. to 9:30 a.m., students reported to their homeroom. Assemblies were held in the auditorium at that time as well. Subject matter classes began at 9:30 a.m. and there were six class periods, 45 minutes each, held each day. There was no written dress code, but a basic conservative dress code was followed. Students were expected to be well groomed and to dress suitably for class. Most of the girls wore dresses or skirts and blouses. The boys wore slacks and shirts and sweaters. Occasionally, they would wear a suit or a coat and tie. Everyone wore socks and shoes, usually loafers and oxfords. Cadets wore their uniforms to classes.

The faculty set the standard for dress in the school. Male and female teachers dressed in business or professional attire every day. Boys did not wear hats indoors. There were no jeans, shorts, sneakers, tank tops, halter tops, sweat pants or sweat suits allowed, nor clothing that was transparent or might be construed to be part of an undergarment.

Racial integration, outstanding physical facilities, or generous financial support were clearly *not* essential to the Dunbar academic performance. It had none of these. Except for a few white teachers in its early days in the 1870's, Dunbar was an all-black school for generation after generation, from students to teachers to administrators. Moreover, school facilities were in a segregated city, where, as recently as 1950, black people were not admitted to most downtown movie theaters or restaurants. Apart from a few years after 1915, the physical facilities of Dunbar were always inadequate; its lunchroom was so small that many students had to eat lunch out on the street, and it was 1950 before the school had a public-address system. Since Dunbar was part of a segregated school system, administered by whites at the top, it was perennially starved for funds. Internally, there were class-conscious and color-conscious cliques among students and resentment of administration favoritism among the teachers. In short, the list of "prerequisites" for success in which educators today indulge themselves was clearly not met at Dunbar.[3]

The local stereotype of Dunbar was that this was the institution where the children of the city's doctors and lawyers went to school; as was probably the case. In a study of class records for the period 1938-1955, the percentage of Dunbar students whose parents' occupations could be identified as "professional" never exceeded six per cent for any of the years studied. Only about half of the parental occupations were identifiable and categorized, so this should be regarded as a high of about 12 per cent of the occupations known and classified. This was exceptionally large for a black school. Former Dunbar principal Charles S. Lofton refers to the middle-class stereotype as "an old wives' tale." "If we took only the children of doctors and lawyers," he asked, "how could we have had 1,400 black students at one time?"[4] Former Dunbar teacher Mary Gibson Hundley wrote: "A large segment of the students had one or more government employees for support. Before the 1940s, these employees were messengers and clerks, with few exceptions."[5]

The alumni survey is enlightening. Responding to the question of what jobs or occupations were held by their parents, the respondents indicated a fairly large number of avocations for their fathers and mothers. A large majority were in the lower socioeconomic strata with government worker (clerk, messenger, etc.) ranking high on both sides; 28 percent for fathers and 26 percent for mothers. The next high percentage for fathers was laborer at 11 percent. However, one-third, 33 percent, of the mothers were listed as "Housewife/home maker." See Table 12-2.

Jobs or Occupations Held by Parents			
Father		Mother	
Occupation	Percent	Occupation	Percent
Post Office	6	Government worker	26
Self-employed	2	Dietitian	2
Government worker	28	Housewife/home maker	33
Chef/Cook	2	Nurse	2
Physician	6	Secretary	2
Dentist	2	Beauty Salon owner	2
Chiropractor/steam engineer	2	Real estate broker	2
Bootblack	2	Housewife/maid	2
Asst. Superintendent, DCPS	2	Domestic	6
Taxi company owner	2	Beautician	2
Vendor (blind)	2	Deceased	4
Security guard, taxicab driver/handy man	2	Seamstress	2
Laborer	11	Computer technician	2
Truck driver	4	Teacher	2
Taxi driver	8	Elevator operator	2
Teacher	6	Public school employee	2
U.S. Army	2	Charwoman	4
Deceased	2	Worked in bakery	2
Fireman	2	Maintenance worker	2

Stationary engineer (Steam/AC)	2		
Road and grounds supervisor	2		
Painter	2		
Construction work and pick-up jobs	2		

Source: Morris, Archie III., "Advancing Urban Educational Policy: Insights from Research on Dunbar High School," *Journal of the Case Studies in Education*, May 2017.

Table 12-2

Black families in the early 20th century exhibited the typical values characteristic of the middle class even when they did not have the financial means to obtain this lifestyle. Typical values associated with a black middle-class lifestyle included a tendency to plan for retirement, a desire to be in control of their future, respect for and adherence to the law, and a desire for a good education for themselves and their children. The way to move forward in socio-economic status was through a good education and hard work. The values consistent with this life style included a desire to protect the family from various hardships such as health issues, financial difficulties, and crime.[6]

Few families of the alumni survey respondents would be considered middle class or higher. The respondents' family household income when they attended the Dunbar High School was clustered between $1,001 and $30,000 with nearly a third at the bottom of the spectrum (see Table 12-3 below). For comparison, in 1940, the mean income in the United States was $1,299 and the median, $2,200.[7]

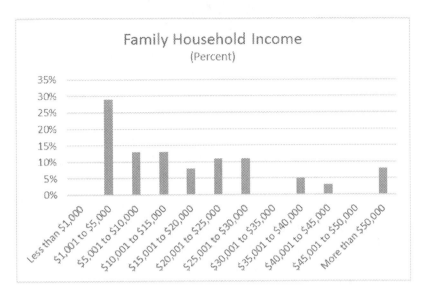

Source: Morris, Archie III., "Advancing Urban Educational Policy: Insights from Research on Dunbar High School," *Journal of the Case Studies in Education*, May 2017.

Table 12-3

Race and Ethnic Background

Given the general predominance of mulattoes among the "free persons of color" and their descendants, it seems probable that the light-skinned mulatto stereotype was applicable to the early M Street and Dunbar students and teachers. This group continued for many years to be over-represented among the schools' students and teachers, but they did not necessarily constitute a majority. A study of old yearbook photographs at Dunbar High School shows the great bulk of the students to have been very much the color of most American blacks. Any bias in the photography of that period, before black was beautiful, would be toward printing the pictures lighter than in life.[8]

The alumni survey respondents could check more than one characteristic under "Race or Ethnic Background." Eleven percent checked "Black/African American" and "White/Caucasian," or these two categories and "Native American." This results in a skewed profile of the students at

Dunbar High School being11 percent white, 92 percent black, and eight percent Native American. There is no evidence of white students attending M Street or Dunbar High School prior to 1954.

In analyzing this situation, two terms appear to warrant consideration, "mulatto" and "mixed race." A mulatto is defined as the first-generation offspring of a black person and a white person. A mixed-race person is one who relates to or has characteristics of people of different ethnic origins. Characterizing those who checked the black and white categories as "mulatto" and those who checked these two categories plus Native American as "mixed race," allows for an adjusted classification which provides for zero white students, 77 percent black students, four percent Native American students, 11 percent mulatto students, and four percent Native American students. See Table 12-4 below.

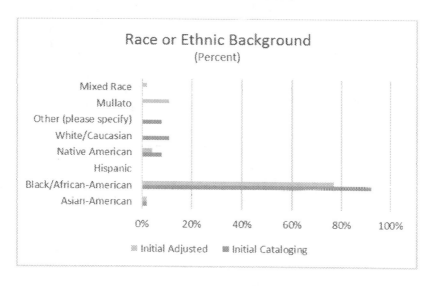

Source: Morris, Archie III., "Advancing Urban Educational Policy: Insights from Research on Dunbar High School," *Journal of the Case Studies in Education*, May 2017.

Table 12-4

ARCHIE MORRIS III, D.P.A.

The Dunbar Experience

The Dunbar experience was unique. Some time ago, Charles L. Morris, who attended the school in the early 1920s, gave this account in a letter he wrote to one of the Washington newspapers:

> I had been exposed to the extraordinary Dunbar milieu, and for me that was a priceless experience. . . .Let me give a hint at this milieu. Immediately on entering Dunbar, the freshman sensed something different from the common street conduct. You lowered your voice and looked at your shoes; maybe you ought to have polished them. . . .The first time in my life that I was ever called "Mister" was as a freshman at Dunbar High—fourteen years old and in knee pants. . . .Faculty excellence was the standard at Dunbar in every aspect. The teachers had not only the paper credentials, but personality and the ability to teach and inspire. The Spanish teachers, in order to perfect their subject, vacationed in Spain when they could. The French teachers went to France. And I would bet that those enthusiastic Latin teachers visited Carthage and Gaul in their dreams. . . .We had two fine teachers who, in their given names, recalled their union sides in the civil War; William Tecumseh Sherman Jackson and Ulysses Simpson Grant Bassett. Both were strict, no-nonsense pedagogues reminiscent of the English public school system. . . .Many felt the magic touch of the old Dunbar, and were given a keen sense of decorum and the love of reading, learning, and thinking. I am proud I was lucky enough to have shared in it.[9]

In his preface to Mrs. Hundley's book on Dunbar, Dr. Robert Weaver (class of 1925) writes:

> My roots in Dunbar High School are deep. My mother was a graduate of the old M Street High School, and my only sibling, an older brother, Mortimer, graduated

from Dunbar, as did I. The efficacy of this high school is certainly expressed in the success of its graduates. My own debt to Dunbar is great. . . .I can recall at least a half dozen outstanding teachers who not only exposed me to the subject matter and instilled a high appreciation for achievement but inspired me as human beings. Perhaps the finest tribute I can pay to Dunbar . . . is the fact that, when I graduated, I went to Harvard College where many of my classmates had been trained in some of the best preparatory schools in the nation. I found myself on the whole about as well able to survive in the college as were they. My brother, who graduated from Williams College, *Phi Beta Kappa*, had a similar experience there, and subsequently at Harvard where he took his Master's degree.[10]

In rating their overall education at the Dunbar High School, 93.1 percent of the survey respondents were satisfied or very satisfied (see Table 12-5 below).

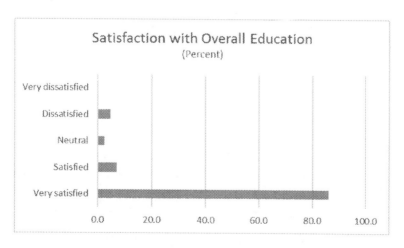

Source: Morris, Archie III., "Advancing Urban Educational Policy: Insights from Research on Dunbar High School," *Journal of the Case Studies in Education*, May 2017.

Table 12-5

Graduates' Educational and Career Attainment

The Dunbar High School was known to have a top college preparatory program. Seventy-two percent of the alumni survey respondents felt the academic and related programs that prepared them for entry into college, the military, and/or the workforce, were excellent or above average. Another 28 percent gave a rating of average or below. See Table 12-6 below.

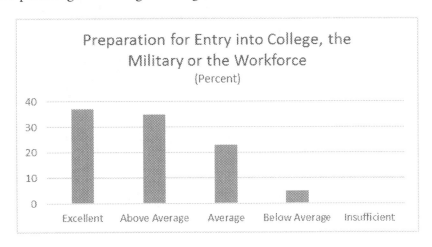

Source: Morris, Archie III., "Advancing Urban Educational Policy: Insights from Research on Dunbar High School," *Journal of the Case Studies in Education*, May 2017.

Table 12-6

During its heyday from 1900 to 1950, Dunbar sent many students to Ivy League and Seven Sisters colleges. Among its graduates were attorneys William Henry Hastie and Charles Hamilton Houston, who went on to Amherst; Judge Robert Terrell, who graduated from Harvard, and historians Rayford Logan and Carter G. Woodson. Moreover, because of Dunbar's prestige and their inability to get job offers from white universities in the North, many of the Dunbar High School teachers were black scholars who had received advanced degrees at Northeastern universities and used Dunbar as a training ground or waiting spot before they went on to college teaching positions at universities like Howard, Fisk, Atlanta, Morehouse, or Spelman.[11]

M Street and Dunbar students attended prestigious Northern colleges and universities because they were encouraged and assisted by teachers who had also attended these schools. Beginning with the emancipation, it was the ideal of most black people to go to places like Harvard. The white teachers who went South in the first years after slavery went there with the idea of "New Englandizing" the South. White Southerners would not let them get away with that in white situations, but they did get away with it where many black people were concerned. Blacks were receptive to that effort, because that was where they thought abolition had been born. Abolitionists were their friends, so their orientation was toward the best standards of a New England education and, sometimes, New England mannerisms. Those blacks, who came back to teach at Dunbar, poured everything they knew into their students' heads.[12]

As far back as 1899, M Street and Dunbar students came in first in citywide tests given in *both* black and white schools. Over the 85-year span, most of Dunbar's graduates went on to college, even though most Americans, white or black, did not. Most Dunbar graduates could afford only to attend low-cost local colleges, either federally supported Howard University or tuition-free Miner Teachers College. However, those graduates who attended Harvard, Amherst, Oberlin, and other prestigious institutions, were usually on scholarships and ran up an impressive record of academic honors. For example, it is known that Amherst admitted 34 M Street and Dunbar graduates between 1892 and 1954. Of these, 74 percent graduated and more than one fourth of these graduates were *Phi Beta Kappas*.[13] Amherst thought so highly of Dunbar graduates that it accepted any student recommended by the school without his even having to take an entrance examination.[14]

Of those graduating, 98 percent of the Dunbar alumni survey respondents attended college. Most of them, 74 percent, attended undergraduate school in Washington, DC, and 26 percent attended out-of-state schools. See Table 12-7 below.

Undergraduate Colleges/Universities Attended	
College/University	Percent
Howard University, Washington, DC	49

North Carolina Agricultural and Technical University, Greensboro, NC	2
D.C. Teachers College, Washington, DC	4
Miner Teachers College, Washington, DC	8
Washington State University, Pullman, WA	6
Pennsylvania State University, University Park, PA	2
Allegheny College, Meadville, PA	6
Columbia College, Columbia University, New York, NY	2
Morgan State University, Baltimore, MD	2
North Carolina College, Chapel Hill, NC	2
California State University, Los Angeles, CA	2
Harvard University, Cambridge, MA	2
Springfield College, Springfield, MA	2
Immaculata and Catholic University, Washington, DC	2
University of San Francisco, San Francisco, CA	2
American University, Washington, DC	4
Howard university/DCTC, Washington, DC	2
Delaware State University, Dover, DE	2
University of the District of Columbia, Washington, DC	2

Source: Morris, Archie III., "Advancing Urban Educational Policy: Insights from Research on Dunbar High School," *Journal of the Case Studies in Education*, May 2017.

Table 12-7

Of those respondents attending undergraduate school, 81 percent went on to graduate school. Thirty-six percent attended graduate school in the District of Columbia and 64 percent attended out-of-state graduate schools. Two percent studied abroad in Brussels, Belgium, and two percent completed an on-line degree from an Australian-based education institution. See Table 12-8 below.

Graduate Colleges/Universities Attended	
College/University	Percent
Catholic University, Law School, Washington, DC	2
Bowie State University, Bowie, MD	2

University of Virginia, Charlottesville, VA	2
George Washington University, Washington, DC	12
Air Force Institute of Technology, Dayton, OH	7
Frostburg State University, Frostburg, MD	2
Howard University, Washington, DC	5
American University, Washington, DC	5
University of Brussels, Brussels, Belgium	2
Howard U., GWU, University Massachusetts, Amherst, MA	2
Miner Teachers College, Washington, DC	2
Howard U. and Virginia Polytechnic Institute and State University, VA	2
Monash University (online), Australia	2
Columbia University, New York, NY	2
Harvard University, Graduate School of Design, Cambridge, MA	2
Decatur and Macon County Hospital of Medical Technology, Decatur, GA	2
Georgetown University, Washington, DC	2
San Francisco State University, San Francisco, CA	2
Pepperdine University, Malibu, CA	2
Lincoln University, Lincoln, PA	2
American College, Bryn Mawr, PA	5
American University, Washington College of Law, Washington, DC	2
Howard U. Nova Southeastern, Ft. Lauderdale, FL	2
Howard U., Catholic U. American U., DC	2
University of the District of Columbia, Washington, DC	2
Did not attend graduate school	19

Source: Morris, Archie III., "Advancing Urban Educational Policy: Insights from Research on Dunbar High School," *Journal of the Case Studies in Education*, May 2017.

Table 12-8

Nineteen percent of the alumni survey respondents did not earn a college degree. A bachelor's degree was earned by 26 percent, a master's degree by 41 percent, a professional degree by nine percent, and a doctorate degree by six percent. See Table 12-9 below.

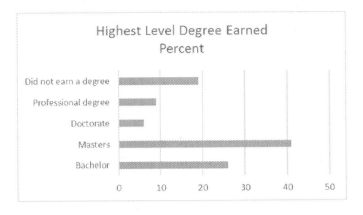

Source: Morris, Archie III., "Advancing Urban Educational Policy: Insights from Research on Dunbar High School," *Journal of the Case Studies in Education*, May 2017.

Table 12-9

In their careers, as well as in their academic work, Dunbar graduates excelled. The first black general (Benjamin O. Davis, Sr.), the first black federal judge (William H. Hastie), the first black Cabinet member (Robert C. Weaver), the discoverer of blood plasma (Charles Drew), and the first black U.S. Senator since Reconstruction (Edward W. Brooke), were all Dunbar graduates. During *World War II*, Dunbar graduates in the Army included "nearly a score of majors, nine colonels and lieutenant colonels, and one brigadier general." This was a substantial percentage of the total number of high-ranking black officers at that time.[15] The academic intelligence of Dunbar students was above average, and their abilities carried over into their careers after graduation. The approach to learning and teaching practiced at M Street/Dunbar High Schools taught them that focusing on how academic subjects (mathematics, science, history, the arts, and basic literacy) can apply to the real world and can be viewed as knowledge supporting practical applications.

Intelligence Quotient

Over 90 percent of the alumni survey respondents rated the academic ability of their fellow Dunbar students to be outstanding or above average. Eight percent of the students were rated average or below by their peers. See Table 12-10.

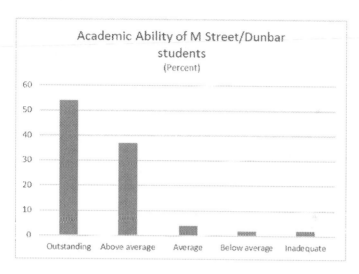

Source: Morris, Archie III., "Advancing Urban Educational Policy: Insights from Research on Dunbar High School," *Journal of the Case Studies in Education*, May 2017.

Table 12-10

Almost by definition, the intelligence quotient (IQ) is a culturally, socially, and ideologically rooted concept. It is intended to predict success (i.e., to predict outcomes that are valued as success by most people) in a large social group carrying its own set of values. Specifically, one's IQ has been found to be the single best predictor of the decision to obtain postsecondary education, and econometric analyses have shown that each additional IQ point may lead to a decision by a student to stay in school a little longer.[16]

Still, the argument has often been made that IQs have little relationship to performance as far as black people are concerned. There is already considerable literature, nonetheless, indicating that IQ tests and similar tests are equally accurate predictors of black and white academic performance. Dunbar provided a somewhat different kind of test of this hypothesis because it is based on a black group with outstanding performances in both academic and career terms. Were Dunbar IQs significantly different from the national average IQ of 85 for black Americans? Table 12-11 below answers that question.[17]

Mean I.Q. of Dunbar Students

Class of	Students	All Graduates Only	Non-Graduates Only
1938	105.5	111.6	97.1
1939	111.2	114.0	101.9
1940	108.5	111.1	100.9
1941	109.3	111.7	101.7
1942	105.2	107.8	101.4
1943	101.3	102.6	98.5
1944	106.0	109.8	97.5
1945	98.8	101.6	93.5
1946	102.1	105.7	102.1
1947	102.0	108.4	94.9
1948	105.3	106.5	98.2
1949	106.1	106.1	104.0
1950	110.9	111.3	99.4
1951	102.7	103.4	98.1
1952	103.1	104.7	94.3
1953	101.3	102.7	93.5
1954	101.7	102.6	98.8
1955	99.6	100.8	96.4

Source: Thomas Sowell, "Black Excellence—the Case of Dunbar High School," *The Public Interest*.

Table 12-11

Dunbar students' average IQs were substantially higher than those of other blacks and, usually, above the national average as well. Even the Dunbar dropouts scored higher than the average of other blacks. However, Dunbar students were *not* selected based on IQ tests. Admission to Dunbar was a matter of individual self-selection.

To put things in perspective, the average score on an IQ test is 100. Sixty-eight percent of IQ scores fall within one standard deviation of the mean. So that means that most people have an IQ score between 85 and 115. Lewis Madison Terman (1916) developed the original notion of IQ and proposed this scale for classifying IQ scores:[18]

Over 140	Genius or near genius
120 – 140	Very superior intelligence
110 – 119	Superior intelligence
90 – 109	Normal or average intelligence
80 – 89	Dullness
70 – 79	Borderline deficiency
Under 70	Definite feeble-mindedness

A bell curve is a graph which depicts a normal distribution of variables, in which most values cluster around a mean, while outliers can be found above and below the mean. In terms of the mental abilities of its students, Dunbar's bell curve was skewed to the right. Moreover, the student population was young, with pupils as young as 12 and 13 years old in the 10th grade, and a few of them graduating at 16 years of age.

Not *everyone* who attended Dunbar had a very high IQ. The pie chart below, done in November 1944, indicates that eight percent of the students had IQs below the national average IQ of 85 for black Americans. Approximately 52 percent were at or above the national average IQ of 100 commonly given for white Americans.[19]

Mental Abilities of Dunbar Pupils
Percentage of distribution According to IQ

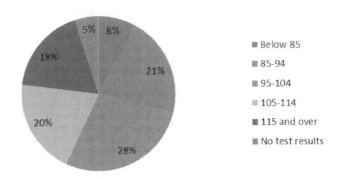

Source: Thomas Sowell, "Black Excellence—the Case of Dunbar High School," *The Public Interest.*

Table 12-12

The high IQs at Dunbar were hardly the whole story. An equal number of black students scattered elsewhere with equal IQs might not have produced an equal number of high academic and career performances unless certain other factors were present: (1) the *motivational* element associated with self-selection for such a school; (2) the benefits of mutual association with high-quality students and with teachers attracted to teaching such students; and (3) the school traditions, including distinguished alumni who were constantly being held up as examples to the students. Certainly, the kind of personal interest, counseling, and extracurricular tutoring that Dunbar students received, is extremely rare for black students even today, whether in all-black or in integrated schools.[20]

A study of class records for the period 1938-1955 also confirms that most Dunbar students' parents were *not* middle-class professionals. Among those students whose parents' occupations could be identified and categorized, the largest single category was consistently "unskilled and semi-skilled," and the median job index was at the level of a white-collar worker. More noteworthy, the differences in mean IQ were relatively slight among students whose parents fell in different occupational categories. For the classes of 1938-1955, the mean IQ of students whose parents were in the "unskilled and semi-skilled" category ranged from 96.1 in 1945 to 113.3 in 1950. The mean IQ of students whose parents were "professionals" ranged from 102.1 in 1942 to 124.2 in 1950. Furthermore, even the academic exclusiveness of Dunbar should not be overstated. Figures available for the period 1938-1948 show that approximately one third of all black students enrolled in D.C. high schools were enrolled in Dunbar.[21]

There also is evidence that Dunbar was at its peak some time *before* the period when IQ scores were recorded. The slight downward shift of IQs over the 1938-1955 period is in keeping with the impression that this was the declining phase of its academic prime. The 1938-1955 period was studied statistically because this is the only period during Dunbar's academic prime for which IQ scores are available. Over the 18-year span, girls outnumbered boys every year. It usually was by about two to one, but it was as much as three to one in the class of 1952. This conforms to a general predominance of females among high-IQ American black people, a baffling phenomenon difficult to explain by either hereditary or environmental theories or by the cultural bias of the tests. Black males and females obviously draw upon the same pool of genes. They are also reared in the same environment.[22]

Segregation and Racial Uplift Activities

Among segregated schools, Dunbar was unique. It became so almost by accident. It was not racially segregated education, *per se*, that made Dunbar the success it was, it was a combination of its students, social class, and a peculiar set of historical circumstances that existed in the early years of its development.[23]

Dunbar strove unceasingly to prepare its pupils for acceptance at non-segregated Northern and Mid-Western universities. However, even considering the academic achievements of the graduates of the high school, there were racially motivated attempts to convert it to a manual arts program as evidenced by the "feud" of Percy M. Hughes, the white director of high schools, with Dr. Anna J. Cooper. The problem of segregation was always a factor for M Street and Dunbar High Schools. [24]

After the end of Reconstruction, which followed from the *Compromise of 1877,* the new Democrat governments in the South instituted state laws to separate black and white racial groups, submitting black Americans to *de facto* second-class citizenship and enforcing white supremacy. Racial segregation of facilities, services, and opportunities, such as housing, medical care, education, and employment, was pretty much the norm in the nation's capital. The expression *de jure* segregation refers primarily to the legally enforced separation of black Americans from other races, but can loosely refer to voluntary social separation and, as well, to separation of other racial or ethnic minorities from the majority mainstream society and communities.[25] During the entire 1870-1955 period, Dunbar drew upon the entire black community of Washington and Georgetown for its student enrollment.

When Neval Thomas became the vice-principal of the M Street High School, president of the Washington branch of the National Association for the Advancement of Colored People (NAACP), and an NAACP executive board member, students could not have helped but to have been struck by his forthright denunciation of segregation. Segregation in Washington and in the civil service was beginning to spread because of Democrat Woodrow Wilson's presidential victory in 1912. Mr. Thomas took up the challenge and, in his various capacities at M Street and in the NAACP, made the fight against segregation a central part of his political and educational activities. A certain bitterness was thought to be evident in Thomas's demeanor.

The spread of Jim Crow in the District of Columbia under Woodrow Wilson and after was enough to embitter any of the Talented Tenth teachers at M Street. Students could not avoid being struck by his forthright denunciation of segregation, even though they were rarely touched directly by the humiliation of Jim Crow. They were more infected by the optimism inherent in a better-quality education[26] that would permit them to wage a revolution based on ideas and individual freedom to raise the race to an equal level with whites.

At the turn of the 20th century, the black American cultural leadership, struggling to articulate a positive black identity, developed a middle-class ideology of racial uplift. Insisting that they were truly representative of the race's potential, black leaders espoused an ethos of self-help and service to the black masses and distinguished themselves from the black majority as agents of civilization; hence the phrase "uplifting the race." A central assumption of the racial uplift ideology was that black Americans' material and moral progress would diminish white racism.[27] This ideology was compatible with the Dunbar culture.

Civil rights, on the other hand, are those rights belonging to an individual by virtue of citizenship, especially the fundamental freedoms and privileges guaranteed by the Thirteenth and Fourteenth Amendments to the *U.S. Constitution* and by subsequent acts of Congress, including civil liberties, due process, equal protection of the laws, and freedom from discrimination. Civil rights, of course, have been blocked by federal and state support of slavery, Jim Crow segregation, and other forms of race prejudice. The fight against racism and discrimination has largely been through nonviolent conflicts, violent confrontations, and bringing civil suits in the courts.

Many Dunbar students were involved in civil rights, racial uplift, suffrage, and the struggle against "Jim Crow," and the school produced several graduates who were involved in civil rights and suffrage. Dr. Anna J. Cooper fought to keep college preparation as a primary goal for her students and was active in the community against racial discrimination. Nannie Helen Buroughs spoke out vigorously about her creed of racial self-help. John Aubrey Davis was a civil rights activist, as were Neval Thomas, Mary Church Terrell and Robert C. Weaver. Charles Hamilton Houston was NAACP Litigation Director and earned the title "The Man Who Killed Jim Crow." Often overlooked in promulgating black history and advancement, is the work of two prominent historians from Dunbar, Carter G. Woodson and Rayford W. Logan.

M Street and Dunbar students also are notable for several "firsts" that paved the way for those following behind them:

- Benjamin O. Davis, Sr., first black U.S. Army general in the American military.
- Edward Brooke, first black U.S. Senator since Reconstruction.
- William Allison Davis, first black American to hold a tenured faculty position at a major white institution of higher learning.

- Robert C. Weaver, first U.S. Secretary of Housing and Urban Development.
- Charles R. Drew, first black surgeon to serve as an examiner on the American Board of Surgery.

The social order prevailing during the glory days of the old M Street and Dunbar High Schools was one of Jim Crow segregation. Some 35 percent of the alumni survey respondents felt that racism and color impacted the success of the school's efforts to function in the mainstream American society. However, they felt that as graduates of the Dunbar High School, they were well prepared to function in the majority American society and to take advantage of any activities and opportunities that became available to them.

Racism and colorism were significant disadvantages for black Americans, but there were some special benefits for those confined to the black community. As a result of racism, for example, M Street and Dunbar were blessed with the best educated teachers in the DC public school system. One was expected to be part of the black community and Dunbar faculty prepared the student to be become a respected and contributing member of that community. Helping fellow classmates and friends was part of the M Street and Dunbar High School training because of the goal of racial uplift.

Thirty percent of the Dunbar alumni survey respondents felt that faculty had an impact on the success of the school's efforts to prepare students to function in the mainstream American society and the black community. For 12.5 percent, it was important that black teachers stressed the importance of education and excellence as a means of improving the status of black people. Another 20 percent felt the students were generally well prepared, despite a lack of resources, because teachers stressed the development of self-confidence, self-discipline, and perseverance as valued traits. Graduates were fortunate to have teachers at the Dunbar High School who were the cream of the crop because the opportunities for jobs in the larger society were limited or nonexistent. A special benefit was that the faculty that taught in the segregated schools also lived in the segregated communities.

Social class or economic status was not perceived to be a major factor for students at the Dunbar High School. Fifty-three percent of the survey respondents said that social class or economic status did not affect their education at the Dunbar High School or that of their fellow students. Elitism did exist, but education and intellectual ability were the more important factors. Those who were not from a privileged background, always felt that the faculty motivated them to succeed despite their economic means. Another 16 percent, however, felt that socioeconomic status did affect them. Seven percent said they were not aware of any problem in that respect.

Comments from 21 percent of the respondents were more explicit. Students whose families had more money and higher positions in the community were afforded greater opportunities because their families could provide them those opportunities. There were students of lower socioeconomic status who did feel disadvantaged because they were exposed to a wide range of lifestyles among their classmates. However, Dunbar High School provided social and cultural activities and opportunities that were free or low cost so that everyone could participate and benefit as much as possible.

Notable Dunbar and M Street High School Alumni

Dunbar and M Street High Schools produced numerous graduates who excelled in many areas of endeavor; scholarship, the arts, business, military, religion, medicine, law, government, and athletics. A list drawn up around 1970 by Edgar R. Sims, Class of 1930, shows that Dunbar:

> ....has sent forth 8,000 federal and District government workers; 2,500 teachers, educators, and specialists; 150 principals at all levels; 1,000 doctors, dentists, pharmacists, medical technicians; 400 lawyers, judges, and court workers; 200 architects, engineers, and scientists; 200 priests, ministers, and religious workers; 200 law enforcement, correctional, and fire officers; 200 musicians and stars of stage, screen, and TV; 200 military officers, from generals to lieutenants; 300 banking, business, industry, and organizational leaders; 300 leaders

in the political arena (local, state, and federal); 100 artists, poets, writers, reporters; 100 participants in the field of sports; 300 craftsmen and tradesmen at journeyman level; 100 foreign-service employees; 1,500 nurses, hygienists, technicians, and assistants.[28]

Below is a list of notable alumni that, by no means, includes all the graduates who warrant special recognition for their achievements.

Scholars and artists:

- James E. Bowman, Ph.D., scientist, physician, pathologist, studied Glucose-6-phosphate. dehydrogenase deficiency (G6PD) and Sickle Cell disease.
- Herman Russell Branson, Ph.D., black physicist, chemist, best known for his research on the alpha helix protein structure, and was the president of two colleges.
- Sterling Allen Brown, black professor, poet, and literary critic.
- Mary P. Burrill, educator and playwright.
- Nannie Helen Burroughs, black educator, orator, religious leader, and businesswoman.
- Elizabeth Catlett, a prominent American-born Mexican sculptor, printmaker, and artist.
- Frank Coleman, professor of physics, founder of Omega Psi Phi Fraternity, Incorporated.
- Anna J. Cooper, Ph.D., author, educator, and one of the most prominent black scholars in United States history.
- Oscar J. Cooper, physician, founder of Omega Psi Phi Fraternity, Incorporated.
- William Allison Davis, Ph.D., Anthropologist, educator, scholar, first black American to hold full tenured faculty position at a major white institution-University of Chicago.
- John Aubrey Davis, Sr., Ph.D., civil rights activist, head academic researcher on *Brown v. Board of Education* (1954), New Negro Alliance co-founder and political science professor.
- James Reese Europe, first black American officer to lead troops in battle in *World War I*, founder and first president of the Clef Club,

leader of the 369th Hellfighters Infantry Regiment Band; American ragtime and early jazz bandleader, arranger, and composer.

- Kelly Miller, a black American mathematician, sociologist, essayist, newspaper columnist, author, and an important figure in the intellectual life of black America for close to half a century.

- May Miller, a black poet, playwright and educator; known as the most widely published female playwright of the Harlem Renaissance, with seven published volumes of poetry during her career as a writer.

- Willis Richardson, playwright, first black dramatist to have a non-musical work staged on Broadway when his play The Chip Woman's Fortune opened in May 1923, the first writer to win two first prizes during the Harlem Renaissance, called by some the "Father of Black Drama".

- Billy Taylor, an American jazz pianist, composer, broadcaster and educator; Robert L. Jones Distinguished Professor of Music at East Carolina University in Greenville, and since 1994, he was the artistic director for jazz at the John F. Kennedy Center for the Performing Arts in Washington, D.C.

- Mary Church Terrell, educator, suffragist and civil rights activist, as well as one of the first black women to earn a college degree.

- Jean Toomer, poet and novelist associated with the Harlem Renaissance.

- Vantile Whitfield, influential arts administrator who helped found several performing arts institutions in the United States.

- Carter G. Woodson, Ph.D., black American historian, author, journalist and the founder of the Association for the Study of African American Life and History.

- George Theophilus Walker, Ph.D., composer and educator, for his work Lilacs for Voice and Orchestra, premiered by the Boston Symphony, first black American composer to win the Pulitzer Prize for Music.

- Rayford W. Logan, Ph.D., a black historian and Pan-African activist.

Government:

- Ionia Rollin Whipper, black American obstetrician and public health outreach worker; during the mid-1920s, worked for the United States Children's Bureau and travelled the rural South training midwives to use sterile delivery techniques and to register births; opened her home to unwed mothers of color and eventually, with the help of donations, she established a separate home for her work with these women which still bears her name.
- Benjamin O. Davis, Sr., first black U.S. Army general in the American military.
- Andrew P. Chambers, Lieutenant General, U.S. Army.
- Roscoe C. Brown, Jr., Ph.D., squadron commander of the 100th Fighter Squadron of the 332nd Fighter Group, Tuskegee Airmen; professor at New York University and President of Bronx Community College.
- Edward Brooke, first black American to be elected by popular vote to the United States Senate.
- Frederick D. Wilkinson Jr., one of the first black executives at Macy's, the City of New York and the American Express Company; executive officer for passenger services for the New York City Transit Authority and executive officer for surface transit with operating responsibilities for the bus system in the five boroughs.
- Elmer T. Brooks, Brigadier General, USAF; second career as a government senior executive, serving in NASA Headquarters as Deputy Associate Administrator, Management and Facilities, and Space Communications.
- Frederic Ellis Davison, Major General, U. S. Army, third black general officer in the history of the US military and the first black man to lead an infantry brigade in combat, commanding officer of the 199th Infantry Brigade in Vietnam and, later, the 8th Infantry Division in Europe, commanding general of the Military District of Washington.
- Robert C. Weaver, Ph.D., appointed by President Franklin D. Roosevelt to his Black Cabinet, he acted as an informal adviser to Roosevelt as well as directing federal programs during the New

Deal; served as the first U.S. Secretary of Housing and Urban Development.

- William H. Hastie, lawyer, judge, educator, public official, and advocate for the civil rights of black Americans.
- Charles Hamilton Houston, Howard Law School Dean and NAACP Litigation Director who played a significant role in dismantling the Jim Crow laws, which earned him the title "The Man Who Killed Jim Crow."
- Hugh G. Robinson, Major General, U. S. Army, first black American general officer in the Corps of Engineers, served as deputy director of Civil Works and assumed command of the Southwestern Division.
- Eleanor Holmes Norton, Delegate to the United States Congress representing the District of Columbia.
- Vincent C. Gray, chairman of the Council of the District of Columbia and mayor of Washington D.C.

Business, religion and professionals:

- Charles R. Drew, an American physician, surgeon and medical researcher who discovered blood plasma and the first black surgeon to serve as an examiner on the American Board of Surgery.
- H. Naylor Fitzhugh, one of the first black American graduates of Harvard Business School and is credited with creating the concept of target marketing, and Vice President for Special Markets at Pepsi-Cola Company.
- Walter E. Fauntroy, pastor, New Bethel Baptist Church; national coordinator for the Poor People's Campaign; chairman, board of directors, Martin Luther King, Jr., Center for Social Change, Atlanta, Ga.; member, Leadership Conference on Civil Rights; Delegate to the United States Congress representing the District of Columbia.

PART V

THE END OF AN ERA

"Maybe all one can do is hope to end up with the right regrets."

—Arthur Miller, (1915-2005)

CHAPTER THIRTEEN

EXTERMINATION OF THE TRADITIONS

It is true that the history and traditions of the M Street and Dunbar high schools were shaped, to a large extent, by members of a few prominent families in Washington's black community. These were, typically, descendants of the antebellum "free persons of color," light-skinned in general, and, in some cases, physically indistinguishable from whites. This group was not numerically dominant and did not intermarry with the masses of blacks during most of the M Street-Dunbar period, so it had little *biological* effect on the rest of the black population. As late as the 1950s, there was a dedicated Dunbar teacher of many years' service who had, herself, graduated from Dunbar, whose mother had graduated in the class of 1885, and whose grandfather had headed the group that set up the original school in the basement of a church in 1870. This kind of involvement had a major and enduring cultural impact on the Dunbar community.[1]

The Setting of the Dunbar Tradition

The story of this school is important because many of the students and teachers of the school went on to become some of the most notable blacks in America. From 1870 until 1955, when the United States Supreme Court declared segregation in the District of Columbia public schools unconstitutional in the landmark case, *Bolling v. Sharpe*, which was also supplemented with *Brown v. Board of Education*, the school had a reputation for being among the best academic high schools in the country. Its teachers were some of the best scholars this country had to offer. Consequently, Dunbar was able to attract teachers with outstanding credentials because most white colleges, at that time, did not hire black professors.

The black people who established that first black Preparatory High School for Colored Youth understood slavery and its consequences. They knew of the troublous days of the *Missouri Compromise*, the hatred and sectional discords that resulted in the *Compromise of 1850* and saw the devastating effects of the *Kansas-Nebraska Bill*, the *Dred Scott Decision*, and the John Brown raid. They lived through the hectic days of slavery, disunion, civil war, and subsequent reconstruction, and they were never again going to subject themselves, their children, or their people to the tender mercies of America's peculiar institution.

The District of Columbia had flirted with the idea of an integrated school system at various times in its past, but the attempts to establish a unitary system were short-lived. The thought of a unitary school system provoked anger among many whites, who chafed at the prospect of their children having intimate social contacts with black children. However, the proposals also distressed the black community. Blacks felt an integrated system would shortchange them. The city, with Miner Teachers College, Howard University, and a relatively prosperous and less restricted black community, had attracted a large number of teachers and others qualified to teach in the public schools. They feared loss of their jobs to white teachers should the classrooms be integrated.[2]

The black middle class set the tone for the black community after the *Civil War* with values and goals typically characteristic of the white middle-class lifestyle; basically, attempting to move from accommodation to assimilation.[3] This lifestyle was much more than simply having a household income. It was a way of life replete with values, desires, and goals to attain a better quality of life. Even blacks with lower incomes sought a middle-class lifestyle and no one aspired to a lifestyle of poverty or dependency on external forces.

Families exhibited the values characteristic of the middle class even when they did not have the financial means to obtain this lifestyle. Typical values associated with the black middle-class lifestyle included a tendency to plan for retirement, a desire to be in control of their future, respect for and abidance of the law, and a desire for a good education for themselves and their children. The way to move forward in socio-economic status was through a good education and hard work. The values consistent with this life style included a desire to protect their families from various hardships such as health issues, financial difficulties, and crime.

The Dunbar Legacy

The black middle-class of Washington resisted the introduction of trade and industrial education courses into the M Street and Dunbar curriculum, fearing they would impinge upon the college-preparatory nature of the school. They did support in 1902, however, the founding of Armstrong Technical High School which was inspired by Booker T. Washington. Mary Church Terrell reproached those who opposed industrial education, but other blacks felt that a formalized education was the best way to improve black living standards. The founding of Armstrong helped settle the argument in that it allowed the separation of the college-bound student from the masses and allowed the academic school to concentrate on the students aspiring to higher education.[4]

The importance of individual parents is often ignored or slighted. Schemes for "open enrollment," voucher systems, or any other form of free choice by black parents of public school children invariably run into the argument that uneducated ghetto parents cannot make informed educational choices. However, the history of Dunbar High School shows that only a relative handful of people need to understand the complexities involved in creating a first-rate education. Once they have created such an education, the others need only be able to *recognize* it. Generations of lower class, working class, and middle-class youngsters were sent to Dunbar for just this reason.[5]

Washington's black society was as stratified as any in white America. Blacks in the city did not consider themselves a monolithic body; indeed, members of the black middle class known, with no insult intended, as "strivers" were more likely to socialize with whites than with black laborers. The Syphax family, for instance, was once among the most prominent families, black or white, in the District.[6]

For decades, members of the clan ran schools, churches, and businesses in Washington. The family's matriarch, Maria Carter Syphax, grew up a slave in Arlington, Virginia, the illegitimate daughter of George Washington Parke Custis and his housekeeper. In 1826, Custis, a wealthy landowner who was Martha Washington's grandson, admitted paternity and freed Maria. In the 1850s, Maria's son, William, moved to the District. In the years before his death in 1891, William Syphax became both the chief messenger at the Interior Department and the first head of the city's black school system. In 1878, even the white-owned *The Washington Post*, in describing his work for the federal government, praised Syphax for his "magnificent" mind and "coolness of intellect." Analogous was the Grimké family, whose patriarchs, brothers Francis and Archibald, graduated at the turn of the century from Princeton Theological Seminary and Harvard Law School, respectively.[7]

The social life of the city's black upper class revolved around voluntary organizations rather than places of employment. The city teemed with black social groups. The Knights of Pythias, Love and Charity, the Sons and Daughters of Moses, all had large chapters in the Washington. At the turn of the century, the District of Columbia supported 11 black Masonic lodges and 24 black Odd Fellows halls, with a combined membership of almost 4,000 members. The city also had many black fraternities and sororities (nearly every black fraternity and sorority in America was founded in Washington), which acted as social service agencies supporting, for instance, the Ionia Whipper Home for unwed mothers.[8]

Founded and maintained on its strength in business and education, Washington's black upper class did not at any time wield or outwardly seek political power. Yet, even before the abolition of slavery, the city's black professionals did agitate for civil rights. In 1850, William Syphax founded the Civil and Statistical Association, which sought to secure legal rights for blacks. Until his death in 1891, Syphax lobbied Congress for equal funding for the city's black schools; often with some degree of success. In the 1890s, the black Union League printed an annual list of "institutions that make no discrimination on account of race." The institutions cited included the G. H. Cardozo pharmacy on K Street, as well as several law practices.[9]

The Changed Black Cultural Environment

In the 1940s, 1950s, and the early 1960s, black communities featured a vertical integration of different segments of the black population. Lower class, working class, and middle-class black families all lived in the same communities, but in different neighborhoods. They sent their children to the same schools, used the same recreational facilities, and shopped at the same stores. Black middle and working classes were confined by racially restrictive covenants to communities also inhabited by the lower class, and their presence provided stability to black communities and inner-city neighborhoods. Black professionals (doctors, teachers, lawyers, social workers, ministers) serviced and lived in higher income neighborhoods in the black community. They reinforced and perpetuated the mainstream patterns of norms and behavior.[10]

The situation began changing in the late 1960s and early 1970s. Black professionals and the stable working class moved to higher-income neighborhoods in other parts of the city and the suburbs, leaving behind the most disadvantaged segments of the black community. The latter were a heterogeneous grouping of families and individuals who were outside the mainstream of the American occupational system. Included in this group were individuals who lacked education, training, and skills. They experienced long-term unemployment or were not in the labor force. Other individuals in this group were engaged in street crime and other forms of aberrant behavior or were incarcerated. Many of the families in this group were single-parent households that experienced long-term spells of poverty and/or welfare dependency. William Julius Wilson, a black scholar, uses the term "underclass" rather than the term "lower class" to suggest that the changes that had taken place in black communities and the groups that have been left behind were collectively different from those who lived in these neighborhoods in earlier years.[11]

Some viewed the use of the term underclass as destructive and misleading, lumping together different people who had different problems. Others denied that an underclass even existed for fear of being accused of being racist or of stigmatizing poor people. Sen. Daniel Patrick Moynihan's unflattering depiction of the black family led a number of people, particularly black liberals, to emphasize in the late 1960s and early

1970s the more positive aspects of the black experience.[12] Early arguments, which asserted that some characteristics of life in the black community were pathological,[13] were rejected in favor of descriptions that emphasized the strengths of the black community. Studies in the 1960s, that described "black ghetto behavior" as pathological, were reinterpreted or redefined as functional because, it was argued, blacks were demonstrating their ability to survive and even flourish in an economically depressed and racist environment.

No one wanted to talk about the underclass or a subculture of poverty anymore, and the problem was swept under the rug with little study and research conducted toward solutions. Most poverty academics have gotten out of the business of talking to poor black people altogether. Tenure passed through data sets, not inner-city streets, and the experts spoke a desiccated, technical language which only they understood.[14] Few social scientists undertook serious research in low-income communities today.

American life has coarsened over the past several decades, but the nature of the beast is still in question. Gertrude Himmelfarb sees it as a struggle between competing elites, in which the Left originated a counterculture that the Right failed to hold back.[15] Sen. Moynihan has given us the phrase "defining deviancy down," to describe a process in which we change the meaning of morality to fit what we are doing anyway.[16] One may add a third voice to the mix, that of the late historian Arnold Toynbee, who would find our recent history no mystery at all. We are witnessing the proletarianization of the dominant minority that now is setting the value standard for the larger society.[17]

The tradition based on love of God, country, and family is viewed as outmoded in the contemporary culture. In April 1966, *Time* magazine created a sensation with a cover article featuring some of the ideas of William Hughes Hamilton III, a tenured professor of church history at a small divinity school in Rochester, New York. Hamilton had been writing about the "death of God" for years in journals read mainly by ministers and theologians, but the *Time* article "Is God Dead?" became an icon of the rebellious and increasingly secular sixties.[18]

The concept of country, the cultural attachment to one's country, has changed substantially in today's culture. Patriotism today is deemed politically incorrect. The inclination of loyalty to country is more in keeping with Karl Marx: "The working men have no country."[19] The intact nuclear family of the 1950s is an endangered species today. Changing family dynamics is a consideration being applauded by progressives and liberals who glorify an increasing diversity of American households; i.e., blended families, same-sex partnerships, or cohabitation. The breakdown of the traditional family is being encouraged, with children viewed as a "weight" or burden because of the cost of raising them.[20]

This appears to support a trend indicated by one national Democrat leader who has as an administration goal, "… to give people life, a healthy life, liberty to pursue their happiness. And that liberty is to not be job-locked, but to follow their passion." She proposes an economy where people can be an artist, a poet, a photographer, or a writer without worrying about keeping their day job in order to have health insurance. People would start a business, be entrepreneurial, and take risks without worrying about job loss because of a child with asthma or someone in the family being bipolar. These conditions are viewed as "job locking."[21] This is a new culture, especially for minorities, predicated upon poverty rather than the middle-class values and aspirations that were the foundation of Dunbar High School from 1870 to 1955.

This culture of poverty is a social phenomenon in economics and sociology under which poverty-stricken individuals exhibit a tendency to remain poor throughout their lifespan, and, in many cases, across generations. The term "subculture of poverty" (later shortened to "culture of poverty") made its first prominent appearance in the work of American anthropologist Oscar Lewis who struggled to show that poverty transformed the lives of "the poor." Lewis listed many characteristics that suggested a presence of the culture of poverty. He argued, however, that not all these characteristics were shared among all the lower classes. The burdens of poverty were systemic and imposed upon poor members of society and this led to the formation of an autonomous subculture. Consequently, children were socialized into behaviors and attitudes that caused the continuation of their inability to escape the underclass.[22]

The people in the culture of poverty have a strong feeling of marginality, of helplessness, of dependency, of not belonging. They are like aliens in their own country, convinced that the existing institutions do not serve their interests and needs. Along with this feeling of powerlessness is a widespread feeling of inferiority, of personal unworthiness. In the United States, the culture of poverty for black people has the additional disadvantage of racial discrimination.[23]

In a chapter of *A Study of History,* entitled "Schism in the Soul," Arnold Toynbee discusses the disintegration of civilizations.[24] He observes that one of the consistent symptoms of disintegration is that the elites, Toynbee's "dominant minority," begin to imitate those at the bottom of society. He argues that the growth phase of a civilization is led by a creative minority with a strong, self-confident sense of style, virtue, and purpose. The uncreative majority follows along through mimesis, "a mechanical and superficial imitation of the great and inspired originals." In a disintegrating civilization, the creative minority has degenerated into elites that are no longer confident, no longer setting the example. Among other reactions are a "lapse into truancy" (a rejection, in effect, of the obligations of citizenship) and a "surrender to a sense of promiscuity" (vulgarizations of manners, the arts, and language) that "are apt to appear first in the ranks of the proletariat and to spread from there to the ranks of the dominant minority, which usually succumbs to the sickness of 'proletarianization.'"[25]

This seems very much like what has been happening in the United States. Toynbee's dominant minority consists of athletes, Hollywood celebrities, entertainers, and middle and upper class "progressives," who are role models for behavior, fashion, and political correctness. Truancy and promiscuity, until a few decades ago, were publicly despised and largely confined to what we used to call "low-class" or "trash." Today, they have transmuted those behaviors into a code that the elites sometimes imitate, sometimes placate, and fear to challenge. The hooker and gangster looks are in fashion. Tattoos and body piercing are the obvious evidence of moral change. Significant, also, is that people wear jeans to church. No one in the public eye calls any of this kind of dress "cheap" or "sleazy" anymore.[26]

Thousands of other non-middle-class black youngsters are being taken out of dreadful ghetto schools, created by those who purportedly understand education, and enrolled in local Catholic schools by Protestant black families. The cost of such schools is typically very low compared to other private schools, but still very high compared to ghetto incomes. Still, many black families are making this sacrifice in cities across the country.[27]

This widespread phenomenon remains a non-event for intellectuals, just as Dunbar High School was a non-event for 85 years. To admit the possibility of widespread individual initiative on the part of those at the bottom of the socioeconomic ladder would be to threaten a whole conception of the world and of the intellectuals' role in it.[28]

A 20th-reunion survey of the class of 1940 indicated that Dunbar graduates apparently shared a striking characteristic of the black privileged. Fertility rates are too low even to replace themselves; the married members of the class of 1940 averaged 1.6 children. Typical of middle-class blacks, they not only have far fewer children than lower-class black people, but they have fewer children than whites of the same income or education level as themselves. This demographic peculiarity means that a great part of the struggle from poverty to middle-class status must be repeated in the next generation. Very few black children are born to parents who could start them off with the benefits won by their own struggle.[29]

The Impact of Brown v. Board of Education

The U.S. Supreme Court decision (*Brown v. Board of Education of the City of Topeka*, 347 U.S. 483) handed down on May 17, 1954, was remarkable both for its simplicity and for the extraordinary fashion in which it avoided all legal and historical complexities. Chief Justice Earl Warren's opinion said that considering conditions in the 20th century, it was obvious that enforced segregation generated "a feeling of inferiority" in children which might well inflict such grave damage to their minds and hearts that it could never be undone. Public school segregation by state violated the equal protection clause of the Fourteenth Amendment. The old *Plessy* "separate but equal" rule was herewith formally overruled.[30] Down the street, not too far from the Supreme Court building, there was no feeling of inferiority among Dunbar teachers or students. They had demonstrated over many years that black students could obtain a superior education even under conditions of government-enforced segregation.

The justices did not order immediate desegregation of Southern schools in the 1954 opinion. Instead, in a subsidiary decision a year later, the Court invoked a principle from equity law to order desegregation carried out under local federal court direction "with all deliberate speed." The Court "legislated" by sweeping aside state decisions and decisions based on mere law and precedent and based its opinion on broad considerations of the national welfare. Thus, the Court has decided questions of the kind it faced in *Brown* in a "political" fashion.[31]

Brown set in motion a series of events, which in a few years destroyed all that had been built up over several decades at Dunbar High School. The whole dual school system in Washington had to be reorganized and, in this reorganization, all D.C. schools became neighborhood schools. The neighborhood, in which Dunbar was located, was one of the poorest multi-problem areas in the Washington, D.C. metropolitan area. For years it had been the pattern that most youngsters who *lived* near Dunbar did not *go* to Dunbar. Now, suddenly, they did and the character of the school began to change drastically. As an interim measure, however, existing Dunbar students could continue in the school until graduation, regardless of where they lived. Most elected to do so. This postponed the inevitable, but not for long.[32]

Teachers used to bright, eager students began to find learning problems and, then, disciplinary problems in their classrooms. Advanced courses in mathematics faced dwindling enrollments, which finally forced their cancellation. Remedial math courses appeared for the first time. Similar trends were apparent in other subjects as well. The Dunbar teaching staff at that time was somewhat advanced in years, and many began retiring, some as early as the minimum age of 55. In the past, it had been common for Dunbar teachers to stay on until the mandatory retirement age of 70. Equally qualified replacements were hard to find, since Dunbar was now rapidly becoming a typical ghetto school. Ironically, the drastic changes forced upon Dunbar in the reorganization that followed, the 1954 Supreme Court decision had virtually no desegregation effect given that the neighborhood in which the school was located was virtually all-black.[33] D.C. Public School records show that Dunbar is still segregated, with a student body composition that is 98 percent black.

The Supreme Court's desegregation decision, as such, did not doom Dunbar High School. Theoretically, it could have remained an academic high school, not tied to neighborhood boundaries, by simply opening to students without regard to race. There have been public schools of this sort in New York, Boston, and other cities, but in the emotionally charged atmosphere of the time, under the strong legal and political pressures to "do something" in the nation's capital, such a resolution was never a realistic possibility. "Neighborhood schools" was the rallying cry of whites resisting total desegregation; "integration" was the battle cry of black leaders. The maintenance of educational quality at a black academic high school had no such emotional appeal or political clout. The school reorganization plan gave something to both sides, a measure of integration and the maintenance of neighborhood schools. Thus, it was a political success, but, for Dunbar, it was an educational catastrophe.[34]

Alumni Thoughts on Replication of the M Street/Dunbar High School Model

From the time the Preparatory High School for Colored Youth was established by a group headed by William Syphax, a freedman and civil rights activist, black parents sent their children to school with a respect for learning and a readiness to work. Consequently, the M Street and Dunbar High Schools, run by a 100 percent black staff and faculty and populated by a 100 percent black student body, was a high-performing educational institution. When asked if they thought the educational and cultural atmosphere of the pre-1960 Dunbar High School model could be replicated in the environment of today, 51 percent of the respondents said no, 22 percent said yes, and 27 percent were ambivalent.

The reasons survey respondents gave to indicate why they thought replication of the Dunbar High School education model could or could not occur, were culture, students, and teachers. Culturally, 49 percent of the respondents indicated it would be difficult, if not impossible, to replicate the high-performance environment of M Street and Dunbar because the factor of segregation was the underpinning of the black community. Education during the "old Dunbar" period was the way to get ahead and compete with white people in the larger society. The middle-class values of God, country, and family were critical to black aspirations. During the period of 1920 to 1955, black neighborhoods were socio-economically diverse, and children were likely to see adults in a variety of positive roles. There was a strong sense of community where parents trusted and supported teachers as true professionals and leaders. Today, the dominant value system of black culture is primarily one of entitlement and the feeling that one is *owed* a good life.

Twenty-nine percent of respondents felt that black students nowadays are less prepared academically in the elementary and middle schools due to various sociological reasons; i.e., more single parent families, less discipline, and more incarceration of black males, and low expectations. Furthermore, the students do not have family support for education, lack self-discipline and a desire to learn, and have too many nonacademic distractions. It was also felt by 22 percent that many of our current teachers are not as well-educated and dedicated as faculty was during the respondents' time at Dunbar. Highly educated black professionals currently have economic options beyond that of teaching, while, for Dunbar faculty with doctorates, master's, and professional degrees, there were rare opportunities, outside of teaching, for other work in their fields of expertise.

Analysis and Discussion

Dunbar High School was the product of unique historical circumstances and its educational and social achievements have continued to have relevance. First, it showed what could be done with black children, including substantial numbers with low-income backgrounds. The question of *how* it was done needs more exploration. Teaching ethnocentric "relevance" did not do it, nor was it achieved with generous financing or with an adequate physical plant and equipment. What Dunbar had was a solid nucleus of parents, teachers, and principals who knew just what kind of education they wanted and how to produce it. They came from one of the oldest and largest urban black middle classes in the nation.[35]

The combination of historical circumstances that created Dunbar High School can never be recreated. Some of those essential circumstances *should not* be recreated; e.g., the racial barriers, which led a scholar, like Carter G. Woodson to teach at Dunbar High School, when he should have been conducting graduate seminars at a major university. Such historical experiences contain important lessons for the present. Dunbar did not seek "grass-roots" teachers who could "relate" to "disadvantaged" students, even though a substantial part of its students were the children of laborers, maids, messengers, and clerks. Dunbar faculty included, in today's parlance, many "overqualified" people. Almost all its principals during its 85-year ascendancy held degrees from the leading colleges and universities in the country instead of teacher's college degrees or education degrees from other institutions. They had been trained in hard intellectual fields and had been held to rigid standards. Their discipline was reflected in the atmosphere and standards of M Street and Dunbar High Schools.[36]

The beneficiaries of this situation were not exclusively, or even predominantly, middle-class students. Because the knowledge and educational values of the black middle-class were institutionalized and traditionalized, they became available to generations of low-income black students. Despite the fashionable, sometimes justified, criticism of the old "black bourgeoisie," they were a source of know-how, discipline, and organization otherwise virtually unavailable to lower-class blacks. The possibilities of transmitting this sophistication from a fortunate segment of the race to a wider range of receptive individuals may now have declined with the exit of the black middle class to the suburbs and with the rise of ideological barriers insulating black youth from such influences.[37]

The average I.Q. scores of Dunbar students were very much higher than those of black students in general, indicating that I.Q.'s and achievement are correlated among blacks as they are among whites. Note that, here, "achievement" means the *subsequent* accomplishments of the students rather than the socioeconomic background of their parents. Dunbar students from homes of low socioeconomic status also had substantially higher I.Q.'s than the black population at large. Dunbar teachers and counselors tutored promising students from such backgrounds and saw to it that both they and their parents understood the importance of a college education. The faculty also made special efforts to help parents and students to navigate the numerous practical details to be taken care of to secure college admission and financial aid. Most black high school students today get nothing resembling this kind of preparation, whether they are in all black or "integrated" schools.[38] A Ford Foundation study, for example, has reported the quality of counseling available nationally to black students during most of Dunbar's history has been "markedly inadequate" in both the North and the South, and the testimony of college recruiters paints an even grimmer picture of neglect or distorted "guidance" given to black students.[39]

The Dunbar experience is by no means an argument for either externally imposed segregation or self-imposed separatism. In fact, the school fought against both these ideas. The founders of the school first tried to secure equal access to all public schools for all students. Only when this failed, did they set about producing the best school they could for black youth. Down through the years, Dunbar teachers sought to break through the imposed insularity of a segregated society by bringing black and white speakers, entertainers, and other cultural attractions to the school.[40] Even a vice president visited and spoke at the school in 1954.[41] While Dunbar promoted racial pride, it was pride in the achievements of outstanding black persons as measured by universal standards, not special "black" achievements or special "black" standards.[42]

There is a tendency among some white critics of American black people to point to particular black "success" models and ask, "Why can't the *others* do it?" If racial barriers and cultural handicaps did not stop men like Ralph Bunche and Edward Brooke, how can they provide a blanket excuse for welfare recipients and hell-raisers? It is no answer to say that Bunche, Brooke, and others were just "exceptions," for that amounts to nothing more than rephrasing the question. What the Dunbar history shows is the enormous importance of time, tradition, and institutional circumstances in providing the essential setting in which individual achievement can flourish. If such achievements were wholly or predominantly a matter of personal ability, then this many outstanding individuals would not have come from one institution.[43]

This concentration of black achievement in a few special settings is not limited to Dunbar. As rare as black doctorates are, empirically they are not *isolated* phenomena. A study of 609 Ph.D.'s awarded to blacks in 1957-1962 showed that, while these black Ph.D.'s had attended 360 different high schools, 5.2 per cent of these high schools had produced 20.8 per cent of the Ph.D.'s. Dunbar was first among these high schools. A more relevant comparison would have included the vast number of black high schools whose alumni earned *no* Ph.D.'s during that period. However, this would only have made the concentration still more extreme.[44]

Another study examined those black families in which someone had earned a doctoral degree of some sort (M.D., Ph.D., etc.) and found that the average number of doctorates per family was 2.25. If the family setting permitted someone to earn a doctorate, it generally permitted more than one to earn a doctorate. Impressionistic evidence on the backgrounds of historic black figures also suggests that black achievements have come out of circumstances very different from those which many black Americans experience. W.E.B. DuBois grew up with aristocratic New England whites, Ralph Ellison grew up in frontier territory, George Washington Carver was raised by a German couple, and even Booker T. Washington, though "up from slavery," was in his youth the protégé of a succession of wealthy, educated, and influential whites. This in no way demeans the achievement of these men, for, ultimately, they had to have the ability to accomplish what they did. It does, however, underline the importance of the special circumstances necessary for individuals to realize their potential and the remoteness of these circumstances from the lives of most American blacks.[45]

Today, kids are playing basketball, getting high, and not taking their education seriously. In fact, if one acts too serious about schoolwork and study, others think there is something wrong. Black kids often pretend they are not smart and do not spend time developing their intellectual talents. Many black people, today, put more emphasis on their ancestors having been slaves than they do on the progress most their ancestors have made to date. This whole attitude of anti-intellectualism in black communities is one of the most damaging things that can be done to young black adults.

Much of the contemporary discussion of teaching methods, educational philosophies, and organizational principles in the school system, seems unreal in the context of the "blackboard jungle" atmosphere in many ghetto schools. While more classroom time is often devoted to trying to maintain order, or contain disorder, than to teaching, more education literature is devoted to philosophy, politics, "black English," and, in fact, almost anything other than the overriding problem of reducing the chaos, disruption, and fear that can prevent *any* teaching method or philosophy from being effective. Yet, it is not considered politic, much less chic, to discuss such things.[46]

During the 1870-1955 period, the self-selection of students freed Dunbar from the incubus of disinterested and disruptive students. After such students ceased to enter Dunbar, following the school reorganization of 1954, the school was destroyed within a few years. Various forms of self-selection can free other institutions from the hard core of disruptive and violent students, but all plans that involve freedom of choice (vouchers, open enrollment, etc.) are damned by critics as inhibiting racial integration. It is an empirical question, however, whether black youngsters will gain more educationally by separation from a hard core of hell-raisers or by integration with whites. Studies of the educational effects of integration show few gains. However, the shibboleth of integration is still powerful enough to thwart fundamental educational reform.[47]

Conclusion

While the Dunbar experience provides some empirical refutation for currently fashionable statements about the "necessary" ingredients of good education for black children, it is not itself a universal model. Part of Dunbar's strength was that it did not try to be all things to all people. The founders of the school intended it to be an institution solely devoted to preparing black students for college and, in that special role, it was unsurpassed. It showed what could be done and some of the ways that it could be done. Moreover, it demonstrated that some of the presumed "prerequisites" of good education are not really essential. What *is* essential is to create and sustain an atmosphere of academic achievement.[48]

Dunbar High School provides no instant formulas for use by "practical" planners. Its example suggests that instant formulas by "practical" planners may not be the way to quality education. What is needed, above all, is *a sense of purpose*, a faith in what can be achieved, and an appreciation of the hard work required to achieve it. As the many flaws of Dunbar indicate, it is not necessary to find ideal people or an ideal setting, but it does require a dedicated nucleus of people in a setting where their dedication can be effectual.[49]

CHAPTER FOURTEEN

EPILOGUE

The *Brown v. Board of Education* desegregation decision was not the sole determinant for the continuation of Dunbar High School as a high performing academic high school. Theoretically, it could have become a magnet school, unconstrained by neighborhood boundaries, and allowed admission to all students without regard to race. However, in the emotionally charged atmosphere of the time, such an option was never a realistic possibility. "Neighborhood schools" was the rallying cry of whites resisting total desegregation, while "integration" was the battle cry of black leaders. The maintenance of educational quality at a black academic high school had no emotional appeal or political clout. The school reorganization plan was a political success, but it was an educational disaster for Dunbar. It gave something to both sides, a measure of integration and the maintenance of neighborhood schools.[1]

The Board of Education, that promulgated the reorganization plan of 1954 that destroyed Dunbar High School, seems to have had no appreciation of or concern about this possibility. In the lengthy and bitter debates recorded in the Board of Education minutes, almost every conceivable problem was argued, other than the consequence of the reorganization on Dunbar High School. This was even more remarkable because the Board's most vocal critic of the school superintendent's plan was a Dunbar alumna. Years later, she could not recall saying a word about Dunbar High School at the time, even in executive sessions not reported in Board minutes. Integration was the cry of the time and the fight of the hour.[2]

Archie Morris III, D.P.A.

The Changing Culture

Before the 1950s, the black family taught values that had changed little between 1880 and 1920. Reinforced by those taught in the church, the values of thrift, hard work, self-respect, and righteousness were the cornerstone of "respectability." As was custom in society at that time, the mother did not work when the family had young children. Fathers, therefore, played a valuable role in the family. They brought home the paychecks that housed and fed the family and keeping the children fed, clothed, housed, and out of poverty was important. Bringing a paycheck home was vital because nothing is more devastating to the lives of children than poverty. Moreover, the father was the family's moral guardian, the symbol of masculinity for his sons, and a disciplinarian.[3]

In the old two-parent black family, the father played many roles including that of companion, care provider, spouse, protector, model, moral guide, and teacher.[4] Parents, mother and father, were the example for children to follow, and if the parents became involved in racial uplift efforts, the children took them at their word.[5] The closeness of these families may have been a defense mechanism in reaction to discrimination from the outside world, but it was undoubtedly legitimate. The warmth created in the home environment provided a shelter, but, correspondingly, it nourished the growth of happy children and provided continuity and hope for the future. Most marriages were partnerships forged to further family goals and perpetuate status. Divorce was not unheard of, but it was rare. Separations were not unusual. The black family in Washington was a line of defense against society, and its values and strategies ensured that family status would continue through succeeding generations.[6]

The late 1960s and early 1970s saw a major cultural revolution in the United States. The Vietnam policies of the Johnson administration unleashed the largest and most effective antiwar movement in the nation's history, a movement that flourished particularly on elite college campuses. The so-called countercultural or "hippie movement," in which young people abandoned middle-class values *en masse* as they "turned on, tuned in, and dropped out," became a political problem on college campuses and in high schools.[7]

Many young Americans let their hair grow long; traded in their high heels and skirts and their ties and button-down shirts for torn jeans, tie-dyed T-shirts, and dirty sneakers. They talked openly about and even practiced "free love." They listened to music that was incomprehensible to their parents, smoked marijuana, and rejected authority. However, while most young Americans were not foul-mouthed hippies, dope users, free-lovers, members of antiwar coalitions, or Marxists, there were enough of telegenic countercultural, anti-establishment types at Columbia, Harvard, and Berkeley, to suggest that the next generation of young Americans might not be like their parents.[8] Unfortunately, this has been particularly true for black young adults.

Today, the neighborhood around Dunbar has a high concentration of low-income families that spawns social problems by bringing together welfare dependent, single-parent families whose fatherless children disproportionately become school dropouts, drug users, nonworkers, and criminals. There are a dozen or so social service agencies in this relatively small area, bringing homeless or indigent people to the area daily. Consequently, potential businesses and house hunters may be deterred when they see people lingering on the streets outside the agencies. Moreover, while crime has dropped in the area, it is not gone. Shootings, stabbings, and home and car break-ins still occur too frequently.[9]

In this kind of community, mothers are predominant and create a maternalistic environment. They may have multiple children, but the children often have different fathers who do not live in the household or provide child support. The profile of family usually shows an unmarried black female in her mid-twenties, with no high school diploma or GED, and three children younger than 10. The concern of the mothers is to have the children completely protected as much as possible from the outer world and to be gratefully attached to the mother for as long as they live. The avoidance of risk gets a very high priority. On the other hand, in a paternalistic environment, it is said that fathers want their children to grow up to be self-reliant, self-supporting, and able to cope with a recalcitrant world.[10] Fathers, however, are not a predominant presence in the homes around Dunbar High School.

The neighborhood did not reap the benefits of the Shaw Area Renewal Plan, as adopted by the National Capital Planning Commission on January 9, 1969. New Jersey Avenue and Florida Avenue seem to be barriers to development, while nearby neighborhoods are constantly sprouting new restaurants, residential projects, and renovated row houses. All that began gradually changing in the early 2000s. The area received a big push a few years ago, when more than 40 row houses clustered around Bates Street went on the market at once. The homes had been serving as Section 8 subsidized rental units and were quite dilapidated. Many wound up in the hands of first-time home buyers. The new homeowners in the community began a serious burst of activity and a group covering much of Truxton Circle, the Bates Area Civic Association, was formed to address issues such as community beautification, crime prevention, and deterrence.[11]

The End of Symbolism for "Old Dunbar"

In the mid-1970s, a highly contested and public debate occurred in Washington, D.C. It centered on the impeding demolition of the vacant 1916 building that had previously housed Dunbar High School. Advocates for demolition, including the school's administration, many city officials, and members of the Board of Education, were adamant that they had in mind the best interests of the students. Instead of a worn-down structure, students would enjoy a highly innovative and completely modernized school plant. The students would gain a home football field where the 1916 building once stood. Because the Dunbar athletics program was now receiving nationwide recognition, the field was an essential addition to the new school grounds.[12]

Many black Washingtonians wanted a clean break with everything they felt Dunbar once represented; i.e., predominantly light-skinned people who thought they were better than others and assumed themselves to have superior intellect, wealth, and membership in the upper echelons of society. They called for the destruction of the old building as soon as the new one was ready, but admirers and older alumni of the old school would have none of it. They demanded the building be preserved as a historical monument to what they achieved there and to the pioneering role the school played in the development of higher education among blacks. Thus, the relatively silent war that pro- and anti-Dunbar factions had been waging for decades erupted into a loud and hostile confrontation.[13]

The spirit and the wishes of the anti-Dunbar faction were championed by the D.C. Board of Education, which wanted no further reminders of what the old school stood for in the life of black Washingtonians. The Board led the fight to have the old building demolished. A good many of its members were young black professionals, politicians, and grass-roots community leaders. Some of them came out of the civil rights movement of the 1960s, were educated in other parts of the country (or in other high schools in Washington), and had no feelings for what many called Dunbar's illustrious past. The point was that the school did not have an adequate athletic field and there was no space for a sports stadium apart from where the old building stood.[14]

Without the skillful maneuvers of Mary Hundley, Dr. W. Montague Cobb, and Senator Edward Brooke, the order to knock down the old Dunbar building would have been swiftly issued, signed, and delivered.[15] Many Dunbar alumni, preservationists, and local historians countered the demolition arguments proposing that keeping the historic Dunbar High School would benefit students. Preservation of the building would provide students with a physical reminder of the rich history of their school, an example how slaves valued education as an integral part of freedom, and black academic excellence despite *de jure* segregation throughout America. The protracted arguments and debates about saving the building were unyielding on both sides, but the pro-Dunbar proponents never had a chance of saving the old 1916 building. It was demolished in July 1977.

A new philosophy had taken root and some blacks were demonstrating their ability to survive and even flourish in an economically depressed racist environment. However, people living in an area predicated upon a culture of poverty have very little sense of history. They are a marginal people who know only their own troubles, their own local conditions, their own neighborhood, or their own way of life. Usually, they have neither the knowledge, the vision, nor the ideology to see the similarities between their problems and those of others like themselves elsewhere in the world. They are not class conscious, but they are very sensitive to status distinctions.[16]

The Open Space Plan Dunbar High School

Mayor Walter Washington first requested funds to replace the 1916 high school in the city's 1972 public schools' budget. Replacing the old

Dunbar, however, had been a topic of interest since the late 1960s when the Board of Education declared the building "had passed its prime."[17]

In 1971, the architectural critic Wolf Von Eckardt proclaimed in *The Washington Post*:

> Washington's school board is at last ready to break through the old, eggcrate classroom walls. . . All of the 11 new public school buildings currently on the drawing boards call for the so-called "open plan" that replaces the rigid physical and intellectual confinement of enclosed classrooms.[18]

Furthermore, *The Washington Post* made public the design for the new Dunbar High School. Von Eckardt contended the innovation was:

> "something that Washington's public school builders have not dared since 1868 when the Franklin School [designed by Adolph Cluss] at Thirteenth and K streets, N.W., was built and won first prize as a model school building at the Vienna Exposition of 1873."[19]

Robert deJongh, a 27-year old native of the Virgin Islands and a graduate of the Howard University School of Architecture, was the Dunbar High School project designer. He ingeniously adapted a prototypical suburban "house" layout, which normally would require a large campus site, to a constricted urban setting. The deJongh design was based on a ninety-foot tower. It would not be divided into ten autonomous, stacked floors, but, instead, offer a continuous flow of space, best experienced in staggered split-level areas. Von Eckardt explained:

The levels are grouped into three "houses," that is, complete schools within the school. Each "house" has four levels, each taking half of the total floor area, which form a complete unit for one age group. Each has its own lecture and instruction areas, studies, laboratories, teacher preparation centers, a kitchenette for food preparation, and a combined lunch and multi-purpose space and an outdoor terrace for lounging and recreation.[20]

The separation of the tower space into smaller schools, "houses," is the urban vertical equivalent to early postwar solutions for suburban school campuses. DeJongh considered site limitations and attempted to create small-scale intimacy within a dense package. The Educational Facilities Laboratories (EFL) supported the incorporation of the house model in urban settings, stating in 1968, "While the facilities could be spread out . . . if the school were built in the suburbs, they need not be: the houses and other buildings could occupy separate floors of a city skyscraper, for example."[21] When the new Dunbar building opened in 1977, students and staff were optimistic about its innovative planning and design. As one 18-year old student stated, "We are proud to have this school . . . and we'll see that it is properly taken care of."[22]

The Dunbar design incorporated other progressive components. It included spacious athletic facilities and up-to-date science labs. Additionally, the dining area featured "wall to wall carpeting, as well as a café styled interior with small four-person tables that stand in marked contrast to the long 'prison' style tables which are mainstays in other school cafeterias."[23] This design was not executed exactly as planned. In the modified plan, the terraces that were prominent in the tower drawing were omitted, creating a more pronounced feeling of fortification or, possibly, defense.

The new Dunbar building was located at 1301 New Jersey Avenue, N.W. Initially, there were 889 students and 56 teachers for grades 9 through 12. Since desegregation, of course, it has been a neighborhood school with a student body that is nearly 100 percent black. As of early 2014, there were 593 students and 47 teachers for grades 9 through 12.

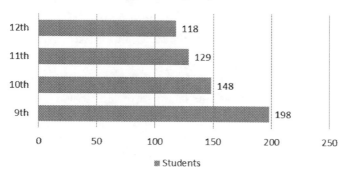

Student Body by Grade

Source: U. S. News and World Report, High Schools, 2016

Table 14-1

The *historical* approach to the new design signified a rejection of the 1916 building's past and a focus on contemporary and future needs. It revealed a strong disconnect between past accomplishments of the old Dunbar and the academically unproductive state of the institution in the 1970s.[24] Instead of the values and culture of middle-class America, it brings to mind the social phenomena in economics and sociology under which poverty-stricken individuals exhibit a tendency to remain poor throughout their lifespan and, in many cases, across generations.[25] In this culture, higher education and higher level professional, managerial, and technology careers are not the usual priorities. The young black adult, especially the male, is forced to base his self-esteem on a stereotyped picture of sexual impulsiveness, irresponsibility, verbal bombast, posturing, and compensatory achievement in entertainment and athletics.[26]

Dunbar is no longer a college preparatory school in the strict sense of its past. Its web site suggests that its mission is to provide an all-inclusive instructional program for students that fosters maximum academic achievement, enabling them to enjoy lifelong learning while becoming productive citizens. It states that Dunbar aims to serve as a learning community where students undergo diverse, meaningful opportunities and experiences and receive a quality education.[27] The school's programs include Academic Enrichment, Wellness and Fitness, Arts and Culture, and Special Education. Dunbar is now best known, however, for its athletic programs. It competes in the D.C. Interscholastic Athletic Association and does particularly well with its football and basketball teams.

It is a painful irony that the original Dunbar High School building, which opened in 1916, accommodated a school with a record of high academic achievements for generations of black students. Despite the inadequacies of the building, *de jure* segregation, and the inadequacies of the financial support that the school received, it was an outstanding academic success. By contrast, the open plan Dunbar High School with its new building and athletic field became just another ghetto school with abysmal standards and low test score results despite the District of Columbia's record of having some of the country's highest levels of money spent per pupil.[28]

Ironically, the open space building itself was widely considered to be a factor in the school's problems. By the early 1970s, the phrase open classrooms dominated educators' vocabularies, even though parents and practitioners found it hard to pin down exactly what open education meant. Many school boards adopted open-education programs and open-space schools were built across the country. However, few superintendents or principals could risk saying aloud that they had neither heard of the innovation nor found it desirable without risking sneers from peers or criticism from superiors. So many schools were adopting the physical attributes of open classrooms that some advocates wondered whether the spirit of informal education was truly being followed.[29]

In his 1973, book *The Open Classroom Reader*, Charles Silberman warned enthusiastic teachers and parents:[30]

> By itself, dividing a classroom into interest areas does not constitute open education; creating large open spaces does not constitute open education; individualizing instruction does not constitute open education . . . . For the open classroom . . . is not a model or set of techniques, it is an approach to teaching and learning.

The artifacts of the open classroom—interest areas, concrete materials, wall displays—are not ends in themselves but rather means to other ends. . . . In addition, open classrooms are organized to encourage:

- Active learning rather than passive learning;
- Learning and expression in a variety of media, rather than just pencil and paper and the spoken word;
- Self-directed, student-initiated learning more than teacher-directed learning.

Just a few years later, however, things transformed. In the mid-1970s, with the economy stagnating and the nation deeply divided over the Vietnam War, critics again trained their sights on the public schools. The national crisis gave rise to a perception, amplified by the media, that academic standards had slipped, that the desegregation movement had failed, and that urban schools were becoming violent places. This time the call was not for open education, but for a return to the basics mirroring general social trends; namely, a conservative backlash against the cultural and political changes of the 1960s and early 1970s.[31]

Traditional schools sprang up in suburbs and cities. Open-space schools rebuilt their walls. States tried to raise academic standards by developing minimum competency tests that high-school students had to pass to receive a diploma. Citations in the media and academic journals indicate that interest in open classrooms peaked somewhere around 1974. By the early 1980s, open classrooms had become a footnote in doctoral dissertations.

Were open classrooms just another fad by "pedagogical progressives?" Perhaps they were, in the sense that, like hula hoops and pet rocks, they soared onto the scene and then disappeared without a trace. Considering them merely a fad, however, would miss the deeper meaning of open classrooms. Open-space classrooms were yet another skirmish in the ideological wars that have split educators and the public since the first tax-supported schools opened their doors in the early 1800s.[32]

A School Building Inspired by History

In December 2010, Adrian Fenty, then mayor of Washington, D.C., announced the highly anticipated plans for the re-design of Paul Laurence Dunbar High School. The Office of Public Education Facilities Management (OPEFM), a city agency created in 2007 to fulfill campaign promises for a complete overhaul of the school system, had conducted two design competitions in two years with the hopes of selecting a winning design for the Dunbar building. After a year-long design competition for the new school, Mayor Fenty announced on December 14, 2010, that the winning proposal was submitted by the architecture team of Ehrenkrantz Eckstut & Kuhn Architects-Engineers (EEK) and Moody-Nolan Architects. Both firms are based in Washington, D.C.[33]

Interviews were conducted with Dunbar alumni to determine what they thought should be incorporated in the forthcoming building. The idea was to create an edifice that would honor the past, the present, and the future.[34] D.C. Mayor Vincent Gray and alumni from Paul Laurence Dunbar High School gathered on August 19, 2013, to celebrate the new $122-million-dollar building that ostensibly draws upon the school's history to inspire students. An alumnus, who graduated in 2002 from the old Dunbar building that still stood next door, used the words "breathtaking" and "refreshing" to describe the new school. The new Dunbar, with 280,000 square feet of space, is located at First and N Streets, N.W., in the Truxton Circle neighborhood and boasts a soaring and light-filled atrium, a new pool and gym, a 600-person auditorium, and four academies featuring classrooms and labs. The design maximizes learning spaces while embracing technology.[35]

Unlike its predecessor, more than to showcase modernity, the new Dunbar, was inspired by its history. In the past, Dunbar graduated generations of black leaders, lawyers, and artists, and their names are inscribed on 118 plaques throughout the school. Another 130 plaques are blank, hinting that any future graduates of the school could see their name featured on them as well.[36] The school's interior features an atrium-like armory that is the "heart of the school," connecting the academic wing, sports fields, gym, pool, auditorium, and cafeteria seating areas. It does not have a rifle range.

The school also features a small museum commemorating its rich history and the accomplishments of its many graduates, which included Nannie Helen Burroughs, Mary Church Terrell, Carter G. Woodson, D.C. Del. Eleanor Holmes Norton, and D.C. Mayor Vince Gray. During the ribbon-cutting, alumni from as far back as the class of 1925 marveled at the new building while remembering their time at Dunbar. District officials hope that the building's transformation will usher in a new era in academic achievement. The new building will accommodate 1,100 students, more than double the 500 that have attended the school in recent years.[37] It officially opened to students August 19, 2013.

The Arguments Continue

There is already a proposal to improve Dunbar High School by converting it to an autonomous and selective school. This has generated widespread debate among teachers, students, alumni and community members. The push for change, which a small group of alumni and parents quietly developed over the past several months, would give Dunbar more freedom to make decisions about whom it hires, how it spends its money and how it designs its academic offerings. It would transform a neighborhood school that is legally obligated to take all comers into an application-only institution that could choose its students. Such an arrangement most likely would give Dunbar the ability to choose not to serve the neediest neighborhood children.[38]

It is an idea the group feels could jump-start a transformation of Dunbar from one of the city's worst-performing schools to an institution that once again would be known for academic excellence. Critics of the proposal, however, say it would be built on the rejection of students who come to class with profound challenges that need to be addressed; i.e., poor reading ability, deficient math skills, and difficult home lives.[39] It is not easy to turn around any low-performing school, particularly a high school. Students come to high school years below grade level in reading, writing, mathematics, and many other subjects. Frequently, they also bring with them dangerous behavioral patterns.

The two most selective public high schools are the School Without Walls (Walls) and Benjamin Banneker Academic High School. Both get far more applicants than they admit. Banneker's student body is 85 percent black and 60 percent low-income. Walls, in contrast, is 45 black and 17 percent low-income. In 2013, Walls, in Foggy Bottom, received over 1,000 applications for a class of 130 to 150. Banneker received about 700 applications that year and, like Walls, ended up with a class of 150. Those figures, standing alone, would indicate that there is room in Washington for another selective school.[40]

However, Banneker takes all applicants who meet the school's qualifications, which are based on grades point average (GPA), test scores, teacher recommendations, and an interview.[41] Walls requires that any student interested in applying must follow an entrance procedure. Students must have a 3.0 GPA in their core subject classes, receive a proficient or advance score on a standardized test (SSAT, DCCAS, Stanford, any State-mandated test, PSAT/SAT, or any other approved standardized test). If a student meets all the requirements above, they are invited to take a standardized, proprietary test that includes multiple choice math (algebra and geometry), multiple choice reading comprehension, and a writing prompt. The test is not timed, and students have as long as they need to complete it. If a student passes the test, he or she is invited, along with their parent(s) or guardian, for a panel interview at the school. The panel consists of faculty, staff, and students.[42]

While it appears there are enough "qualified" students to fill up Dunbar, which has a capacity of 1,100, as well as the existing selective schools, the applicant pool may not be as large as it appears. One may assume that many students apply to both Banneker and Walls, along with another application-only school, McKinley Tech, which is almost as selective as Banneker. Dunbar would in all probability end up offering admission to students who, rather than being truly gifted or advanced, are the ones who show up for school, do the work, do not cause discipline problems, and are not classified as special education or English language learners.[43]

There is the possibility of giving the Dunbar group much of what it is asking for, just not the right to be selective in admissions.[44] The old Dunbar was not a "selective" school in the sense in which we normally use that term. There were no tests to take to for admission. Undoubtedly, there was *self-selection* in the sense that students who were serious about college preparation went to Dunbar. Those who were not serious, had to find other places where they could while away their time without having to meet high academic standards.[45] The Dunbar group is also seeking more autonomy for the school in hiring and spending decisions. In this respect, one is reminded that the M Street and Dunbar High faculty and principals were noted for high qualifications and educational backgrounds and, accordingly, they were paid good salaries.[46]

One can argue that parents may be more educated and more sophisticated today than they were in the past. However, it is not clear that their political activism or community involvement in schools and education has been a net benefit in the black community. At the very least, history shows that their involvement beyond the concerns of their individual children has never been essential. Today, education is politics and, politically, failure becomes a reason to demand more money, smaller classes, and more trendy courses and programs, ranging from "black English" to bilingualism and "self-esteem." [47]

ARCHIE MORRIS III, D.P.A.

A New Way of life

Even the best things come to an end. The past cannot be recaptured and there is much in the past that we do not want to recapture. When education was the chief means of ameliorating problems of race and class, Dunbar travelled with black people through the long journey and rigors of making the adjustment from slavery to freedom, through the travails of dealing with segregation as blacks attempted to assimilate into the American mainstream society. The academic achievements of the M Street and Dunbar education model, between 1870 and 1955, cannot be replicated in the current DC public high school environment. Emulating the high-performance environment of the M Street and Dunbar High Schools would be difficult in the best of times. Yet, through the travails of dealing with segregation as blacks attempted to assimilate into the American mainstream society, the school had an open admissions policy. Children from all neighborhoods were granted entry without questions concerning the families' socio-economic level. A Dunbar education was an important part of the recurring salient thematic element blacks still needed in their fight for freedom.

Furthermore, M Street and Dunbar strove unceasingly to prepare its pupils for acceptance at non-segregated northern and mid-western universities. There were many racially motivated attempts to convert it to a manual arts program by whites, including public school officials. Percy M. Hughes, the white director of high schools, recommended an increase in manual training, particularly for M Street students, who needed to learn the "dignity of labor." They would be "better educated men and women and therefore better fitted to win out in life's battle if properly trained in the use of tools as well as books."[48] Future scholars also may well find that this past racism is strongly associated with the reasons why Dunbar has been ignored in urban educational policy and research.

Black neighborhoods are no longer socio-economically diverse, and children are not likely to see adults in a variety of positive roles. Today, the dominant value system of black culture is one of low expectations dominated by more single parent families, less discipline, and more incarceration of black males. Consequently, black students are less prepared academically in the elementary and middle schools for entrance into high school. Entering students do not have family support for education, lack self-discipline, and have little desire to learn. Finally, teachers are not as well qualified and committed as the past M Street and Dunbar faculty and well-educated blacks have economic alternatives to teaching. To match the faculties of pre-1955, a minimum requirement for teaching at Dunbar today would require, on average, a master's degree in the field a faculty member is teaching, with preference given to a doctorate or A.B.D. (all but dissertation). Equally important, however, is the concept of a professional ethos among teachers.

Being a professional in one's chosen field means more than wearing a coat and tie or possessing a college degree. The M Street and Dunbar faculties were true professionals who created a workplace environment that reflected high standards. Faculty and students were neat in their appearance and polite and well-spoken when interacting with each other and with parents. Moreover, they could be counted on to find a way to get the job done, and set themselves apart from other teachers, black and white, by taking courses to continue their education, attending seminars, publishing written works, and obtaining any related professional designations.

The culture of poverty has been institutionalized through expanded welfare assistance and government dependency. The new entitlement beneficiaries are not employed and, instead, receive Food Stamps, welfare checks, Section 8 vouchers, and Medicaid. In this age of what some may term to be neo-slavery, the old Dunbar is passé. These social, political, and cultural factors mitigate against replicating in the 21th century the high-performance environment that existed at the M Street and Dunbar High Schools prior to 1955.

We cannot return to the past, even if we wanted to, but let us hope that we can learn something from the past to make for a better present and future. If nothing else, history shows what can be achieved, even in the face of adversity. Most people in the inner-cities of America, today, do not feel an excellent education or professional job skills and qualifications are required to realize the American dream. The nation's value system has been significantly altered. The aim of social workers once was to help people get off the welfare rolls as quickly as possible. Now, social workers have the opposite aim, to try to get as many people on welfare as possible. The persistence of the underclass is advertised as a positive lifestyle, no matter how deviant and dysfunctional, and members of the class proclaim their "right" to be subsidized to an even greater extent by the government. The nation's value system has been significantly altered, but the new progressive urban education policies do not appear to have made our country a better place to live; especially, for those caught up in the culture of poverty.

Unfortunately, the black community owns this cultural transformation and, consequently, the legacy of academic excellence no longer prevails at Dunbar. Hence, the journey from slavery to freedom is unfinished.

NOTES

Preface

1   Jean Jacques Rousseau, *Emile, On Philosophy of Education* (New York: Promethus Books, 2003), p. 2.
2   Jervis Anderson, "A Very Special Monument," *The New Yorker*, March 20, 1978, p. 105.
3   Anderson, *op. cit.*, p. 93.
4   Thomas Sowell, "Black Excellence—the Case of Dunbar High School," *The Public Interest*, pp. 26-27.

Chapter One - Slavery and Bondage

1   Edward Burnett Tylor, *Primitive Culture: Researches into the Development of Mythology, Philosophy, Religion, Art, and Custom* (New York: Gordon Press, 1971), p. 1.
2   Seymour Drescher, *Abolition: A History of Slavery and Antislavery* (New York: Cambridge University Press, 2009) pp 4–5.
3   Paul Finkelman, "Laws" in Paul Finkelman and Joseph C. Miller, eds., *Macmillan Encyclopedia of World Slavery* (New York: MacMillan Reference, 1998) Vol. 2, pp. 477-478.
4   Aaron Sheehan-Dean, "A Book for Every Perspective: Current Civil War and Reconstruction Textbooks," *Civil War History*, Vol, 51, No. 3, September 2005, pp 317–324.
5   J. Dyneley Prince, "The Code of Hammurabi," *The American Journal of Theology*, Vol. 8, No. 3 (Jul. 1904), pp. 601–609. Published by: The University of Chicago Press Stable URL: http://www.jstor.org/stable/3153895
6   Thomas Sowell, *Black Rednecks and White Liberals* (San Francisco: Encounter Books, 2005), p. 115; Daniel Evans, Daniel, "Slave Coast of Europe," *Slavery and Abolition*, Vol. 6, No. 1 (May 1985), p. 42.

7   Robert C. Davis, *Christian Slaves, Muslim Masters: White Slavery in the Mediterranean, the Barbary Coast, and Italy, 1500-1800* (New York: Palgrave Macmillan, 2003, p 23; Philip D. Curtin, *The Atlantic Slave Trade: A Census* (Madison, University of Wisconsin Press, 1969), pp. 72, 75, 97.

8   Paul Johnson (1997). *A History of the American People* (New York: HarperCollins Publishers, Inc.), p. 4.

9   *Ibid.*

10 August Meier and Elliott Rudwick, *From Plantation to Ghetto* (New York: Hill and Wang, 1970), p. 27.

11 *Ibid.*, pp. 25-27; Johnson, *op. cit.*, pp. 4-5.

12 Bernard Lewis, *Race and slavery in the Middle East: an historical enquiry* (New York: Oxford University Press, 1992), pp. 52-53.

13 *Ibid.*, p. 53.

14 Johnson, *op. cit.*, p. 9.

15 Mier and Rudwick, op. cit., p.36.

16 Sowell, *op. cit.*, p. 115.

17 John Henderson Russell, *The Free Negro in Virginia, 1619-1865* (unpublished Doctoral dissertation, The Johns Hopkins University, Baltimore, 1913); James Curtis Ballagh, *A History of Slavery in Virginia*, (Baltimore: The Johns Hopkins Press, 1902); John Codman Hurd, *The Law of Freedom and Bondage in the United States*, in two volumes (Boston: Little, Brown and Company, 1858).

18 Ira Berlin, *Many Thousands Gone: The First Two Centuries of Slavery in North America* (Cambridge, MA: Harvard University, Press 1998), p. 8.

19 *Ibid.*

20 Frank Tannenbaum, *Slave and Citizen: The Classic Comparative Study of Race Relations in the Americas* (Boston: Beacon Press, 1946), p. 117.

21 25 Berlin, op. cit., pp. 8-10.

22 Woodbury Lowery, *Spanish Settlements within the Present Limits of the United States* (2 Vols., New York, 1903-1905).

23 A fragment of Fray Sabastian Canete of DeSoto's Expedition appeared in a journal of that era and it described an advanced state of development among the Cofitachiqui. This translation was made by Eugene Lyon and published in Clayton, Lawerence A, Venon James Knight, Jr., Edward C. Moore. *The De Soto Chronicles: The Expedition of Hernando De Soto to North America 1539 – 1543.* Volume I and II. (Tuscaloosa: University of Alabama Press, 1994.

24 David Hackett Fischer, *Albion's Seed: Four British Folkways in America* (New York: Oxford University Press, 1991), pp. 387-388.

25 William Thorndale, "The Virginia Census of 1619," *Magazine of Virginia Genealogy*, Vol. 33, (1995), pp. 155-70.

26 Johnson, *op. cit.*, p. 27.

27 *Ibid.*

28 A. Leon Higginbotham, Jr., In *the Matter of Color; Race and the American Legal Process: The Colonial Period* (New York: Oxford University Press, 1978), pp. 19-21.

29 Carl Degler, "Slavery and the Genesis of American Race Prejudice," *Comparative Studies in Sociology and History* (October 6, 1959), p. 52.

30 Higginbotham, *op. cit.*, p. 20.

31 John C. Hotten, *Original Lists of Persons of Quality, 1600-1700* (Baltimore, MD: Genealogical Publishing Company, 1980), p. 244.

32 36 *Ibid.*, pp. 173-174, 178, 224, 229.

33 Gary B. Nash, *Red, White and Black: The Peoples of Early America* (Englewood, NJ: Prentis-Hall, 1974), pp. 194-195.

34 Ariela Gross, "Of Portuguese Origin: Litigating Identity and Citizenship among the 'Little Races' in Nineteenth-Century America," *Law and History Review*, Vol. 25, No. 3, Fall 2007.

35 Paul Heinegg, *Free African Americans of North Carolina, Virginia, and South Carolina from the Colonial Period to about 1820*, Vol. 2 (Baltimore, MD: Genealogical Publishing, 2005), p. 705.

36 Breen, *op. cit.*, p.12.

37 *Ibid.*

38 John B. Boles, The Blackwell Companion to the American South (Oxford, UK: Blackwell Publishing, 2004).

39 Henry Read McIlwaine, ed., *Minutes of Council and General Court of Colonial Virginia* (Richmond, VA: The Library Board, 1924), pp. 22-23.

40 *Ibid.*, pp. 35-38.

41 *Ibid.*, p. 38.

42 *Ibid.*, pp. 39-41.

43 *Ibid.*, pp. 40-43.

44 Johnson, *op. cit.*, pp. 27-28.

45 Edward Arber, ed., *1910 Travels and Works of Captain John Smith, President of Virginia and Admiral of New England, 1580-1631*, 2 vols. (Edinburg, England: John Grant, 1910), pp. 541-542.

46 Susan M. Kingsbury, *Records of the Virginia Company of London* (Washington, DC: Government Printing Office, 1906-1935), Vol. III, p. 93.

47 *Ibid.*, Vol. I, p. 334.

48 McIlwaine, *op. cit.*, p. 62.

49 Kingsbury, *op. cit.*, Vol. III, p. 668; Vol. IV, pp. 58, 229.

50 Alexander Brown, *The Genesis of the United States*, 2 Vols. (Boston and New York: Houghton, Mifflin and Company, 1890), p. 446.

51 "An Account of the Ancient Planters," [1624]. *In Colonial Records of Virginia*. (Richmond, VA: Commonwealth of Virginia, 1871), pp.75-76.

52 Edward W. Haile, *Jamestown Narratives: Eyewitness Accounts of the Virginia Colony, the First Decade: 1607-1617* (Champlain, VA: Roundhouse, 1998), p. 913.

53 Junius P. Rodriguez, ed., *Slavery in the United States: A Social, Political, and Historical Encyclopedia, Volume 2* (Santa Barbara, CA: ABC-CLIO, Inc., 2007), p. 193.

54 James Oliver Horton and Lois E. Horton, *Hard Road to Freedom: The Story of African America*, Vol. 1, African Roots through the Civil War (New Brunswick, NJ: Rutgers University Press, 2002), p. 29.

55 Timothy H. Breen and Stephen Innes, *Myne Owne Ground: Race and Freedom on Virginia's Eastern Shore, 1640-1676* (New York: Oxford University Press, 1980), p. 8.

56 Horton, *op. cit.*, p. 26.

57 Frederic W. Gleach, Powhatan's World and Colonial Virginia: A Conflict of Cultures (Lincoln, NB: The University of Nebraska Press, 1997), pp. 4-5.

58 Breen, *op. cit.*, p.10.

59 *Ibid.*

60 Rodriguez, *op. cit.*, p. 352.

61 Heinegg, op. cit., p. 705.

62 Juliet Walker, *The History of Black Business in America: Capitalism, Race, Entrepreneurship*, Vol. 1 (Chapel Hill, NC: University of North Carolina Press, 2009), p. 49.

63 Frank W. Sweet, *Legal History of the Color Line: The Rise and Triumph of the One-Drop Rule* (Palm Coast, FL: Backintyme Publishing, 2005), p. 117.

64 Darrell J. Kozlowski, *Colonialism: Key Concepts in American History* (New York: Chelsea House Publications, 2010), p. 78; Warren M. Billings, ed., *The Old Dominion in the Seventeenth Century: A Documentary History of Virginia, 1606–1689* (Chapel Hill: The University of North Carolina Press, 1975), P. 180–181.

65 Anthony Johnson and his servant, Commonwealth of Virginia, Northampton County Deeds, Wills, Etc., March 8, 1654/5, 7 (1655–1668), fol. 10.

66 R. Halliburton, Jr., "Free Black Owners of Slaves: A Reappraisal of the Woodson Thesis, *The South Carolina Historical Magazine*, Vol. 76, No. 3 (Jul. 1975), pp. 129-142.

67 Loren Schweninger, *Black Property Owners in the South, 1790-1915* (Chicago, IL: University of Illinois, 1990).

68 Halliburton, *op. cit.*, pp. 131-140.

69 Larry Koger. *Black Slaveowners: Free Black Slave Masters in South Carolina 1790-1860* (Columbia, SC: University of South Carolina Press, 1985).

70 Carter G. Woodson, *Free Negro Owners of Slaves in The United States in 1830.* (Washington, DC: The Association for the Study of Negro Life and History, 1924).

71   *Ibid.*, pp. vi-vii.

72   John Hope Franklin and Evelyn Higginbotham, From Slavery to Freedom: A History of African Americans, 9th Edition (New York: McGraw-Hill Higher Education, 2010).

73   Lorenzo G. Greene, *The Negro in Colonial New England, 1620-1776* (New York: Columbia University Press, 1942), p. 17.

74   Colonial Laws of Massachusetts Rep. From 1660 Supp. to 1672: Containing Also, the Body of Liberties (Boston: Rockwell and Churchill, 1889).

75   *Ibid.*, p. 91.

76   Sowell, *op. cit.*, p. 145.

77   Thomas Jefferson (1853-1854). *The Writings of Thomas Jefferson: Being His Autobiography, Correspondence, Reports, Messages, Addresses, and other Writings, Official and Private* (Washington, D.C.: Taylor & Maury); http://www.blackpast.org/primary/declaration-independence-and-debate-over-slavery#sthash.s4aQftZQ.dpuf

78   Johnson, *op. cit.*, p. 169.

79   Samuel H. Williamson and Louis P. Cain, "Measuring Slavery in 2011 Dollars," *MeasuringWorth.com*, 2015; http://www.measuringworth.com/slavery.php

80   Robert William Fogel and Stanley L. Engerman, *Time on the Cross: The Economics of American Slavery* (New York: Little, Brown and Company, Inc., 2013).

81   Johnson, *op. cit.*, pp. 155-156.

82   U.S. Constitution. Article 1, Section 8.

83   Johnson, *op. cit.*, p. 188.

84   Catherine Drinker Bowen, *Miracle at Philadelphia* (New York: Little, Brown and Company, 1966), p. 201.

85   U.S. Constitution. Article 1, Section 9.

86   U.S. Constitution. Article 4, Section 2, Clause 3.

87   Gunnar Myrdal, *An American Dilemma; the Negro Problem and Modern Democracy*, Vol. I (New York: Pantheon Books, 1972), p. 85.

88   *Ibid.*

89   Paul Leicester Ford (ed.), *The Writings of Thomas Jefferson*, Vol, I, (New York: G. P. Putnam's Sons, 1892), p. 68.

90   Don E. Fehrenbacher, *Slavery, Law and Politics: The Dred Scott Case in Historical Perspective*, (New York: Oxford University Press, 1981), pp. 33-34.

Chapter Two - Pre-Civil War Education of Black People

1   Shmoop Editorial Team, "Narrative of the Life of Frederick Douglass Theme of Education," *Shmoop University, Inc.*, Last modified November 11, 2008, http://www.shmoop.com/life-of-frederick-douglass/education-theme.html.

2 Frederick Douglass, *Narrative of the Life of Frederick Douglass* (New York: Dover Publications, Inc., 1995), pp. 22-23.

3 Frederick Douglass, Harriet Ann Jacobs, and Kwame Anthony Appiah, *Narrative of the Life of Frederick Douglass, an American Slave & Incidents in the Life of a Slave Girl.* (New York: Random House USA, Inc., 2004).

4 *Ibid.*

5 Stephanie P. Browner, ed., "Classroom," *The Charles Chesnutt Digital Archive,* http://faculty.berea.edu/browners/chesnutt/classroom/education.html

6 Carter Godwin Woodson, *The Education of the Negro Prior to 1861: A History of the Education of the Colored People of the United States from the Beginning of Slavery to the Civil War* (Whitefish, MT: Kessinger Publishing's Rare Reprints, 1915), p. 3; http://andromeda.rutgers.edu/~natalieb/ The_Education_Of_The_Negro_P.pdf

7 Cotton Mather, *The Negro Christianized, An Essay to Execute and Assist that Good Work, The Instruction of Negro Servants in Christianity* (Boston: B. Green, 1706), pp. 4-5, 28. http://digitalcommons.unl.edu/cgi/viewcontent. cgi?article=1028&context=etas

8 Woodson, *loc. cit.*

9 Robert E. Park and Ernest W. Burgess, *Introduction to the Science of Sociology* (Chicago: University of Chicago Press, 2009), p. 738; www.gutenberg.net

10 *Ibid.*, p. 764.

11 Woodson, *op. cit.*, p. 3.

12 Gunnar Myrdal, *An American Dilemma; the Negro Problem & Modern Democracy,* Vol. II (New York: Pantheon Books, 1972), p. 887.

13 Harry Morgan, *Historical Perspective on the Education of Black Children* (Connecticut: Praeger, 1995), p. 36.

14 108 Gates, Henry Louis Jr. *The Trials of Phillis Wheatley: America's First Black Poet and Her Encounters with the Founding Fathers,* (New York: Basic Civitas Books, 2003), p. 5.

15 Hammon, Jupiter. *America's First Negro Poet: The Complete Works of Jupiter Hammon of Long Island* (Associated Faculty Press, Inc., Kenniket Press, Empire State Historical Publications Series, 1983, Port Washington, NY.); Wallace, George. "Jupiter Hammon, the Father of African American Poetry." ThoughtCo, Mar. 2, 2017, thoughtco.com/jupiter-hammon-african-american-poetry-2725264.

16 *Ibid.*

17 O'Brien, Michael. *Intellectual Life and the American South, 1810-1860.* (Chapel Hill, NC: The University of North Carolina Press, 2010), p. 181.

18 August Meier and Elliott Rudwick, From Plantation to Ghetto (New York: Hill and Wang, 1970), p. 93.

19 Morgan, *op. cit.*, pp. 59-60.

20 A. Leon Higginbotham, Jr. *In the Matter of Color; Race and the American Legal Process: The Colonial Period* (New York: Oxford University Press, 1978), p. 200.

21 Morgan, *op. cit.*, p. 73.

22 E. Jennifer Monaghan, *Learning to Read and Write in Colonial America* (Boston: University of Massachusetts Press, 2005), pp. 47-48.

23 *Ibid.*

24 Carleton Mabee, *Black Education in New York State from Colonial to Modern Times* (Syracuse, N. Y.: Syracuse University Press, 1979), pp. 1-13.

25 *Ibid.*

26 Higginbotham, *op. cit.*, pp. 200-201.

27 Browner, *op. cit.*

28 Thomas Sowell, *Black Rednecks and White Liberals* (San Francisco: Encounter Books, 2005), p. 145.

29 Johnson, *op. cit.*, p. 169.

30 Higginbotham, *op. cit.*, pp. 258-259.

31 Stephan Thernstrom and Abrigail Thernstrom, *America in Black and White; One Nation Indivisible.* (New York: Touchstone, 1997), p. 32.

32 U.S. Bureau of the Census, Historical States of the United States: Colonial Times to 1970 (Washington, D.C.: U.S. Government Printing Office, 1975), p. 382.

33 John K. Nelson, *A Blessed Company: Parishes, Parsons, and Parishioners in Anglican Virginia, 1690-1776* (Chapel Hill, NC: University of North Carolina Press, 2001), p. 261.

34 *Ibid.*, p. 263.

35 Woodson, *op. cit.*

36 *Ibid.*, pp. 3-4.

37 *Ibid.*, p. 4.

38 Morgan, *op. cit.*, p. 11.

39 Morgan, *op. cit.*, pp. 44, 46.

40 Harry A. Ploski and James Williams, *The Negro Almanac*, 5th ed. (Detroit: Gale Research Inc., 1989), p. 5.

41 *Ibid.*, p. 48.

42 Meier and Rudwick, op. cit., p. 93

43 *Ibid.*, pp. 93-94.

44 *Ibid.*, p. 94.

45 *Ibid.*, pp. 94-95.

46 *Ibid.*, p. 95.

47 *Ibid.*

48 Stuart Brown, ed., *British Philosophy and the Age of Enlightenment* (New York: Routledge, 2003).

49 Woodson, *op. cit.*, p. 4.

50 Vincent P. Franklin, *The Education of Black Philadelphia* (Philadelphia: University of Pennsylvania Press, 1979).

51 *Ibid.*, p. 31.

52 Gary B. Nash, *Forging Freedom* (Cambridge: Harvard University Press, 1988), pp. 202-209.

53 Woodson, *op. cit.*

54 E. Delorus Preston, Jr., "William Syphax, a Pioneer in Negro Education in the District of Columbia," *The Journal of Negro History*, Vol. 20, No. 4, October 1935, pp. 462-464.

55 *Ibid.*

Chapter Three - Sparking the Inevitable War

1 Francis A. Walker, *Political Economy* (New York, 1887), p. 92.

2 Bradford, James C. *A Companion to American Military History*, Vol. 1, (Malden, MA: Blackwell Publishing Ltd., 2010), p. 101.

3 152 Keegan, John (2009). *The American Civil War: A Military History* (New York: Alfred A. Knopf, 2009), p. 73.

4 153 Perman, Michael and Taylor, Amy M. *Major Problems in the Civil War and Reconstruction: Documents and Essays* (Boston, MA: Wadsworth, Cengage Learning, 2010), p. 177.

5 154 Walker, *op. cit.*

6 "The Missouri Compromise." 123HelpMe.com. 10 Oct 2012 <http://www.123HelpMe.com/view.asp?id=23329>.

7 *Dred Scott v. Sanford* (1857), 19 Howard, 393.

8 *Ibid.*

9 "Address by Charles L. Remond", April 3, 1857, in Herbert Aptheker, *Documentary History of Negro People in the United States* (New York: Citadel Press, 1951), p. 394.

10 "The Dred Scott Decision", a speech delivered before the American AntiSlavery Society, New York, May 11, 1857, in Philip S. Foner, ed., *The Life and Writings of Frederick Douglass*, vol. 2 (New York: International Publishers, 1950), pp. 421, 4.

11 National Anti-Slavery Standard, May 23, 1857, p. 1.

12 161 Carter G. Woodson, *Free Negro Owners of Slaves in the United States in 1830; Together with Absentee Ownership of Slaves in the United States in 1830* (Washington, D. C.: The Association for the Study of Negro Life and History, 1924), p. iii.

13 *Ibid.*, p. v.

14 Larry Koger, *Black Slaveowners: Free Black Slave Masters in South Carolina, 1790-1860* (Jefferson, NC: McFarland & Company, Inc., 1958), p. 85.

15 *Ibid.*, p. 1.

16 Woodson, *op. cit.*, pp. vi-vii.

17 "A Standard Maxim for Free Society," Springfield, Ill., June 26, 1857, in Mario M. Cuomo and Harold Holzer, eds., *Lincoln and Democracy* (New York: HarperCollins, 1990), pp. 90-91.

18 *Ibid.*

19 *Ibid.*, p. 90.

20 David Zarefsky, *Lincoln, Douglas and Slavery: In the Crucible of Public Debate* (Chicago: University of Chicago Press, 1990).

21 Horton and Lois E. Horton, *In Hope of Liberty: Culture, Community, and Protest among Northern Free Blacks, 1700-1860* (Oxford University Press, 1998), p. 264.

22 Steven E. Woodworth, Cultures in Conflict: The American Civil War (Westport, CT: Greenwood Press, 2000), p. 3.

23 Shelby Foote, *The Civil War: Fort Sumter to Perryville, Vol. 1* (New York: Random House, 1958), p. 34.

24 James McPherson, *Battle Cry of Freedom: The Civil War Era* (New York: Oxford University Press, 1988), pp. 114, 143.

25 *Ibid.*, p. 184.

26 Woodworth, *op. cit.*, p. 3.

27 Woodworth, *Ibid.*, p. 4.

28 Woodworth, *Ibid.*

29 McPherson, *op. cit.*, p. 245.

30 Abraham Lincoln, House Divided Speech, Springfield, Illinois, June 16, 1858.

31 Woodworth, *op. cit.*, pp. 4-5.

32 "Jane Stuart Woolsey to a friend, May 10, 1861", in Henry Steele Commager, ed., The Blue and the Gray: Volume 1: From the Nomination of Lincoln to the Eve of Gettysburg, (Plume, rev. and abridged ed., New York, 1973), p. 48.

33 *Ibid.*

34 George Ticknor; *Life, Letters, and Journals of George Ticknor*, 2. vols. (Boston: James R. Osgood and Co., 1876), II, pp. 433-34; Jane Stuart Woolsey to a friend, May 10, 1861", in Henry Steele Commager, ed., *The Blue and the Gray*, 2 vols. (rev. and abridged ed., New York: The Fairfax Press, 1973), I, p. 48.

35 Philip S. Foner, *Business and Slavery: The New York Merchants and the Irrepressible Conflict* (Chapel Hill, 1941), p. 207.

36 Woodworth, *op. cit.*, p. 5.

37 Woodworth, *Ibid.*, pp. 5-6.

38 *Ibid.*, p. 6.

39 *Ibid.*

40 McPherson, *op. cit.*, p. 313.

41 James A. Rawley, *Turning Points of the Civil War* (Lincoln, NE: University of Nebraska Press, 1989), p. 49.

42 191 W. E. Burghardt Du Bois, "The Freedmen's Bureau," *Atlantic Monthly* 87 (1901), p. 355.

43 *Ibid.*

44 *Ibid.*

45 For a listing of the number of men engaged and losses incurred by both sides, see Grady McWhiney and Perry D. Jamieson, *Attack and Die: Civil War Military Tactics and the Southern Heritage* (Tuscaloosa, AL: University of Alabama Press, 1984), p. 8.

46 Woodworth, *op. cit.*, p. 6.

47 McWhiney and Jamieson, *op. cit.*, p.8.

48 Woodworth, *op. cit.*, p. 6.

49 Francis B. Carpenter, *The Inner Life of Abraham Lincoln: Six Months at The White House* (New York, 1866), p. 22.

50 David Donald, ed., *Inside Lincoln's Cabinet: The Civil War Diaries of Salmon P. Chase* (New York, 1954), pp. 149-152; Howard K. Beale, ed., *Diary of Gideon Welles*, 3 vols. (New York, 1960), I, pp. 142-145.

51 Roy P. Basler (ed.), Proclamation of Amnesty and Reconstruction, December 8, 1863, *Collected Works of Abraham Lincoln*, Vol. 7, pp. 53-56; http://www.lincolnstudies.com/documents/12081863.html

52 201 Eric Foner, *Forever Free: The Story of Emancipation & Reconstruction* (New York: Vintage Books, 2005), pp. 61-62.

53 Michael Vorenberg; "'The Deformed Child: Slavery and the Election of 1864," *Civil War History*, Vol. 47, 2001.

54 *Ibid.*

55 Michael Vorenberg, *Final Freedom: The Civil War, the Abolition of Slavery, and the Thirteenth Amendment* (Cambridge: Cambridge University Press, 2001), chap. 2.

56 Handwritten copy of Wade-Davis Bill as originally submitted 1846; Records of Legislative Proceedings; Records of the United States House of Representatives 1789-1946; Record Group 233; National Archives; http://www.ourdocuments.gov/doc.php?flash=true&doc=37

57 A more detailed comparison of presidential and congressional initiatives is given in Herman Belz, *Reconstructing the Union: Theory and Practice during the Civil War* (Ithaca, N.Y.: Cornell University Press, 1969), pp. 126-243.

58 Vorenberg, *loc. cit.*

59 William Frank Zornow, *Lincoln and the Party Divided* (Norman: University of Oklahoma Press, 1954), pp. 72-86.

60 209 *Ibid.*

61 *Biography of Andrew Johnson*, The White House, Washington, D.C. http://www.whitehouse.gov/history/presidents/aj17.html

62 Zornow, *op. cit.*, pp. 99-103.

63 Edward Chase Kirkland, *Peacemakers of 1864* (New York: The Macmillan Company, 1927), pp. 135-136.

64 *Ibid.*, p. 112.

65 Paul Johnson, *A History of the American People* (New York: Harper Prennial, 1977), p. 485.

66 McPherson, *op. cit.*, pp. 821-822.

67 Alexander H. Stephens, *A Constitutional View of the War between the States*, 2 vols. (Philadelphia: The National Publishing Co., 1868-70), II, p. 619.

68 *Ibid.*

69 McPherson, *op. cit.*, p. 823.

70 Richard N. Current, *The Lincoln Nobody Knows* (New York: McGraw-Hill Book Company, Inc., 1958), pp. 243-247.

71 Stephens, *op. cit.*, pp. 584-619.

72 Hudson Strode, *Jefferson Davis: Tragic Hero* (New York: Harcourt, Brace and World, 1964), pp. 140-143.

73 Kirkland, *op. cit.*, pp. 109.

74 *Ibid.*, pp. 109-110.

75 *Ibid.*

76 Henry J. Raymond, *The Life and Public Services of Abraham Lincoln* (New York: Derby and Miller, 1865), p. 670.

Chapter Four - From Accommodation to Conflict

1 Robert E. Park and Ernest W. Burgess, *Introduction to the Science of Sociology* (Chicago: The University of Chicago Press, 1921), p. 735; http://www.gutenberg.org/files/28496/28496-h/28496-h.htm

2 *Ibid.*, p. 5.

3 Paul Johnson. *A History of the American People* (New York: Harper Perennial, 1997), p. 88.

4 Winthrop D. Jordan, *White Over Black: American Attitudes Toward the Negro, 1550-1812*, 2nd Ed. (Published for the Omohundro Institute of Early American Hist) (Chapel Hill: The University of North Carolina Press, 1968), p. 120.

5 Peter H. Wood. *Black Majority: Negroes in Colonial South Carolina from 1670 through the Stono Rebellion* (W. W. Norton & Company, Inc., 1974), pp. 314-323.

6 *Ibid.*

7 *Acts of the General Assembly of the State of South Carolina from 1791 to December 1794* (1808). Vol. 1, Columbia, S.C.: D. & J.J. Faust, State Printers. www.slaveryinamerica.org/geography/slave_laws_SC.htm

8 *Ibid.*

9 A. Leon Higginbotham, Jr. *In the Matter of Color; Race and the American Legal Process: The Colonial Period* (New York: Oxford University Press, 1978), pp. 198-199, 258-259.

10 Woodson, *op. cit.*, p. 5.

11 236 Pulliam, Ted. 2001. "The Dark Days of Black Codes." *Legal Times* 24.

12 237 Paul Moreno. "Racial Classifications and Reconstruction Legislation," *The Journal of Southern History* Vol. 61, No. 2 (May 1995): pp. 271-305; Wilson, Theodoe Branter Wilson. *The Black Codes of South Carolina* (Tuscalossa: University of Alabama Press, 1967), pp. 111-113.

13 Roy P. Basler (ed.), Emancipation Proclamation, January 1, 1863, *Collected Works of Abraham Lincoln*, Vol. 6, pp. 28-31; http://www.lincolnstudies.com/documents/01011863.html

14 Emancipation Proclamation, January 1, 1863; Presidential Proclamations, 1791-1991; Record Group 11; General Records of the United States Government; National Archives; http://www.ourdocuments.gov/doc.php?flash=true&doc=34

15 *Ibid.*

16 Kirkland, *op. cit.*, pp. 17-18.

17 McPherson, op. cit., p. 853.

18 *Ibid.*

19 Whitelaw Reid, *After the War: A Tour of the Southern States, 1865-1866* (New York: Harper Torchbooks, 1965), p. 44.

20 Hans L. Trefousse, *Andrew Johnson: A Biography* (New York: W.W. Norton, 1989), p. 215, citing Petition from Colored People of Alexandria, April 29, 1865, From Frederick, Maryland, Citizens, April 24, 1865, Burnham Wardwell to Johnson, April 21, 1865, *PJ* 7:656-58, 626-27, 608-9; Thomas J. Durant to Johnson, May 1, 1865, Carl Schurz Papers, LC.

21 Henry W. Brands, *The Man Who Saved the Union: Ulysses S. Grant in War and Peace* (New York: Doubleday, 2012), pp. 397-398.

22 Eric Foner and Olivia Mahoney, "America's Reconstruction: People and Politics after the Civil War," *Digital History*, 2003; http://www.digitalhistory.uh.edu/exhibits/reconstruction/introduction.html

23 History, com Staff, "The Failure of Reconstruction," A+E Networks, 2009; http://www.history.com/topics/american-civil-war/reconstruction

24 *Ibid.*, pp. 392, 396.

25 *Ibid.*, p. 396.

26 Jean Edward Smith, *Grant* (New York: Simon & Schuster, 2001), pp. 369-397; Brands, op. cit., p. 389.

27 *Ibid.*, pp. 398-399.

28 U.S. Constitution. Article IV, Section 4.

29 Woodworth, *op. cit.*

30 Trefousse, *op. cit.*, pp. 219-220.

31 Steven E. Woodworth, *Cultures in Conflict: The American Civil War* (Westport, CT: Greenwood Press, 2000), p. 18.

32 W. E. Burghardt Du Bois, *Black Reconstruction in America, 1860-1880* (New York: The Free Press, 1962), p. 348.

33 *Ibid.*

34 John Hope Franklin, *Reconstruction after the Civil War* (Chicago: University of Chicago Press, 1994).

35 Gitlin, Martin (2009), *The Ku Klux Klan: A Guide to an American Subculture* (Santa Barbara, CA. Greenwood Press) p. 1-2.

36 Paul Johnson, *A History of the American People* (New York: Harper Perennial, 1977), p. 506.

37 Allen Trelease, *White Terror: The Ku Klux Klan Conspiracy and Southern Reconstruction* (New York: Harper & Row, Publishers, 1971), p. 18.

38 Parsons, Elaine Frantz, *Ku-Klux: The Birth of the Klan during Reconstruction* (Chapel Hill, NC: Publisher: University of North Carolina Press, 2015), pp. 5-6.

39 *Ibid.*, p. 6.

40 *Ibid.*

41 "An Act to enforce the Right of Citizens of the United States to vote in the several States of this Union, and for other Purposes," 41st Congress, Sess. 2, ch. 114, 16 Stat. 140.

42 Nicholas Lemann, *Redemption: The Last Battle of the Civil War* (New York: Farrar, Strauss & Giroux, 2007), pp. 75-77.

43 *Ibid.*

44 Gitlin, *op. cit.*, p. 17.

45 *Ibid.*, p. 18.

46 *Ibid.*, pp. 19-20.

47 *Ibid.*, p. 20.

48 *Ibid.*, p. 21.

49 *Ibid.*, p. 22.

50 *Ibid.*, pp. 22-23.

51 *Ibid.*, p. 27.

52 *Ibid.*, pp. 27-28.

53 *Ibid.*, p. 28.

54 1866 Civil Rights Act, 14 Stat. 27-30, April 9, 1866.

55 Westin, *op. cit.*, p. 142.

56 History, com Staff, *op. cit.*

57 Johnson, *op. cit.*, p. 507.

58 Richard H. Pildes, "Democracy, Anti-Democracy, and the Canon", *Constitutional Commentary*, Vol.17, 2000, pp.12-13, 27; Michael Perman, *Struggle for Mastery: Disfranchisement in the South, 1888-1908*, Chapel Hill: University of North Carolina Press, 2001, pp. 208-210.

59 David Blight, *Race and Reunion: The Civil War in American Memory*, Cambridge: Harvard University Press, 2002.

60 Alan F. Westin, "The Case of the Prejudiced Doorkeeper" (*U.S. v. Singleton, etc.*, [The Civil Rights Cases], 109 U.S. 3), *Quarrels that Have Shaped the Constitution* (New York: Harper & Row, Publishers, 1987), pp. 141-142.

61 *Ibid.*, p. 142.

62 1866 Civil Rights Act, 14 Stat. 27-30, April 9, 1866.

63 Gordon Harvey, "Public Education During the Civil War and Reconstruction Era," The *Encyclopedia of Alabama*, 2010; http://www.encyclopediaofalabama. org/article/h-2600

64 Ronald E. Butchart, "Freedmen's Education during Reconstruction," *New Georgia Encyclopedia*, 2002; http://www.georgiaencyclopedia.org/articles/ history-archaeology/freedmens-education-during-reconstruction

65 Harvey, *op. cit.*

66 Butchart, *op. cit.*

67 Harvey, *op. cit.*

68 Harvey, *op. cit.*

69 Edward A. Hatfield, "Freedman's Bureau," *New Georgia Encyclopedia*, 2009; http://www.georgiaencyclopedia.org/articles/history-archaeology/ freedmens-bureau

70 *Ibid.*

71 *Ibid.*

72 The Editors of Encyclopedia Britannica, "Freedman's Bureau," *Encyclopedia Britannica*, 2015; http://www.encyclopedia.com/history/ united-states-and-canada/us-history/freedmens-bureau

Chapter Five - The Philosophy of Education

1 Robert E. Park and Ernest W. Burgess, *Introduction to the Science of Sociology* (Chicago: The University of Chicago Press, 1921), p. 735; http://www.gutenberg. org/files/28496/28496-h/28496-h.htm

2 *Ibid.*

3 Carter Godwin Woodson, *The Education of the Negro Prior to 1861: A History of the Education of the Colored People of the United States from the Beginning of Slavery to the Civil War* (Whitefish, MT: Kessinger Publishing's Rare Reprints, 1915), p. 4; http://andromeda.rutgers.edu/~natalieb/ The_Education_Of_The_Negro_P.pdf

4 James Oliver Horton and Lois E. Horton, *In Hope of Liberty: Culture, Community, and Protest among Northern Free Blacks, 1700-1860* (Oxford University Press, 1998), p. 192.

5 302 Rosalind Cobb Wiggins, ed., *Captain Paul Cuffee's Logs And Letters, 1808-1817: A Black Quaker's "Voice From Within The Veil"* (Washington: Howard University Press, 1996), p. xi.

6 Abigail Mott, *Biographical Sketches and Interesting Anecdotes of Persons of Colour* (printed and sold by W. Alexander & Son; sold also by Harvey and Darton, W. Phillips, E. Fry, and W. Darton, London; R. Peart, Birmingham; D.F. Gardiner, Dublin, 1826), pp. 31-43 (accessed on Google Books); http://books.google.com/books?id=vQ2qZk0hdlsC

7 Lamont D. Thomas, *Paul Cuffee: Black Entrepreneur and Pan-Africanist* (Chicago: University of Illinois Press, 1988), p. 110.

8 *Ibid.,* p. 111.

9 Tonya Bolden, "Strong Men Keep Coming" *The Book of African American Men* (New York: John Wiley & Sons, Inc., 1999). p. 31.

10 *Ibid.*, pp 192-193.

11 *Ibid.*

12 Jacqueline M. Moore, *Leading the race: The Transformation of the Black in the Nation's Capital, 1880-1920* (Charlottesville and London: University Press of Virginia, 1999, p. 21.

13 Butchart, *op. cit.*

14 *Ibid.*

15 *Ibid.*

16 *Ibid.*

17 *Ibid.*

18 Woodson, *loc. cit.*

19 *Ibid.*

20 *Ibid.*

21 Gunnar Myrdal, *An American Dilemma: The Negro Problem and Modern Democracy*, Vol. II, New York: Harper & Row Publishers, Incorporated, 1973, p. 880.

22 *Ibid.*

23 *Ibid.*, pp. 880-881.

24 *Ibid.*; Sandra Fitzpatrick and Maria R. Goodwin, *The Guide to Black Washington: Places and Events of Historical and Cultural Significance in the Nation's Capital*, New York: Hippocrene Books, 1990, p. 156.

25 The Smithsonian Anacostia Museum and Center for African American History and Culture, *The Black Washingtonians: The Anacostia Museum Illustrated Chronology*, Hoboken, New Jersey: John Wiley & Sons, Inc., 2005, p. 349.

26 Report of the District of Columbia Board of Trustees, 1876-1877, pp. 140.-141.

27 Moore, *op. cit.*, p. 22.

28 Gunnar Myrdal, *An American Dilemma: The Negro Problem and Modern Democracy*, Vol. II, New York: Harper & Row Publishers, Incorporated, 1973, p. 888.

29 Ibid., p. 889.

30 *Ibid.*; J. M. Heffron, "Armstrong, Samuel Chapman," *American National Biography Online*, February 2000; http://www.anb.org/articles/09/09-00034.html

31 Myrdal, *loc. cit.,* p. 889.

32 Frederick Douglass, *The life and times of Frederick Douglass: his early life as a slave, his escape from bondage, and his complete history*, Hartford, Conn: Park Publishing, Co., 1882, p. 357.

33 Thomas C. Holt "Du Bois, W. E. B.," *American National Biography Online*, February 2000; http://www.anb.org/articles/15/15-00191.html

34 *Ibid.*

35 *Ibid.*

36 Myrdal, *op. cit.,* pp. 889-890.

37 Thomas Sowell, *Black Rednecks and White Liberals* (San Francisco: Encounter Books, 2005), p. 232.

38 W. E. B. Du Bois, "The Hampton Idea," *The Education of Black People: Ten Critiques, 1906-1960*, edited by Herbert Aptheker (Amherst: University of Massachusetts Press, 1973), pp. 6-7.

39 W.E.B. Du Bois, *The Philadelphia Negro; A Social Study* (New York: gramercy Books, 1970), p. 395.

40 W.E.B. Du Bois, *The Souls of Black Folk* (New York: Dover Publications, Inc., 1994), p. 42.

41 Sowell, *op. cit.,* p. 232.

42 Booker T. Washington, *Up From Slavery* (New York: Dover Publications, Inc., 1995), p. 109.

43 *Ibid.*, p.108.

44 C. Eric Lincoln, "The Negro College and Cultural Change," *Daedalus*, Summer 1971, p. 614.

45 See Charles W. Chestnut et al, *The Negro Problem* (Memphis, Tennessee: General Books, reprinted 2010), pp. 6-20.

46 W. E. B. Du Bois, "Education and Work," The *Education of Black People*, edited by Herbert Aptheker, p. 68.

47 Sowell, *op. cit.,* p. 233.

48 Louis R. Harlan, *Booker T. Washington: The Wizard of Tuskegee 1901-1915* (New York: Oxford University Press, 1983), p. 138.

49 Booker T. Washington, *The Future of the American Negro* (New York: The New American Library, Inc., 1969), pp. 80-81.

50 Willard B. Gatewood, *Aristocrats of Color: The Black, 1880-1920* (Bloomington: Indiana University Press, 1990), p. 266.

51 Harlan, *op. cit.*, p. 280.

52 Du Bois, *op. cit.*, p. 63.

53 *Ibid.*, p. 203.

54 Washington, *The Future of the American Negro*, p. 80.

55 Washington, *Up from Slavery*, p. 93.

56 Washington, *The Future of the American Negro*, p. 141.

57 Louis R. Harlan, *Booker T. Washington*, pp. 291, 297-298, 302-303, *idem.*, *Booker T. Washington: The Wizard of Tuskegee, 1901-1915*, p. 244-250.

58 James M. McPherson, *The Abolitionist Legacy: From Reconstruction to the NAACP* (Princeton: Princeton University Press, 1975), pp. 352-363.

59 Harlan, *op. cit.*, p. 361.

60 *Ibid.*, p. 134.

61 A fuller discussion of Booker T. Washington can be found in Thomas Sowell's article, "Up from Slavery" in the December 5, 1994 issue of *Forbes* magazine, as well as in the already cited two-volume biography of Booker T. Washington by Louis R. Harlan.

62 Kelly Miller, "Washington's Policy," *Booker T. Washington and His Critics: The Problem of Negro Leadership* edited by Hugh Hawkins (Lexington: D.C. Heath and Co., 1962), p. 51.

63 Washington, *Up from Slavery*, p. 270.

64 Lillian Gertrude Dabney, *The History of Schools for Negroes in the District of Columbia, 1807-1947: a Dissertation.* (Washington: Catholic University Press of America, 1949), pp. 195-200, 216-217.

65 E. Delorus Preston, Jr., "William Syphax, a Pioneer in Negro Education in the District of Columbia," *The Journal of Negro History*, Vol. 20, No. 4, October 1935, pp. 462-464.

66 *Ibid.*, p. 448.

67 *Ibid.*, p. 458

68 *Ibid.*, pp. 463-464.

69 Robert E. Park and Ernest W. Burgess, *Introduction to the Science of Sociology* (Chicago: The University of Chicago Press, 1921), p. 626; http://www.gutenberg.org/files/28496/28496-h/28496-h.htm

70 G. Smith Wormley, "Educators of the first Half Century of Public Schools of the District of Columbia," *The Journal of Negro History*, Vol. 17, No. 2, April 1932, p. 124.

Chapter Six - The Culture of the Black Community Prior to 1960

1   C. Vann Woodward, "The Case of the Louisiana Traveler" (*Plessy v. Ferguson*, 163 U.S. 537), *Quarrels that Have Shaped the Constitution* (New York: Harper & Row, Publishers, 1987), pp. 158.

2   *Ibid.*, p. 157.

3   *Ibid.*, p. 174.

4   Elgin F. Hunt and David C. Colander, *Social Science: An Introduction to the Study of Society*, 14th Ed., (New York: The Macmillan Company, 2010), pp. 38-39, 44.

5   Melville J. Herskovits. "Social of the Negro," in Carl Murchison, ed., *A Handbook for Psychology* (Worcester, Mass.: Clark university press, 1935), pp. 234-240.

6   Gunnar Myrdal, *An American Dilemma; the Negro Problem and Modern Democracy* (New York: Harper & Brothers, 1944), p. 859.

7   *Ibid.* pp. 859-860.

8   *Ibid.* p. 860.

9   William Edward Burghardt Du Bois, *The Negro* (New York: Henry Holt and Company, 1915), p. 227.

10 Allison Davis, "The Negro church and associations in the lower South" (unpublished manuscript, Carnegie-Myrdal study of *The Negro in America*, 1945), pp. 36-37.

11 Myrdal, *op. cit.*, p. 861.

12 Jacqueline M. Moore, *Leading the race: The Transformation of the Black in the Nation's Capital, 1880-1920*, Charlottesville and London: University Press of Virginia, 1999, p. 71.

13 *Ibid.*

14 *Ibid.*

15 *Ibid.*, pp. 71-72.

16 Evelyn Brooks Higginbotham, *Righteous Discontent: The Women's Movement in the Black Baptist Church, 1880-1920* (Cambridge, MA: Harvard University Press, 1994), pp. 23, 52-53.

17 See Richard S. Newman, *Freedom's Prophet: Bishop Richard Allen, the AME Church, and the Black Founding Fathers* (New York: New York University Press, 2008), pp.14-15, 184.

18 Moore, *op. cit.*, p. 73.

19 John Wesley Cromwell, Sr., "First Negro Churches in the District of Columbia," pp. 12-13, folder 37, box 2, Cromwell family Papers, Moorland-Spingarn Research Center, Howard University.

20 Dickson D. Bruce, Jr., *Archibald Grimké, Portrait of a Black Independent* (Baton Rouge: Louisiana State University Press, 1993); "Francis Grimke," American

National Biography, Volume 9 (New York: Oxford University Press, 1999), p. 627; http://www.westminster-stl.org/Sermons/050220.htm

21   Paul E. Sluby, Sr., *Sessional Minutes*, Vol. 1-111 of the fifteenth Street Presbyterian Church, 1980, pp. 157-165,170, 184, 193, 205, 210-211.

22   Francis J. Grimké, "Equality of Rights for All Citizens, Black and White Alike," sermon delivered March 27, 1909, in *Grimké, Works*, 1:418-419.

23   Moore, *op. cit.*, pp. 73-74.

24   Francis J. Grimké, *A Look Backward*, pp. 2-3, Francis J. Grimké Sermons, April 7, 1895, folder 663.

25   Francis J. Grimké, "God and Prayer as factors in the Struggle," *ibid.*, pp. 274-290.

26   Moore, *op. cit.*, p. 75.

27   Booker T. Washington, "The Religious Life of the Negro," *The North American Review*, Vol. 181, No. 584 (Jul., 1905), pp. 20-23; http://www.jstor.org/stable/pdfplus/25105424.pdf?acceptTC=true

28   Moore, *op. cit.*, pp. 84-85.

29   *Black Americans in Defense of Our Nation*, (Department of Defense, 1985). http://www.shsu.edu/~his_ncp/AfrAmer.html

30   Robert L. Scribner, *Revolutionary Virginia, the Road to Independence*. (Charlottesville, VA: University of Virginia Press, 1983). pp. *xxiv*.

31   Benjamin Quarles, *The Negro in the American Revolution*. (Chapel Hill: University of North Carolina Press, 1961), p. i.

32   Michael Lanning. *African Americans in the Revolutionary War* (New York: Kensington Publishing, 2000), p.177.

33   *American Revolution — African Americans in the Revolutionary Period* (Washington, D.C.: National Park Service); http://www.nps.gov/revwar/about_the_revolution/african_americans.html

34   Budge Weidman, *The Fight for Equal Rights: Black Soldiers in the Civil War* (Washington, D.C.: The U.S. National Archives and Records Administration); http://www.archives.gov/education/lessons/blacks-civil-war/article.html

35   *Ibid.*

36   *Ibid.*

37   *Black Americans in Defense of Our Nation, op. cit.*

38   *The African American Odyssey: World War I and Postwar Society* (Washington, D.C.: Library of Congress); http://memory.loc.gov/ammem/aaohtml/exhibit/aopart7.html

39   Cameron McWhirter, *Red Summer: The Summer of 1919 and the Awakening of Black America* (New York: Henry Holt, 2011), p.13.

40   *Ibid.*, p.15.

41 Rawn James, Jr., "The Forgotten Washington Race War of 1919," *George Mason University History News Network*, February 28, 2010; http://www.hnn.us/article/123811#sthash.1KA4P9V0.dpuf

42 Peter Perl, "Race Riot of 1919 Gave Glimpse of Future Struggles," *The Washington Post*, March 1, 1999; Page A1.

43 *Ibid.*

44 James, *op. cit.*

45 *Ibid.*

46 Kenneth D. Ackerman, Young J. Edgar: *Hoover, the Red Scare, and the Assault on Civil Liberties* (New York: Da Capo Press, 2007), pp. 60-62.

47 *Black Americans in Defense of Our Nation, op. cit.*

48 Lisa Krause, "Black Soldiers in WW II: Fighting Enemies at Home and Abroad," National *Geographic News*, February 15, 2001; http://news.nationalgeographic.com/news/2001/02/0215_tuskegee.html

49 *Ibid.*

50 *Ibid.*

51 Frederick Douglass speech, unidentified typescript, folder 351, box 19, Archibald H. Grimké Papers, Moorland-Spingarn Research Center, Howard University.

52 Moore, *op. cit.*, p. 33.

53 Myrdal, *op. cit.*, p. 134.

54 Paul Raeburn, Do Fathers Matter? What Science is Telling Us About the Parent We've Overlooked (New York: Scientific American/Farrar, Straus and Girous, 2014), pp. 5-6.

55 *Ibid.*, p. 14.

56 Moore, *op. cit.*, p. 33.

57 Moore, *ibid.*, p. 34.

58 Although the official title of the document is *The Negro Family: The Case for National Action* (Washington, D.C.: Office of Policy Planning and Research, U.S. Department of Labor, 1965), it is known by the name of its principal author, Daniel Patrick Moynihan.

59 E. Franklin Frazier, *The Negro Family in the United States* (Chicago: University of Chicago Press, 1939).

60 Summarized in Andrew J. Cherlin, *Marriage, Divorce. Remarriage* (Cambridge, Mass.: Harvard University Press, 1981).

61 For recent reincarnations of this argument, see Nicholas Lemann, "The Origins of the Underclass." *Atlantic,* June 1986, pp. 31-35, and July 1986, pp. 54-68; Leon Dash, *When Children Want Children* (New York: William Morrow, 1989).

62 Erol Ricketts, "The Origin of Black Female-Headed Families," *Focus*, Spring/Summer 1989, pp 32-37; http://www.irp.wisc.edu/publications/focus/pdfs/foc121e.pdf

63 *Ibid.*, p. 33.

64 *Ibid.*, p. 34.

65 Fred Siegal, *The Future Once Happened Here: New York, D.C., L.A., and the Fate of America's Big* Cities (New York: The Free Press, 1997).

66 Mickey Kaus, *The End of Equality* (New York: Basic Books, 1998), p. 111.

67 Lyndon B. Johnson, "Great Society Speech, 1964," Public Papers of the Presidents of the United States, *Lyndon B. Johnson, Book I* (1963-64), p. 704-707. http://coursesa.matrix.msu.edu/~hst306/documents/great.html

68 Kaus, *op. cit.*, pp. 110-112.

69 Ricketts, *op. cit.*, pp. 32-37.

70 Thomas Sowell, *The Vision of the Anointed: Self-Congratulations as a Basis for Social Policy* (New York: Basic Books, 1995), p. 61.

71 Ricketts, *loc. cit.*, pp. 32-37.

72 Melvin Small, *The Presidency of Richard Nixon* (Lawrence, KS: University Press of Kansas, 1999), p. 12.

73 Arnold Toynbee and David Churchill Somervell, A *Study of History: Abridgement of Volumes 1-VI* (New York: Oxford University Press, 1946.

74 Small, op. cit., pp. 12-13.

75 John Elson, "Is God Dead?" *Time*, Vol. 87, No. 14, Apr. 8, 1966.

76 Karl Marx and Friedrich Engel, *The Communist Manifesto* (Chiron Academic Press - The Original Authoritative Edition) (2016), p. 23.

77 Daniel Patrick Moynihan, "Defining Deviancy Down," *American Scholar*, Vol. 62, No. 1, Winter 1993, pp. 17-30.

Chapter Seven - The Washington-Georgetown Localities

1 For references to Professor Robert E, Park's theories of competition, conflict, accommodation, and assimilation, see Gunnar Myrdal, *An American Dilemma; the Negro Problem and Modern Democracy* (New York: Harper & Brothers, 1944), p.662; also, Brewton Berry, Race Relations (Boston: Hougth Mifflin Company, 1951), p. 134.

2 Mary Mitchell, *Glimpses of Georgetown, Past and Present* (Washington, DC: The Road Street Press, 1983), pp. 14-15.

3 Delany, Kevin, *A Walk Through Georgetown*. (Washington, D.C.: Kevin Delany Publications. 1971).

4 Grace Dunlop Ecker, *A Portrait of old Georgetown* (Richmond, Va., Garrett & Massie, Inc., 1933), pp. 1-6.

5 Richard Plummer Jackson, *The Chronicles of Georgetown, D.C., from 1751-1878.* (Washington, D.C.: R. O. Polkinhorn, 1878), pp. 3–4; http://books.google.com/books?id=VFUUAAAAYAAJ.

6   Kathleen M. Lesko, Valerie Babb and Carroll R. Gibbs, *Black Georgetown Remembered: A History of Its Black Community from The Founding of "The Town of George"*. (Washington, D.C.: Georgetown University Press, 1991), p. 1.

7   Grace Dunlop Ecker, *A Portrait of old Georgetown* (Richmond, Va., Garrett & Massie, Inc., 1933), p. 12.

8   Lesko, *op. cit.*, pp. 1-2.

9   Ecker, *op. cit.*, p. 8.

10 Ron Chernow, *Alexander Hamilton* (New York: Penguin Press, 2004), pp. 321-331.

11 Oliver W. Holmes, "Suter's Tavern: Birthplace of the Federal City," *Records of the Columbia Historical Society* 73-74: 1–34.

12 Oliver W. Holmes, "The City Tavern: A Century of Georgetown History, 1797-1898," *Records of the Columbia Historical Society*, 50: 1–35.

13 "An Old City's History: The Simple Annals of Our Venerable Suburb," *The Washington Post*, July 24, 1878.

14 *Ibid.*

15 Ecker, *op. cit.*, p. 47.

16 Lonn Taylor, Kathleen M. Kendrick, and Jeffrey L. Brodie, *The Star-Spangled Banner: The Making of an American Icon* (New York: HarperCollins, for the Smithsonian Institution, 2008), p. 40.

17 From its beginning to December 1876, the canal earned $35,659,055 in revenue, while expending $35,746,301. - "An Old City's History: The Simple Annals of Our Venerable Suburb". *The Washington Post*, July 24, 1878.

18 *Ibid.*

19 Frederick Albert Gutheim and Antoinette J. Lee, *Worthy of the Nation: Washington, DC, from L'Enfant to the National Capital* (Baltimore, MD: Johns Hopkins University Press, 2006), p. 49.

20 Lesko, *op. cit.*, p. 2.

21 Gutheim and Lee, op. cit., p. 51.

22 *District of Columbia Emancipation Act*, April 16, 1862 [For the Release of Certain Persons Held to Service or Labor in the District of Columbia], 04/16/1862 (ARC Identifier: 299814); General Records of the United States Government; Record Group 11; National Archives.

23 Lesko, *op. cit.*, p. 2.

24 Mary Mitchell, *Glimpses of Georgetown: Past and Present* (Washington, D.C.: The Road Street Press, 1983), p. 10.

25 Washington, DC-Mt. Zion Cemetery.

26 George P. Sanger, Counselor at Law, ed., *The United States Statutes at Large and Proclamations of the United States of America, from December 1869 to March 1871, and Treaties and Postal Conventions,* Vol. 16, p. 428, §40.

27 *The United States Statutes at Large of the United States of America, from August 1893 to March 1895, and Recent Treatie*s, Conventions, and Executive Proclamations, edited, printed, and published by authority of Congress, under the direction of the Secretary of State (Washington, D.C.: Government Printing Office, 1895) p. 679.

28 Gutheim and Lee, *op. cit.*, p. 58.

29 *Ibid.*, p. 94.

30 A. Robert Smith and Eric Sevareid, *Washington: Magnificent Capital* (New York: Doubleday & Company, 1965), p. 154.

31 Mitchell, *op. cit.*, p. 2.

32 Gutheim and Lee, op. cit., p. 199.

33 *District of Columbia Emancipation Act, op. cit.*

34 Lesko, *op. cit.*, p. 95.

35 *Old Georgetown Act*, Public Law 808, 81st Congress, H.R. 7670, D.C. Code 5-801, 64 Stat. 903.

36 Thomas Sowell, "Black Excellence—the Case of Dunbar High School," *The Public Interest*, Vol. 43, Spring 1976, p. 30.

37 C. Vann Woodward, "The Case of the Louisiana Traveler" (*Plessy v. Ferguson*, 163 U.S. 537), *Quarrels that Have Shaped the Constitution* (New York: Harper & Row, Publishers, 1987), pp. 158-159.

38 *Ibid.*

39 *Ibid.*

40 U Street Corridor, Washington, DC, http://www.ustreetcorridor.com/u-street-history/

41 Robert G. Kaiser, "A City of Splendid Spaces, Great Events; 4 Landmarks Offer Washingtonians Gateways to a Capital Adventure," *The Washington Post*, April 22, 2004.

42 Tracey Gold Bennett, *Washington, D.C. 1861-1962* (Charleston, SC: Arcadia Publishing, 2006), pp. 13.

43 *Ibid.*

44 National Capital Parks and Planning Commission, Reports and Plans, Washington Region, 1928, pp. 2, 56.

45 *Ibid.*, pp. 11, 52.

46 Washington D.C., Department of Urban Renewal, Washington's Far Southeast '70 Report, 1970, p. 23.

47 See George Lipsitz, *The Possessive Investment in Whiteness: How White People Profit from Identity Politics* (Philadelphia, PA: Temple University Press, 2006); Douglas S. Massey, *Categorically Unequal: The American Stratification System* (New York: Russell Sage Foundation, 2007); and, Douglas S. Massey and Nancy A. Denton, *American Apartheid: Segregation and the Making of the Underclass* (Cambridge, MA: Harvard University Press, 1998).

48 Archie Morris III., "Advancing Urban Educational Policy: Insights from Research on Dunbar High School," *Journal of the Case Studies in Education*, May 2017.

49 Sowell, *op. cit.*, p. 31.

50 *Ibid.*, p. 34.

51 Myrdal, *op. cit.*

52 Jervis Anderson, "A Very Special Monument," *The New Yorker*, March 20, 1978, p. 105.

53 Patricia Sullivan, Charles Sumner Lofton; Principal at Dunbar During Civil Rights Era, *The Washington Post*, August 10, 2006, p. B06.

Chapter Eight – Living a Segregated Life in the Nation's Capital

1 Constance McLaughlin Green, *The Secret City: A History of Race Relations in the Nation's Capital* (Princeton, N.J.: Princeton University Press, 1967), pp. 119-134.

2 *Plessy vs. Ferguson*, Judgement, Decided May 18, 1896; Records of the Supreme Court of the United States; Record Group 267; *Plessy v. Ferguson*, 163, #15248, National Archives; https://www.ourdocuments.gov/doc.php?flash=true&doc=52.

3 Cooper, John Milton Jr., ed., *Reconsidering Woodrow Wilson: Progressivism, Internationalism, War, and Peace.* (Washington D.C.: Woodrow Wilson International Center for Scholars, 2008).

4 Desmond King, *Separate and Unequal: Black Americans and the U.S. Federal Government* (Oxford: Clarendon Press, 1997), pp. 10-13.

5 Green, op. *cit.*, p.154.

6 Kenneth Robert Janken, *Rayford W. Logan and the Dilemma of the African-American Intellectual* (Amherst: University of Massachusetts Press, 1993), p.18.

7 Janken, *op. cit.*, p. 17.

8 *Ibid.*, pp. 17-18.

9 Isaac Weld, *Travels Through the States of North America and the Providences of Upper and Lower Canada*, vol. I (London: J. Stockdale, 1799), pp. 145-152.

10 James Weldon Johnson, *Along the Way* (New York: Viking, 1937), p. 32.

11 Ignatius Holoe to the Secretary of the Navy, circa 1840, NARA RG45.

12 Henry B. Hibben, *Original History of the Washington Navy Yard* (Washington, D.C.: Naval District Washington, 1890), p. 37.

13 John Stephen Durham, "The Labor Union and the Negro," *Atlantic Monthly*, February 1898, p. 226.

14 *Ibid.*, pp. 132-133.

15 Tucker Carlson, "Washington's Lost Black Aristocracy," *City Journal*, Autumn 1996; http://www.city-journal.org/html/6_4_urbanities-washingtons_los.html

16 *Ibid.*

17 *Ibid.*

18 Phyllis Field, "Union League," in Nina Mjagkij, ed., *Organizing Black America: An Encyclopedia of African American Associations* (New York: Garland Publishing, 2001); Michael Fitzgerald, T*he Union League Movement in the Deep South: Politics and Agricultural Change During Reconstruction* (Baton Rouge: Louisiana State University Press, 1989).

19 *Ibid.*

20 "Daniel Freeman: The Man behind the Camera," The Historical Society of Washington, D.C., O*ctober 26, 2009 to January 18, 2010;* http://www.historydc.org/pastexhibits.aspx

21 *Ibid.*, p. 132.

22 *Ibid.*

23 *Ibid.*, pp. 132-133.

24 *Ibid.*, pp. 133-134.

25 Robert Kinzer and Edward Sagarin, "Roots of the Integrationist-Separatist Dilemma," in Bailey, *Black Business Enterprise*, pp. 52-53, 55-56; Joseph A. Pierce, "The Evolution of Negro Business," in Bailey, *Black Business Enterprise*, p. 36.

26 Thomas Hudson McKee, *The National Conventions and Platforms of All Political Parties, 1789-1905* (New York: Burt Franklin, 1971), pp. 18-20.

27 Eugene V. Smalley, *A Brief History of the Republican Party. From Its Organization to the Presidential Campaign of 1884* (New York: John Alden, Publisher, 1885), p. 30.

28 McKee, *National Conventions and Platforms*, pp. 108-109.

29 *Ibid.*

30 *Democratic National Committee* online, "Brief History of the Democratic Party" (at http://www.democrats.org/ about/history.html).

31 Robert L. Zangrando, *The NAACP Crusade Against Lynching, 1909-1950* (Philadelphia: Temple University Press, 1980), pp. 139-165; Harvard Sitkoff, *A New Deal for Blacks: The Emergence of Civil Rights as a National Issue* (New York: Oxford University Press, 1978), pp. 289-295.

32 *Executive Order 8802* dated June 25, 1941, General Records of the United States Government; Record Group 11; National Archives.

33 Samuel Lubell, (1956). *The Future of American Politics, 3rd ed.* (New York: Anchor Press. 1956), p. 232.

34 Melvyn Dubofsky. "Rustin, Bayard"; *American National Biography Online*, February 2000; http://www.anb.org/articles/15/15-00935.html.

35 Lawrence Otis Graham, *Our Kind of People: Inside America's Black Upper Class*, (New York: HarperCollins Publishers, 2000), p. 10.

36 Graham, *ibid*, p. 10; Tracey Gold Bennett, *Washington, D.C. 1861-1962* (Charleston, SC: Arcadia Publishing, 2006), p. 13; *Biographical Directory of the*

American Congress 1774-1949 (Washington, D.C.: U.S. Government Printing Office, 1950), pp. 1729-1730.

37   Graham, *ibid*, pp. 10-11; Bennett, Ibid. p. 26; *Biographical Directory 1774-1949, ibid.*, pp. 1713-1714.

38   Graham, *ibid*, pp. 10-11; *Biographical Directory 1774-1949, ibid.*, p. 1723.

39   Graham, *ibid*, pp. 10-11; Bennett, Ibid. p. 27; *Biographical Directory 1774-1949, ibid.*, p. 1822.

40   Graham, *ibid*, pp. 10-11; Bennett, Ibid. p. 34; *Biographical Directory 1774-1949, ibid.*, pp. 904-905.

41   Graham, *ibid*, p. 11.

42   *Biographical Directory of the American Congress 1774-1949* (Washington, D.C.: U.S. Government Printing Office, 1950).

43   *Ibid.*

44   Office of History and Preservation, Office of the Clerk, *Black Americans in Congress, 1870–2007.* Washington, D.C.: U.S. Government Printing Office, 2008.

45   William B. Gatewood, *Aristocrats of Color: The Black, 1880-1920* (Fayetteville: University of Arkansas Press, 1990), p.66.

46   *Ibid.*, pp. 66-67.

47   Steven Mintz, "A Historical Ethnography of Black Washington, D.C.", *Records of the Columbia Historical Society of Washington, D.C. 52*, 1989, pp. 239-240.

48   David L. Lewis, *The District of Columbia: A Bicentennial History* (New York: W. W. Norton, 1976), pp. 72-73.

49   Federal Writers' Project, *City and Capital: Federal Writers' Project, Works Progress Administration* (Washington, DC: U. S. Government Printing Office, 1937), p. 1076.

50   Karen Tanner Allen, *Alley, Alley in Free,* The Washington Post, January 7, 2006, p. F05.

51   James Borchert, *Alley Life in Washington: Family, Community, Religion, and Folklife in the City, 1850–1970* (Urbana: University of Illinois Press, 1980), pp. 45-47.

52   National Capital Parks and Planning Commission, Reports and Plans, Washington Region, 1930, p. 76.

53   *Ibid.*

54   National Capital Parks and Planning Commission, Washington Present and Future, 1950, p. 20.

55   Mintz, *op. cit.*, p. 236.

56   Janken, *op. cit.*, pp. 12-13.

57   Thomas Sowell, "Black Excellence—the Case of Dunbar High School," *The Public Interest*, Vol. 43, Spring 1976, p. 39.

58   Moore, *op. cit.*, p. 51.

59 William H. Jones, *Recreation and Amusement Among Negroes in Washington, D.C.: A Sociological Analysis of the Negro in an Urban Environment* (Washington: Howard University Press, 1927), pp. 98-99.

60 Paul K. Williams, *Images of America; Greater U Stre*et (Chicago: Arcadia Publishing, 2002), p. 27.

61 *Ibid.*, p. 51.

62 *Ibid.*

63 Moore, *op. cit.*, p. 61.

64 *Ibid.*

65 Jones, *op. cit.*, pp. 29-34.

66 Moore, op. cit., p. 61.

Chapter Nine - The Commencement of Liberation

1 Kevin Gaines, Uplifting the Race: Black Leadership, Politics, and Culture in the Twentieth Century (Chapel Hill, University of North Carolina Press, 1996), 1-2.

2 *Ibid.*

3 *Report of Board of Education, 1867-1868.*

4 *Report of Board of Education, 1899-1900*, pp. 54-59.

5 G. Smith Wormley, "Educators of the first Half Century of Public Schools of the District of Columbia," *The Journal of Negro History*, Vol. 17, No. 2, April 1932, pp. 124-125.

6 *Ibid.*, pp. 126-127.

7 *Ibid.*, p. 127.

8 *Ibid.*, pp. 127-128.

9 *Ibid.*, pp. 124-125.

10 Gaines, *op. cit.*, p. 2.

11 Jacqueline M. Moore, *Leading the race: The Transformation of the Black in the Nation's Capital, 1880-1920*, Charlottesville and London: University Press of Virginia, 1999, p. 22.

12 Antoinette J. Lee, "Magnificent Achievements - The M Street High School," *CRM Magazine: African-American History and Culture*, Vol. 20, No 02, 1997, p 24; http://crm.cr.nps.gov/20-2/20-2-16.pdf

13 E. Delorus Preston, Jr., "William Syphax, a Pioneer in Negro Education in the District of Columbia," *The Journal of Negro History*, Vol. 20, No. 4, October 1935, p. 470; Mary Gibson Hundley, *The Dunbar Story* (New York: Vintage Press Hundley, 1965), pp. 15-16.

14 Kenneth Robert Janken, *Rayford W. Logan and the Dilemma of the African-American Intellectual* (Amherst: University of Massachusetts Press, 1993), pp. 18-19.

15 W.E.B. Du Bois, *The Negro Problem* (New York: James Pott and Company, 1903).

16 Mary Church Terrell, "History of the High School for Negroes in Washington," *The Journal of Negro History*, Vol. 2, No. 3, July 1917, pp. 252-254.

17 Moore, *op. cit.,* p. 25.

18 Hundley, *op. cit.,* p. 16.

19 Terrell, *op. cit.,* pp. 254-255.

20 Hundley, *op. cit.,* p.16; Preston, *op. cit.,* pp. 470-471.

21 Hundley, *ibid.,* pp. 16-17.

22 Terrell, *op. cit.,* pp. 255-256.

23 *Ibid.,* p. 256.

24 *Ibid.,* p. 257.

25 Hundley, *ibid.,* p. 17; Lee, *op. cit.,* p. 24; G. Smith Wormley, "Educators of the first Half Century of Public Schools of the District of Columbia," *The Journal of Negro History*, Vol. 17, No. 2, April 1932, p. 137.

26 Hundley, *op. cit.,* p.17.

27 Terrell, *op. cit.,* p. 257; Hundley, *loc. cit.,* p.17.

28 Wormley, *op. cit.,* p. 137.

29 *Ibid.,* p. 124.

30 Terrell, *op. cit.,* p. 258.

31 Lee, *op. cit.,* p. 24.

32 Lee, *op. cit.,* pp. 24-25.

33 Note: The Boston Latin School was both the first public school and oldest existing school in the United States. The Public Latin School was a bastion for educating the sons of the Boston, resulting in the school claiming many prominent Bostonians as alumni. Its curriculum followed that of the 18th century Latin-school movement which holds the classics to be the basis of an educated mind. Four years of Latin was mandatory for all pupils who entered the school in 7th grade, three years for those who entered in 9th.

34 *Ibid.,* p 25.

35 Rayford W. Logan, "Growing Up in Washington: A Lucky Generation," *Records of the Columbia Historical Society*, Vol. 50, 1980, p.503.

36 Thomas Sowell, "Black Excellence—the Case of Dunbar High School," *The Public Interest*, Vol. 43, Spring 1976, p. 31.

37 Terrell, *op. cit.,* p. 258; G. Smith Wormley, "A Great Educator in a Great City," *Howard University Record* 18 (1923-24), pp. 230-232.

38 *Ibid.,* p. 259.

39 *Ibid.,* p. 259; Sowell, *op. cit.,* p. 31.

40 Terrell, *op. cit.,* p. 259.

41 Kenneth R. Manning, *Black Apollo of Science: The Life of Ernest Everett Just* (New York: Oxford University Press, 1983), p. 18 and p. 27.

42 Henry S. Robinson, "The M Street High School, 1891-1916," *Records of the Columbia Historical Society, Washington, D.C.*, Vol. 51, [The 51ˢᵗ separately bound book] (1984), pp. 122-123, citing *Washington Post*, August 10, 1958, p. A-23; *Colored American*, October 20, 1900, p.8, October 3, 1903; *Report of the Board of Trustees of Public Schools of the District of Columbia to the Commissioners of the District of Columbia: 1898-1899* (Washington: Government Printing Office, 1900), pp. 7, 11..

43 Thomas Sowell, *Black Rednecks and White Liberals* (San Francisco: Encounter Books, 2005), pp. 39-40, 204-211, 213-214.

44 Louise Daniel Hutchinson, *Anna J. Cooper: A Voice from the South* (Washington, D. C.: Smithsonian Institution Press, 1981), pp. 57-58.

45 Leona C. Gabel, *From Slavery to the Sorbonne and Beyond: The Life & Writings of Anna J. Cooper* (Northampton, Mass.: Department of History of Smith College, 1982), p. 49.

46 Moore, *op. cit.*, p. 95.

47 Moore, *op. cit.*, pp. 94-95; Robinson, pp. 122-123, citing *Washington Post*, September 29, 1905, p. 2.

48 *Ibid.*

49 Robinson, p. 123, citing *ibid.*, September 19, 1905, p. 1 pt. 2, September 29, 1905, p. 2.

50 Lee, *op. cit.*, p. 25.

51 Robinson, *op. cit.*, p. 123.

52 Robinson, *op. cit.*, p. 123-124.

53 *Report of the Board of Education, 1902-1903*, pp. 196-197; *1903-1904*, pp. 187-188.

54 Robinson, pp. 123-124, citing ibid., October 31, 1905, p. 2; interview, Paul Cooke, December 19, 1979. Dr. Cooper returned to teach at the M Street High School in 1910.

55 Moore, *op. cit.*, pp. 161-162.

56 Robinson, *op. cit.*, p. 124.

57 Evan J. Albright, "A Slice of History," *Amherst Magazine*, Winter 2007. http://www3.amherst.edu/magazine/issues/07winter/blazing_trail/slice.html

58 Terrell, *op. cit.*, pp. 259-260.

59 Jessie Carney Smith, Ed. "Edward Christopher Williams," *Notable Black American Men, Book II* (Detroit: Thomson Gale, 2007).

60 E. J. Josey, *The black librarian in America* (Metuchen, NJ: Scarecrow Press, 1970).

61 E. J. Josey and A. A. Shockley, *Handbook of Black Librarianship* (Littleton, CO: Libraries Unlimited, 1977).

62 Terrell, *ibid.*, p. 260.

63 Robinson, *op. cit.*, p. 124.

64 Terrell, *op. cit.*, p. 260.

65 Robinson, *op. cit.*, pp. 124-125.

66 *The Crisis*, Vol. 27, No. 4, (New York: The Crisis Publishing Company, Inc., Feb 1924); Faustine C. Jones-Wilson, *Encyclopedia of African American Education* (Connecticut: Greenwood Publishing Company, 1996); http://encyclopedia. jrank.org/articles/pages/4144/Browne-Hugh-M-1851-1923.html#ixzz0bzcyIaRl

67 *Ibid.*

68 Robinson, *op. cit.*, p. 125; The Smithsonian Anacostia Museum and Center for African American History and Culture, *The Black Washingtonians: The Anacostia Museum Illustrated Chronology*, Hoboken, New Jersey: John Wiley & Sons, Inc., 2005, p.118; Moore, *op. cit.*, pp. 93,108.

69 The Smithsonian Anacostia Museum and Center for African American History and Culture, *ibid.*, pp. 138-139, 354; Moore, *ibid.*, pp. 11, 152; Grimké, Angelina Weld. Papers of Angelina Weld Grimké. Moorland-Spingarn Research Center, Howard University, Washington, D.C.

70 *Ibid.*

71 *Ibid.*

72 Robinson, *op. cit.*, pp. 127-128; Fitzpatrick and Goodwin, *op. cit.*, pp 94-95.

73 *Ibid.*; Adam Spencer, "Edwin B. Henderson Elected to Basketball Hall of Fame; Grandfather of Black Basketball Finally Elected to Hall of Fame," *Yahoo Contributor Network*, Aug 28, 2013; http://voices.yahoo.com/edwin-b-henderson-elected-basketball-hall-fame-12301217.html

74 Charlynn Spencer Pyne, "The Burgeoning 'Cause,' 1920-1930," *Library of Congress Information Bulletin*, Vol 53, No.3, February 7, 1994.

75 *Ibid.*

76 *Ibid.*

77 *Ibid.*

78 *Ibid.*

79 *Ibid.*

80 The Smithsonian Anacostia Museum and Center for African American History and Culture, *ibid.*, pp. 148, 150, 174, 177, 364; Moore, op. cit., pp. 93, 109-110; Robinson, *op. cit.*, p. 128; Fitzpatrick and Goodwin, *op. cit.*, pp 76, 120, 152.

81 Robinson, *op. cit.*, p. 128; Moore, *op. cit.*, p. 93.

82 Moore, *ibid.*, p. 93.

83 Lawrence Otis Graham, *The Senator and the Socialite: The True Story of America's First Black Dynasty* (New York: HarperCollind Publishers, 2006), pp. 166-167.

Chapter Ten - The Paul Laurence Dunbar High School

1   Mary Church Terrell, "History of the High School for Negroes in Washington," *The Journal of Negro History*, Vol. 2, No. 3, July 1917, pp. 252-253; Mary Gibson Hundley, *The Dunbar Story* (New York: Vintage Press Hundley, 1965), p. 145.

2   Terrell, *Ibid.*, p. 252.

3   *Ibid.*, pp. 252–253.

4   *Ibid.*, pp. 66-67.

5   Mary Gibson Hundley, *The Dunbar Story (1870-1955)* (Vantage Press, Inc., 1965), p. 66.

6   A proprietary system of library classification developed by Melvil Dewey in 1876 while working as a librarian at Amherst College. The system classified books using numbers from 000-999, dividing nonfiction books into 10 broad categories. By the time of his death, the system was being used in over 96% of all American libraries.

7   Hundley, *op. cit.*, p. 67.

8   *Ibid.*, p. 68.

9   *Ibid.*

10 *Ibid.*, p. 67.

11 Terrell, *op. cit.*, p. 253.

12 Hundley, *op. cit.*, pp. 33-34.

13 Thomas Sowell, "Black Excellence—the Case of Dunbar High School," *The Public Interest*, Vol. 43, Spring 1976, p. 50.

14 660 Jervis Anderson, "A Very Special Monument," *The New Yorker*, March 20, 1978, p. 107.

15 N. Graham Nesmith, "William Branch: (A Conversation) Reminiscence," *African American Review*, Vol. 38, 2004.

16 Sowell, *op. cit.*, pp. 33-34.

17 Terrell, *op. cit.*, pp. 260-261.

18 Cyndy Bittinger, "Black Women in Vermont History: The Story of Nettie Anderson," *Vermont Public Radio*, March 8, 2010; http://www.vpr.net/episode/48106/

19 Hundley, *op. cit.*, p. 61.

20 *Ibid.*, pp. 18, 140.

21 *Ibid.*, pp. 18-19.

22 *Ibid.*

23 The Catholic University of America, *The Haynes-Lofton Family Papers, 1882-1974*, (Washington, D.C.: The American Catholic Research Center and University Archives). http://archives.lib.cua.edu/findingaid/Haynes-Lofton.cfm

24 Patricia Sullivan, "Charles Sumner Lofton; Principal at Dunbar During Civil Rights Era," *The Washington Post*, August 10, 2006, p. B06.

25 *Ibid.*

26 *Ibid.*

27 Kenneth Robert Janken, *Rayford W. Logan and the Dilemma of the African-American Intellectual* (Amherst: University of Massachusetts Press, 1993), p. 20.

28 Hundley, *op. cit.*, pp. 64-65.

29 Hundley, *op. cit.*, p. 131.

30 *Ibid.*

31 *Ibid.*, p. 132.

32 Harry E. Groves, "Separate but Equal — The Doctrine of Plessy v. Ferguson" *Phylon (1940-1956)*, Vol. 12, No. 1. (1st Qtr., 1951), pp. 66-72.

33 Evelyn Boyd Granville, "The Lives We Lead: Evelyn Boyd Granville '45," *Smith College Alumni Relations*; http://alumnae.smith.edu/spotlight/3632-2/

34 Hundley, *op. cit.*, pp. 131-132.

35 *Ibid.*

36 *Ibid.*, p. 138.

37 *Ibid.*, pp. 135, 145.

38 Kathy A. Perkins (Ed.), (1990). *Black Female Playwrights: An Anthology of Plays Before 1950* (Bloomington & Indianapolis, Indiana: Indiana University Press. 1990), pp. 53–56.

39 Hundley, *op. cit.*, p. 139.

40 *Ibid.*, pp. 132-133.

41 Perkins, *op. cit.*, pp. 53-56.

42 Hundley, *op. cit.*, p. 133.

43 *Ibid.*, p. 133.

44 *Ibid.*, p. 136.

45 *Ibid.*, pp. 133-134.

46 *Ibid.*, p. 144.

47 *Ibid.*

48 *Ibid.*, p. 134.

49 *Ibid.*, p. 136.

50 *Ibid.*, p. 134.

51 *Ibid.*, p. 136.

Chapter Eleven – The Dunbar Paradigm

1 Jervis Anderson, "A Very Special Monument," *The New Yorker*, March 20, 1978, p. 108.

2 N. Graham Nesmith, "William Branch: (A Conversation) Reminiscence," *African American Review*, Vol. 38, 2004, pp. 22-23.

3 *Ibid.*, pp. 23-24.

4 *Ibid.*, p. 24.

5   Gunnar Myrdal, *An American Dilemma: The Negro Problem and Modern Democracy*, Vol. II, New York: Harper & Row Publishers, Incorporated, 1973, p. 889.

6   Mary Gibson Hundley, *The Dunbar Story (1870-1955)* (Vantage Press, Inc., 1965), p. 24

7   *Ibid.*, pp. 29-30.

8   *Ibid.*, p. 13.

9   Susan Wise Bauer, Jessie Wise, *The Well-Trained Mind: A Guide to Classical Education at Home* (New York: W.W. Norton & Company, Inc., 2009), pp. 13-15. Douglas Wilson, Classical Education, Printed in PHS #6, 1994; http://www.home-school.com/Articles/ClassicalEducation.html

10 *Ibid.*, p. 15.

11 *Ibid.*

12 *Ibid.*, p. 16.

13 Hundley, *op. cit.*, pp. 26-29.

14 *Ibid.*, p. 28.

15 *Ibid.*

16 Robert J. Schneller, Jr., *Breaking the Color Barrier: The U.S. Naval Academy's First Black Midshipmen and the Struggle for Racial Equality* (New York: New York University Press, 2005), p. 77.

17 *Ibid.*, p. 78; Tracey Gold Bennett, *Washington, D.C. 1861-1962* (Charleston, SC: Arcadia Publishing, 2006), p. 13.

18 William H. Jones, *Recreation and Amusement Among Negroes in Washington, D.C.: A Sociological Analysis of the Negro in an Urban Environment* (Washington, D.C.: Howard University Studies in Urban Sociology, 1927).

19 Schneller, *op. cit.*, pp. 77-78.

20 *Ibid.*, p. 78.

21 Kenneth Robert Janken, *Rayford W. Logan and the Dilemma of the African-American Intellectual* (Amherst: University of Massachusetts Press, 1993), pp. 22-23.

22 Schneller, *op. cit.*, p. 174.

23 Hundley, *op. cit.*, p. 57.

24 *Ibid.*, pp. 51-52.

25 *Ibid.*, pp. 50-51.

26 Hundley, *loc. cit.*, pp. 51.

27 Hundley, *op. cit.*, pp. 67-68.

28 *Ibid.*, pp. 51-52.

29 *Ibid.*, pp. 52-53.

Chapter Twelve, The Dunbar Milieu

1 Thomas Sowell, "Black Excellence—the Case of Dunbar High School," *The Public Interest*, Vol. 43, Spring 1976, p. 33.

2 *Ibid.*, p. 34.

3 *Ibid.*, pp. 36-37.

4 *Ibid.*, p. 40.

5 Mary Gibson Hundley, *The Dunbar Story* (New York: Vintage Press Hundley, 1965), p. 31.

6 Gunnar Myrdal, *An American Dilemma; the Negro Problem and Modern Democracy* (New York: Harper & Brothers, 1944), p. 662; also, Brewton Berry, Race Relations (Boston: Houghton Mifflin Company, 1951), p. 134.

7 U.S. Census Bureau, *Historical Income Tables: Households* (Washington, DC: U.S. Department of Commerce, June 2, 2016); https://www.census.gov/data/tables/time-series/demo/income-poverty/historical-income-households.html

8 Sowell, Excellence, *op. cit.*, p. 39.

9 Anderson, *op. cit.*, pp. 104-105.

10 *Ibid.*, pp. 105-106.

11 Lawrence Otis Graham, *Our Kind of People: Inside America's Black Upper Class*, (New York: HarperCollins Publishers, 2000), p. 61.

12 Anderson, *op. cit.*, p. 108.

13 Sowell, Excellence, *op. cit.*, p. 27.

14 Robert Lichello, *Pioneer in Blood Plasma: Dr. Charles Richard Drew* (New York: Simon and Schuster, 1968), p. 13.

15 Sowell, Excellence, *loc. cit.*, p. 27.

16 R. F. Kronick and C. H. Hargis, *Dropouts: Who Drops Out and Why—and the Recommended Action* (Springfield, Ill.: Charles C. Thomas, 1990).

17 Sowell, Excellence, *op. cit.*, pp. 33-34.

18 Lewis M. Terman, *The Measurement of Intelligence: An Explanation of and a Complete Guide for the Use of the Stanford Revision and Extension of the Binet-Simon Intelligence Scale* (San Francisco: Houghton-Mifflin Company, 1916).

19 Hundley, *op. cit.,* p. 25.

20 Sowell, Excellence, *op. cit.*, pp. 359.

21 Sowell, Excellence, *op. cit.*, pp. 39-40.

22 *Ibid.*, pp. 36-37.

23 *Ibid.*, p. 106.

24 Jacqueline M. Moore, *Leading the race: The Transformation of the Black in the Nation's Capital, 1880-1920,* Charlottesville and London: University Press of Virginia, 1999, pp. 94-95.

25 Douglas S. Massey and Nancy A. Denton (1993). *American Apartheid* (Cambridge, MA: Harvard University Press, 1993).

26 Kenneth Robert Janken, *Rayford W. Logan and the Dilemma of the African-American Intellectual* (Amherst: University of Massachusetts Press, 1993), pp. 21-22.

27 Kevin K. Gaines, *Uplifting the Race: Black Leadership, Politics, and Culture in the Twentieth Century* (Chapel Hill: University of North Carolina Press, 1966); Jacqueline M. Moore. *Booker T. Washington, W. E. B. DuBois, and the Struggle for Racial Uplift.* (Wilmington: Scholarly Resources, 2003).

28 Anderson, *op. cit.*, p. 101.

Chapter Thirteen - Extermination of the Traditions

1   Thomas Sowell, "Black Excellence—the Case of Dunbar High School," *The Public Interest*, Vol. 43, Spring 1976, p. 41.

2   Kenneth Robert Janken, *Rayford W. Logan and the Dilemma of the African-American Intellectual* (Amherst: University of Massachusetts Press, 1993), pp. 18-19.

3   For references to Professor Robert E, Park's theories of competition, conflict, accommodation, and assimilation, see Gunnar Myrdal, *An American Dilemma; the Negro Problem and Modern Democracy* (New York: Harper & Brothers, 1944), p. 662; also, Brewton Berry, Race Relations (Boston: Hougth Mifflin Company, 1951), p. 134.

4   Constance McLaughlin Green, *The Secret City: A History of Race Relations in the Nation's Capital* (Princeton, N.J.: Princeton University Press, 1967), p.168.

5   Sowell, Excellence, *op. cit.*, pp. 52-53.

6   *Ibid.*

7   Tucker Carlson, "Washington's Lost Black Aristocracy," *City Journal*, Autumn 1996; http://www.city-journal.org/html/6_4_urbanities-washingtons_los.html

8   *Ibid.*

9   *Ibid.*

10 William Julius Wilson, *The Truly Disadvantaged: The Inner City, the Underclass, and Public Policy* (Chicago: University of Chicago Press, 1987), p. 7.

11 Ibid.

12 Daniel Patrick Moynihan, *The Negro Family: The Case for National Action* (Washington, D.C.: Office of Policy Planning and Research, U.S. Department of Labor, 1965).

13 Kenneth B. Clark, *Dark Ghetto: Dilemmas of Social Power* (New York: Harper and Row, Publishers, Incorporated, 1965).

14 Jason Deparle, *American Dream: Three Women, Ten Kids, and A Nation's Drive to End Welfare* (New York: Penguin Group, 2004), p. 95.

15 Gertrude Himmelfarb, *One Nation, Two Cultures* (New York: Alfred A. Knopf, 1999).

16   Daniel Patrick Moynihan, "Defining Deviancy Down," *American Scholar*, Vol. 62, No. 1, Winter 1993, pp. 17-30.

17   Arnold Toynbee, *A Study of History: Abridgement of Volumes 1-VI (Great Britain:* Oxford University Press, 1946).

18   John T. Elson, "Is God Dead?" *Time*. April 8, 1966.

19   Karl Marx and Friedrich Engels (1848). *The Communist Manifesto*, p. 28.

20   Natalie Angier, *"The Changing American Family,"* The New York Times, November 25, 2013.

21   Democratic Leader Nancy Pelosi (February 6, 2014), *Transcript of Pelosi Press Conference Today in the Capitol Visitor Center*, Washington, D.C.; http://www.democraticleader.gov/ Transcript_of_Pelosi_Weekly_Press_Conference_on_ACA_Immigration

22   Lewis, Oscar, *La Vida: A Puerto Rican family in The Culture of Poverty.* (San Juan and New York, 1966).

23   *Ibid.*

24   Toynbee, *op. cit.*

25   *Ibid.*

26   Charles Murray, "Role Models: America's Elites Take Their Cues from the Underclass," *Wall Street Journal*, February 6, 2001.

27   Sowell, Excellence, *op. cit.*, pp. 53-54.

28   *Ibid.*

29   *Ibid.*, p. 42.

30   Alfred H. Kelly, "The School Desegregation Case" (*Brown v. Board of Education of the City of Topeka*, 347 U.S. 483), *Quarrels that Have Shaped the Constitution* (New York: Harper & Row, Publishers, 1987), p. 331.

31   *Ibid.*, pp. 331-333.

32   Sowell, Excellence, *op. cit.* p. 43.

33   *Ibid.*, pp. 43-44.

34   *Ibid.*, pp. 44-45.

35   *Ibid.*, pp. 45-46.

36   *Ibid.*, pp. 54-55.

37   *Ibid.*, p. 46; Antoinette J. Lee, "Magnificent Achievements - The M Street High School," *CRM Magazine: African-American History and Culture*, Vol. 20, No 02, 1997, p 25; http://crm.cr.nps.gov/20-2/20-2-16.pdf

38   Sowell, Excellence, *op. cit.*, pp. 46-47; Mary Gibson Hundley, *The Dunbar Story* (New York: Vintage Press Hundley, 1965), pp. 64-65.

39   Thomas Sowell, *Black Education: Myths and Tragedies* (New York: David McKay Co., 1972), p.143.

40   Sowell, Excellence, *op. cit.*, pp. 47-48; E. Delorus Preston, Jr., "William Syphax, a Pioneer in Negro Education in the District of Columbia," *The Journal of Negro History*, Vol. 20, No. 4, October 1935, pp. 462-464.

41 The Nixon Library and Museum (March 17, 1954), Pre-Presidential Papers of Richard M. Nixon Series 207, Appearances, 1948-1962, Box 19. Dunbar High School; http://www.nixonlibrary.gov/forresearchers/find/textual/findingaids/findingaid_lagunaniguel_series207.pdf

42 Sowell, Excellence, *op. cit.*, p. 48.

43 *Ibid.*

44 *Ibid.*, pp. 48-49.

45 *Ibid.*

46 *Ibid.*, p. 50.

47 *Ibid.*, p. 54.

48 *Ibid.*, p. 55; Kenneth Robert Janken, *Rayford W. Logan and the Dilemma of the African-American Intellectual* (Amherst: University of Massachusetts Press, 1993), pp. 18-19; Preston, *op. cit.*, pp. 463-464.

49 Sowell, Excellence, *op. cit.*, pp. 55-56.

Chapter Fourteen - Epilogue

1 Thomas Sowell, "Black Excellence—the Case of Dunbar High School," *The Public Interest*, Vol. 43, Spring 1976, p. 45.

2 *Ibid.*

3 Paul Raeburn, *Do Fathers Matter? What Science is Telling Us About the Parent We've Overlooked* (New York: Scientific American/Farrar, Straus and Girous, 2014), pp. 5-6.

4 *Ibid.*, p. 14.

5 Jacqueline M. Moore, *Leading the race: The Transformation of the Black in the Nation's Capital, 1880-1920*, Charlottesville and London: University Press of Virginia, 1999, p. 33.

6 Moore, *ibid.*, p. 34.

7 Melvin Small, *The Presidency of Richard Nixon* (Lawrence, KS: University Press of Kansas, 1999), pp. 12-13.

8 *Ibid.*

9 Amanda Abrams, "An identity reclaimed," *The Washington Post*, May 27, 2011; http://www.washingtonpost.com/realestate/2011/05/13/AGjO6mCH_story.html

10 Irving Kristol, (October 19, 2000). "The Two Welfare States." *The Wall Street Journal.*

11 *Ibid.*

12 Jervis Anderson, "A Very Special Monument," *The New Yorker*, March 20, 1978, p. 111.

13 *Ibid.*

14 *Ibid.*

15 *Ibid.*

16 Lewis, Oscar, "The Culture of Poverty." George Gmelch and Walter Zenner, eds. *Readings in Urban Anthropology* (Prospect Heights, IL: Waveland Press, 1998).

17 Peter Milius, "'72 D.C. School Budget May Mean Larger Classes and Fewer Electives," *The Washington Post,* November 10, 1970, A1.

18 Wolf Von Eckardt, "No Eggcrate, This," *The Washington Post,* March 27, 1971, C1.

19 Wolf Von Eckardt, "Design for an Urban Setting," *The Washington Post,* December 11, 1971, E1.

20 *Ibid.*

21 Ronald Gross and Judith Murphy, *Educational Facilities Laboratories Educational Change and Architectural Consequences: A Report on Facilities for Individualized Instruction* (New York: Educational Facilities Laboratories, Inc., 1968), 71.

22 Lawrence Feinberg, "We Must Have Pride In It," *The Washington Post,* April 13, 1977, C1.

23 R. C. Newell, "New Dunbar High School Opens, Still Facing Same Old Problems," *The Washington Afro American,* April 16, 1977, C1.

24 Michael Kiernan, "Razing Fight Begins Anew," *Washington Star,* February 28, 1975.

25 See Oscar Lewis, *La Vida: A Puerto Rican family in the Culture of Poverty* (San Juan and New York, 1966).

26 Archie Morris III, "Race, Class, and the Subculture of Poverty," *Journal of the Center for Research on African American Women*, Vol. 2, No. 1, 2007.

27 District of Columbia Public Schools (2011), Dunbar High School. http://profiles.dcps.dc.gov/dunbar+high+school

28 Terence P. Jeffrey (May 14, 2014). "DC Schools: $29,349 Per Pupil, 83% Not Proficient in Reading," *CNSNews.com*; http://cnsnews.com/commentary/terence-p-jeffrey/dc-schools-29349-pupil-83-not-proficient-reading

29 Larry Cuban, "The Open Classroom," *Education Next*, Vol. 4, No. 2, Spring 2004; http://educationnext.org/theopenclassroom/

30 Charles Silberman, *The Open Classroom Reader* (New York: Random House, 1973).

31 Cuban, *op. cit.*

32 *Ibid.*

33 "Mayor Fenty and OPEFM Director Lew Announce Dunbar HS Design Competition Winner," *District of Columbia Public Schools*, December 14, 2010; http://dc.gov/DCPS/About+DCPS Press+Releases+and+Announcements/Press+Releases/ Mayor+Fenty+and+OPEFM+Director+Lew+Announce+Dunbar+HS+Design+ Competion+Winner

34   Dunbar High School Alumni Federation, "New Dunbar: Honors Past, Present, and Future," *The Vine*, Spring 2011, p. 7.

35   Martin Austermuhle, "D.C. Officials Celebrate Completion Of New Dunbar High School," *American University Radio*, August 20, 2013; http://wamu.org/news/13/08/20/dc_officials_celebrate_completion_of_new_dunbar_high_school

36   *Ibid.*

37   *Ibid.*

38   Emma Brown, "Dunbar High autonomy proposal stirs debate in D.C.," *The Washington Post*, January 18, 2014; http://www.washingtonpost.com/local/education/dunbar-high-school-autonomy-proposal-stirs-debate-in-dc/2014/01/18/63c4c442-7fad-11e3-93c1-0e888170b723_story.html

39   *Ibid.*

40   Natalie Wexler, "Do we need another selective DCPS high school? A group at Dunbar thinks so," *The Washington Post*, February 12, 2014.

41   *Ibid.*

42   "School Without Walls of Washington, DC," Home and School Association, Quick Facts; http://www.swwhs.org/about-us/quick-facts/

43   Wexler, *op. cit.*

44   Brown, *op. cit.*

45   Thomas Sowell, "The Education of Minority Children," *The Hoover Institute*, 2001, p. 81; http://search.aol.com/aol/search?enabled_terms=&s_it=comsearch&q=The+Education+of+Minority+Children

46   *Ibid.*, pp. 81-85.

47   *Ibid.*, p. 91.

48   Report of the Board of Education, 1902-1903, 196-197; 1903-1904, 187-188.

Printed in the United States
By Bookmasters